My Little Pony
Friendship is Magic

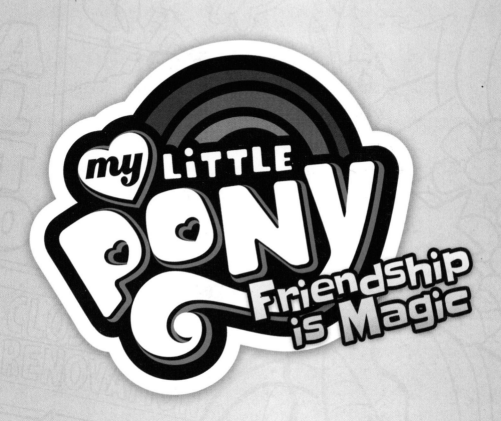

COLLECTION EDITS BY
Justin Eisinger and Alonzo Simon

COLLECTION DESIGN BY
Neil Uyetake

PUBLISHER
Ted Adams

Special thanks to Meghan McCarthy, Eliza Hart, Ed Lane, Beth Artale, and Michael Kelly.

For international rights, contact licensing@idwpublishing.com

ISBN: 978-1-63140-815-1

20 19 18 17   1 2 3 4

Licensed By:

Ted Adams, CEO & Publisher • Greg Goldstein, President & COO • Robbie Robbins, EVP/Sr. Graphic Artist • Chris Ryall, Chief Creative Officer • David Hedgecock, Editor-in-Chief • Laurie Windrow, Senior Vice President of Sales & Marketing • Matthew Ruzicka, CPA, Chief Financial Officer • Dirk Wood, VP of Marketing • Lorelei Bunjes, VP of Digital Services • Jeff Webber, VP of Licensing, Digital and Subsidiary Rights • Jerry Bennington, VP of New Product Development

Facebook: facebook.com/idwpublishing • Twitter: @idwpublishing • YouTube: youtube.com/idwpublishing
Tumblr: tumblr.idwpublishing.com • Instagram: instagram.com/idwpublishing

  You Tube

www.IDWPUBLISHING.com

Ponies of Dark Water

WRITTEN BY
Thom Zahler

ART BY
Tony Fleecs

COLORS BY
Heather Breckel

Election

WRITTEN BY
Ted Anderson

ART BY
Agnes Garbowska

COLORS ASSIST BY
Lauren Perry

LETTERS BY
Neil Uyetake

SERIES EDITS BY
Bobby Curnow

COVER BY
Tony Fleecs

art by Tony Fleecs

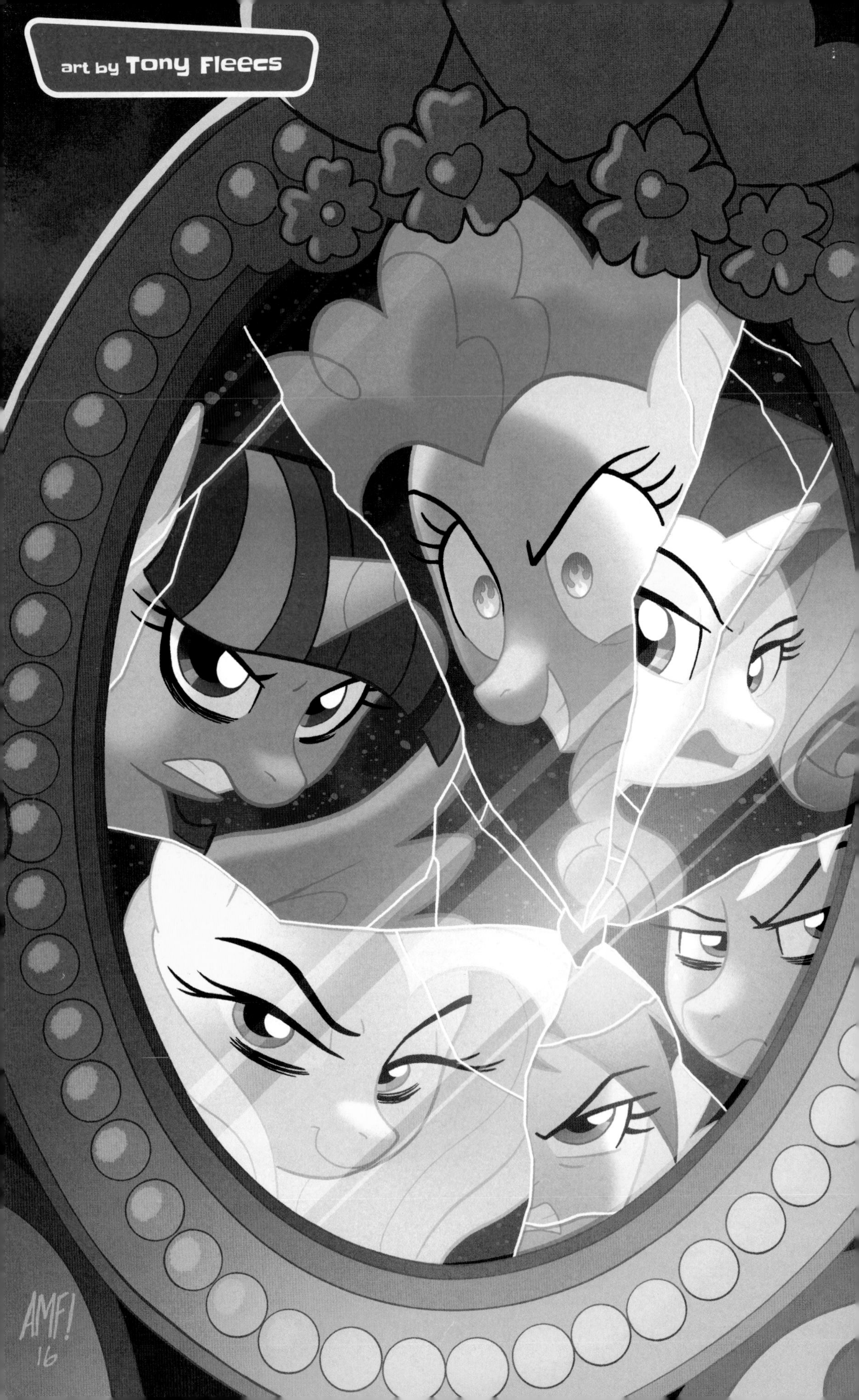
AMF!
16

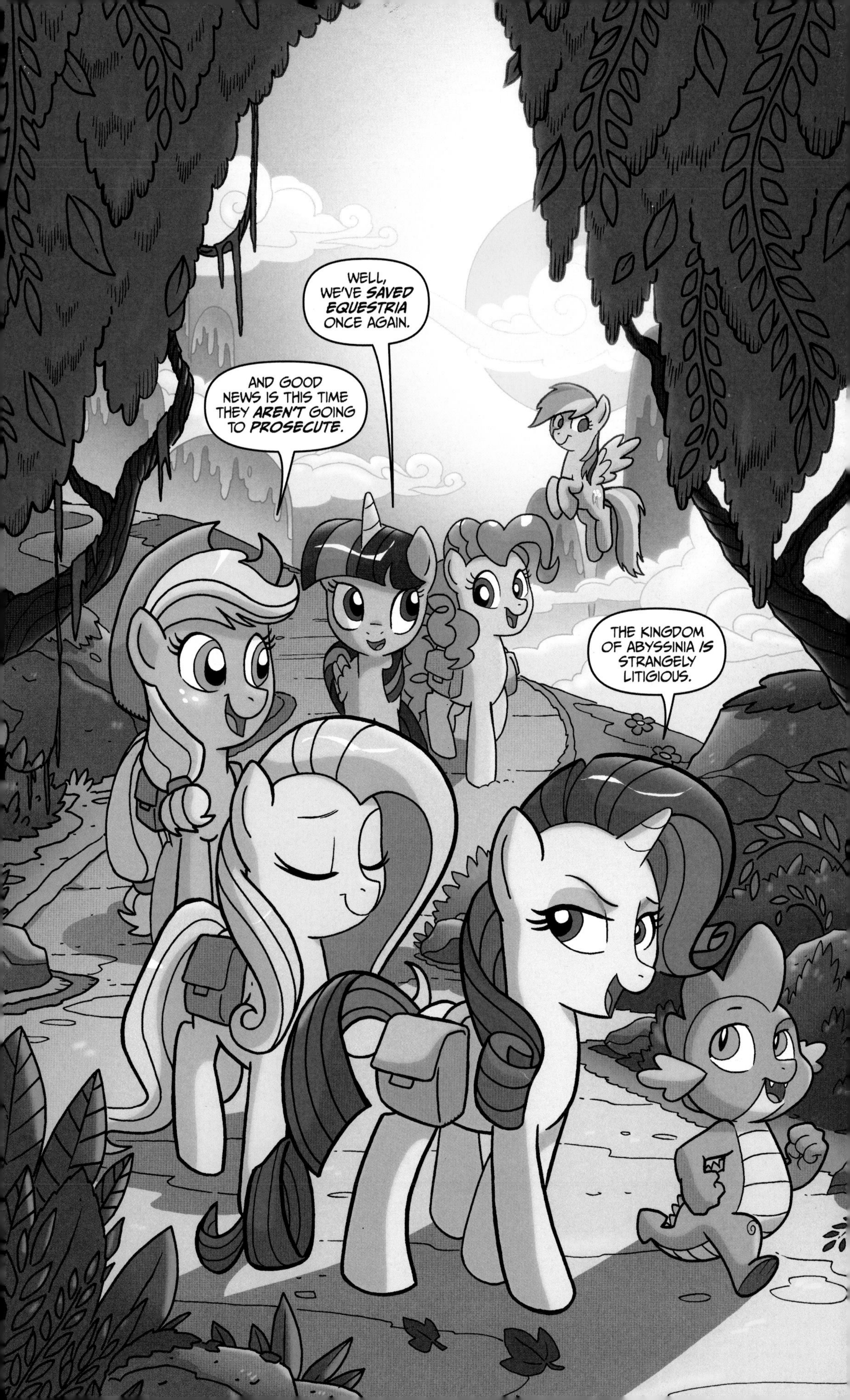
WELL, WE'VE SAVED EQUESTRIA ONCE AGAIN.
AND GOOD NEWS IS THIS TIME THEY AREN'T GOING TO PROSECUTE.
THE KINGDOM OF ABYSSINIA IS STRANGELY LITIGIOUS.

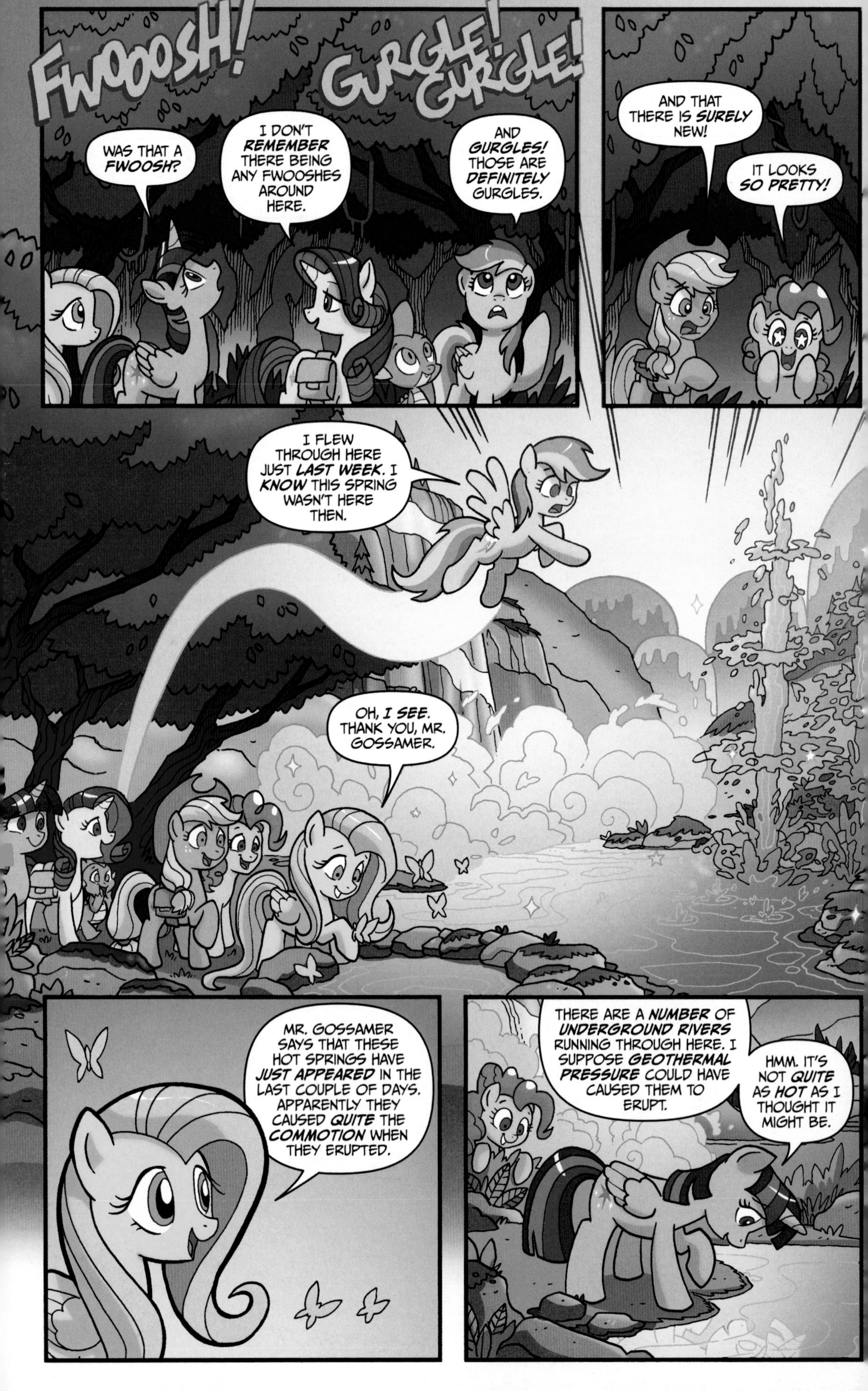
FWOOOSH!
GURGLE! GURGLE!
WAS THAT A FWOOSH?
I DON'T REMEMBER THERE BEING ANY FWOOSHES AROUND HERE.
AND GURGLES! THOSE ARE DEFINITELY GURGLES.
AND THAT THERE IS SURELY NEW!
IT LOOKS SO PRETTY!
I FLEW THROUGH HERE JUST LAST WEEK. I KNOW THIS SPRING WASN'T HERE THEN.
OH, I SEE. THANK YOU, MR. GOSSAMER.
MR. GOSSAMER SAYS THAT THESE HOT SPRINGS HAVE JUST APPEARED IN THE LAST COUPLE OF DAYS. APPARENTLY THEY CAUSED QUITE THE COMMOTION WHEN THEY ERUPTED.
THERE ARE A NUMBER OF UNDERGROUND RIVERS RUNNING THROUGH HERE. I SUPPOSE GEOTHERMAL PRESSURE COULD HAVE CAUSED THEM TO ERUPT.
HMM. IT'S NOT QUITE AS HOT AS I THOUGHT IT MIGHT BE.

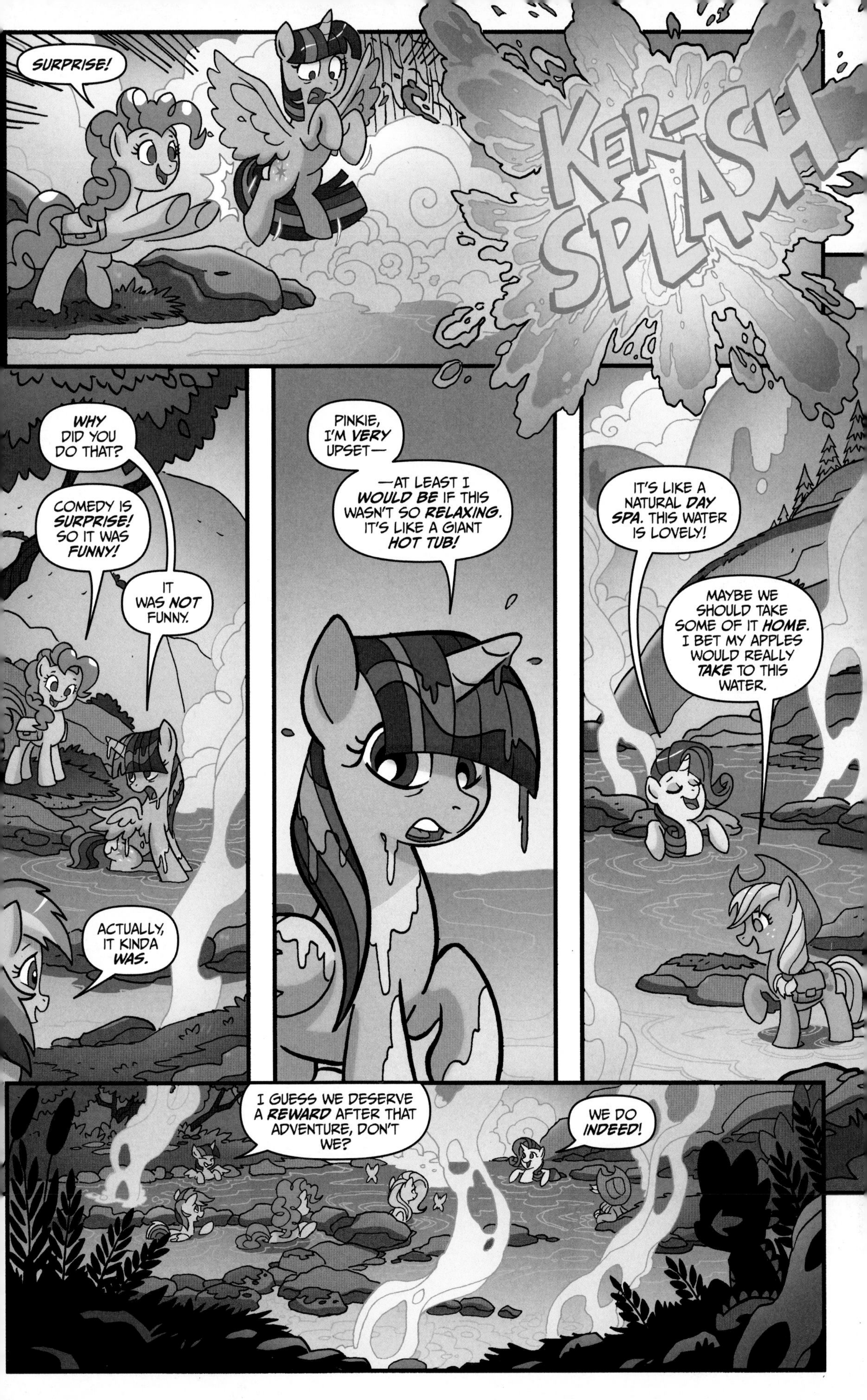
SURPRISE!
KER-SPLASH
WHY DID YOU DO THAT?
COMEDY IS SURPRISE! SO IT WAS FUNNY!
IT WAS NOT FUNNY.
ACTUALLY, IT KINDA WAS.
PINKIE, I'M VERY UPSET—
—AT LEAST I WOULD BE IF THIS WASN'T SO RELAXING. IT'S LIKE A GIANT HOT TUB!
IT'S LIKE A NATURAL DAY SPA. THIS WATER IS LOVELY!
MAYBE WE SHOULD TAKE SOME OF IT HOME. I BET MY APPLES WOULD REALLY TAKE TO THIS WATER.
I GUESS WE DESERVE A REWARD AFTER THAT ADVENTURE, DON'T WE?
WE DO INDEED!

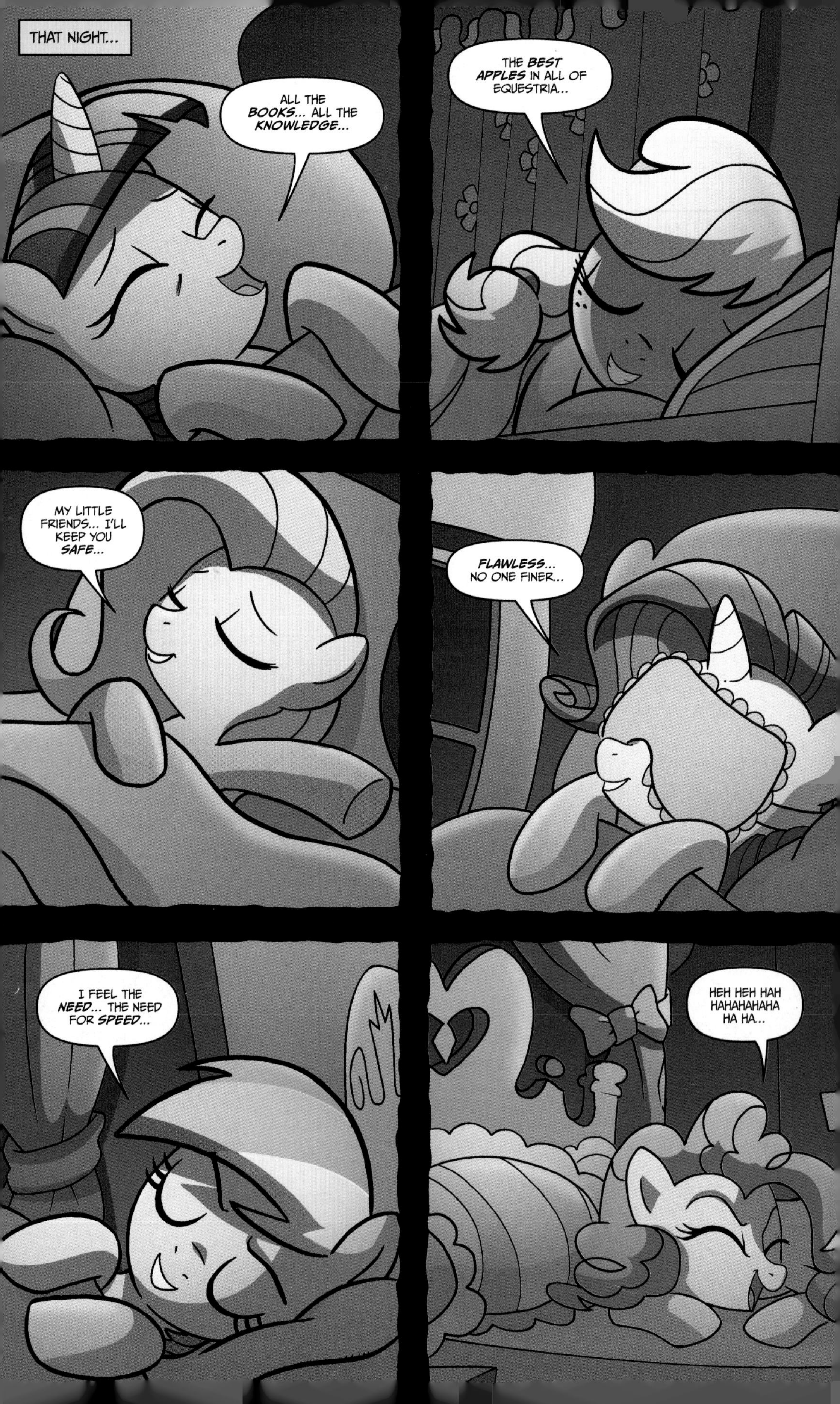
THAT NIGHT...
ALL THE BOOKS... ALL THE KNOWLEDGE...
THE BEST APPLES IN ALL OF EQUESTRIA...
MY LITTLE FRIENDS... I'LL KEEP YOU SAFE...
FLAWLESS... NO ONE FINER...
I FEEL THE NEED... THE NEED FOR SPEED...
HEH HEH HAH HAHAHAHAHA HA HA...

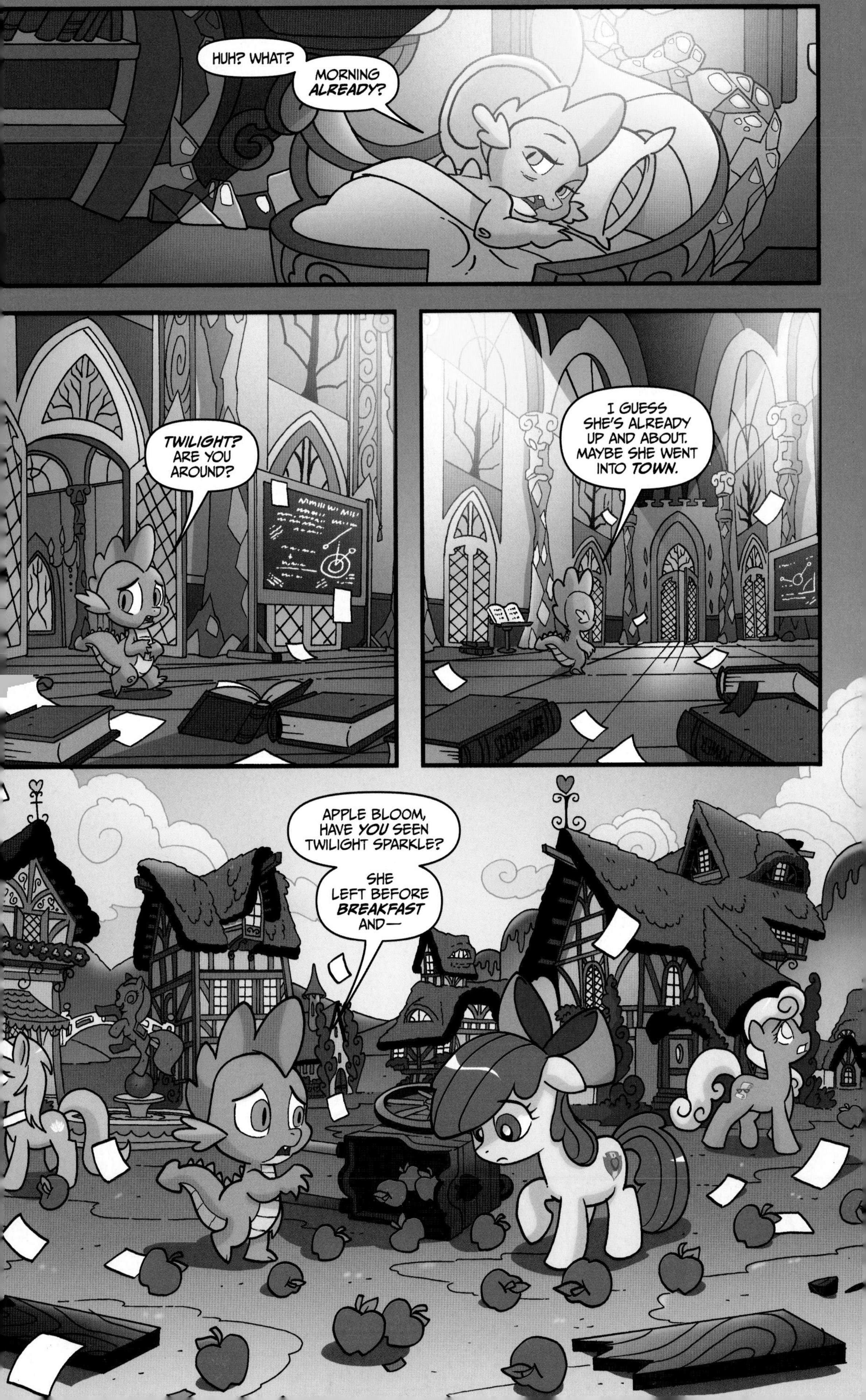
HUH? WHAT?
MORNING *ALREADY?*
TWILIGHT? ARE YOU AROUND?
I GUESS SHE'S ALREADY UP AND ABOUT. MAYBE SHE WENT INTO *TOWN.*
APPLE BLOOM, HAVE *YOU* SEEN TWILIGHT SPARKLE?
SHE LEFT BEFORE *BREAKFAST* AND—

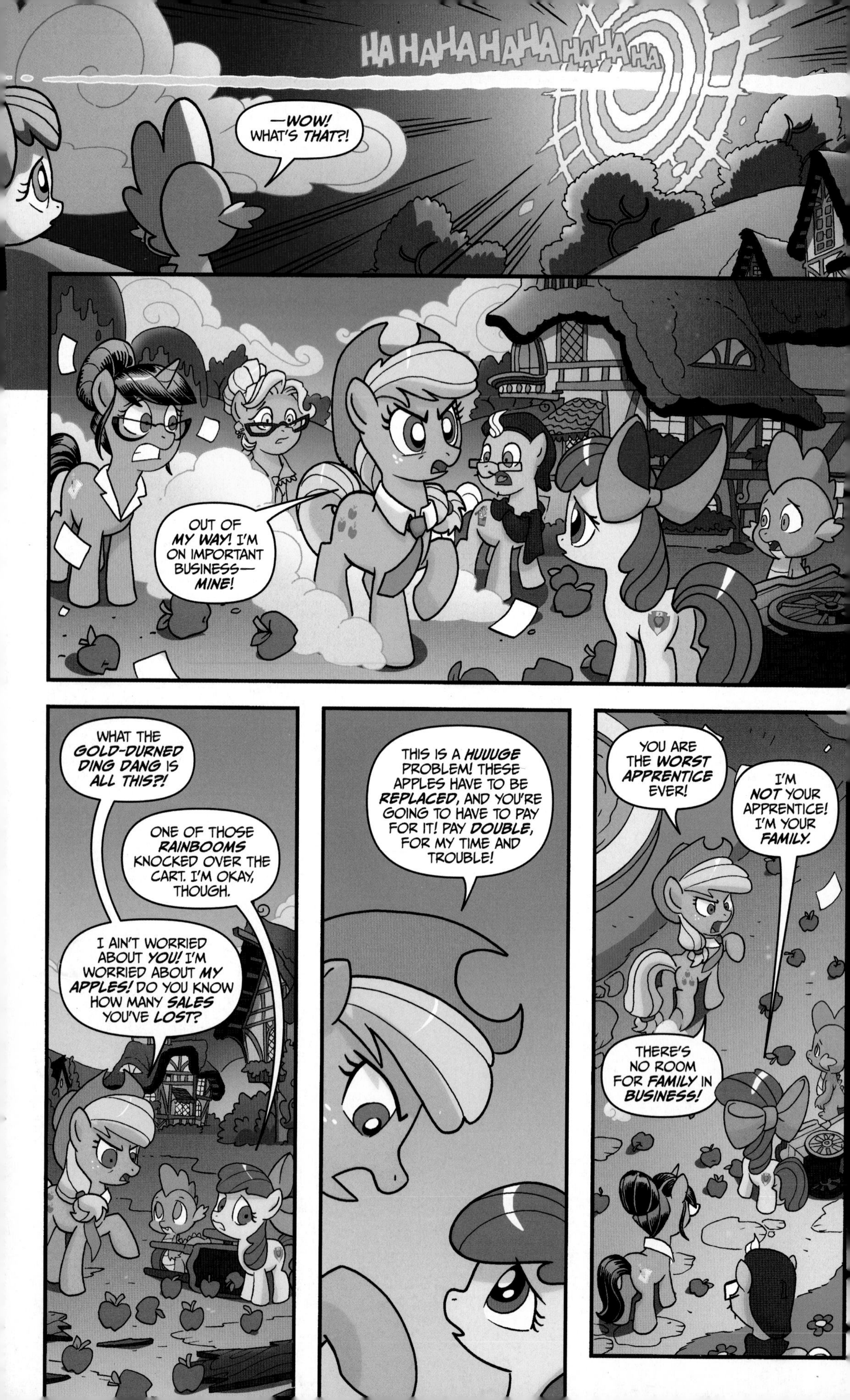
HA HAHA HAHA HAHA HAHA HA
—WOW! WHAT'S THAT?!
OUT OF MY WAY! I'M ON IMPORTANT BUSINESS— MINE!
WHAT THE GOLD-DURNED DING DANG IS ALL THIS?!
ONE OF THOSE RAINBOOMS KNOCKED OVER THE CART. I'M OKAY, THOUGH.
I AIN'T WORRIED ABOUT YOU! I'M WORRIED ABOUT MY APPLES! DO YOU KNOW HOW MANY SALES YOU'VE LOST?
THIS IS A HUUUGE PROBLEM! THESE APPLES HAVE TO BE REPLACED, AND YOU'RE GOING TO HAVE TO PAY FOR IT! PAY DOUBLE, FOR MY TIME AND TROUBLE!
YOU ARE THE WORST APPRENTICE EVER!
I'M NOT YOUR APPRENTICE! I'M YOUR FAMILY.
THERE'S NO ROOM FOR FAMILY IN BUSINESS!

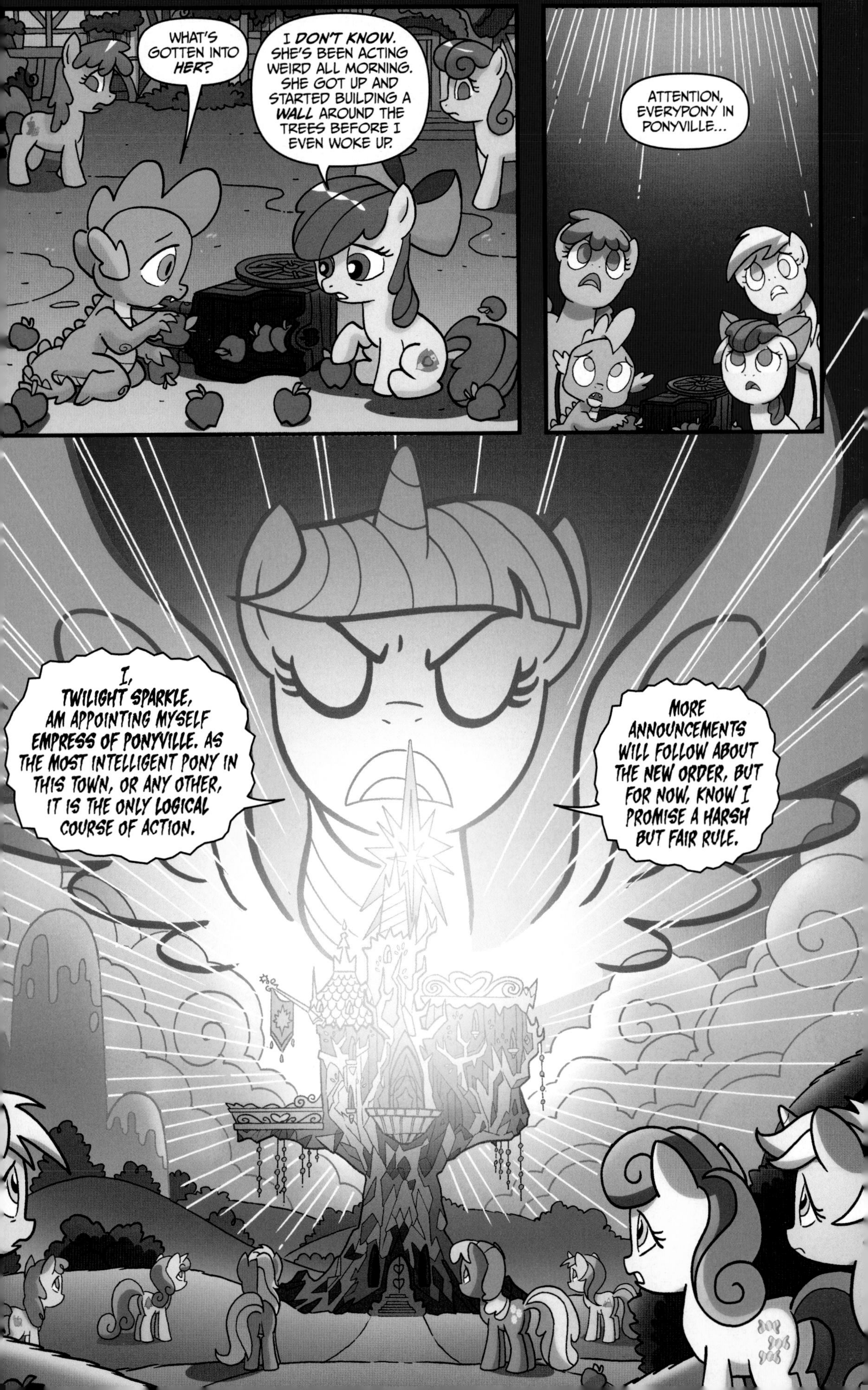
WHAT'S GOTTEN INTO *HER?*
I *DON'T KNOW.* SHE'S BEEN ACTING WEIRD ALL MORNING. SHE GOT UP AND STARTED BUILDING A *WALL* AROUND THE TREES BEFORE I EVEN WOKE UP.
ATTENTION, EVERYPONY IN PONYVILLE...
I, TWILIGHT SPARKLE, AM APPOINTING MYSELF EMPRESS OF PONYVILLE. AS THE MOST INTELLIGENT PONY IN THIS TOWN, OR ANY OTHER, IT IS THE ONLY LOGICAL COURSE OF ACTION.
MORE ANNOUNCEMENTS WILL FOLLOW ABOUT THE NEW ORDER, BUT FOR NOW, KNOW I PROMISE A HARSH BUT FAIR RULE.

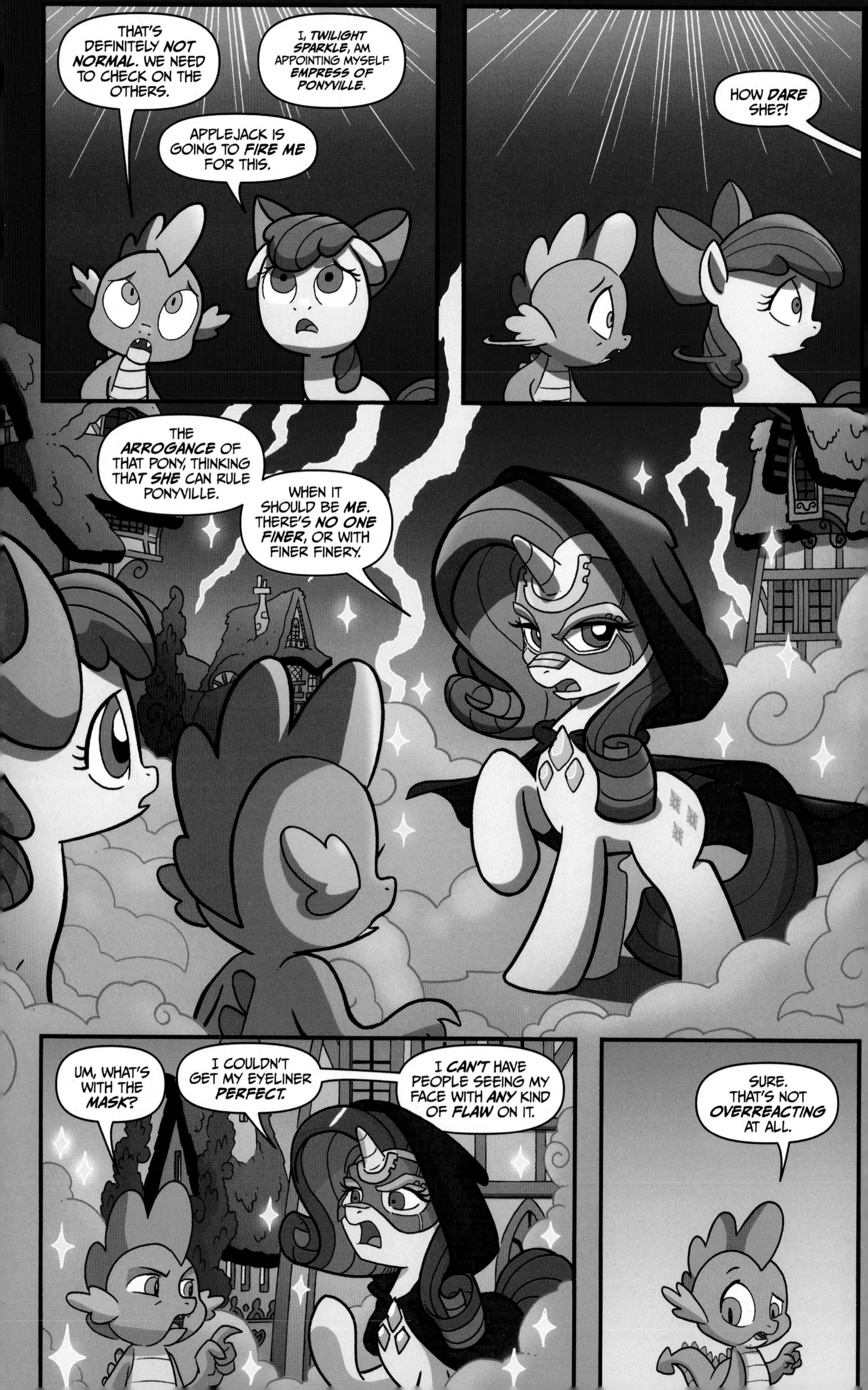
THAT'S DEFINITELY NOT NORMAL. WE NEED TO CHECK ON THE OTHERS.
I, TWILIGHT SPARKLE, AM APPOINTING MYSELF EMPRESS OF PONYVILLE.
APPLEJACK IS GOING TO FIRE ME FOR THIS.
HOW DARE SHE?!
THE ARROGANCE OF THAT PONY, THINKING THAT SHE CAN RULE PONYVILLE.
WHEN IT SHOULD BE ME. THERE'S NO ONE FINER, OR WITH FINER FINERY.
UM, WHAT'S WITH THE MASK?
I COULDN'T GET MY EYELINER PERFECT.
I CAN'T HAVE PEOPLE SEEING MY FACE WITH ANY KIND OF FLAW ON IT.
SURE. THAT'S NOT OVERREACTING AT ALL.

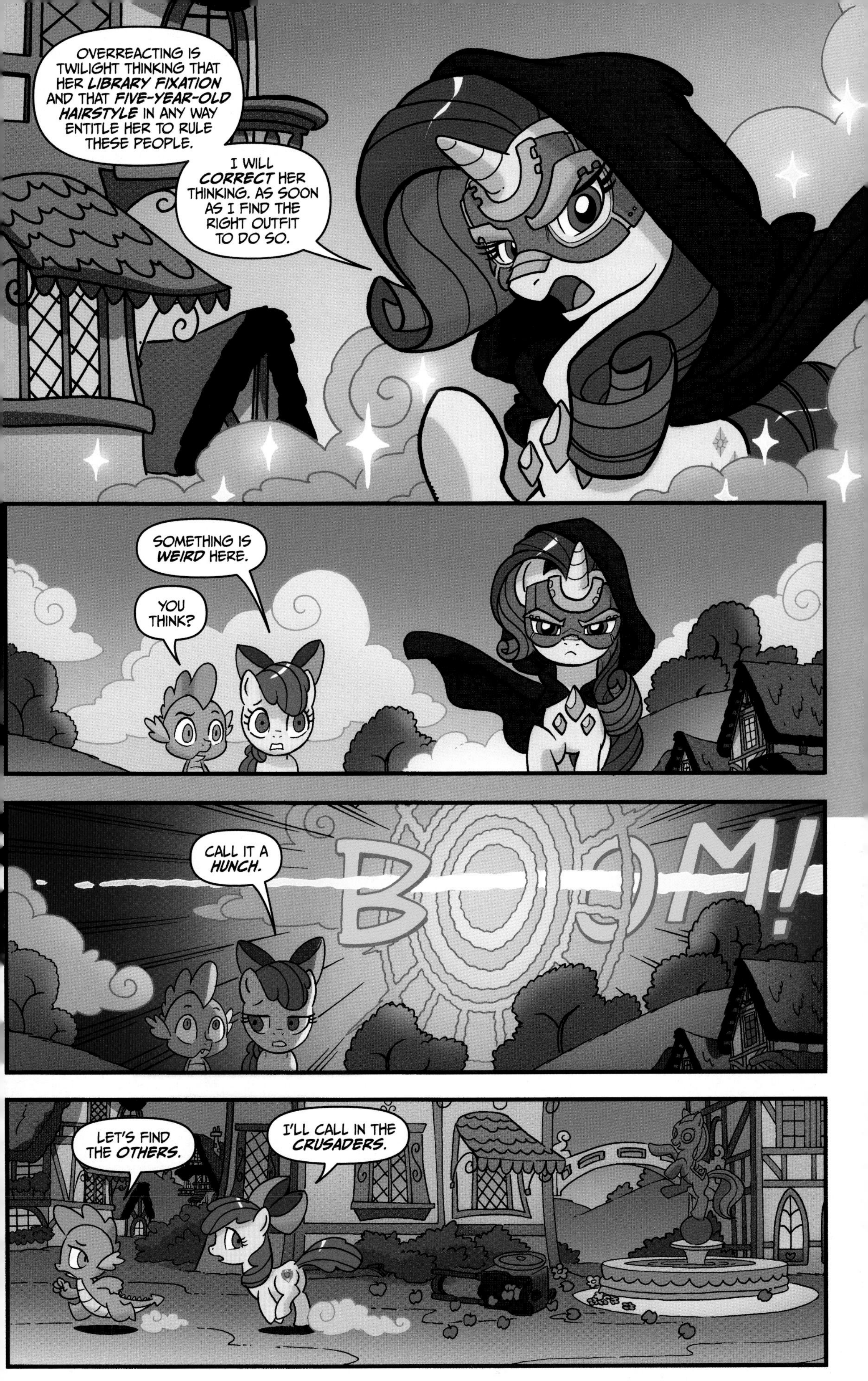
OVERREACTING IS TWILIGHT THINKING THAT HER LIBRARY FIXATION AND THAT FIVE-YEAR-OLD HAIRSTYLE IN ANY WAY ENTITLE HER TO RULE THESE PEOPLE.
I WILL CORRECT HER THINKING. AS SOON AS I FIND THE RIGHT OUTFIT TO DO SO.
SOMETHING IS WEIRD HERE.
YOU THINK?
CALL IT A HUNCH.
BOOM!
LET'S FIND THE OTHERS.
I'LL CALL IN THE CRUSADERS.

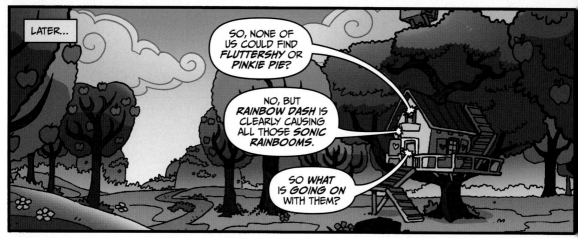

LATER...

SO, NONE OF US COULD FIND *FLUTTERSHY* OR *PINKIE PIE?*

NO, BUT *RAINBOW DASH* IS CLEARLY CAUSING ALL THOSE *SONIC RAINBOOMS.*

SO *WHAT* IS *GOING ON* WITH THEM?

THEY'VE *ALL* BEEN DIFFERENT SINCE WE GOT BACK FROM *ABYSSINIA.*

DID SOMETHING HAPPEN TO THEM *THERE?*

I *DON'T* THINK SO. THEY WERE NORMAL THE WHOLE TRIP BACK. WE EVEN TOOK A BREAK AT THOSE *NEW HOT SPRINGS.*

NEW?

HOT?

SPRINGS?

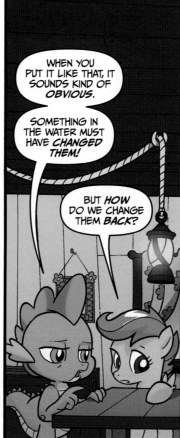

WHEN YOU PUT IT LIKE THAT, IT SOUNDS KIND OF *OBVIOUS.*

SOMETHING IN THE WATER MUST HAVE *CHANGED* THEM!

BUT *HOW* DO WE CHANGE THEM *BACK?*

I DON'T KNOW. BUT YOU KNOW WHO *WILL? PRINCESS CELESTIA!*

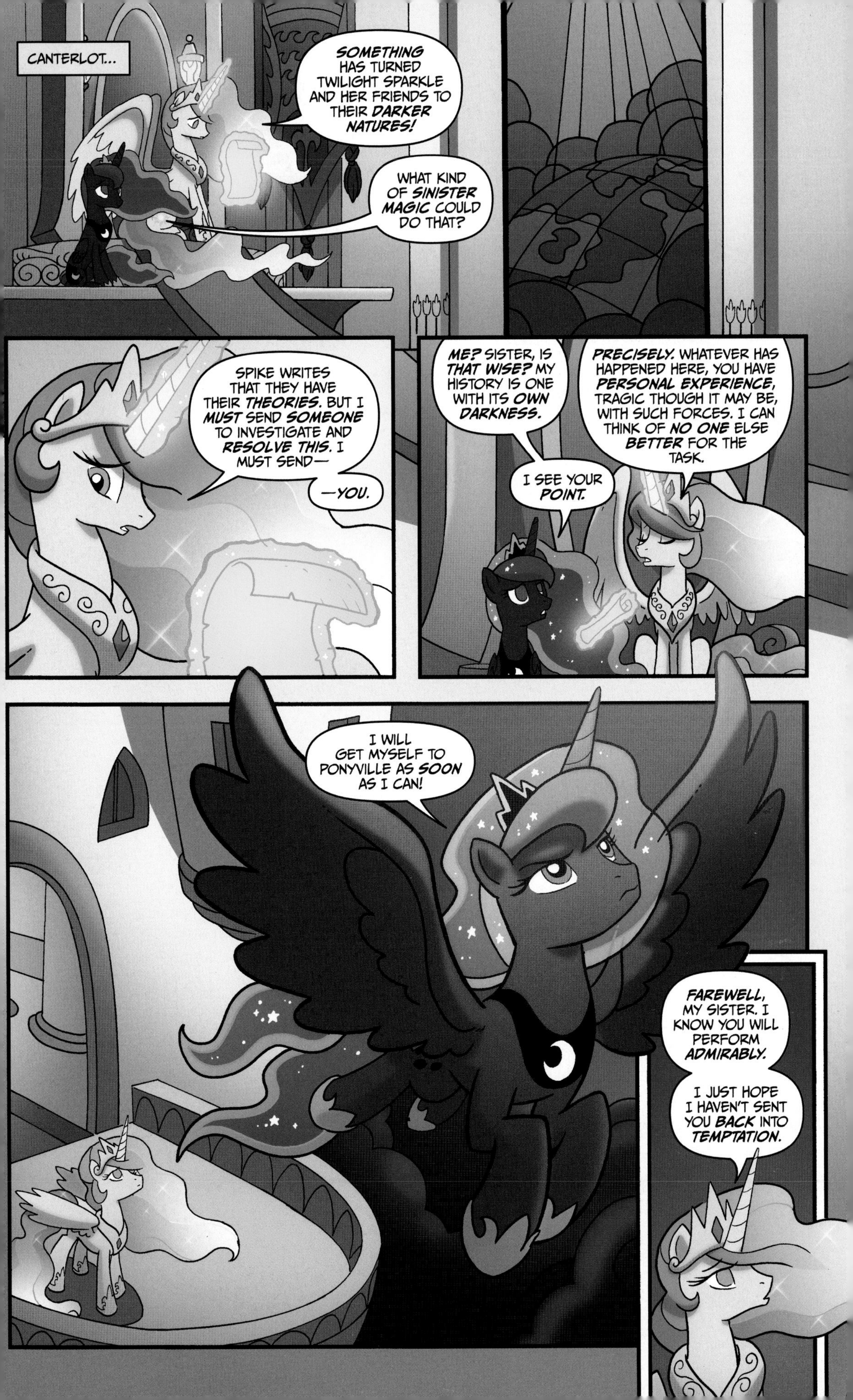

CANTERLOT...
SOMETHING HAS TURNED TWILIGHT SPARKLE AND HER FRIENDS TO THEIR DARKER NATURES!
WHAT KIND OF SINISTER MAGIC COULD DO THAT?
SPIKE WRITES THAT THEY HAVE THEIR THEORIES. BUT I MUST SEND SOMEONE TO INVESTIGATE AND RESOLVE THIS. I MUST SEND—
—YOU.
ME? SISTER, IS THAT WISE? MY HISTORY IS ONE WITH ITS OWN DARKNESS.
PRECISELY. WHATEVER HAS HAPPENED HERE, YOU HAVE PERSONAL EXPERIENCE, TRAGIC THOUGH IT MAY BE, WITH SUCH FORCES. I CAN THINK OF NO ONE ELSE BETTER FOR THE TASK.
I SEE YOUR POINT.
I WILL GET MYSELF TO PONYVILLE AS SOON AS I CAN!
FAREWELL, MY SISTER. I KNOW YOU WILL PERFORM ADMIRABLY.
I JUST HOPE I HAVEN'T SENT YOU BACK INTO TEMPTATION.

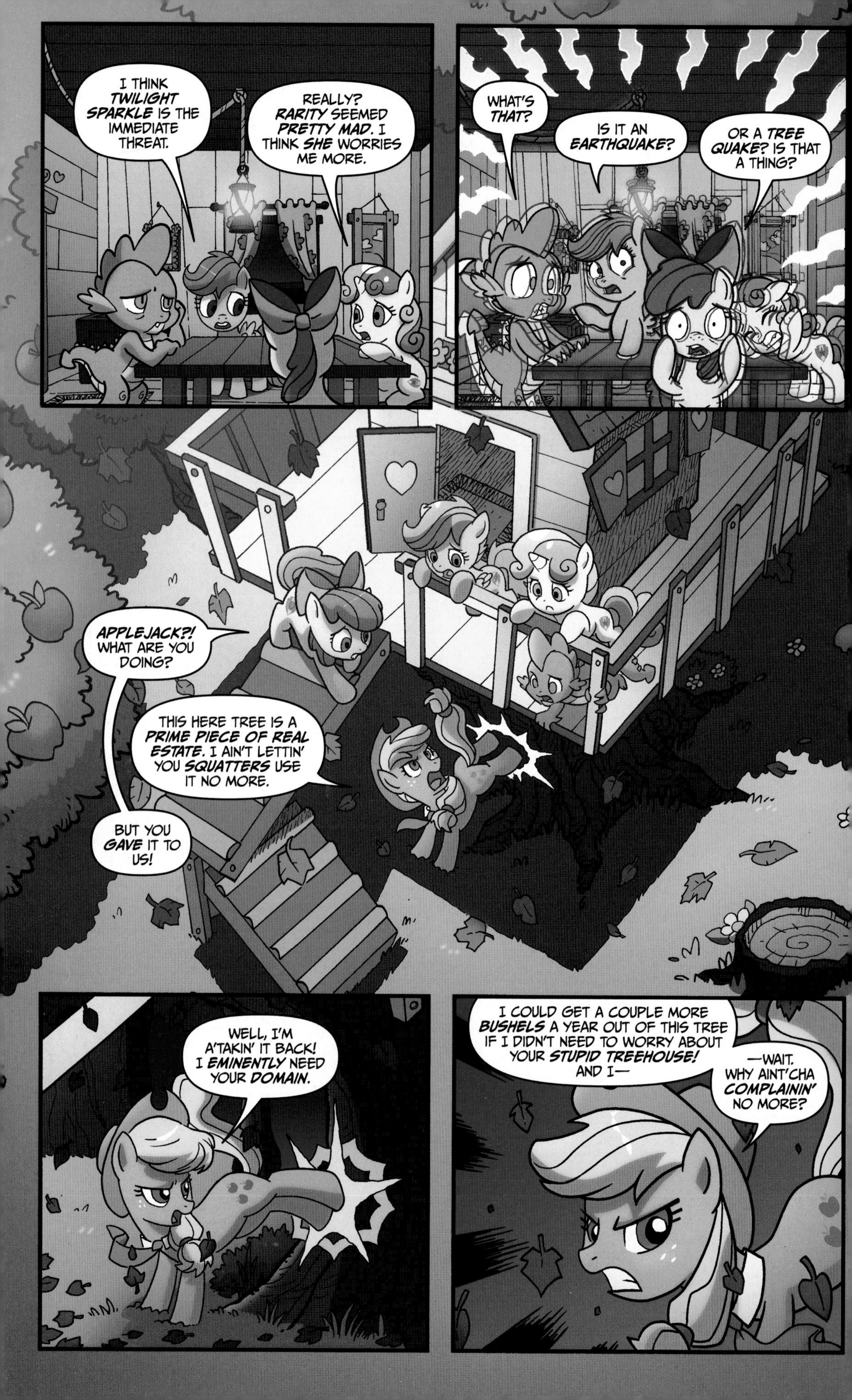

I THINK TWILIGHT SPARKLE IS THE IMMEDIATE THREAT.
REALLY? RARITY SEEMED PRETTY MAD. I THINK SHE WORRIES ME MORE.
WHAT'S THAT?
IS IT AN EARTHQUAKE?
OR A TREE QUAKE? IS THAT A THING?
APPLEJACK?! WHAT ARE YOU DOING?
THIS HERE TREE IS A PRIME PIECE OF REAL ESTATE. I AIN'T LETTIN' YOU SQUATTERS USE IT NO MORE.
BUT YOU GAVE IT TO US!
WELL, I'M A'TAKIN' IT BACK! I EMINENTLY NEED YOUR DOMAIN.
I COULD GET A COUPLE MORE BUSHELS A YEAR OUT OF THIS TREE IF I DIDN'T NEED TO WORRY ABOUT YOUR STUPID TREEHOUSE! AND I—
—WAIT. WHY AINT'CHA COMPLAININ' NO MORE?

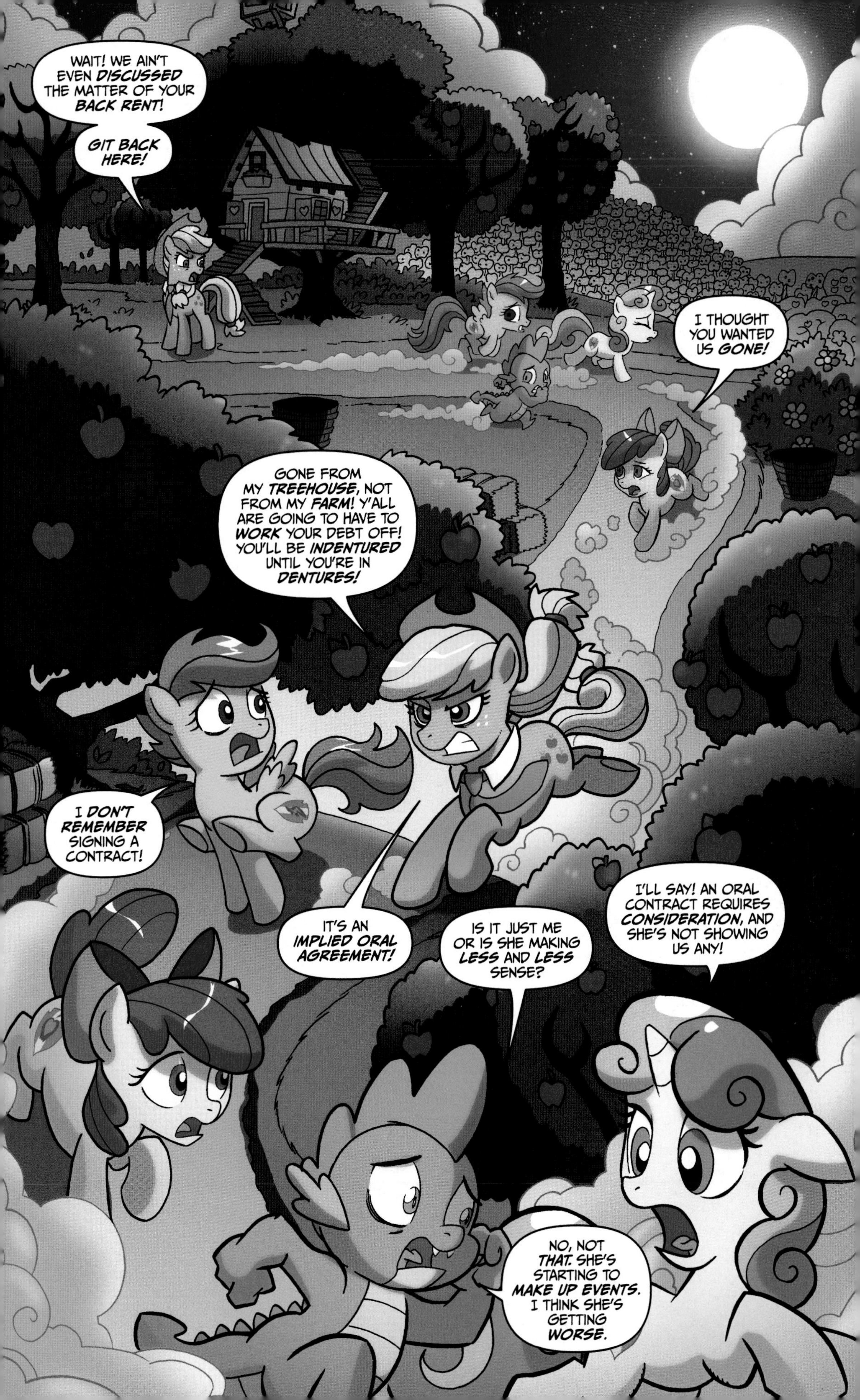
WAIT! WE AIN'T EVEN DISCUSSED THE MATTER OF YOUR BACK RENT!
GIT BACK HERE!
I THOUGHT YOU WANTED US GONE!
GONE FROM MY TREEHOUSE, NOT FROM MY FARM! Y'ALL ARE GOING TO HAVE TO WORK YOUR DEBT OFF! YOU'LL BE INDENTURED UNTIL YOU'RE IN DENTURES!
I DON'T REMEMBER SIGNING A CONTRACT!
IT'S AN IMPLIED ORAL AGREEMENT!
IS IT JUST ME OR IS SHE MAKING LESS AND LESS SENSE?
I'LL SAY! AN ORAL CONTRACT REQUIRES CONSIDERATION, AND SHE'S NOT SHOWING US ANY!
NO, NOT THAT. SHE'S STARTING TO MAKE UP EVENTS. I THINK SHE'S GETTING WORSE.

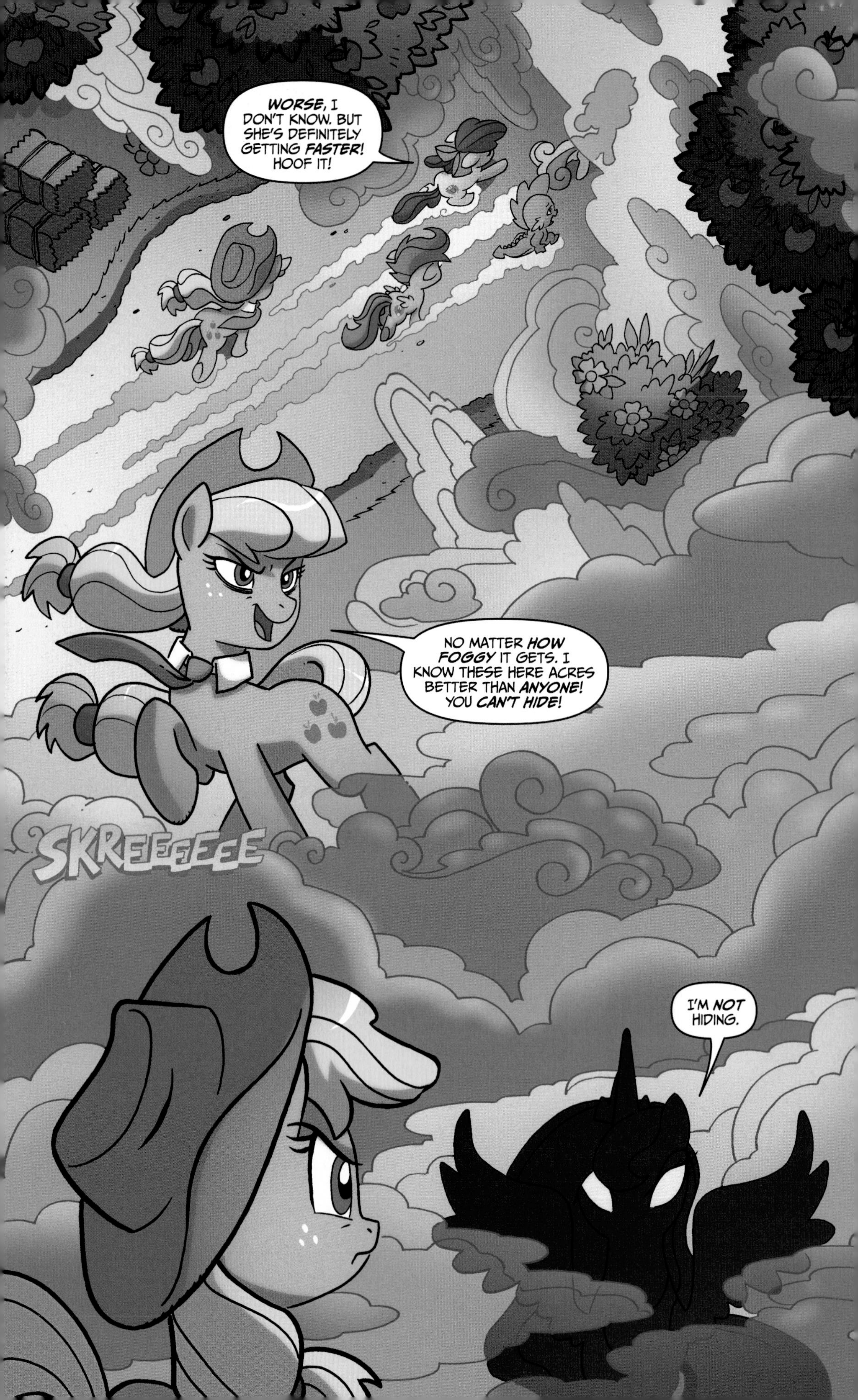
WORSE, I DON'T KNOW. BUT SHE'S DEFINITELY GETTING FASTER! HOOF IT!
NO MATTER HOW FOGGY IT GETS. I KNOW THESE HERE ACRES BETTER THAN ANYONE! YOU CAN'T HIDE!
SKREEEEEEE
I'M NOT HIDING.

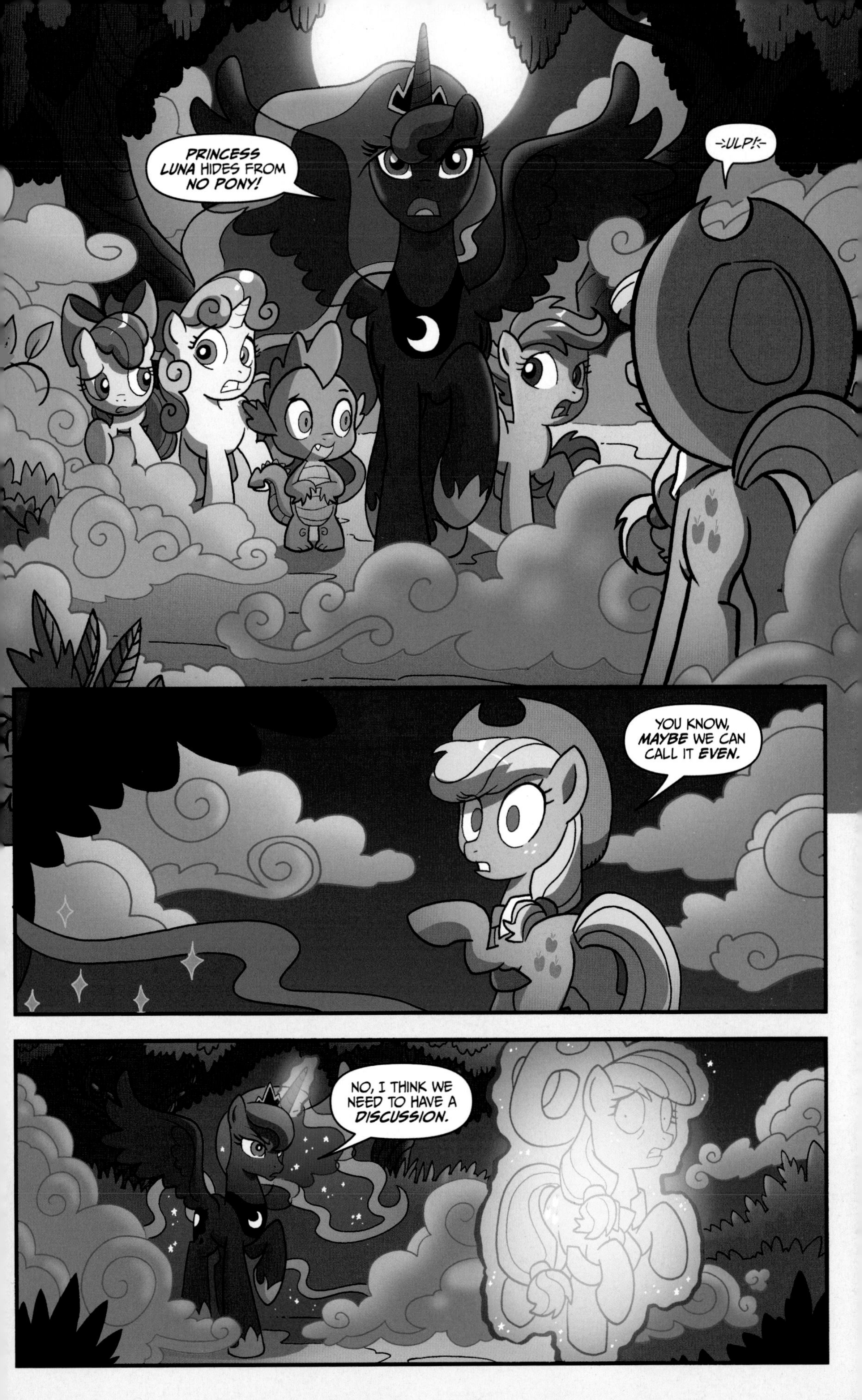
PRINCESS LUNA HIDES FROM NO PONY!
-ULP!-
YOU KNOW, MAYBE WE CAN CALL IT EVEN.
NO, I THINK WE NEED TO HAVE A DISCUSSION.

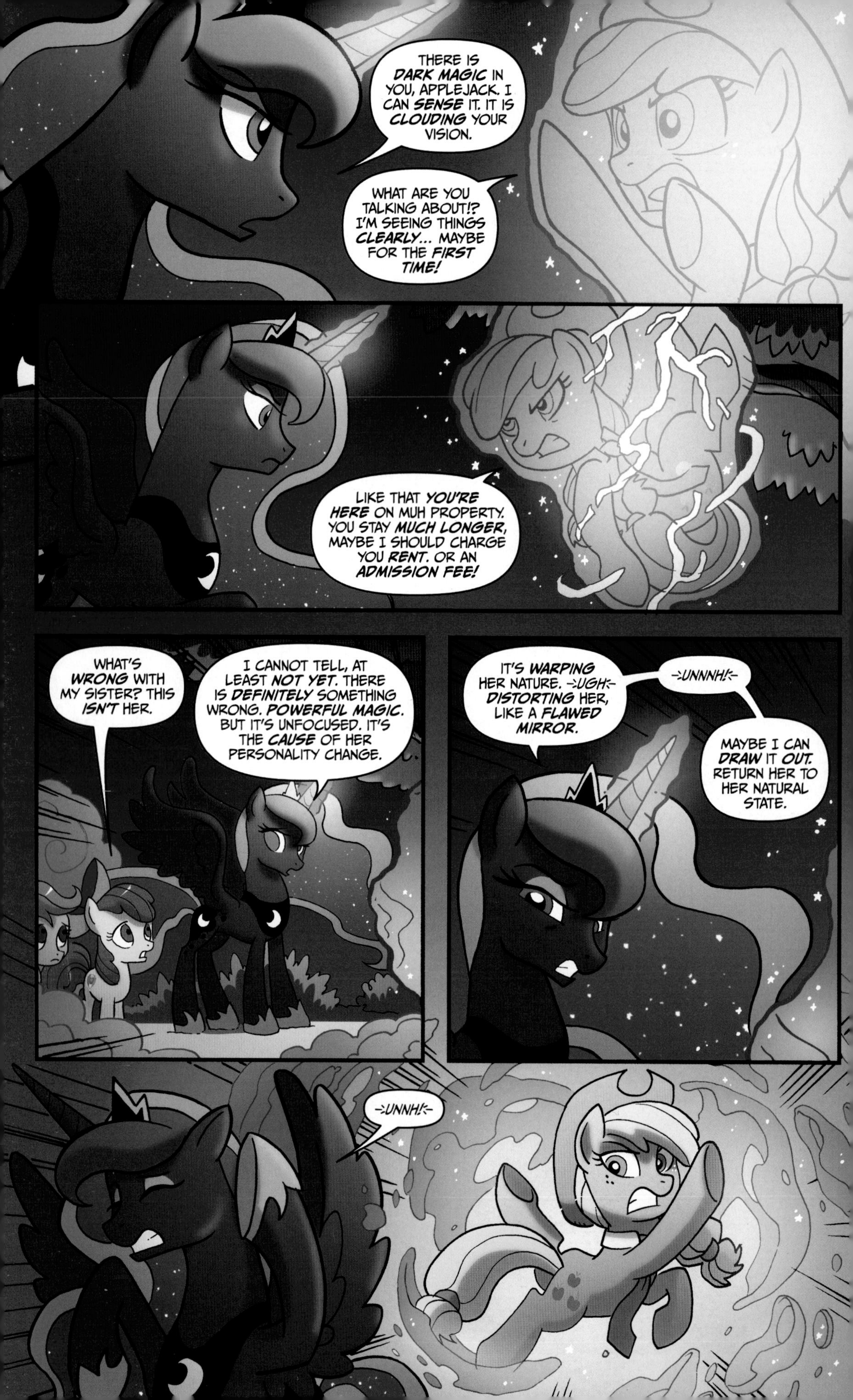
THERE IS DARK MAGIC IN YOU, APPLEJACK. I CAN SENSE IT. IT IS CLOUDING YOUR VISION.
WHAT ARE YOU TALKING ABOUT!? I'M SEEING THINGS CLEARLY... MAYBE FOR THE FIRST TIME!
LIKE THAT YOU'RE HERE ON MUH PROPERTY. YOU STAY MUCH LONGER, MAYBE I SHOULD CHARGE YOU RENT. OR AN ADMISSION FEE!
WHAT'S WRONG WITH MY SISTER? THIS ISN'T HER.
I CANNOT TELL, AT LEAST NOT YET. THERE IS DEFINITELY SOMETHING WRONG. POWERFUL MAGIC. BUT IT'S UNFOCUSED. IT'S THE CAUSE OF HER PERSONALITY CHANGE.
IT'S WARPING HER NATURE. -UGH- DISTORTING HER, LIKE A FLAWED MIRROR.
-UNNNH!-
MAYBE I CAN DRAW IT OUT. RETURN HER TO HER NATURAL STATE.
-UNNH!-

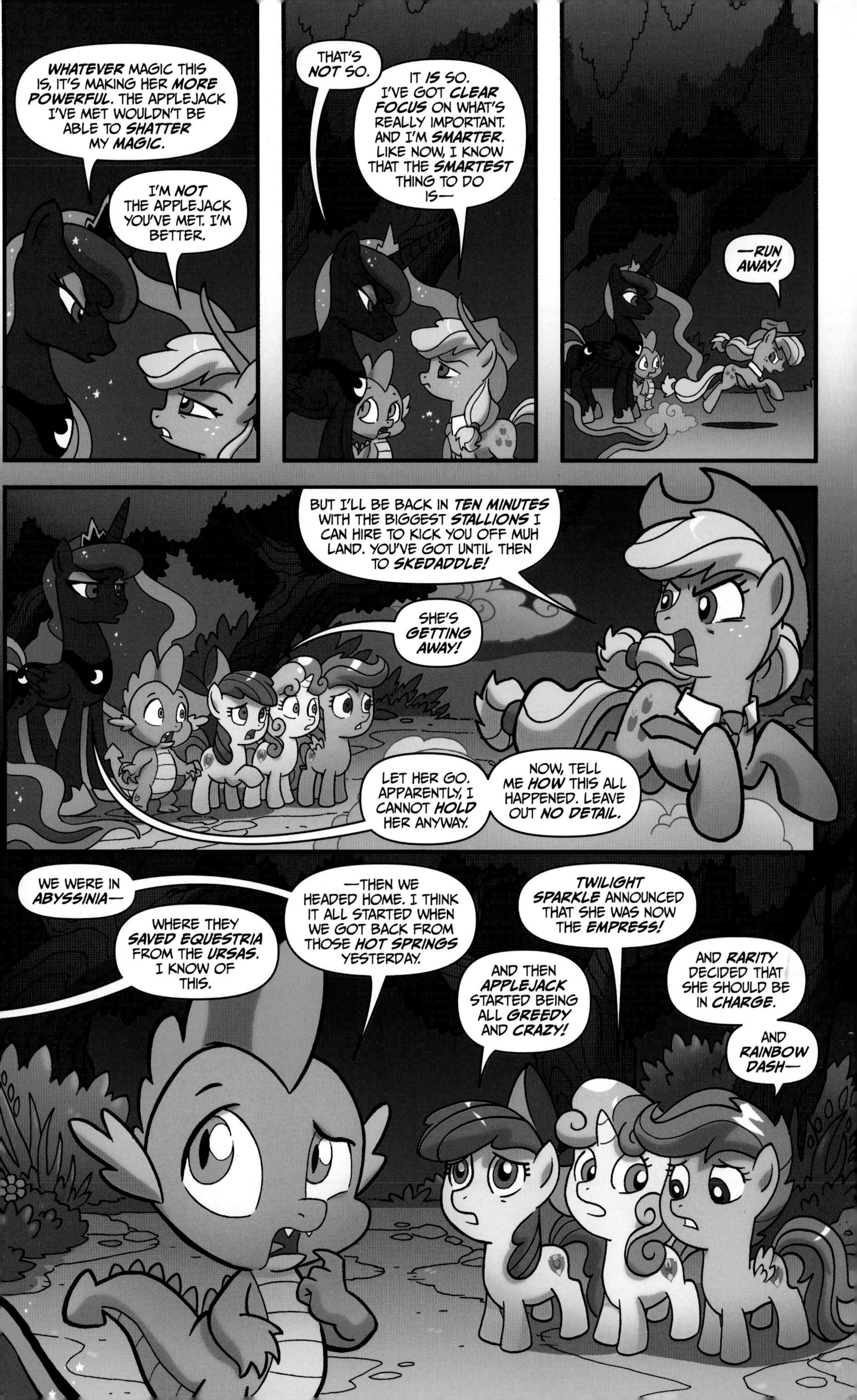
WHATEVER MAGIC THIS IS, IT'S MAKING HER MORE POWERFUL. THE APPLEJACK I'VE MET WOULDN'T BE ABLE TO SHATTER MY MAGIC.
I'M NOT THE APPLEJACK YOU'VE MET. I'M BETTER.
THAT'S NOT SO.
IT IS SO. I'VE GOT CLEAR FOCUS ON WHAT'S REALLY IMPORTANT. AND I'M SMARTER. LIKE NOW, I KNOW THAT THE SMARTEST THING TO DO IS—
—RUN AWAY!
BUT I'LL BE BACK IN TEN MINUTES WITH THE BIGGEST STALLIONS I CAN HIRE TO KICK YOU OFF MUH LAND. YOU'VE GOT UNTIL THEN TO SKEDADDLE!
SHE'S GETTING AWAY!
LET HER GO. APPARENTLY, I CANNOT HOLD HER ANYWAY.
NOW, TELL ME HOW THIS ALL HAPPENED. LEAVE OUT NO DETAIL.
WE WERE IN ABYSSINIA—
WHERE THEY SAVED EQUESTRIA FROM THE URSAS. I KNOW OF THIS.
—THEN WE HEADED HOME. I THINK IT ALL STARTED WHEN WE GOT BACK FROM THOSE HOT SPRINGS YESTERDAY.
TWILIGHT SPARKLE ANNOUNCED THAT SHE WAS NOW THE EMPRESS!
AND THEN APPLEJACK STARTED BEING ALL GREEDY AND CRAZY!
AND RARITY DECIDED THAT SHE SHOULD BE IN CHARGE.
AND RAINBOW DASH—

KA-BOOM!

—WELL, *THAT*.

WHATEVER MAGIC WAS IN THOSE SPRINGS HAS *CORRUPTED* OUR FRIENDS, AND I MAY NOT BE ABLE TO CHANGE THEM *BACK*. I TRIED WITH APPLEJACK AND WE SAW WHAT HAPPENED.

WE NEED A *DIFFERENT* PLAN.

SPIKE, YOU AND I WILL *STAY HERE* AND TRY TO KEEP THOSE *AFFECTED* FROM CAUSING TOO MUCH *DAMAGE*.

THE REST OF YOU WILL GO INTO THE *EVERFREE FOREST* AND FIND *ZECORA*. WHERE *MY MAGIC* HAS *FAILED* AGAINST THIS WATER, PERHAPS *HER KNOWLEDGE* OF *POTIONS* WILL *SUCCEED*.

THE *CUTIE MARK* CRUSADERS ARE ON OUR WAY!

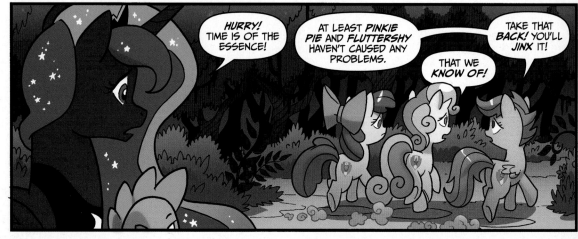

HURRY! TIME IS OF THE ESSENCE!

AT LEAST *PINKIE PIE* AND *FLUTTERSHY* HAVEN'T CAUSED ANY PROBLEMS.

THAT WE *KNOW OF*!

TAKE THAT *BACK*! YOU'LL *JINX* IT!

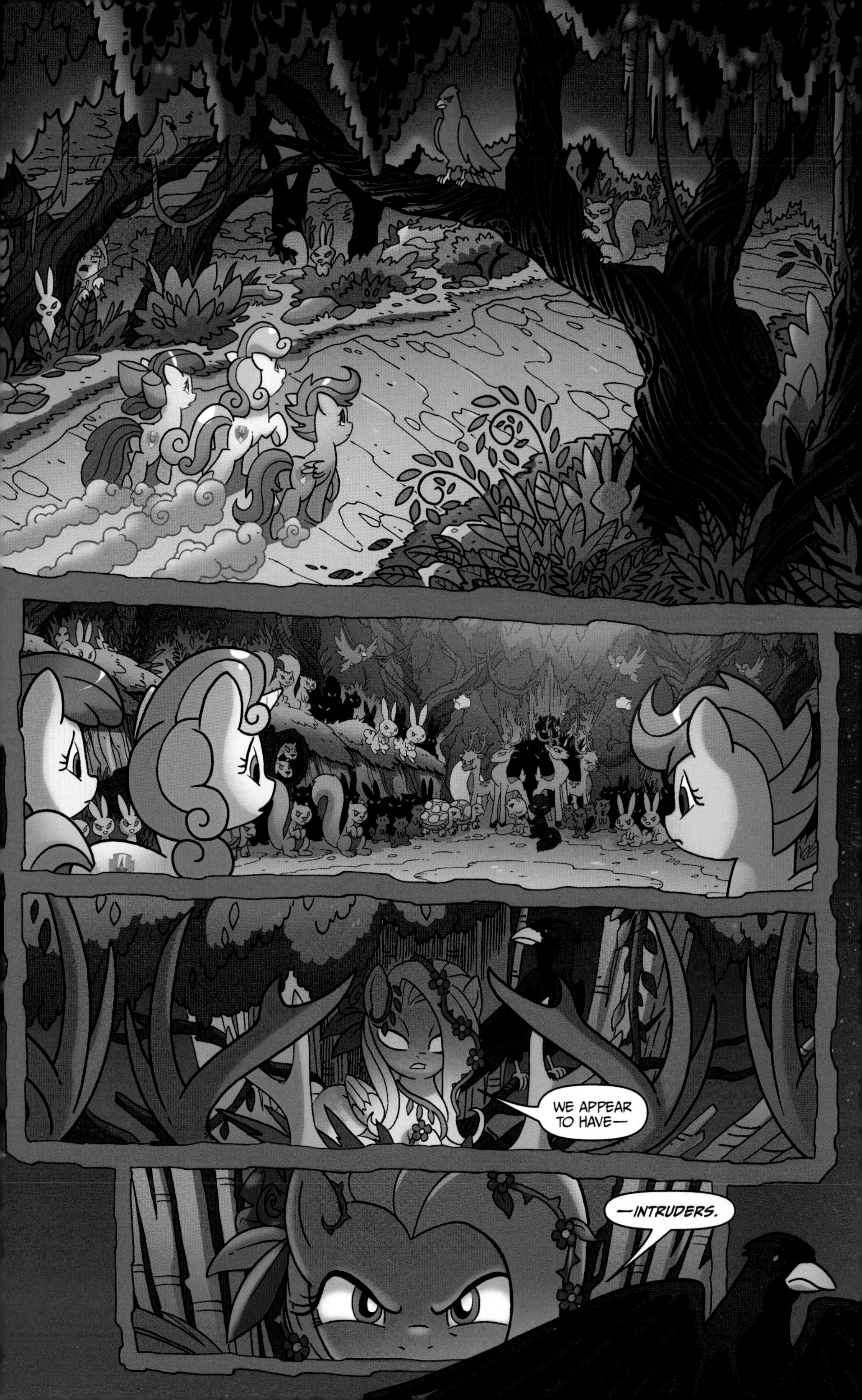
WE APPEAR TO HAVE—
—INTRUDERS.

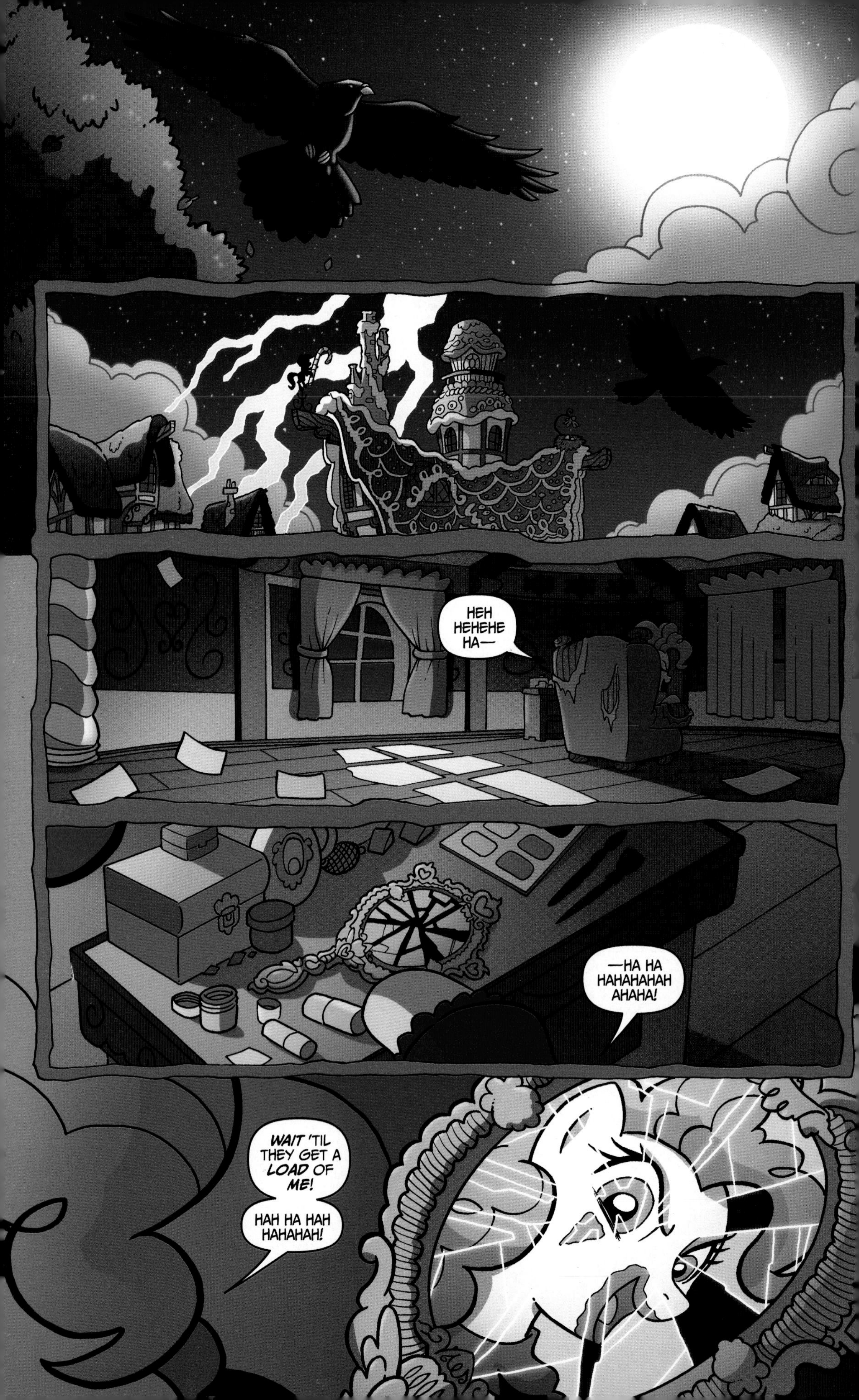
HEH HEHEHE HA—
—HA HA HAHAHAHAH AHAHA!
WAIT 'TIL THEY GET A LOAD OF ME!
HAH HA HAH HAHAHAH!

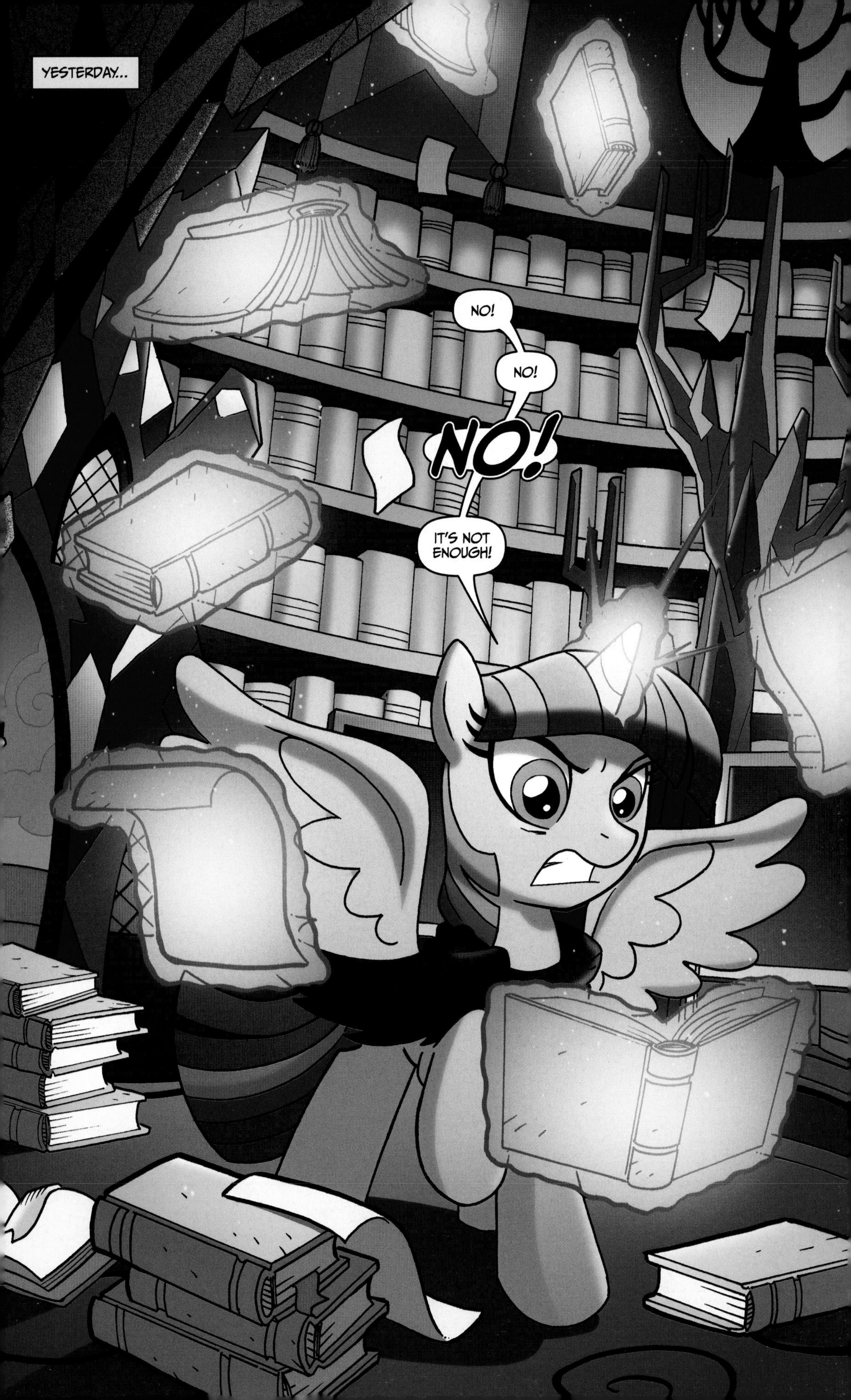
YESTERDAY...
NO!
NO!
NO!
IT'S NOT ENOUGH!

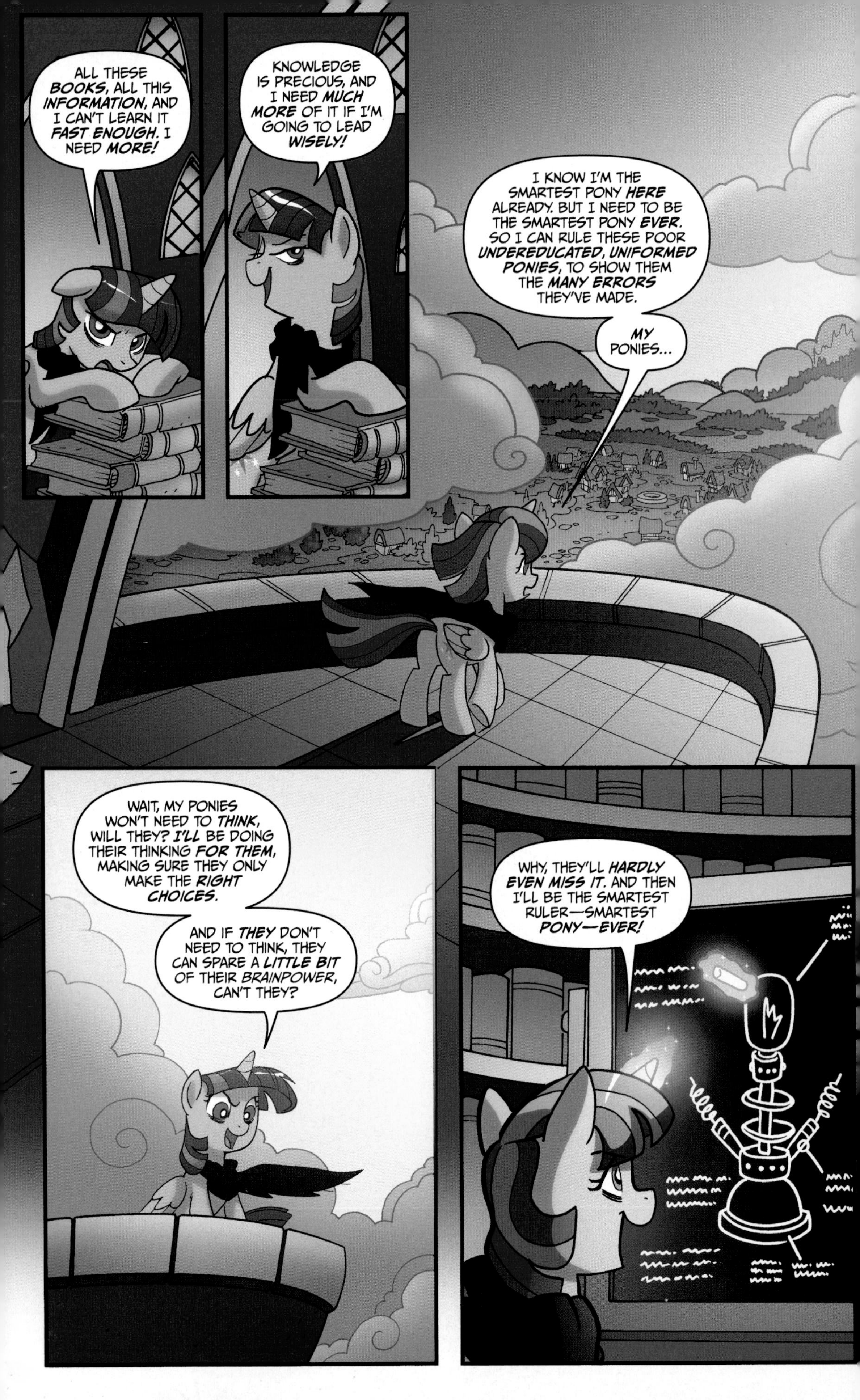
ALL THESE BOOKS, ALL THIS INFORMATION, AND I CAN'T LEARN IT FAST ENOUGH. I NEED MORE!
KNOWLEDGE IS PRECIOUS, AND I NEED MUCH MORE OF IT IF I'M GOING TO LEAD WISELY!
I KNOW I'M THE SMARTEST PONY HERE ALREADY. BUT I NEED TO BE THE SMARTEST PONY EVER. SO I CAN RULE THESE POOR UNDEREDUCATED, UNIFORMED PONIES, TO SHOW THEM THE MANY ERRORS THEY'VE MADE.
MY PONIES...
WAIT, MY PONIES WON'T NEED TO THINK, WILL THEY? I'LL BE DOING THEIR THINKING FOR THEM, MAKING SURE THEY ONLY MAKE THE RIGHT CHOICES.
AND IF THEY DON'T NEED TO THINK, THEY CAN SPARE A LITTLE BIT OF THEIR BRAINPOWER, CAN'T THEY?
WHY, THEY'LL HARDLY EVEN MISS IT. AND THEN I'LL BE THE SMARTEST RULER—SMARTEST PONY—EVER!

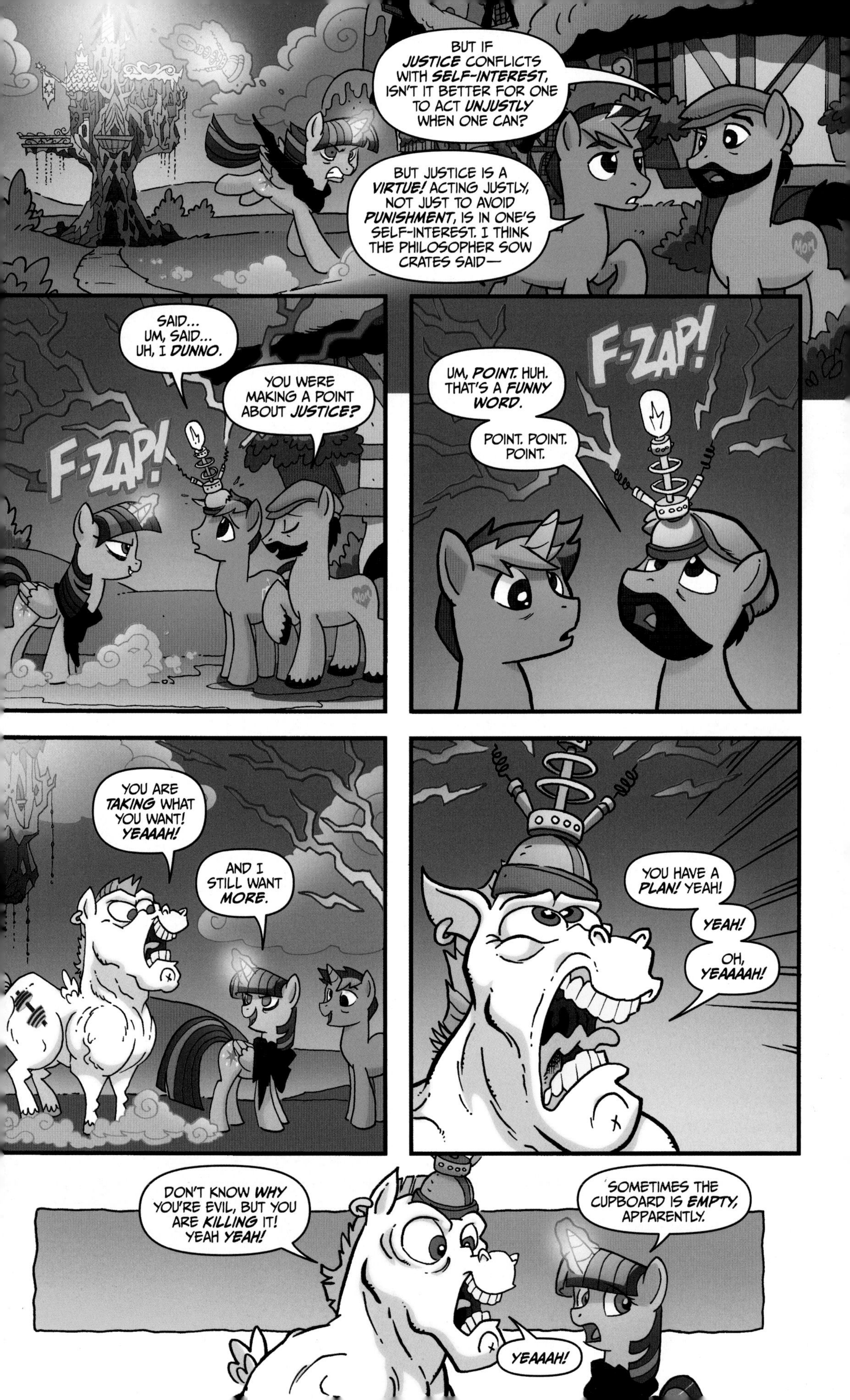
BUT IF JUSTICE CONFLICTS WITH SELF-INTEREST, ISN'T IT BETTER FOR ONE TO ACT UNJUSTLY WHEN ONE CAN?
BUT JUSTICE IS A VIRTUE! ACTING JUSTLY, NOT JUST TO AVOID PUNISHMENT, IS IN ONE'S SELF-INTEREST. I THINK THE PHILOSOPHER SOW CRATES SAID—
MOM
SAID... UM, SAID... UH, I DUNNO.
YOU WERE MAKING A POINT ABOUT JUSTICE?
F-ZAP!
MOM
F-ZAP!
UM, POINT. HUH. THAT'S A FUNNY WORD.
POINT. POINT. POINT.
YOU ARE TAKING WHAT YOU WANT! YEAAAH!
AND I STILL WANT MORE.
YOU HAVE A PLAN! YEAH!
YEAH!
OH, YEAAAAH!
DON'T KNOW WHY YOU'RE EVIL, BUT YOU ARE KILLING IT! YEAH YEAH!
SOMETIMES THE CUPBOARD IS EMPTY, APPARENTLY.
YEAAAH!

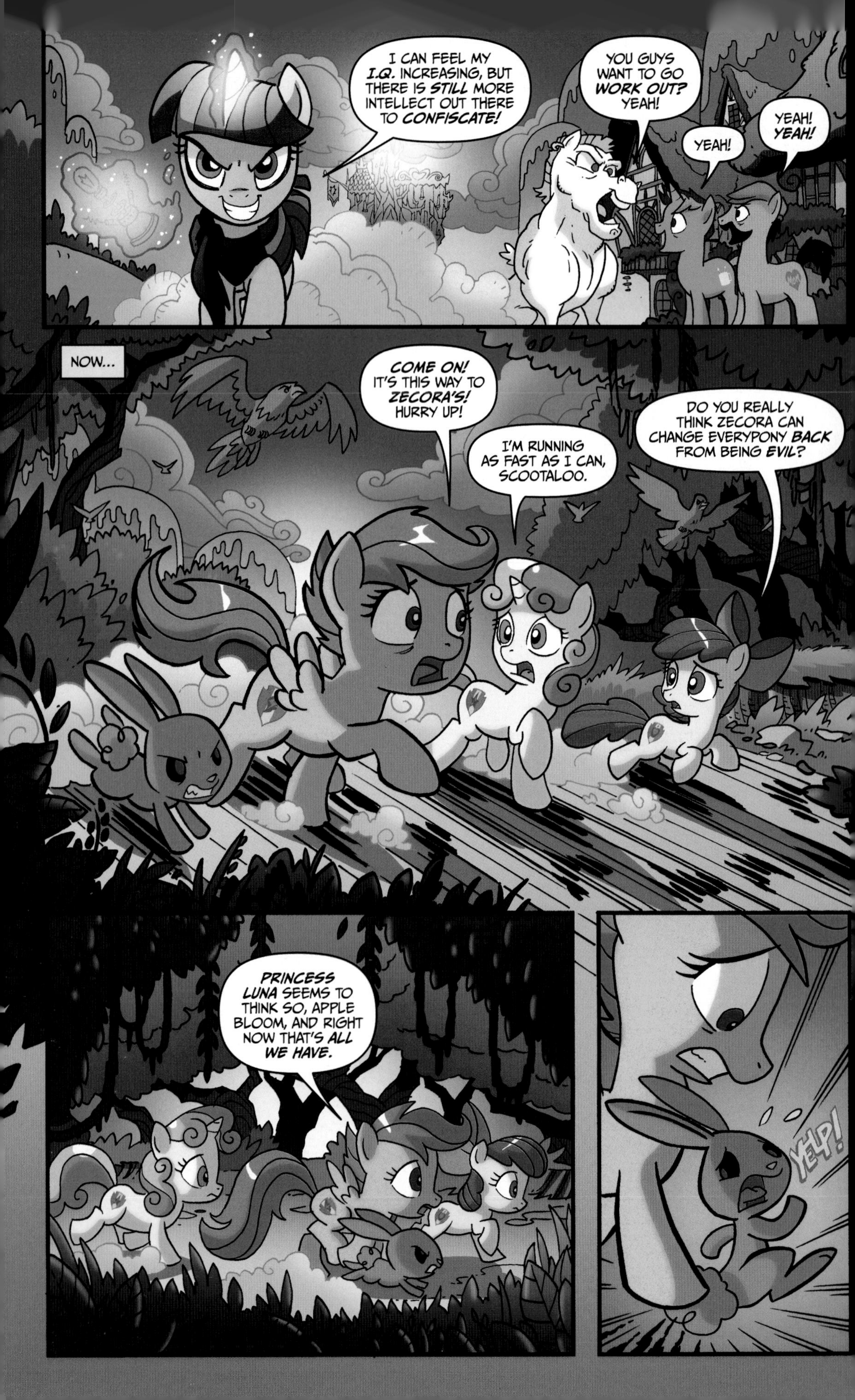
I CAN FEEL MY I.Q. INCREASING, BUT THERE IS STILL MORE INTELLECT OUT THERE TO CONFISCATE!
YOU GUYS WANT TO GO WORK OUT? YEAH!
YEAH!
YEAH! YEAH!
NOW...
COME ON! IT'S THIS WAY TO ZECORA'S! HURRY UP!
I'M RUNNING AS FAST AS I CAN, SCOOTALOO.
DO YOU REALLY THINK ZECORA CAN CHANGE EVERYPONY BACK FROM BEING EVIL?
PRINCESS LUNA SEEMS TO THINK SO, APPLE BLOOM, AND RIGHT NOW THAT'S ALL WE HAVE.
YELP!

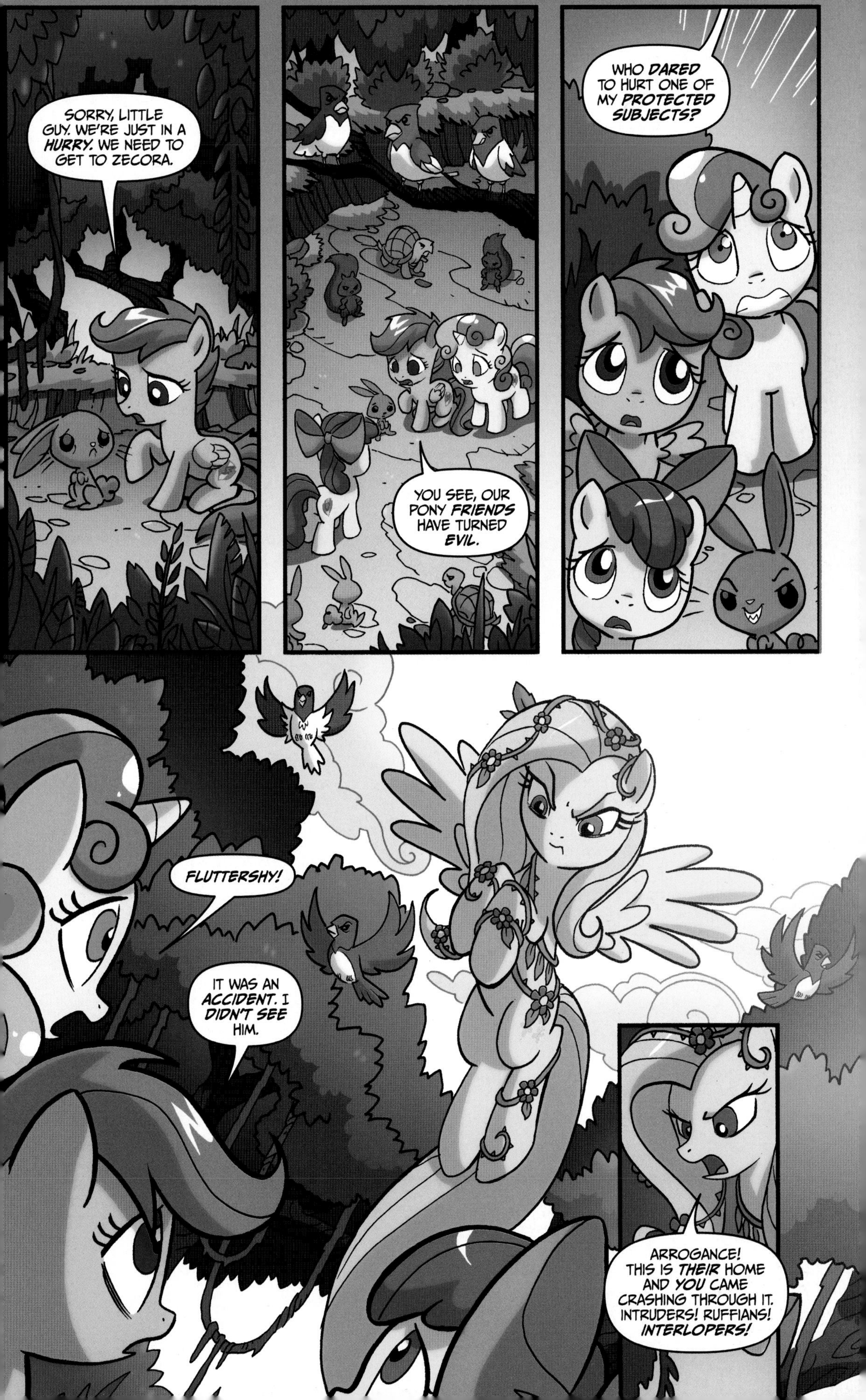
SORRY, LITTLE GUY. WE'RE JUST IN A HURRY. WE NEED TO GET TO ZECORA.
YOU SEE, OUR PONY FRIENDS HAVE TURNED EVIL.
WHO DARED TO HURT ONE OF MY PROTECTED SUBJECTS?
FLUTTERSHY!
IT WAS AN ACCIDENT. I DIDN'T SEE HIM.
ARROGANCE! THIS IS THEIR HOME AND YOU CAME CRASHING THROUGH IT. INTRUDERS! RUFFIANS! INTERLOPERS!

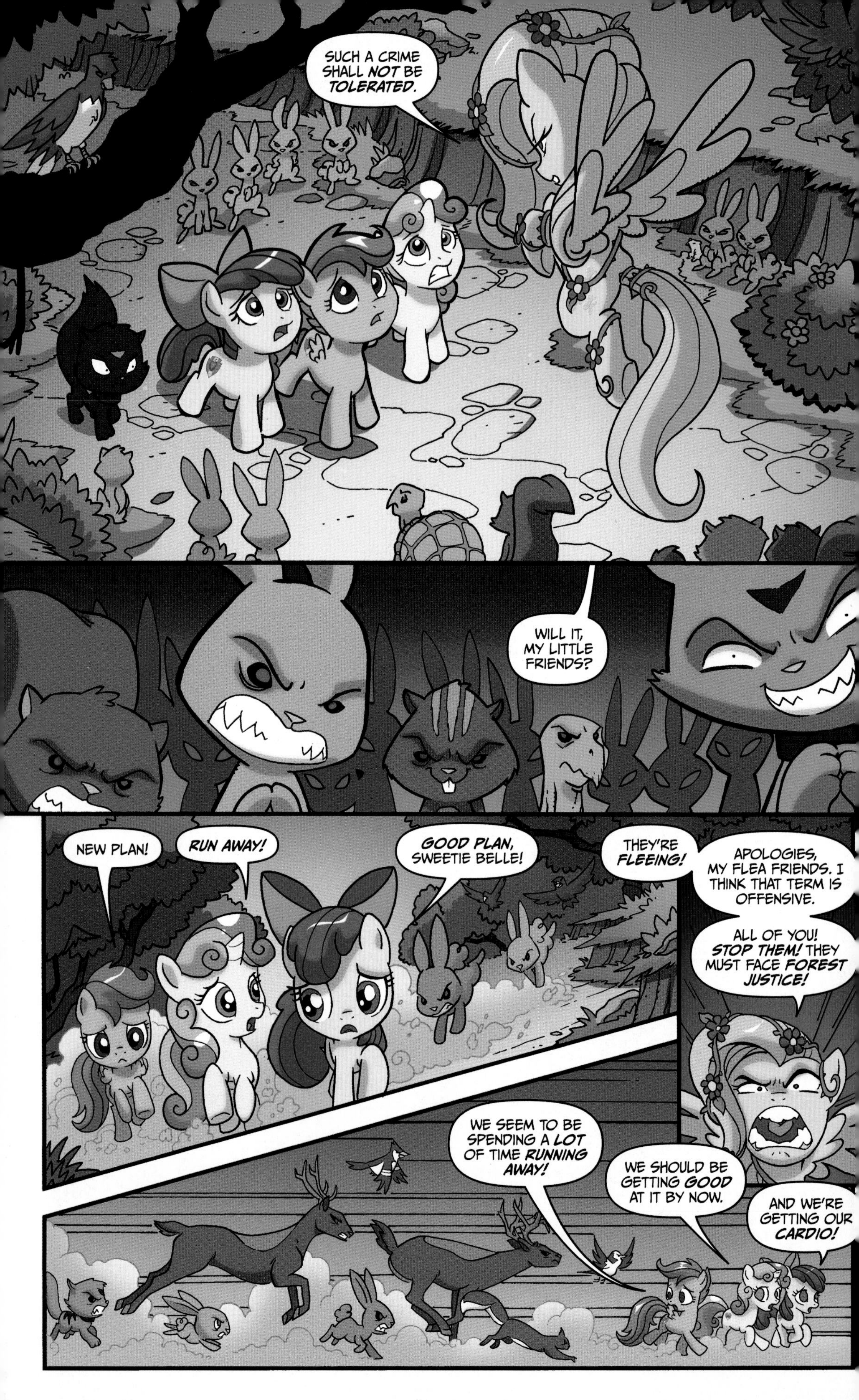
SUCH A CRIME SHALL NOT BE TOLERATED.
WILL IT, MY LITTLE FRIENDS?
NEW PLAN!
RUN AWAY!
GOOD PLAN, SWEETIE BELLE!
THEY'RE FLEEING!
APOLOGIES, MY FLEA FRIENDS. I THINK THAT TERM IS OFFENSIVE.
ALL OF YOU! STOP THEM! THEY MUST FACE FOREST JUSTICE!
WE SEEM TO BE SPENDING A LOT OF TIME RUNNING AWAY!
WE SHOULD BE GETTING GOOD AT IT BY NOW.
AND WE'RE GETTING OUR CARDIO!

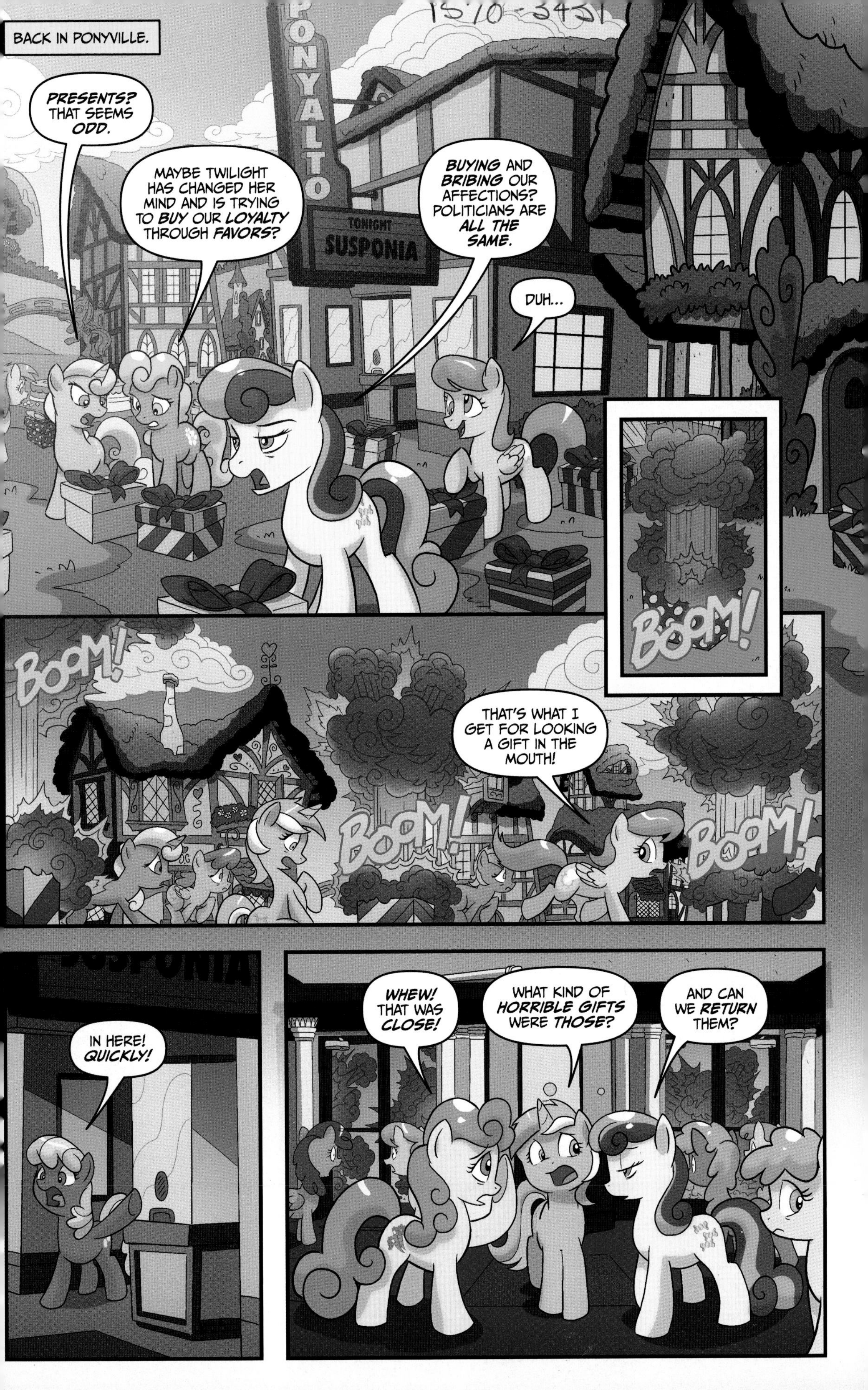
BACK IN PONYVILLE.
PONYALTO
PRESENTS? THAT SEEMS ODD.
MAYBE TWILIGHT HAS CHANGED HER MIND AND IS TRYING TO BUY OUR LOYALTY THROUGH FAVORS?
TONIGHT SUSPONIA
BUYING AND BRIBING OUR AFFECTIONS? POLITICIANS ARE ALL THE SAME.
DUH...
BOOM!
BOOM!
THAT'S WHAT I GET FOR LOOKING A GIFT IN THE MOUTH!
BOOM!
BOOM!
SUSPONIA
IN HERE! QUICKLY!
WHEW! THAT WAS CLOSE!
WHAT KIND OF HORRIBLE GIFTS WERE THOSE?
AND CAN WE RETURN THEM?

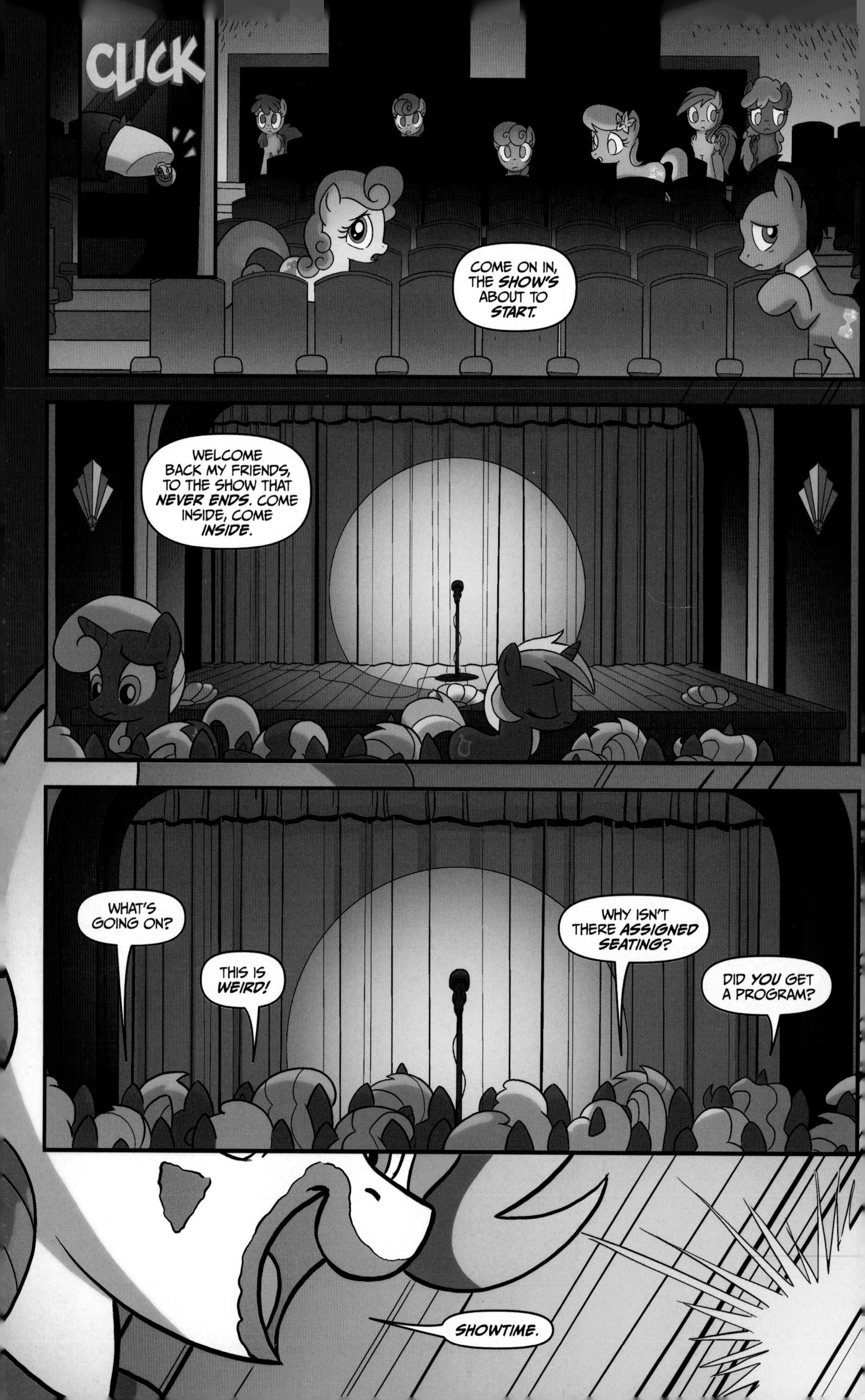
CLICK
COME ON IN, THE SHOW'S ABOUT TO START.
WELCOME BACK MY FRIENDS, TO THE SHOW THAT NEVER ENDS. COME INSIDE, COME INSIDE.
WHAT'S GOING ON?
THIS IS WEIRD!
WHY ISN'T THERE ASSIGNED SEATING?
DID YOU GET A PROGRAM?
SHOWTIME.

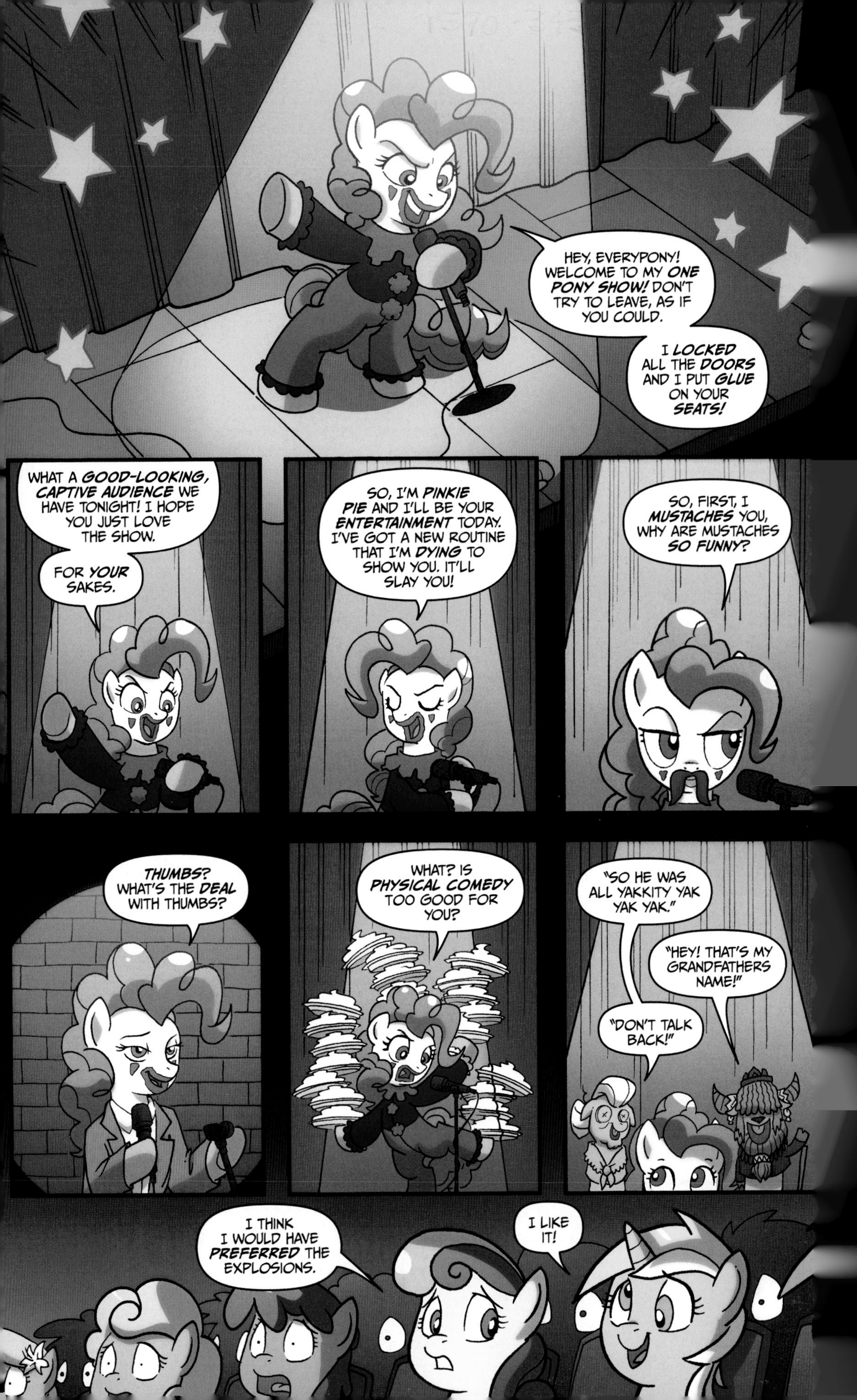

HEY, EVERYPONY! WELCOME TO MY ONE PONY SHOW! DON'T TRY TO LEAVE, AS IF YOU COULD.
I LOCKED ALL THE DOORS AND I PUT GLUE ON YOUR SEATS!
WHAT A GOOD-LOOKING, CAPTIVE AUDIENCE WE HAVE TONIGHT! I HOPE YOU JUST LOVE THE SHOW.
FOR YOUR SAKES.
SO, I'M PINKIE PIE AND I'LL BE YOUR ENTERTAINMENT TODAY. I'VE GOT A NEW ROUTINE THAT I'M DYING TO SHOW YOU. IT'LL SLAY YOU!
SO, FIRST, I MUSTACHES YOU, WHY ARE MUSTACHES SO FUNNY?
THUMBS? WHAT'S THE DEAL WITH THUMBS?
WHAT? IS PHYSICAL COMEDY TOO GOOD FOR YOU?
"SO HE WAS ALL YAKKITY YAK YAK YAK."
"HEY! THAT'S MY GRANDFATHERS NAME!"
"DON'T TALK BACK!"
I THINK I WOULD HAVE PREFERRED THE EXPLOSIONS.
I LIKE IT!

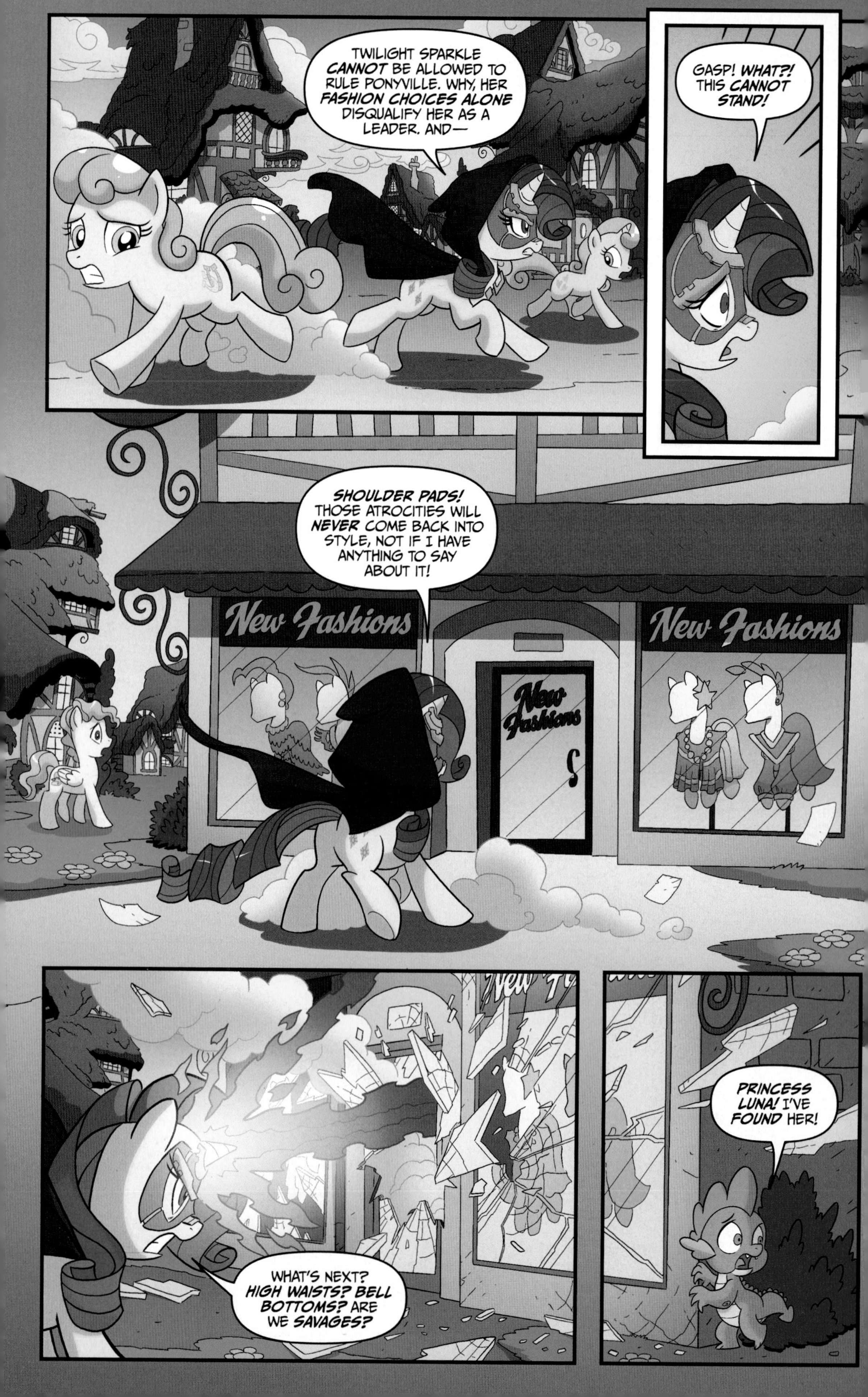
TWILIGHT SPARKLE CANNOT BE ALLOWED TO RULE PONYVILLE. WHY, HER FASHION CHOICES ALONE DISQUALIFY HER AS A LEADER. AND—
GASP! WHAT?! THIS CANNOT STAND!
SHOULDER PADS! THOSE ATROCITIES WILL NEVER COME BACK INTO STYLE, NOT IF I HAVE ANYTHING TO SAY ABOUT IT!
New Fashions
New Fashions
New Fashions
WHAT'S NEXT? HIGH WAISTS? BELL BOTTOMS? ARE WE SAVAGES?
PRINCESS LUNA! I'VE FOUND HER!

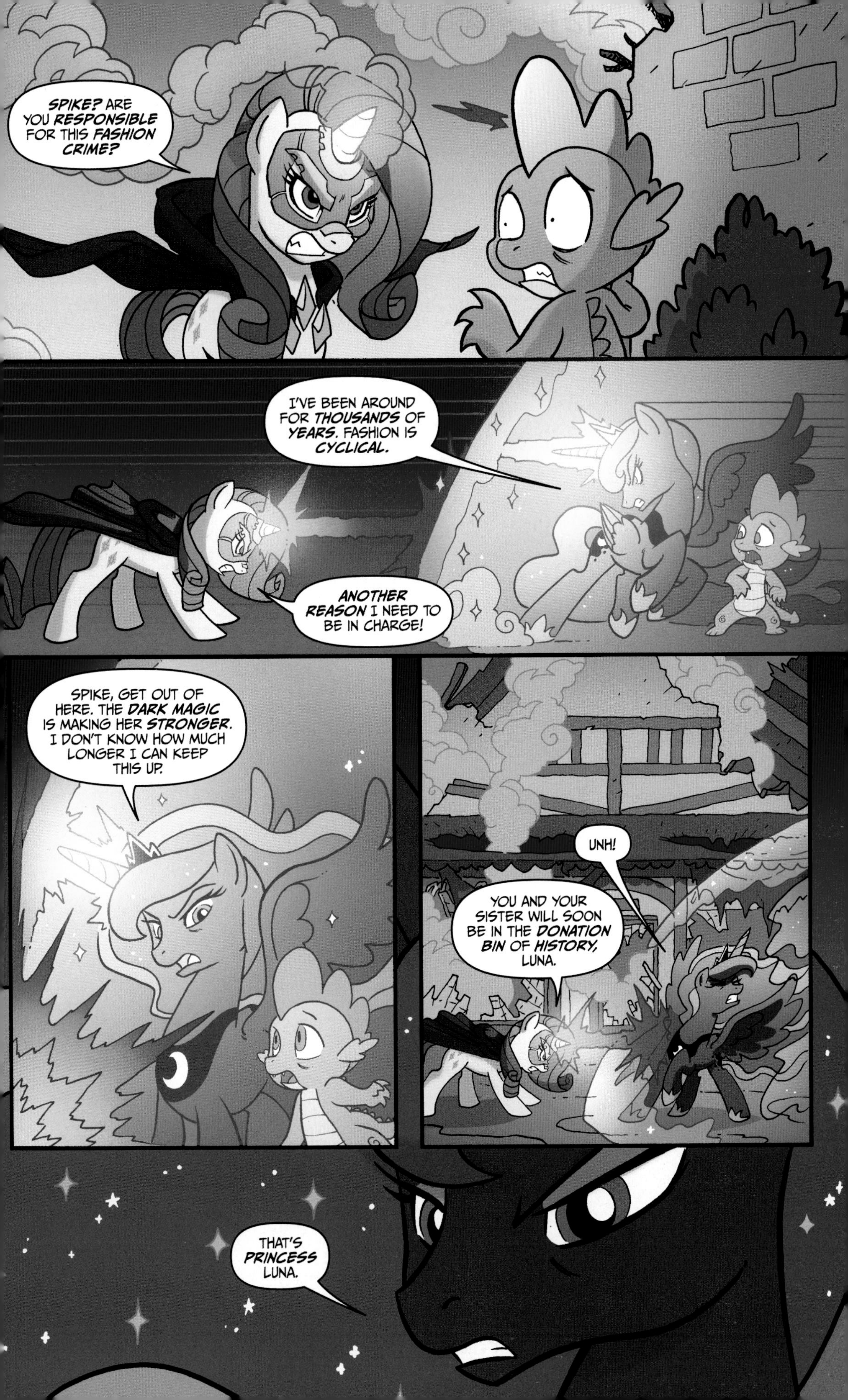
SPIKE? ARE YOU RESPONSIBLE FOR THIS FASHION CRIME?
I'VE BEEN AROUND FOR THOUSANDS OF YEARS. FASHION IS CYCLICAL.
ANOTHER REASON I NEED TO BE IN CHARGE!
SPIKE, GET OUT OF HERE. THE DARK MAGIC IS MAKING HER STRONGER. I DON'T KNOW HOW MUCH LONGER I CAN KEEP THIS UP.
UNH!
YOU AND YOUR SISTER WILL SOON BE IN THE DONATION BIN OF HISTORY, LUNA.
THAT'S PRINCESS LUNA.

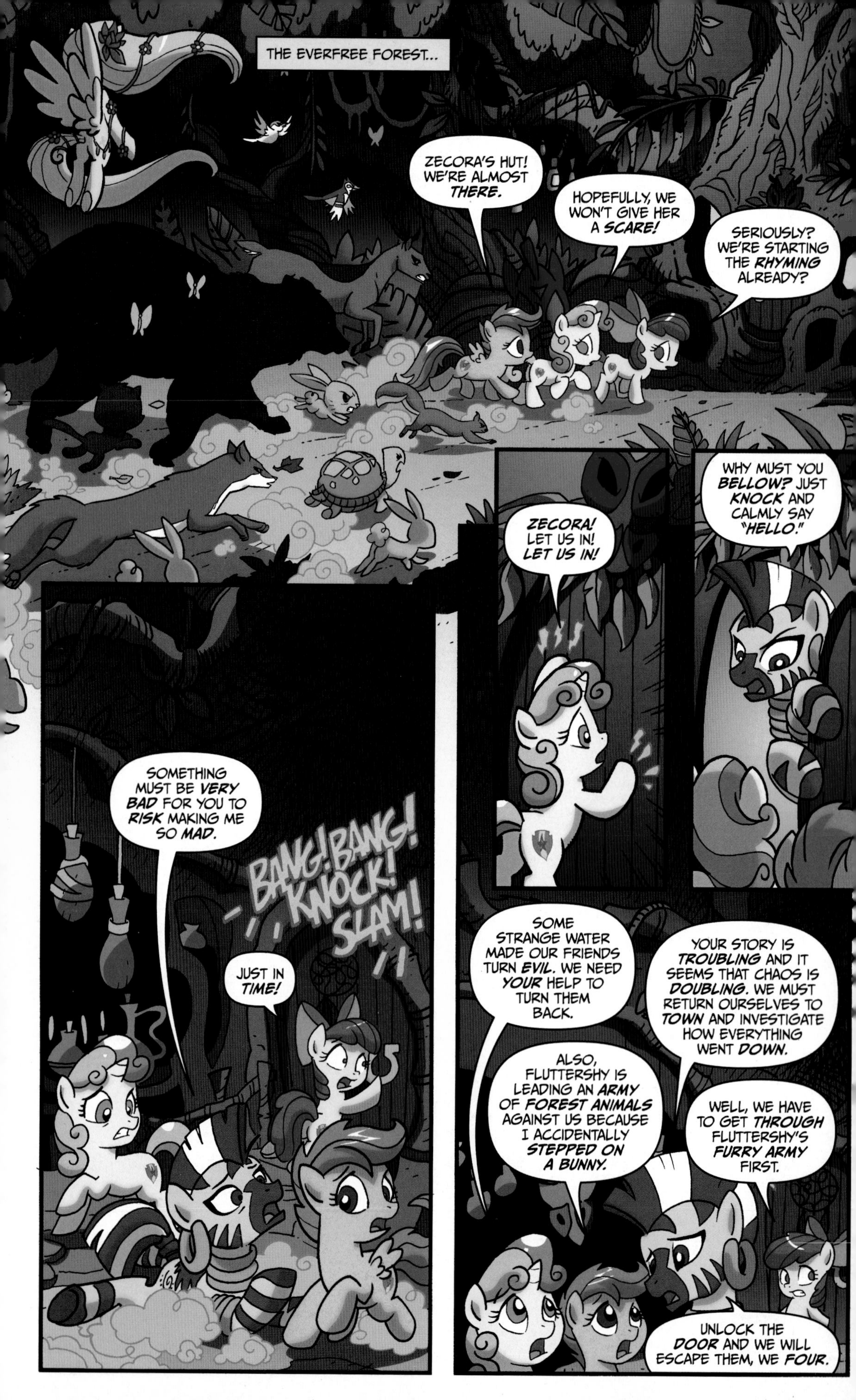
THE EVERFREE FOREST...
ZECORA'S HUT! WE'RE ALMOST THERE.
HOPEFULLY, WE WON'T GIVE HER A SCARE!
SERIOUSLY? WE'RE STARTING THE RHYMING ALREADY?
ZECORA! LET US IN! LET US IN!
WHY MUST YOU BELLOW? JUST KNOCK AND CALMLY SAY "HELLO."
SOMETHING MUST BE VERY BAD FOR YOU TO RISK MAKING ME SO MAD.
BANG! BANG! KNOCK! SLAM!
JUST IN TIME!
SOME STRANGE WATER MADE OUR FRIENDS TURN EVIL. WE NEED YOUR HELP TO TURN THEM BACK.
YOUR STORY IS TROUBLING AND IT SEEMS THAT CHAOS IS DOUBLING. WE MUST RETURN OURSELVES TO TOWN AND INVESTIGATE HOW EVERYTHING WENT DOWN.
ALSO, FLUTTERSHY IS LEADING AN ARMY OF FOREST ANIMALS AGAINST US BECAUSE I ACCIDENTALLY STEPPED ON A BUNNY.
WELL, WE HAVE TO GET THROUGH FLUTTERSHY'S FURRY ARMY FIRST.
UNLOCK THE DOOR AND WE WILL ESCAPE THEM, WE FOUR.

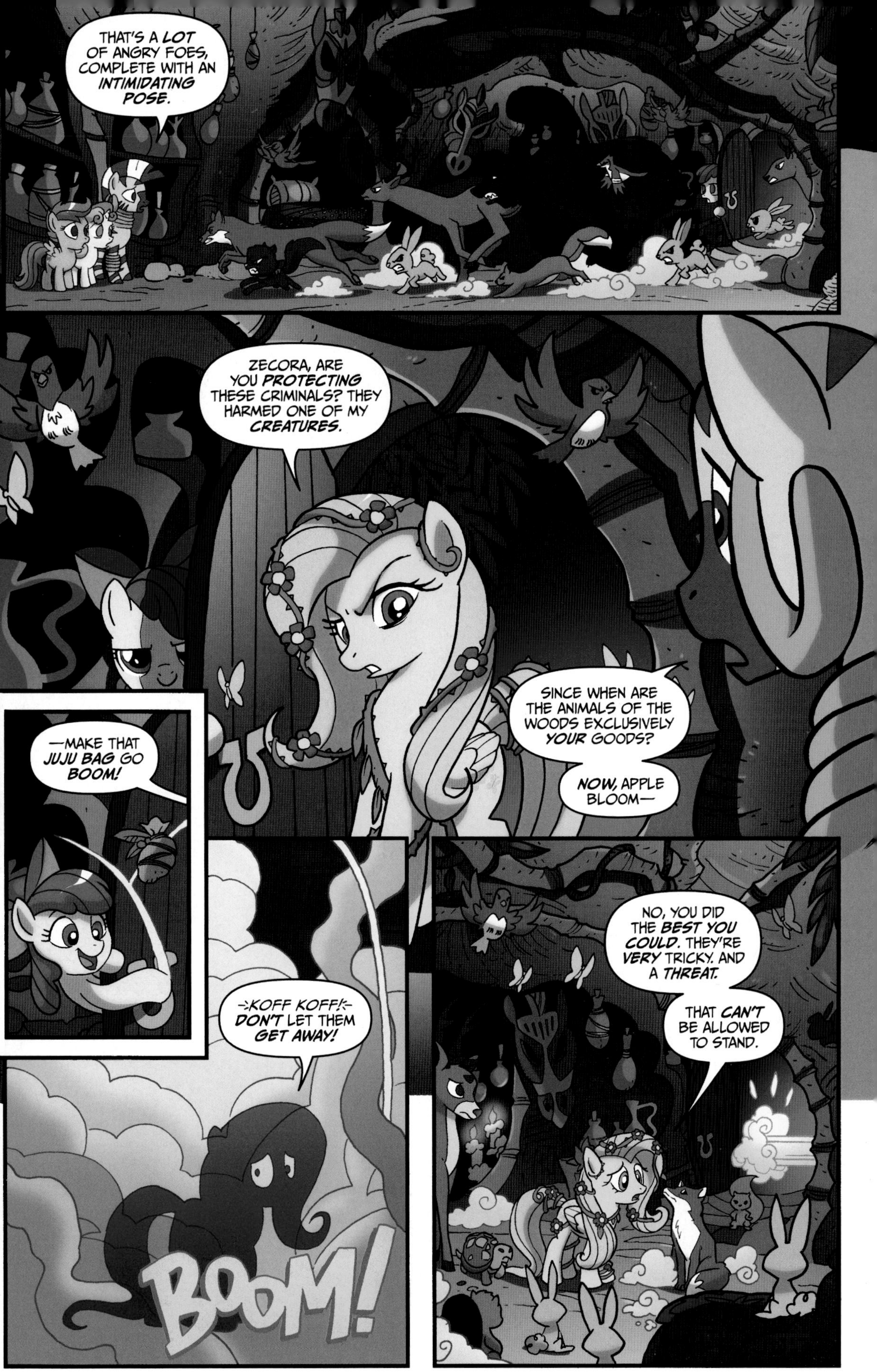
THAT'S A LOT OF ANGRY FOES, COMPLETE WITH AN INTIMIDATING POSE.
ZECORA, ARE YOU PROTECTING THESE CRIMINALS? THEY HARMED ONE OF MY CREATURES.
SINCE WHEN ARE THE ANIMALS OF THE WOODS EXCLUSIVELY YOUR GOODS?
NOW, APPLE BLOOM—
—MAKE THAT JUJU BAG GO BOOM!
KOFF KOFF! DON'T LET THEM GET AWAY!
BOOM!
NO, YOU DID THE BEST YOU COULD. THEY'RE VERY TRICKY. AND A THREAT.
THAT CAN'T BE ALLOWED TO STAND.

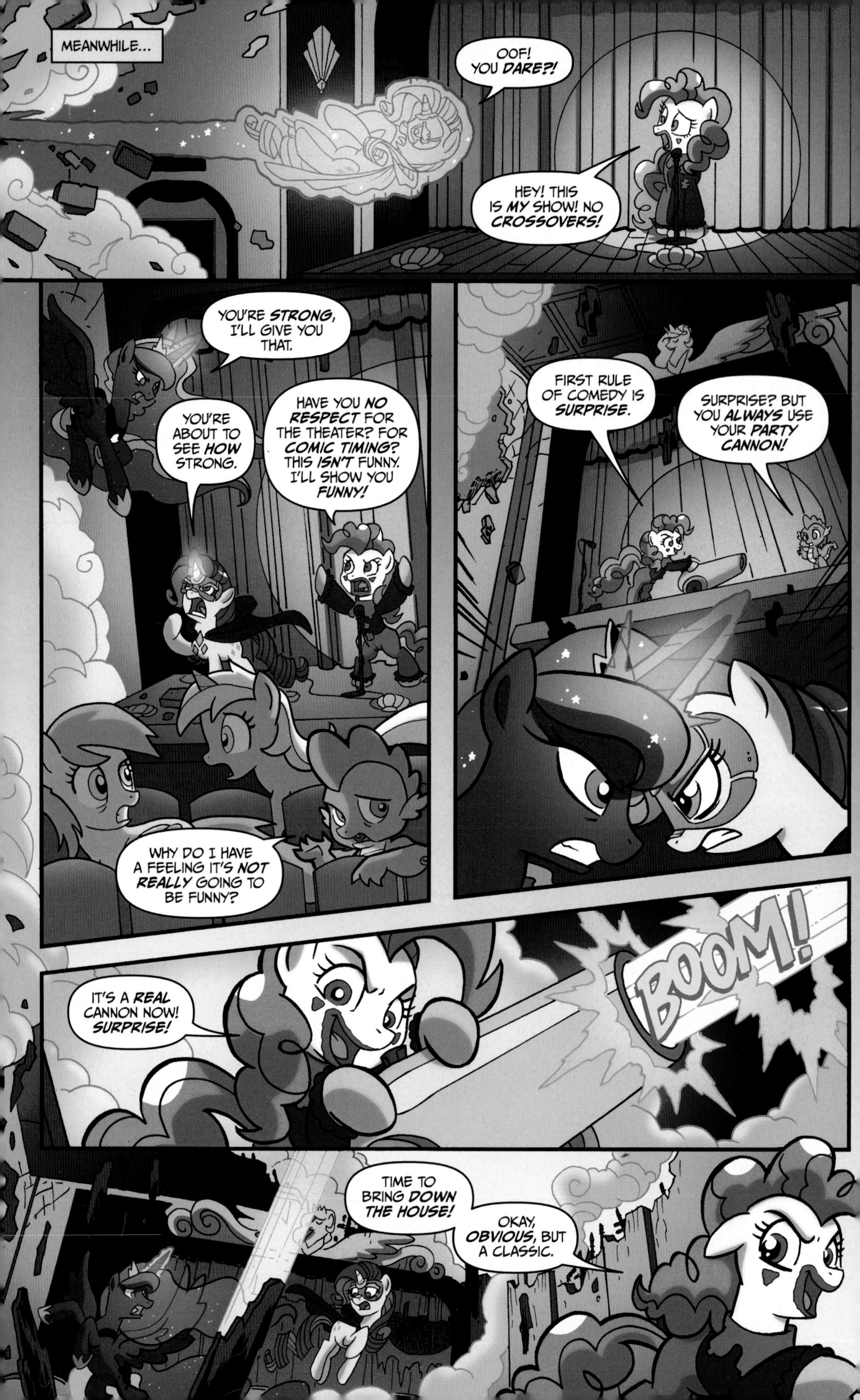
MEANWHILE...
OOF! YOU DARE?!
HEY! THIS IS MY SHOW! NO CROSSOVERS!
YOU'RE STRONG, I'LL GIVE YOU THAT.
YOU'RE ABOUT TO SEE HOW STRONG.
HAVE YOU NO RESPECT FOR THE THEATER? FOR COMIC TIMING? THIS ISN'T FUNNY. I'LL SHOW YOU FUNNY!
WHY DO I HAVE A FEELING IT'S NOT REALLY GOING TO BE FUNNY?
FIRST RULE OF COMEDY IS SURPRISE.
SURPRISE? BUT YOU ALWAYS USE YOUR PARTY CANNON!
IT'S A REAL CANNON NOW! SURPRISE!
BOOM!
TIME TO BRING DOWN THE HOUSE!
OKAY, OBVIOUS, BUT A CLASSIC.

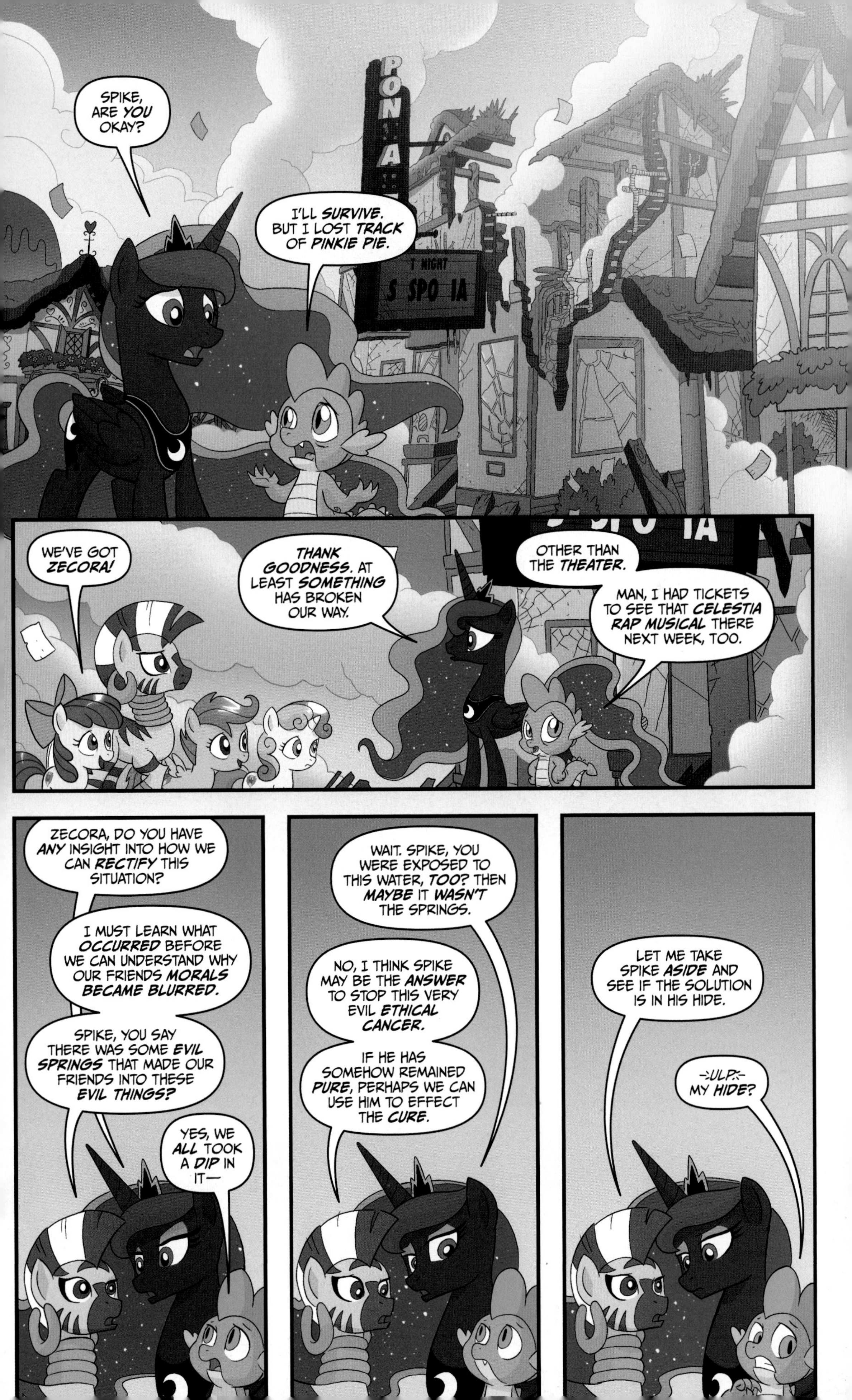
SPIKE, ARE YOU OKAY?
I'LL SURVIVE. BUT I LOST TRACK OF PINKIE PIE.
WE'VE GOT ZECORA!
THANK GOODNESS. AT LEAST SOMETHING HAS BROKEN OUR WAY.
OTHER THAN THE THEATER.
MAN, I HAD TICKETS TO SEE THAT CELESTIA RAP MUSICAL THERE NEXT WEEK, TOO.
ZECORA, DO YOU HAVE ANY INSIGHT INTO HOW WE CAN RECTIFY THIS SITUATION?
I MUST LEARN WHAT OCCURRED BEFORE WE CAN UNDERSTAND WHY OUR FRIENDS MORALS BECAME BLURRED.
SPIKE, YOU SAY THERE WAS SOME EVIL SPRINGS THAT MADE OUR FRIENDS INTO THESE EVIL THINGS?
YES, WE ALL TOOK A DIP IN IT—
WAIT. SPIKE, YOU WERE EXPOSED TO THIS WATER, TOO? THEN MAYBE IT WASN'T THE SPRINGS.
NO, I THINK SPIKE MAY BE THE ANSWER TO STOP THIS VERY EVIL ETHICAL CANCER.
IF HE HAS SOMEHOW REMAINED PURE, PERHAPS WE CAN USE HIM TO EFFECT THE CURE.
LET ME TAKE SPIKE ASIDE AND SEE IF THE SOLUTION IS IN HIS HIDE.
ULP! MY HIDE?

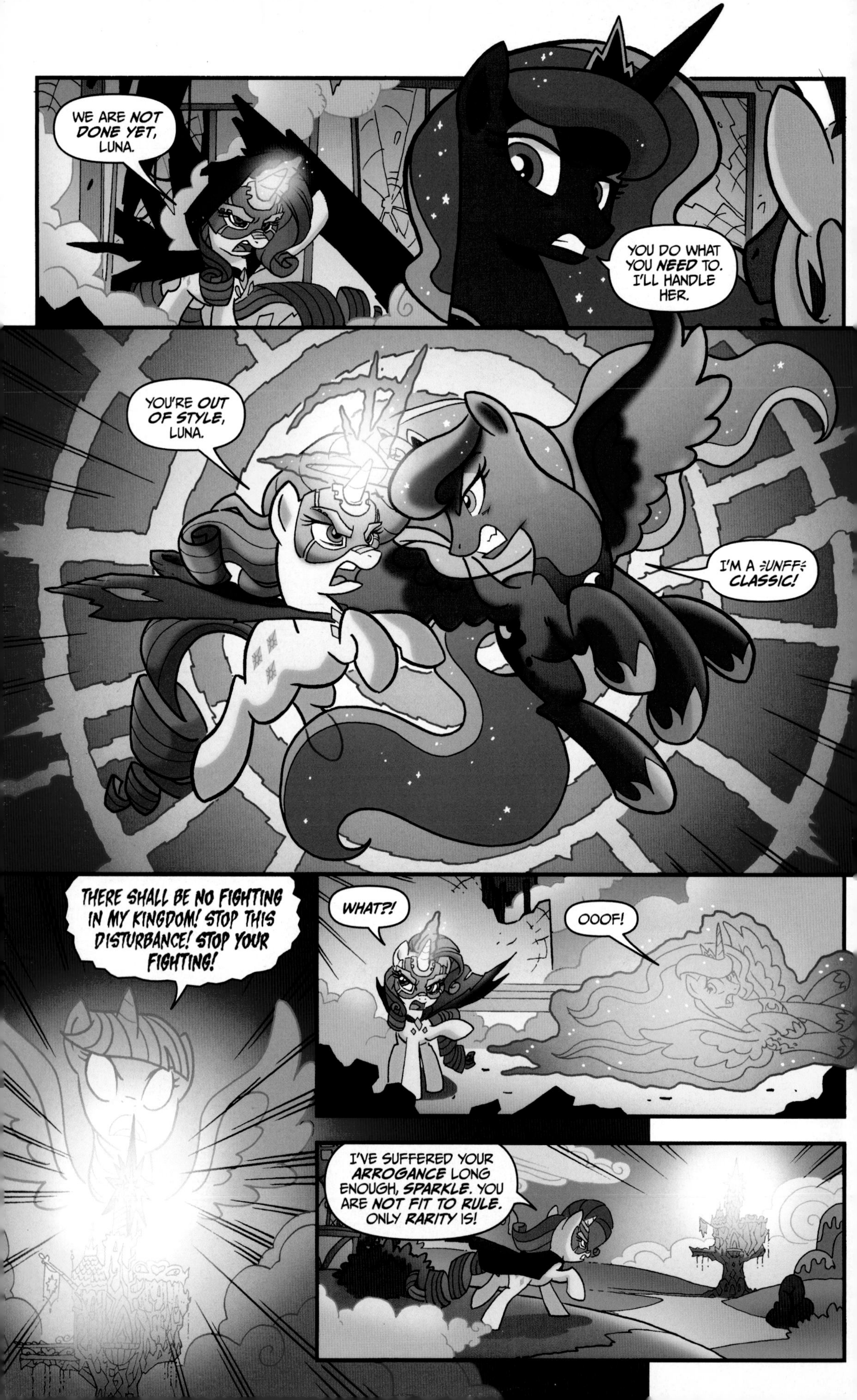
WE ARE NOT DONE YET, LUNA.
YOU DO WHAT YOU NEED TO. I'LL HANDLE HER.
YOU'RE OUT OF STYLE, LUNA.
I'M A ≈UNFF≈ CLASSIC!
THERE SHALL BE NO FIGHTING IN MY KINGDOM! STOP THIS DISTURBANCE! STOP YOUR FIGHTING!
WHAT?!
OOOF!
I'VE SUFFERED YOUR ARROGANCE LONG ENOUGH, SPARKLE. YOU ARE NOT FIT TO RULE. ONLY RARITY IS!

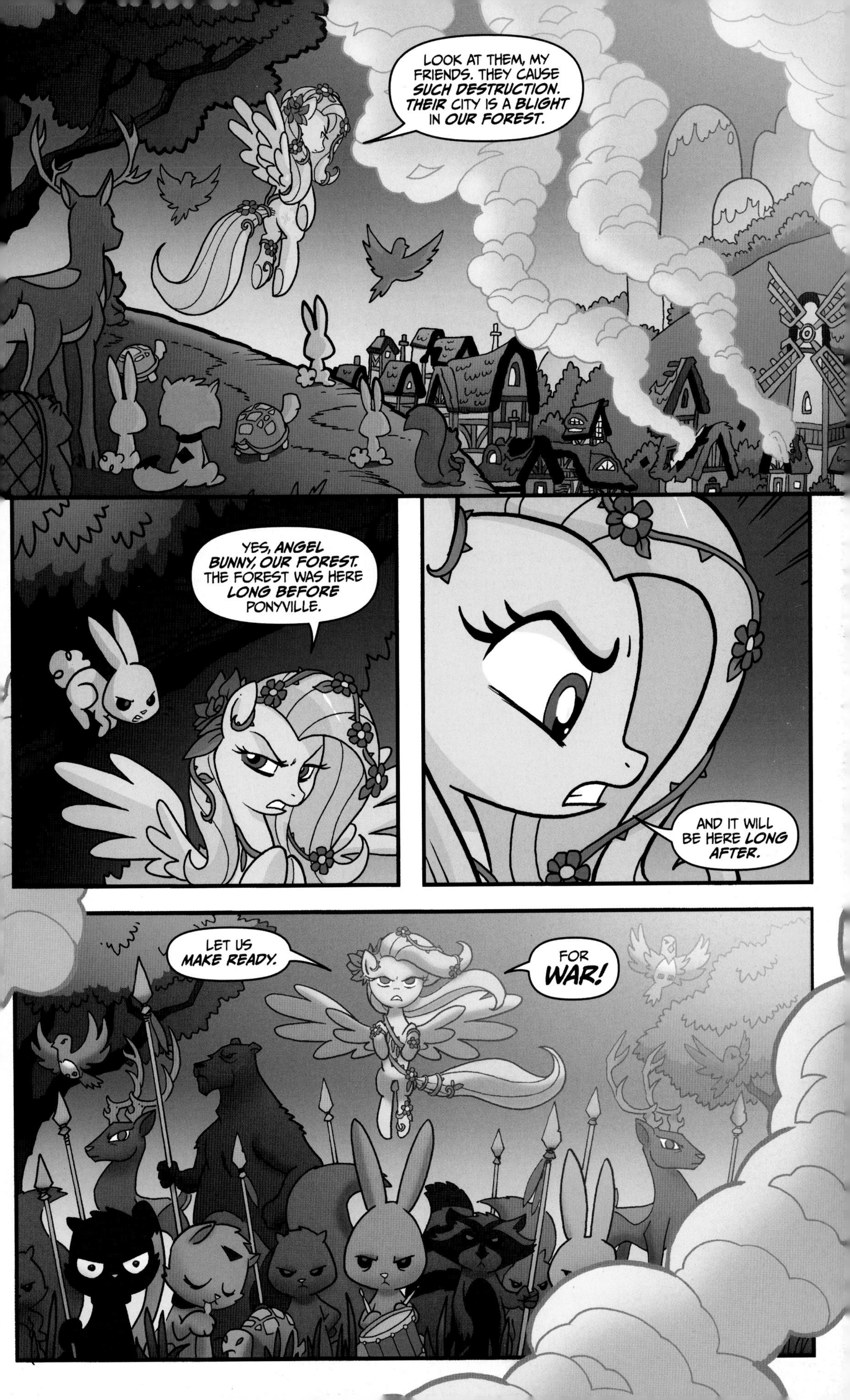
LOOK AT THEM, MY FRIENDS. THEY CAUSE SUCH DESTRUCTION. THEIR CITY IS A BLIGHT IN OUR FOREST.
YES, ANGEL BUNNY, OUR FOREST. THE FOREST WAS HERE LONG BEFORE PONYVILLE.
AND IT WILL BE HERE LONG AFTER.
LET US MAKE READY.
FOR WAR!

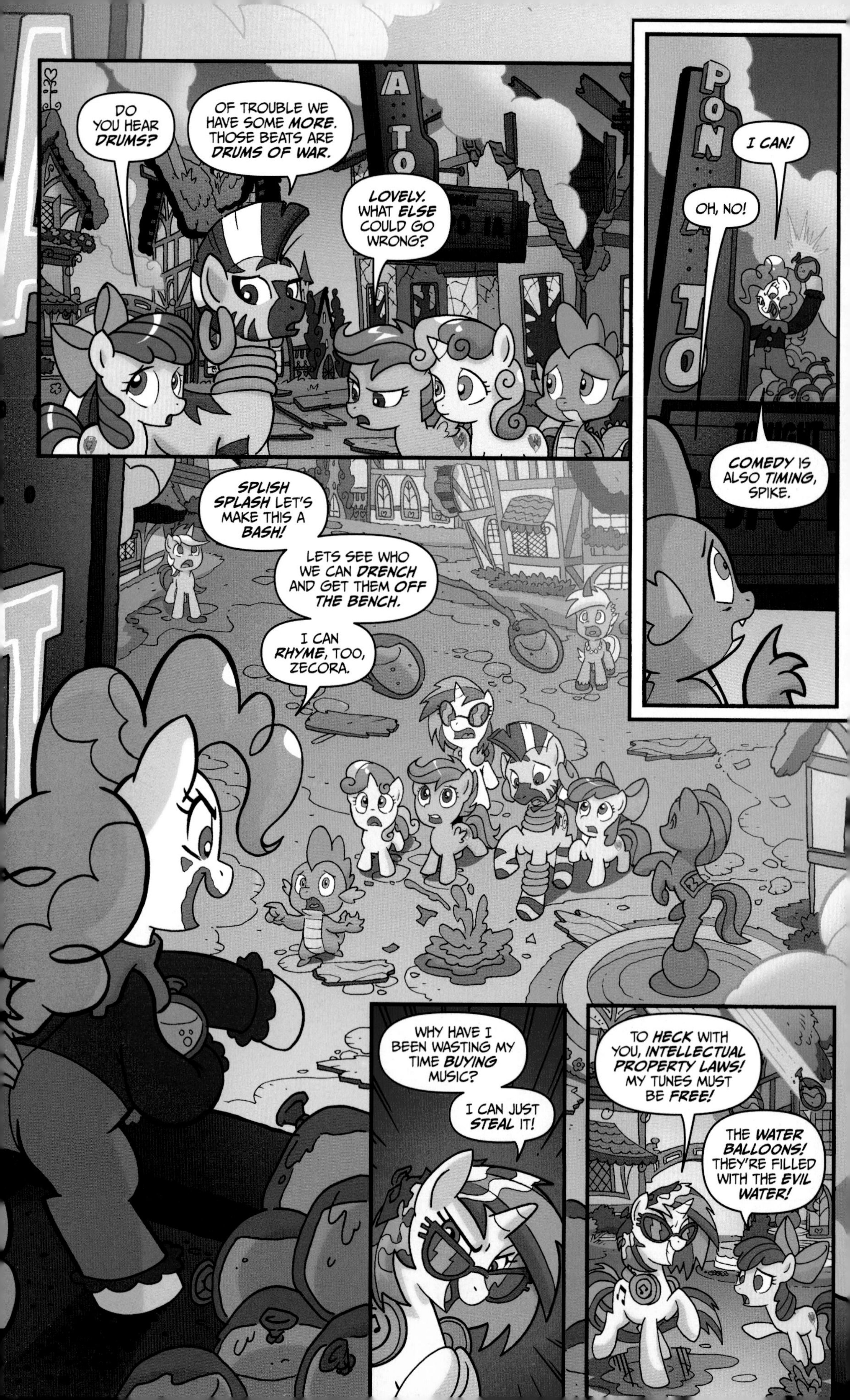
DO YOU HEAR DRUMS?
OF TROUBLE WE HAVE SOME MORE. THOSE BEATS ARE DRUMS OF WAR.
LOVELY. WHAT ELSE COULD GO WRONG?
I CAN!
OH, NO!
COMEDY IS ALSO TIMING, SPIKE.
SPLISH SPLASH LET'S MAKE THIS A BASH!
LETS SEE WHO WE CAN DRENCH AND GET THEM OFF THE BENCH.
I CAN RHYME, TOO, ZECORA.
WHY HAVE I BEEN WASTING MY TIME BUYING MUSIC?
I CAN JUST STEAL IT!
TO HECK WITH YOU, INTELLECTUAL PROPERTY LAWS! MY TUNES MUST BE FREE!
THE WATER BALLOONS! THEY'RE FILLED WITH THE EVIL WATER!

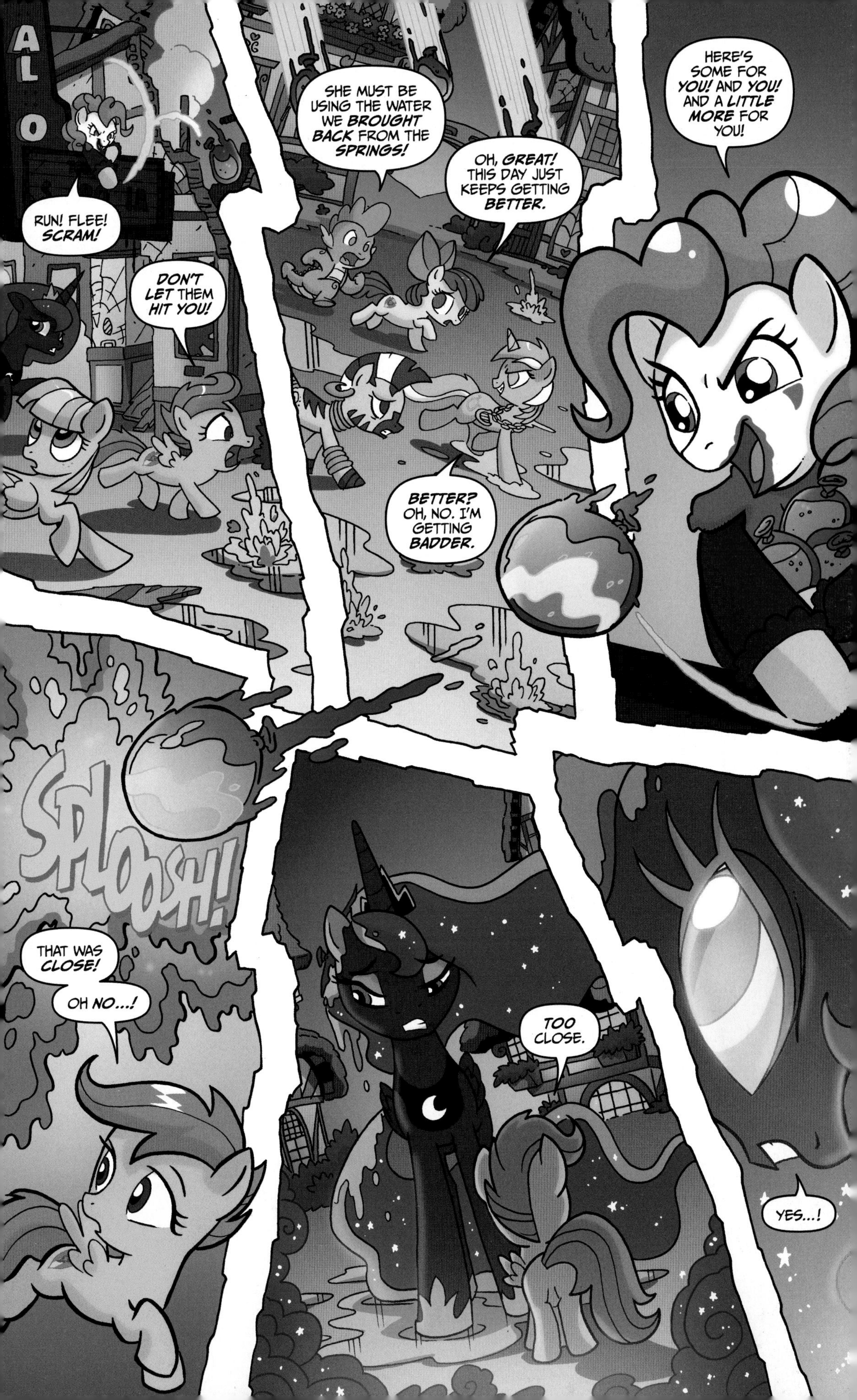

RUN! FLEE! SCRAM!
DON'T LET THEM HIT YOU!
SHE MUST BE USING THE WATER WE BROUGHT BACK FROM THE SPRINGS!
OH, GREAT! THIS DAY JUST KEEPS GETTING BETTER.
BETTER? OH, NO. I'M GETTING BADDER.
HERE'S SOME FOR YOU! AND YOU! AND A LITTLE MORE FOR YOU!
SPLOOSH!
THAT WAS CLOSE!
OH NO...!
TOO CLOSE.
YES...!

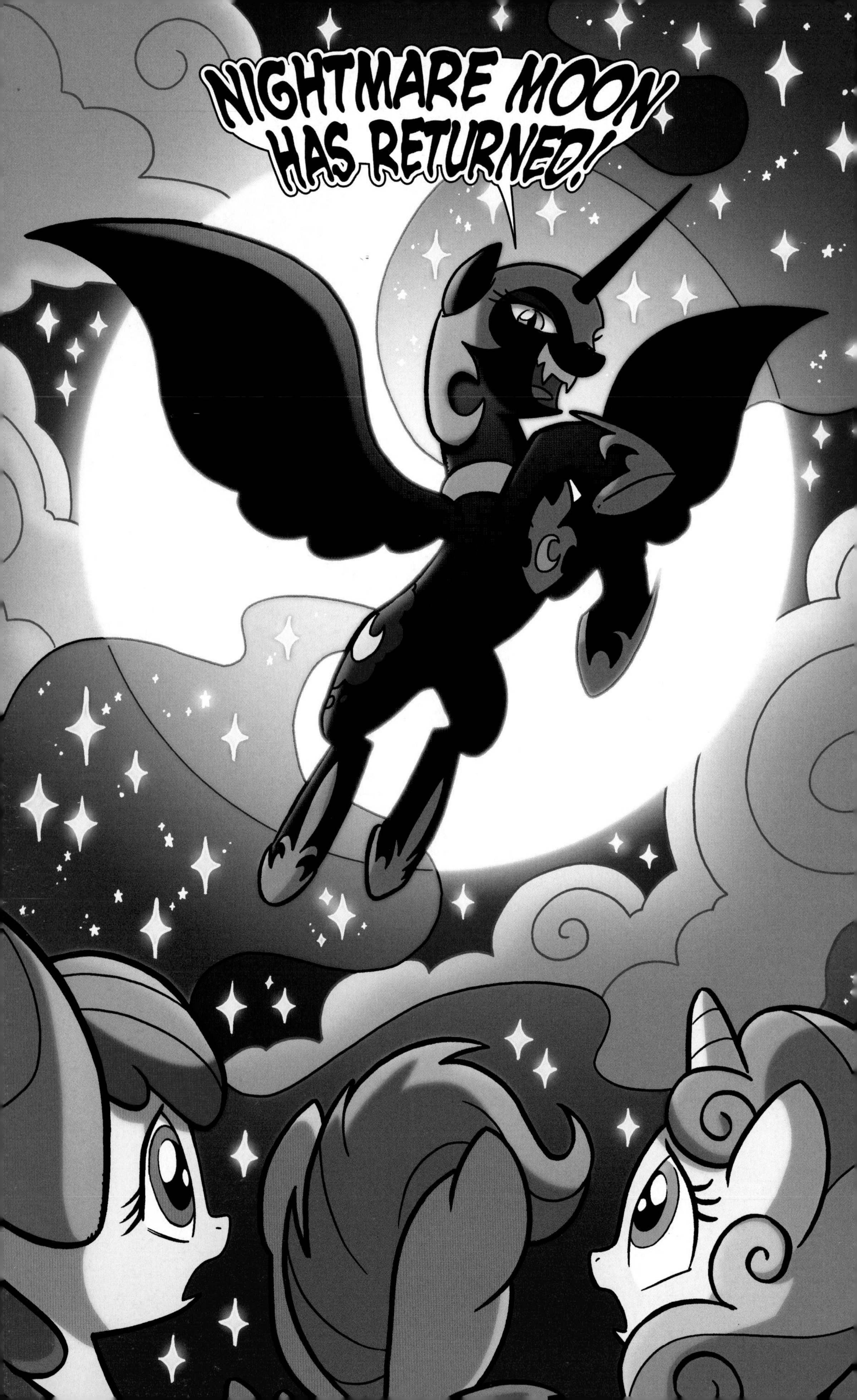
NIGHTMARE MOON HAS RETURNED!

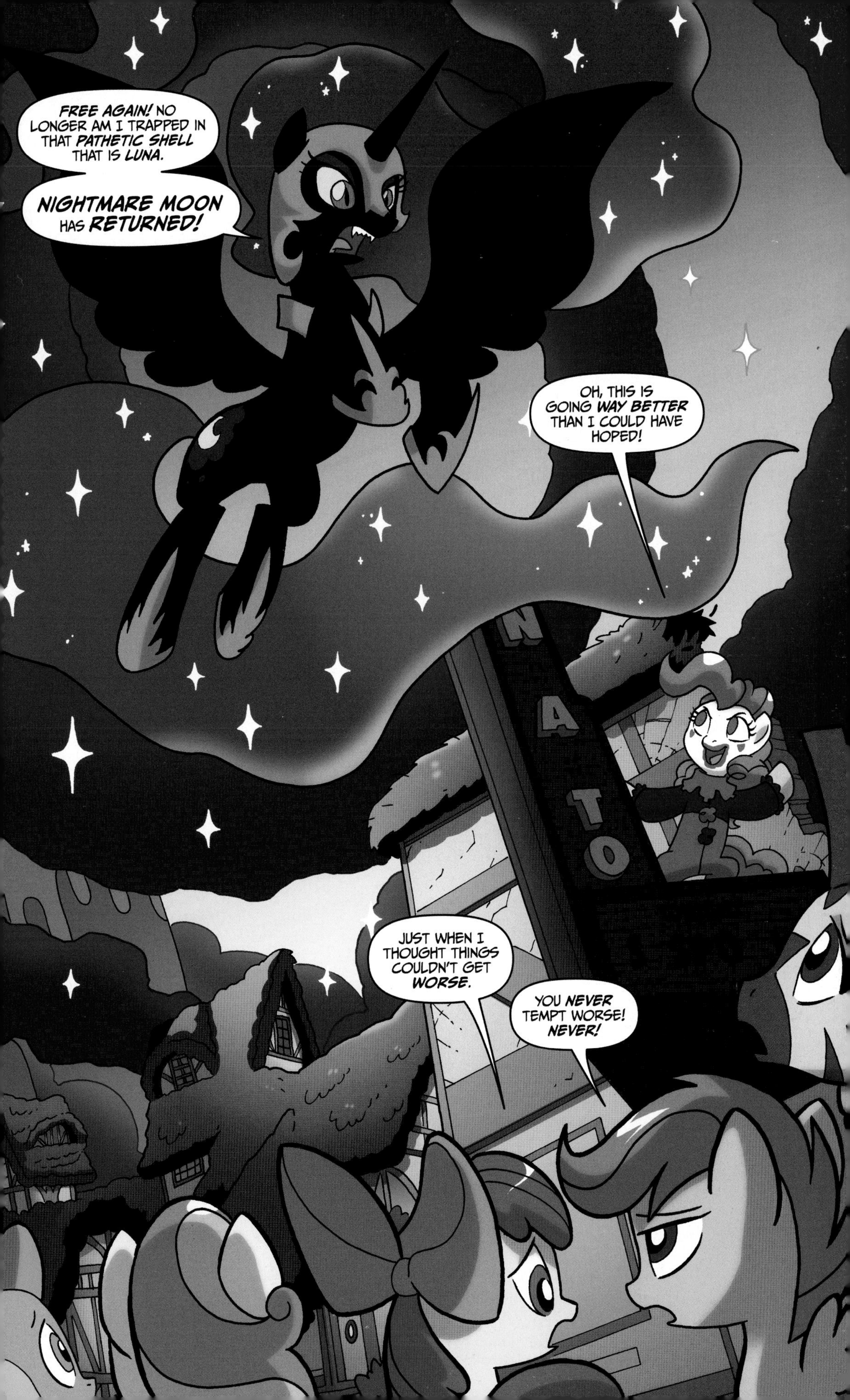
FREE AGAIN! NO LONGER AM I TRAPPED IN THAT PATHETIC SHELL THAT IS LUNA.
NIGHTMARE MOON HAS RETURNED!
OH, THIS IS GOING WAY BETTER THAN I COULD HAVE HOPED!
JUST WHEN I THOUGHT THINGS COULDN'T GET WORSE.
YOU NEVER TEMPT WORSE! NEVER!

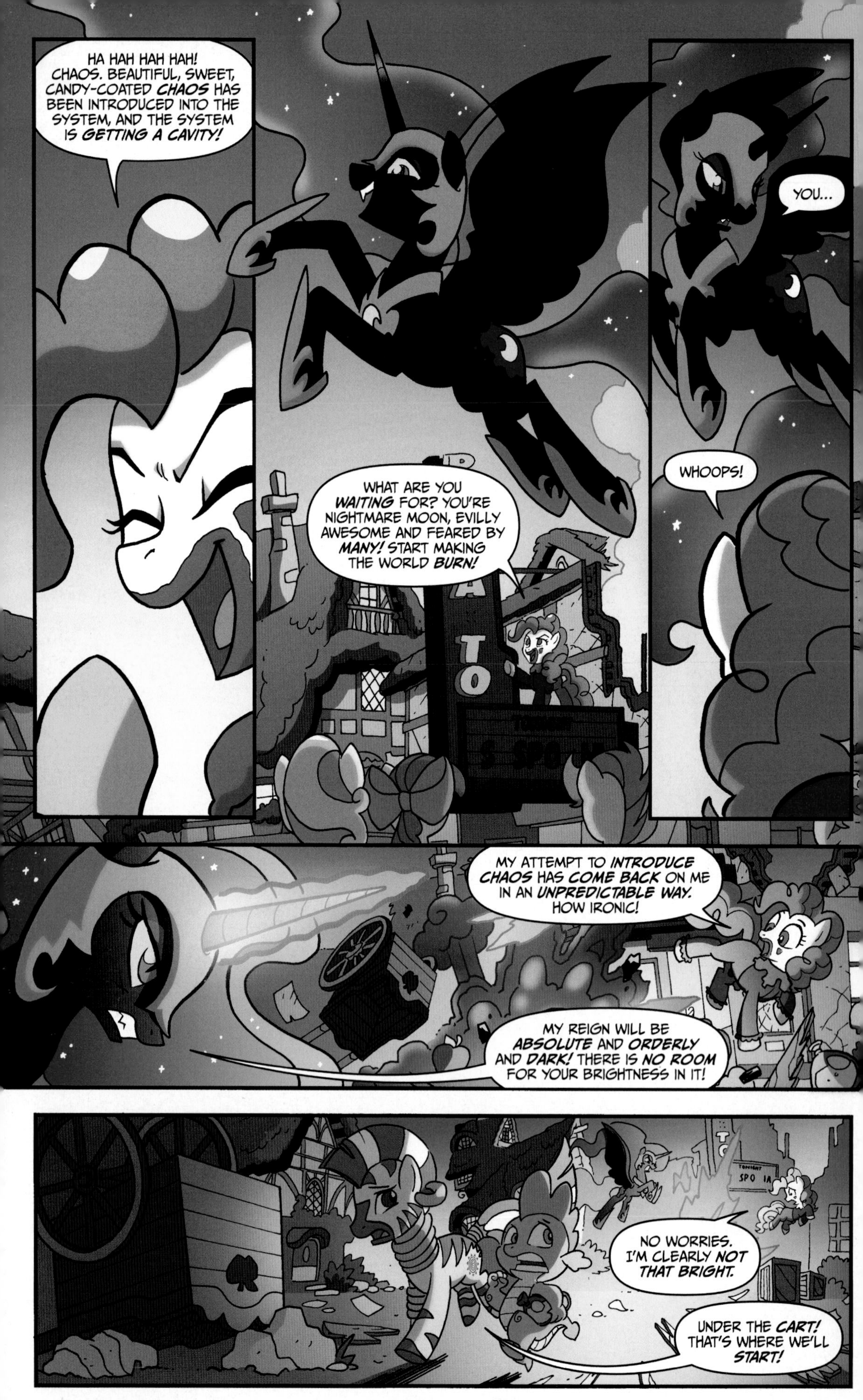
HA HAH HAH HAH! CHAOS. BEAUTIFUL, SWEET, CANDY-COATED *CHAOS* HAS BEEN INTRODUCED INTO THE SYSTEM, AND THE SYSTEM IS *GETTING A CAVITY!*
WHAT ARE YOU *WAITING* FOR? YOU'RE NIGHTMARE MOON, EVILLY AWESOME AND FEARED BY *MANY!* START MAKING THE WORLD *BURN!*
YOU...
WHOOPS!
MY ATTEMPT TO *INTRODUCE CHAOS* HAS *COME BACK* ON ME IN AN *UNPREDICTABLE WAY.* HOW IRONIC!
MY REIGN WILL BE *ABSOLUTE* AND *ORDERLY* AND *DARK!* THERE IS *NO ROOM* FOR YOUR BRIGHTNESS IN IT!
NO WORRIES. I'M CLEARLY *NOT THAT BRIGHT.*
UNDER THE *CART!* THAT'S WHERE WE'LL *START!*

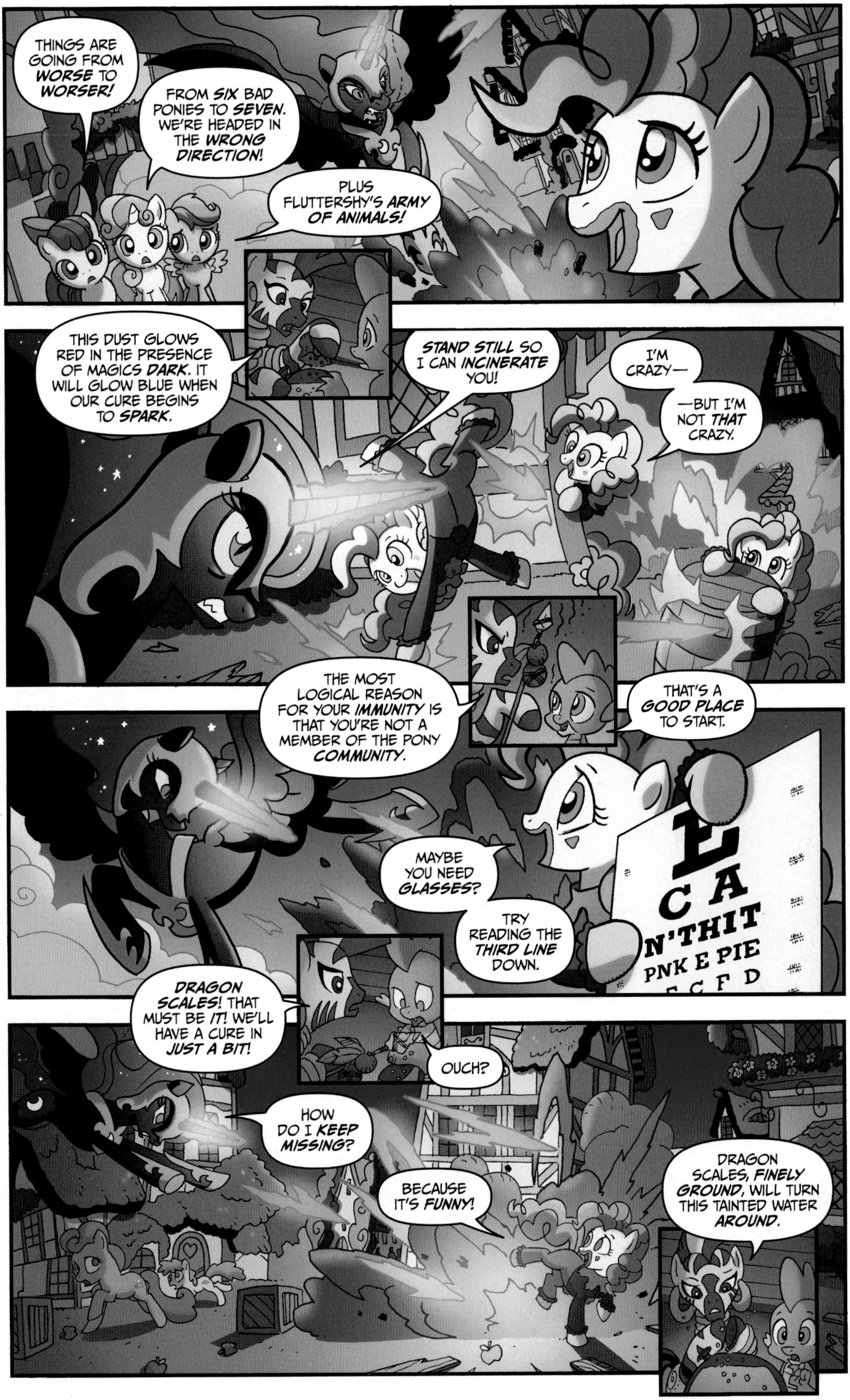

THINGS ARE GOING FROM WORSE TO WORSER!
FROM SIX BAD PONIES TO SEVEN. WE'RE HEADED IN THE WRONG DIRECTION!
PLUS FLUTTERSHY'S ARMY OF ANIMALS!
THIS DUST GLOWS RED IN THE PRESENCE OF MAGICS DARK. IT WILL GLOW BLUE WHEN OUR CURE BEGINS TO SPARK.
STAND STILL SO I CAN INCINERATE YOU!
I'M CRAZY—
—BUT I'M NOT THAT CRAZY.
THE MOST LOGICAL REASON FOR YOUR IMMUNITY IS THAT YOU'RE NOT A MEMBER OF THE PONY COMMUNITY.
THAT'S A GOOD PLACE TO START.
MAYBE YOU NEED GLASSES?
TRY READING THE THIRD LINE DOWN.
E
C A
N'THIT
PNK E PIE
DRAGON SCALES! THAT MUST BE IT! WE'LL HAVE A CURE IN JUST A BIT!
OUCH?
HOW DO I KEEP MISSING?
BECAUSE IT'S FUNNY!
DRAGON SCALES, FINELY GROUND, WILL TURN THIS TAINTED WATER AROUND.

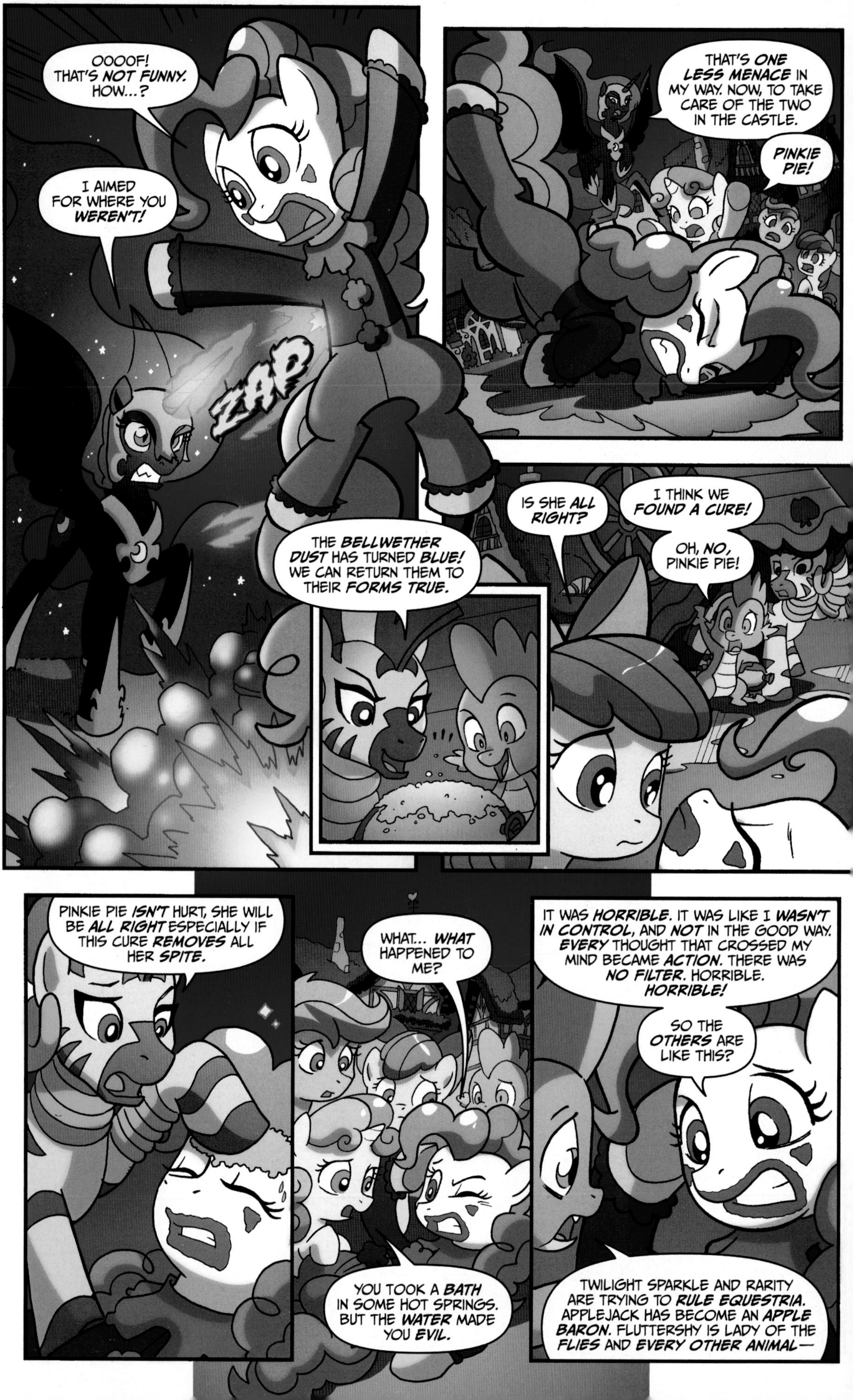

OOOOF! THAT'S NOT FUNNY. HOW...?
I AIMED FOR WHERE YOU WEREN'T!
ZAP
THAT'S ONE LESS MENACE IN MY WAY. NOW, TO TAKE CARE OF THE TWO IN THE CASTLE.
PINKIE PIE!
IS SHE ALL RIGHT?
I THINK WE FOUND A CURE!
OH, NO, PINKIE PIE!
THE BELLWETHER DUST HAS TURNED BLUE! WE CAN RETURN THEM TO THEIR FORMS TRUE.
PINKIE PIE ISN'T HURT, SHE WILL BE ALL RIGHT ESPECIALLY IF THIS CURE REMOVES ALL HER SPITE.
WHAT... WHAT HAPPENED TO ME?
YOU TOOK A BATH IN SOME HOT SPRINGS. BUT THE WATER MADE YOU EVIL.
IT WAS HORRIBLE. IT WAS LIKE I WASN'T IN CONTROL, AND NOT IN THE GOOD WAY. EVERY THOUGHT THAT CROSSED MY MIND BECAME ACTION. THERE WAS NO FILTER. HORRIBLE. HORRIBLE!
SO THE OTHERS ARE LIKE THIS?
TWILIGHT SPARKLE AND RARITY ARE TRYING TO RULE EQUESTRIA. APPLEJACK HAS BECOME AN APPLE BARON. FLUTTERSHY IS LADY OF THE FLIES AND EVERY OTHER ANIMAL—

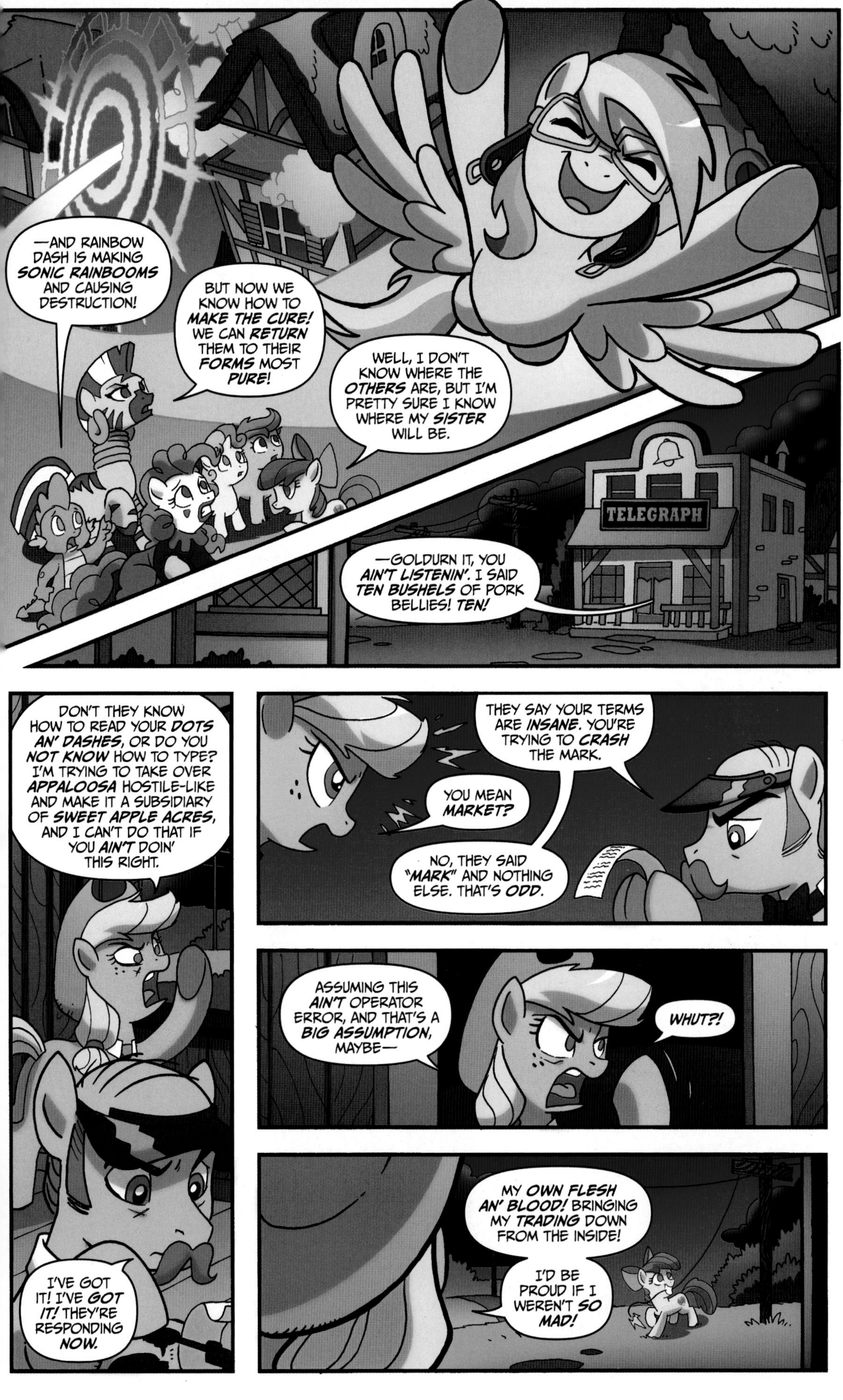

—AND RAINBOW DASH IS MAKING SONIC RAINBOOMS AND CAUSING DESTRUCTION!
BUT NOW WE KNOW HOW TO MAKE THE CURE! WE CAN RETURN THEM TO THEIR FORMS MOST PURE!
WELL, I DON'T KNOW WHERE THE OTHERS ARE, BUT I'M PRETTY SURE I KNOW WHERE MY SISTER WILL BE.
TELEGRAPH
—GOLDURN IT, YOU AIN'T LISTENIN'. I SAID TEN BUSHELS OF PORK BELLIES! TEN!
DON'T THEY KNOW HOW TO READ YOUR DOTS AN' DASHES, OR DO YOU NOT KNOW HOW TO TYPE? I'M TRYING TO TAKE OVER APPALOOSA HOSTILE-LIKE AND MAKE IT A SUBSIDIARY OF SWEET APPLE ACRES, AND I CAN'T DO THAT IF YOU AIN'T DOIN' THIS RIGHT.
I'VE GOT IT! I'VE GOT IT! THEY'RE RESPONDING NOW.
THEY SAY YOUR TERMS ARE INSANE. YOU'RE TRYING TO CRASH THE MARK.
YOU MEAN MARKET?
NO, THEY SAID "MARK" AND NOTHING ELSE. THAT'S ODD.
ASSUMING THIS AIN'T OPERATOR ERROR, AND THAT'S A BIG ASSUMPTION, MAYBE—
WHUT?!
MY OWN FLESH AN' BLOOD! BRINGING MY TRADING DOWN FROM THE INSIDE!
I'D BE PROUD IF I WEREN'T SO MAD!

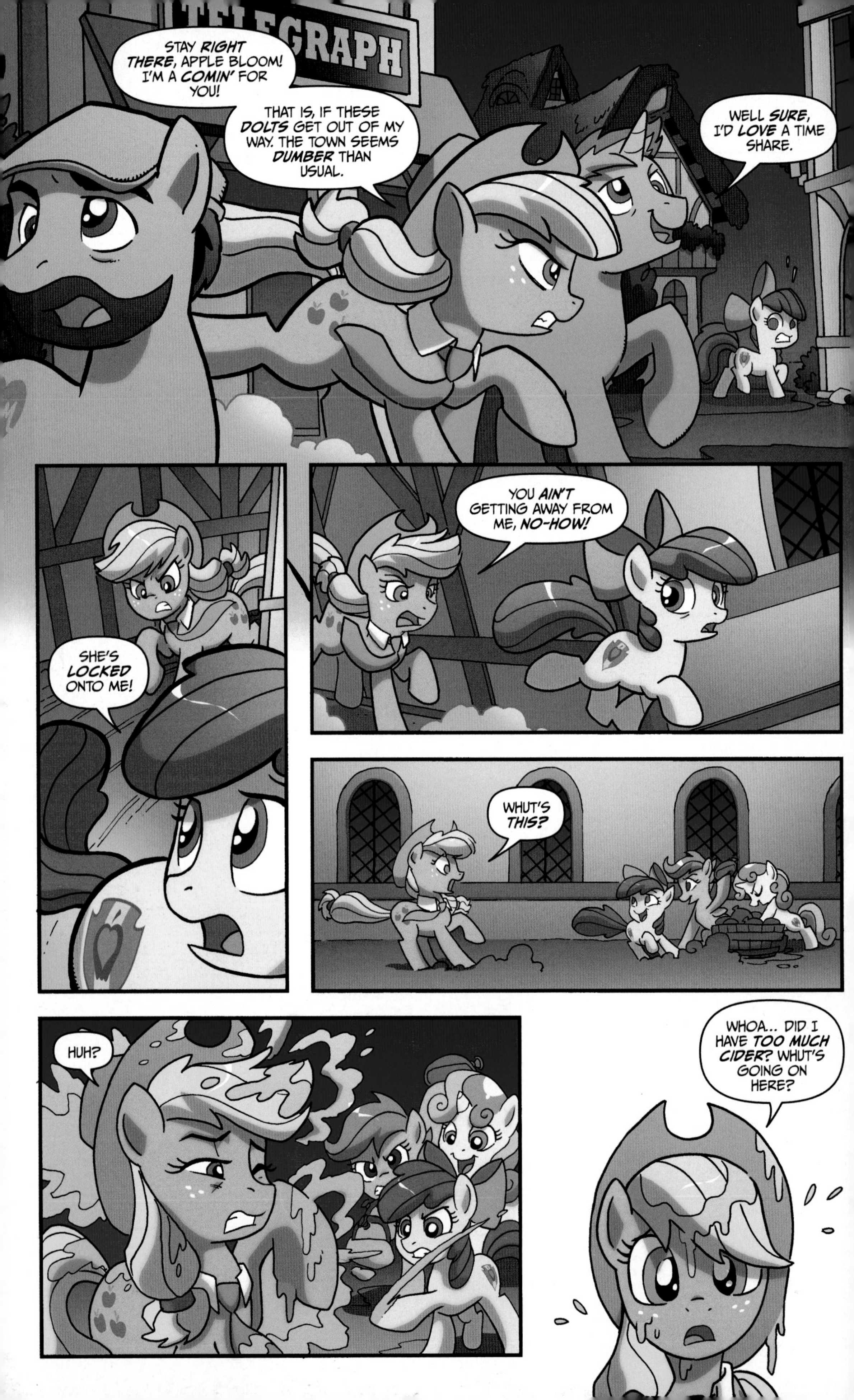
TELEGRAPH
STAY RIGHT THERE, APPLE BLOOM! I'M A COMIN' FOR YOU!
THAT IS, IF THESE DOLTS GET OUT OF MY WAY. THE TOWN SEEMS DUMBER THAN USUAL.
WELL SURE, I'D LOVE A TIME SHARE.
SHE'S LOCKED ONTO ME!
YOU AIN'T GETTING AWAY FROM ME, NO-HOW!
WHUT'S THIS?
HUH?
WHOA... DID I HAVE TOO MUCH CIDER? WHUT'S GOING ON HERE?

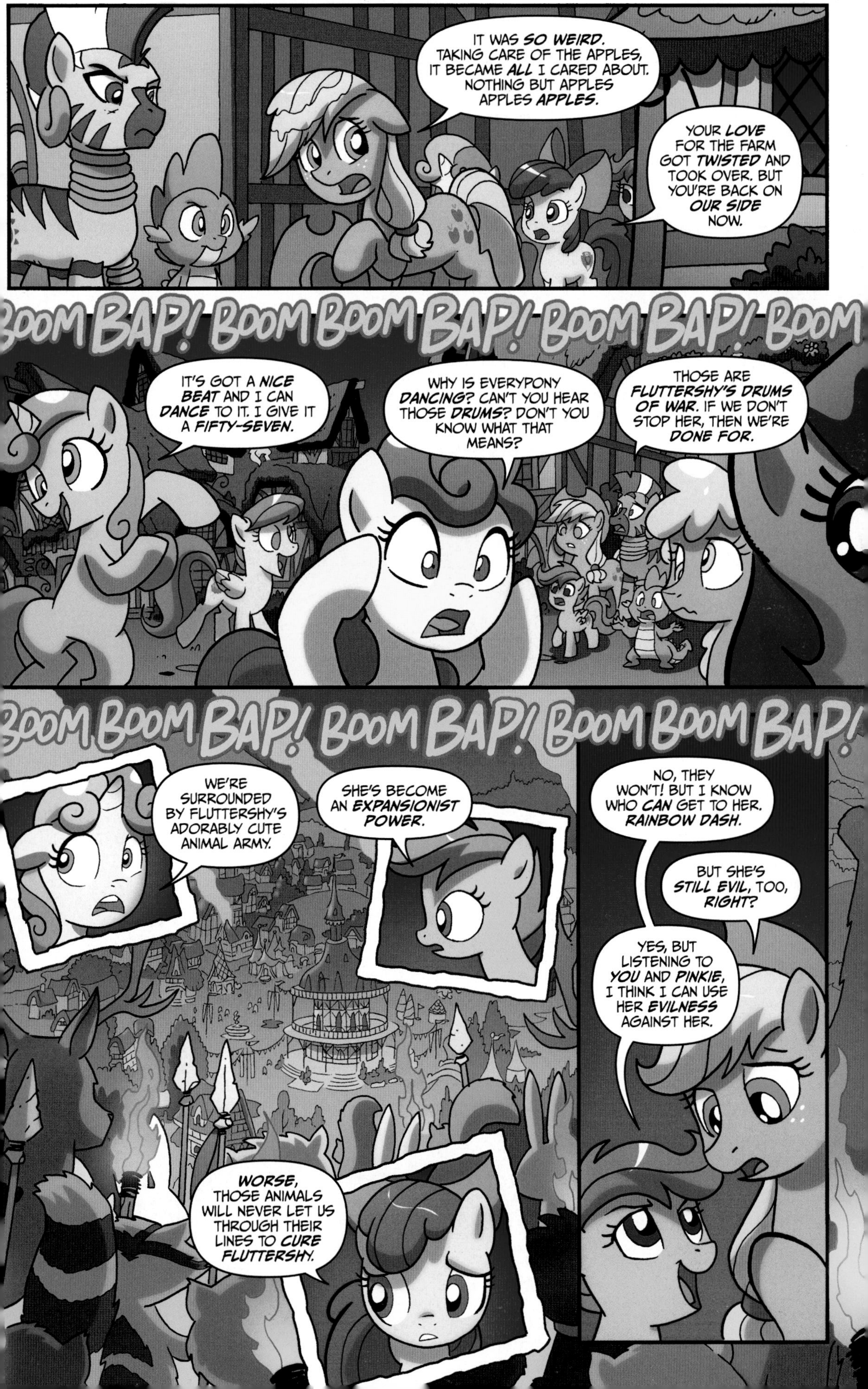
IT WAS SO WEIRD. TAKING CARE OF THE APPLES, IT BECAME ALL I CARED ABOUT. NOTHING BUT APPLES APPLES APPLES.
YOUR LOVE FOR THE FARM GOT TWISTED AND TOOK OVER. BUT YOU'RE BACK ON OUR SIDE NOW.
BOOM BAP! BOOM BOOM BAP! BOOM BAP! BOOM
IT'S GOT A NICE BEAT AND I CAN DANCE TO IT. I GIVE IT A FIFTY-SEVEN.
WHY IS EVERYPONY DANCING? CAN'T YOU HEAR THOSE DRUMS? DON'T YOU KNOW WHAT THAT MEANS?
THOSE ARE FLUTTERSHY'S DRUMS OF WAR. IF WE DON'T STOP HER, THEN WE'RE DONE FOR.
BOOM BOOM BAP! BOOM BAP! BOOM BOOM BAP!
WE'RE SURROUNDED BY FLUTTERSHY'S ADORABLY CUTE ANIMAL ARMY.
SHE'S BECOME AN EXPANSIONIST POWER.
WORSE, THOSE ANIMALS WILL NEVER LET US THROUGH THEIR LINES TO CURE FLUTTERSHY.
NO, THEY WON'T! BUT I KNOW WHO CAN GET TO HER. RAINBOW DASH.
BUT SHE'S STILL EVIL, TOO, RIGHT?
YES, BUT LISTENING TO YOU AND PINKIE, I THINK I CAN USE HER EVILNESS AGAINST HER.

I *DON'T GET IT.* ARE WE GOING TO *SWING* THE EVIL OUT OF HER?

THE EVIL WATER IS *TWISTING* THEIR VIRTUES INTO *VICES.* APPLEJACK'S *LOVE OF APPLES,* FLUTTERSHY *PROTECTING THE ANIMALS,* AND SO ON.

WELL, RAINBOW DASH HAS BEEN CAUSING SONIC RAINBOOMS. BECAUSE SHE'S *SHOWING OFF.* WE JUST HAVE TO GET HER TO SHOW OFF *HERE.*

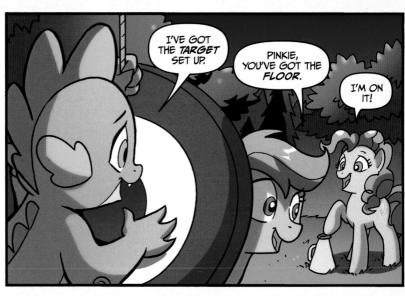

I'VE GOT THE *TARGET* SET UP.

PINKIE, YOU'VE GOT THE *FLOOR.*

I'M ON IT!

NO, YOU'RE **RIGHT!** THERE'S NO WAY EVEN **RAINBOW DASH** COULD HIT THAT **MOVING TARGET!**

I DON'T KNOW! SHE'S PRETTY FLY!

NOPE! THAT TARGET IS MOVING WAY TOO MUCH FOR HER TO CATCH IT!

YOU'D HAVE TO BE SOME KIND OF WONDERBOLT TO DO THAT!

SOME KIND OF WONDERBOLT?

I'M BETTER THAN *ALL* THE WONDERBOLTS! *ADDED UP!*

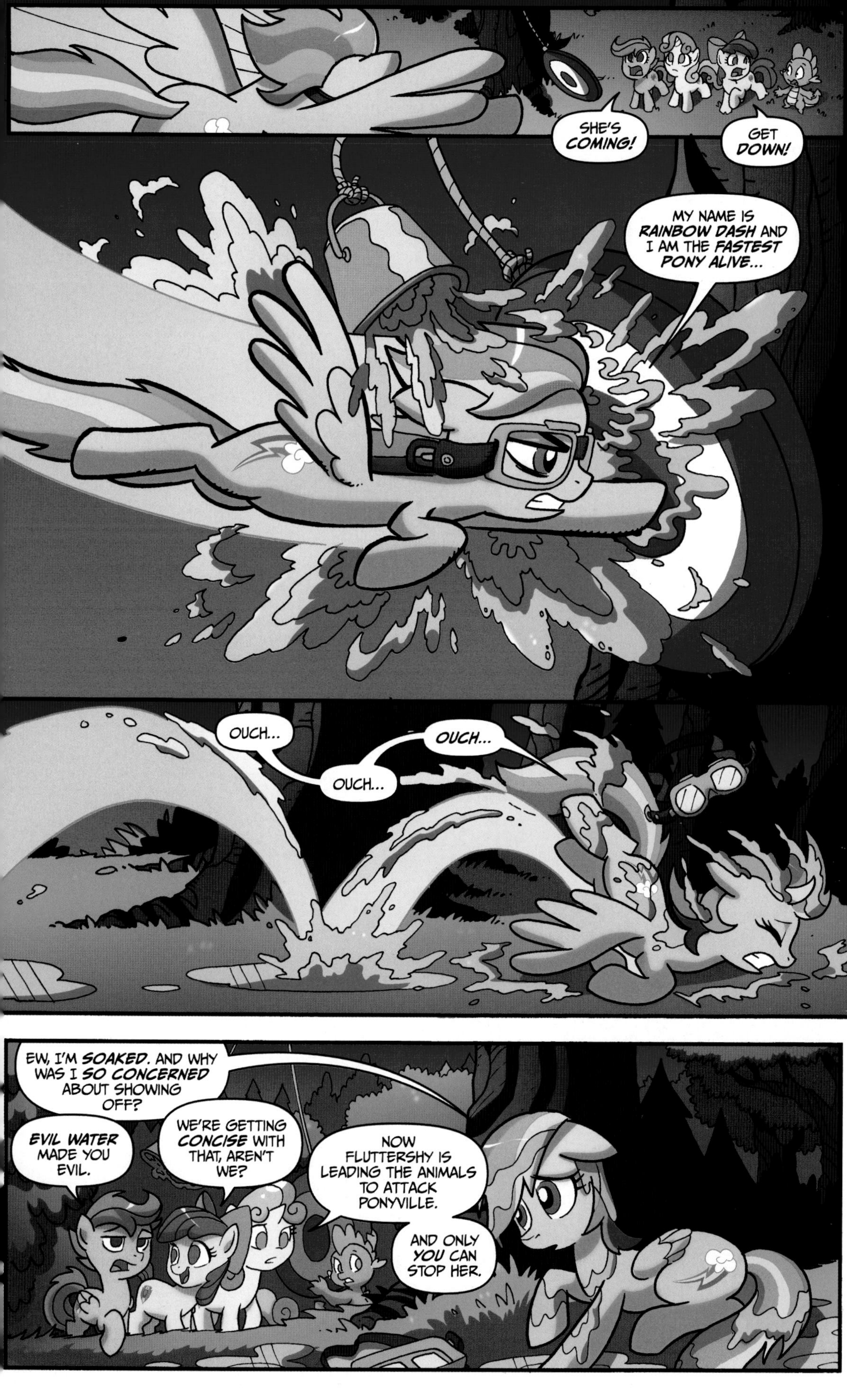

SHE'S COMING!
GET DOWN!
MY NAME IS RAINBOW DASH AND I AM THE FASTEST PONY ALIVE...
OUCH...
OUCH...
OUCH...
EW, I'M SOAKED. AND WHY WAS I SO CONCERNED ABOUT SHOWING OFF?
EVIL WATER MADE YOU EVIL.
WE'RE GETTING CONCISE WITH THAT, AREN'T WE?
NOW FLUTTERSHY IS LEADING THE ANIMALS TO ATTACK PONYVILLE.
AND ONLY YOU CAN STOP HER.

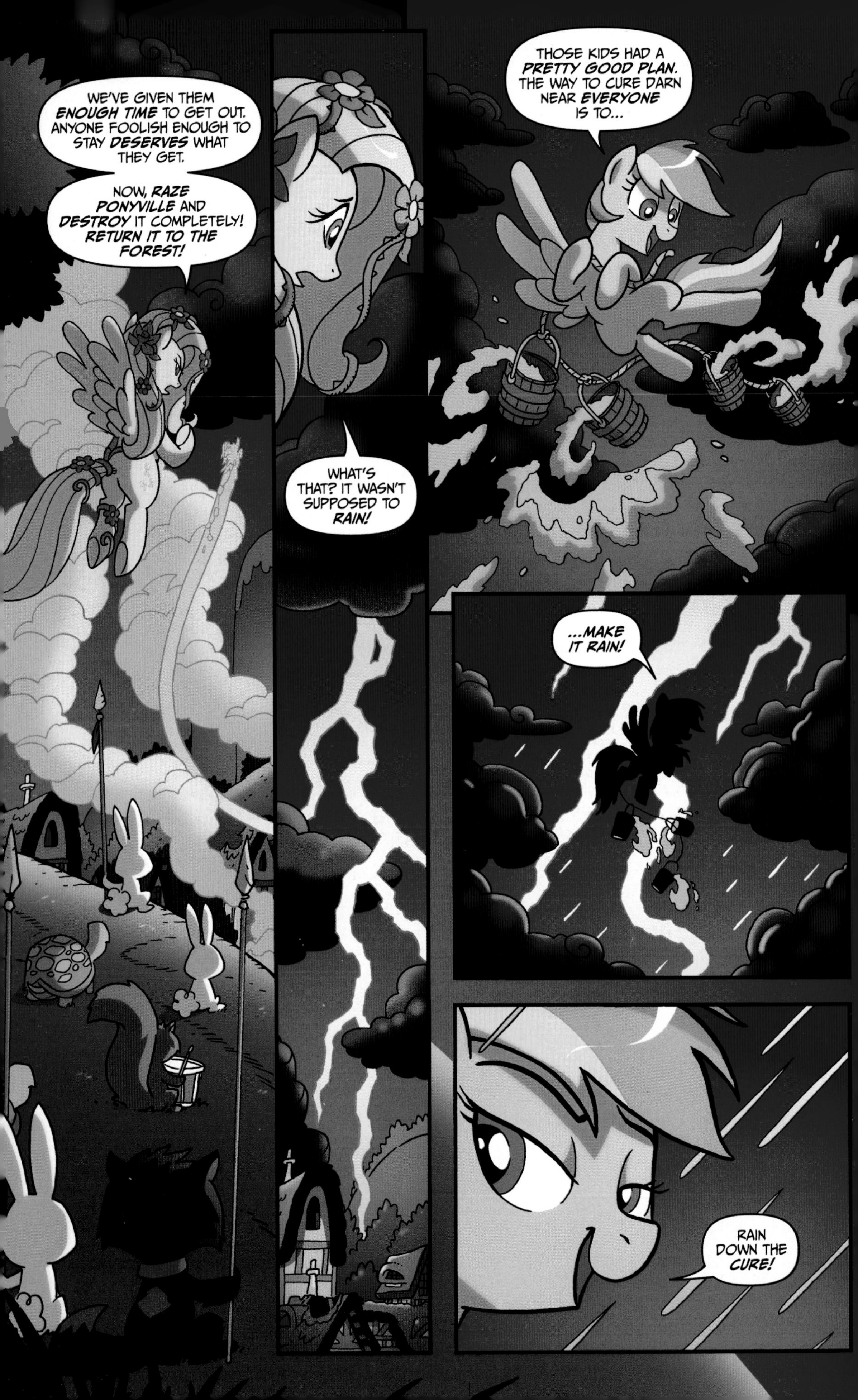
WE'VE GIVEN THEM ENOUGH TIME TO GET OUT. ANYONE FOOLISH ENOUGH TO STAY DESERVES WHAT THEY GET.
NOW, RAZE PONYVILLE AND DESTROY IT COMPLETELY! RETURN IT TO THE FOREST!
WHAT'S THAT? IT WASN'T SUPPOSED TO RAIN!
THOSE KIDS HAD A PRETTY GOOD PLAN. THE WAY TO CURE DARN NEAR EVERYONE IS TO...
...MAKE IT RAIN!
RAIN DOWN THE CURE!

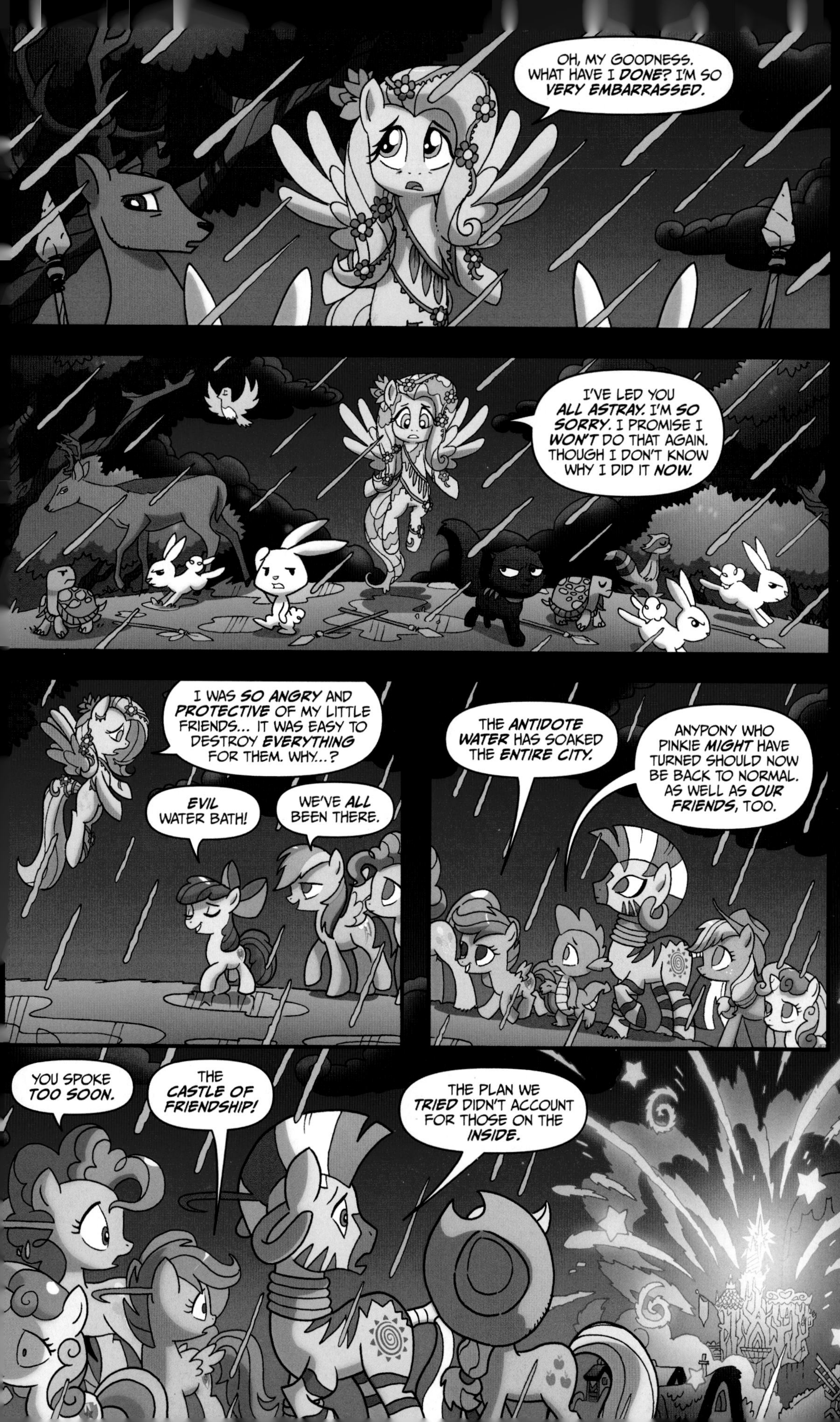
OH, MY GOODNESS. WHAT HAVE I DONE? I'M SO VERY EMBARRASSED.
I'VE LED YOU ALL ASTRAY. I'M SO SORRY. I PROMISE I WON'T DO THAT AGAIN. THOUGH I DON'T KNOW WHY I DID IT NOW.
I WAS SO ANGRY AND PROTECTIVE OF MY LITTLE FRIENDS... IT WAS EASY TO DESTROY EVERYTHING FOR THEM. WHY...?
EVIL WATER BATH!
WE'VE ALL BEEN THERE.
THE ANTIDOTE WATER HAS SOAKED THE ENTIRE CITY.
ANYPONY WHO PINKIE MIGHT HAVE TURNED SHOULD NOW BE BACK TO NORMAL. AS WELL AS OUR FRIENDS, TOO.
YOU SPOKE TOO SOON.
THE CASTLE OF FRIENDSHIP!
THE PLAN WE TRIED DIDN'T ACCOUNT FOR THOSE ON THE INSIDE.

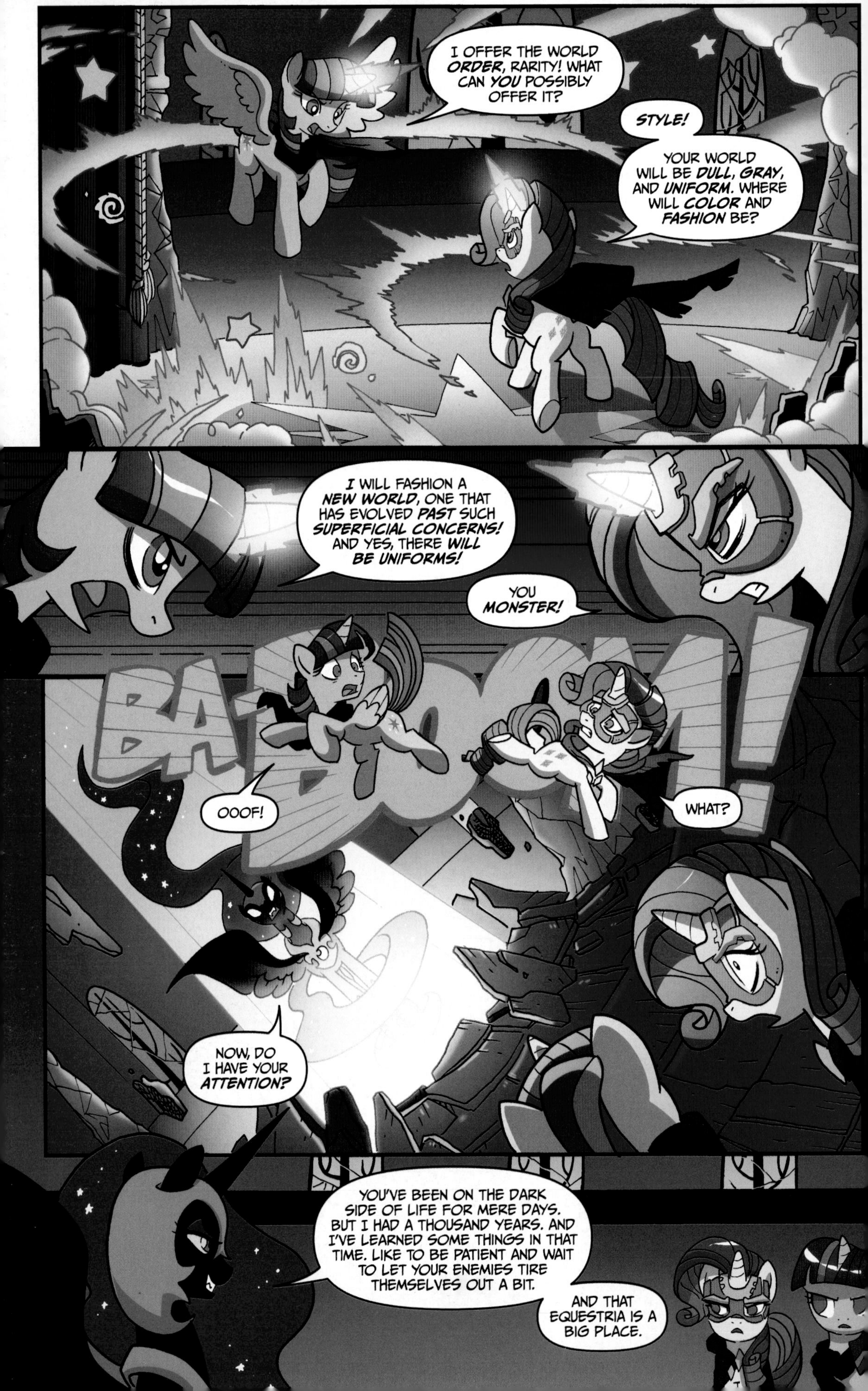

I OFFER THE WORLD ORDER, RARITY! WHAT CAN YOU POSSIBLY OFFER IT?
STYLE!
YOUR WORLD WILL BE DULL, GRAY, AND UNIFORM. WHERE WILL COLOR AND FASHION BE?
I WILL FASHION A NEW WORLD, ONE THAT HAS EVOLVED PAST SUCH SUPERFICIAL CONCERNS! AND YES, THERE WILL BE UNIFORMS!
YOU MONSTER!
OOOF!
WHAT?
NOW, DO I HAVE YOUR ATTENTION?
YOU'VE BEEN ON THE DARK SIDE OF LIFE FOR MERE DAYS. BUT I HAD A THOUSAND YEARS. AND I'VE LEARNED SOME THINGS IN THAT TIME. LIKE TO BE PATIENT AND WAIT TO LET YOUR ENEMIES TIRE THEMSELVES OUT A BIT.
AND THAT EQUESTRIA IS A BIG PLACE.

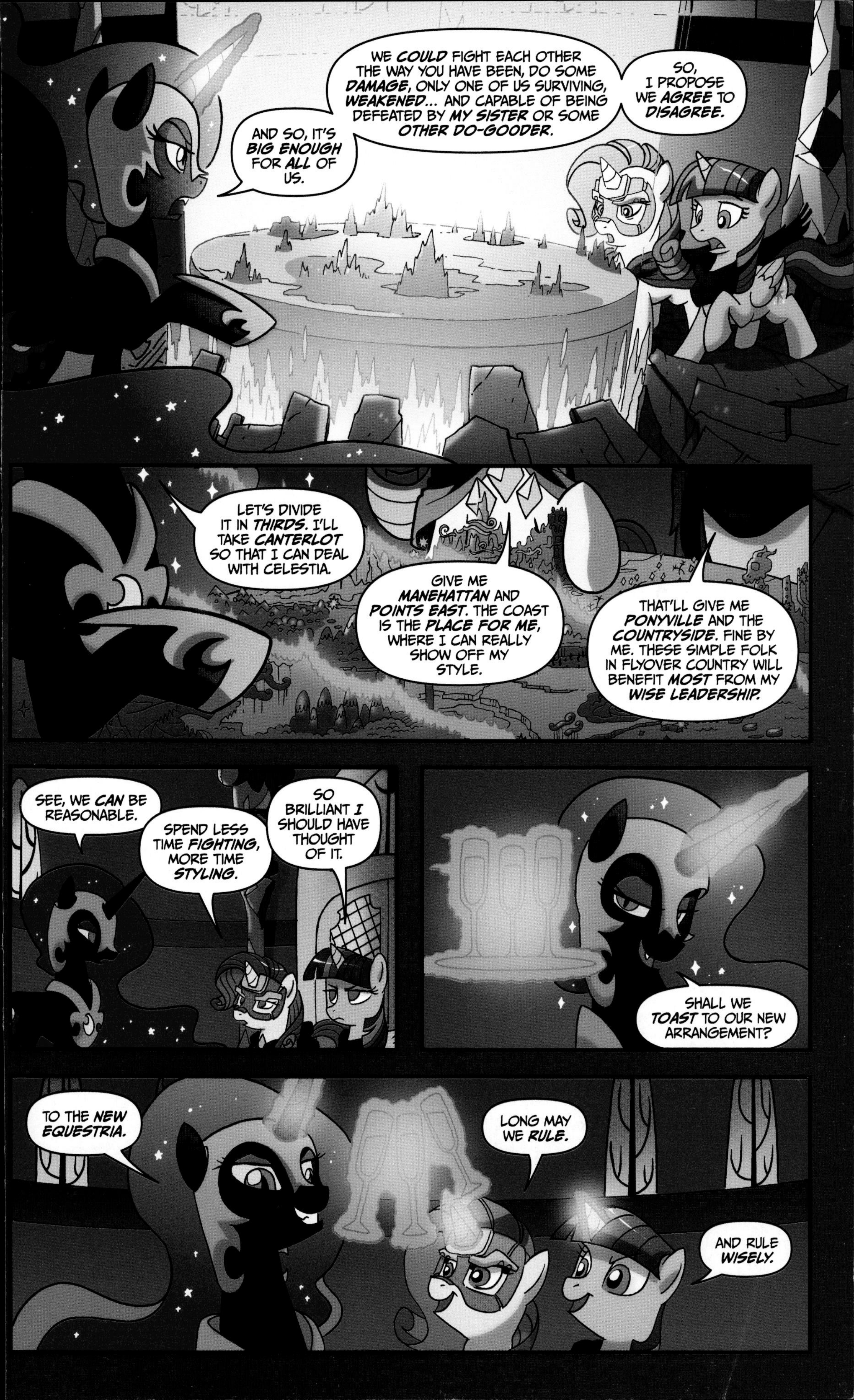
AND SO, IT'S BIG ENOUGH FOR ALL OF US.
WE COULD FIGHT EACH OTHER THE WAY YOU HAVE BEEN, DO SOME DAMAGE, ONLY ONE OF US SURVIVING, WEAKENED... AND CAPABLE OF BEING DEFEATED BY MY SISTER OR SOME OTHER DO-GOODER.
SO, I PROPOSE WE AGREE TO DISAGREE.
LET'S DIVIDE IT IN THIRDS. I'LL TAKE CANTERLOT SO THAT I CAN DEAL WITH CELESTIA.
GIVE ME MANEHATTAN AND POINTS EAST. THE COAST IS THE PLACE FOR ME, WHERE I CAN REALLY SHOW OFF MY STYLE.
THAT'LL GIVE ME PONYVILLE AND THE COUNTRYSIDE. FINE BY ME. THESE SIMPLE FOLK IN FLYOVER COUNTRY WILL BENEFIT MOST FROM MY WISE LEADERSHIP.
SEE, WE CAN BE REASONABLE.
SPEND LESS TIME FIGHTING, MORE TIME STYLING.
SO BRILLIANT I SHOULD HAVE THOUGHT OF IT.
SHALL WE TOAST TO OUR NEW ARRANGEMENT?
TO THE NEW EQUESTRIA.
LONG MAY WE RULE.
AND RULE WISELY.

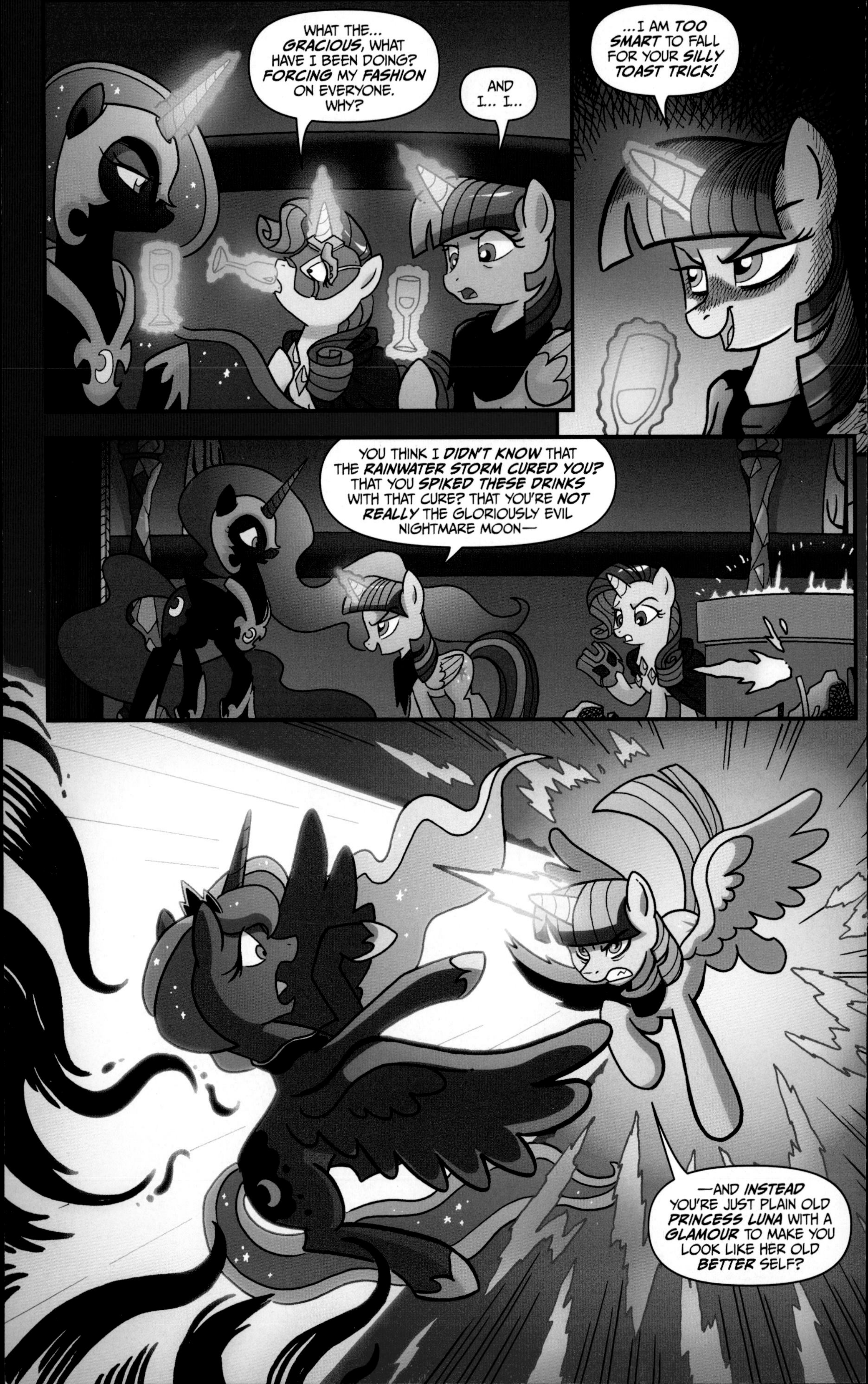
WHAT THE... GRACIOUS, WHAT HAVE I BEEN DOING? FORCING MY FASHION ON EVERYONE. WHY?
AND I... I...
...I AM TOO SMART TO FALL FOR YOUR SILLY TOAST TRICK!
YOU THINK I DIDN'T KNOW THAT THE RAINWATER STORM CURED YOU? THAT YOU SPIKED THESE DRINKS WITH THAT CURE? THAT YOU'RE NOT REALLY THE GLORIOUSLY EVIL NIGHTMARE MOON—
—AND INSTEAD YOU'RE JUST PLAIN OLD PRINCESS LUNA WITH A GLAMOUR TO MAKE YOU LOOK LIKE HER OLD BETTER SELF?

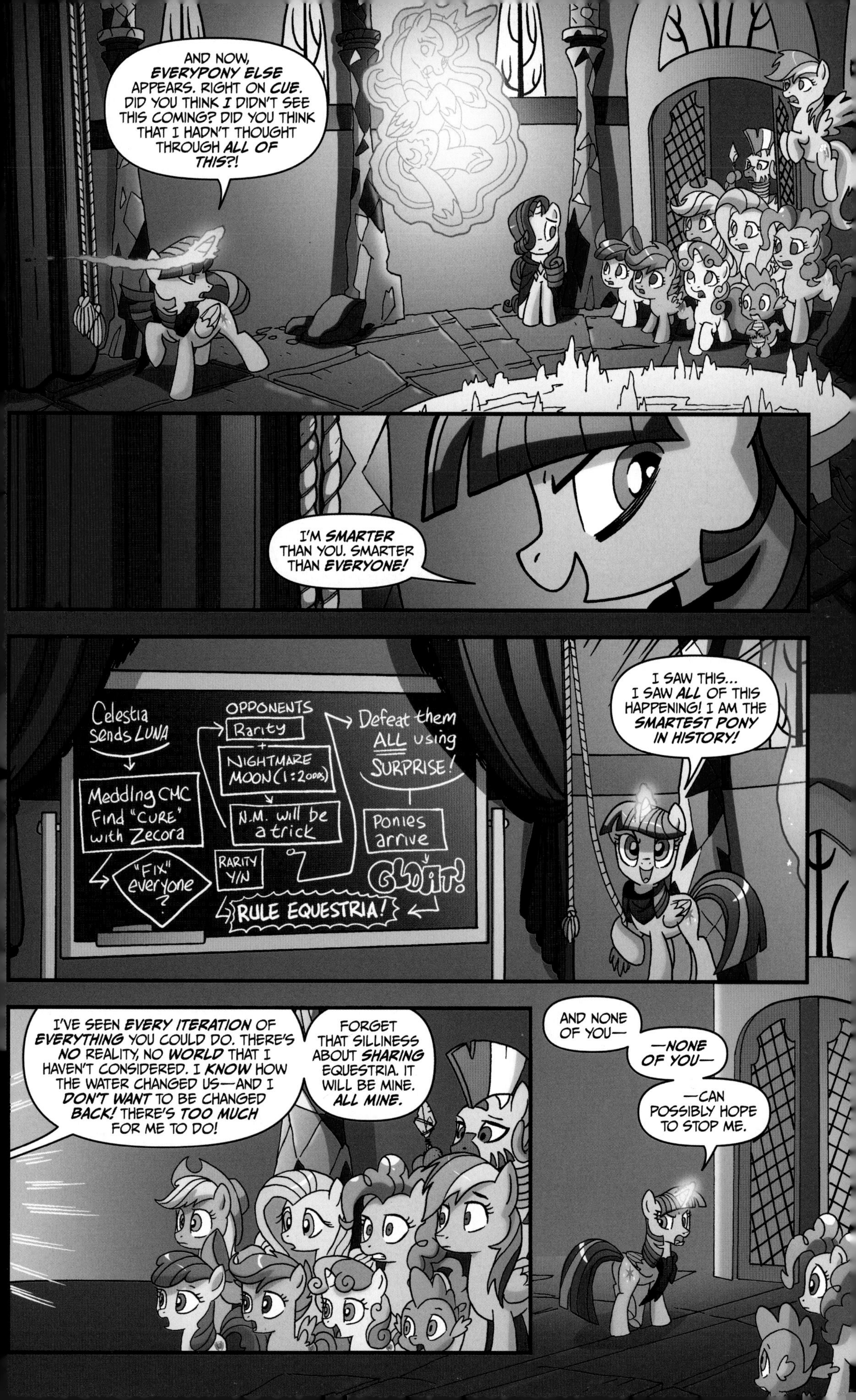
AND NOW, EVERYPONY ELSE APPEARS. RIGHT ON CUE. DID YOU THINK I DIDN'T SEE THIS COMING? DID YOU THINK THAT I HADN'T THOUGHT THROUGH ALL OF THIS?!
I'M SMARTER THAN YOU. SMARTER THAN EVERYONE!
Celestia sends LUNA
Medding CMC Find "CURE" with Zecora
"FIX" everyone ?
OPPONENTS
Rarity
+
NIGHTMARE MOON (1:2000s)
N.M. will be a trick
RARITY Y/N
Defeat them ALL using SURPRISE!
Ponies arrive
GLOAT!
RULE EQUESTRIA!
I SAW THIS... I SAW ALL OF THIS HAPPENING! I AM THE SMARTEST PONY IN HISTORY!
I'VE SEEN EVERY ITERATION OF EVERYTHING YOU COULD DO. THERE'S NO REALITY, NO WORLD THAT I HAVEN'T CONSIDERED. I KNOW HOW THE WATER CHANGED US—AND I DON'T WANT TO BE CHANGED BACK! THERE'S TOO MUCH FOR ME TO DO!
FORGET THAT SILLINESS ABOUT SHARING EQUESTRIA. IT WILL BE MINE. ALL MINE.
AND NONE OF YOU—
—NONE OF YOU—
—CAN POSSIBLY HOPE TO STOP ME.

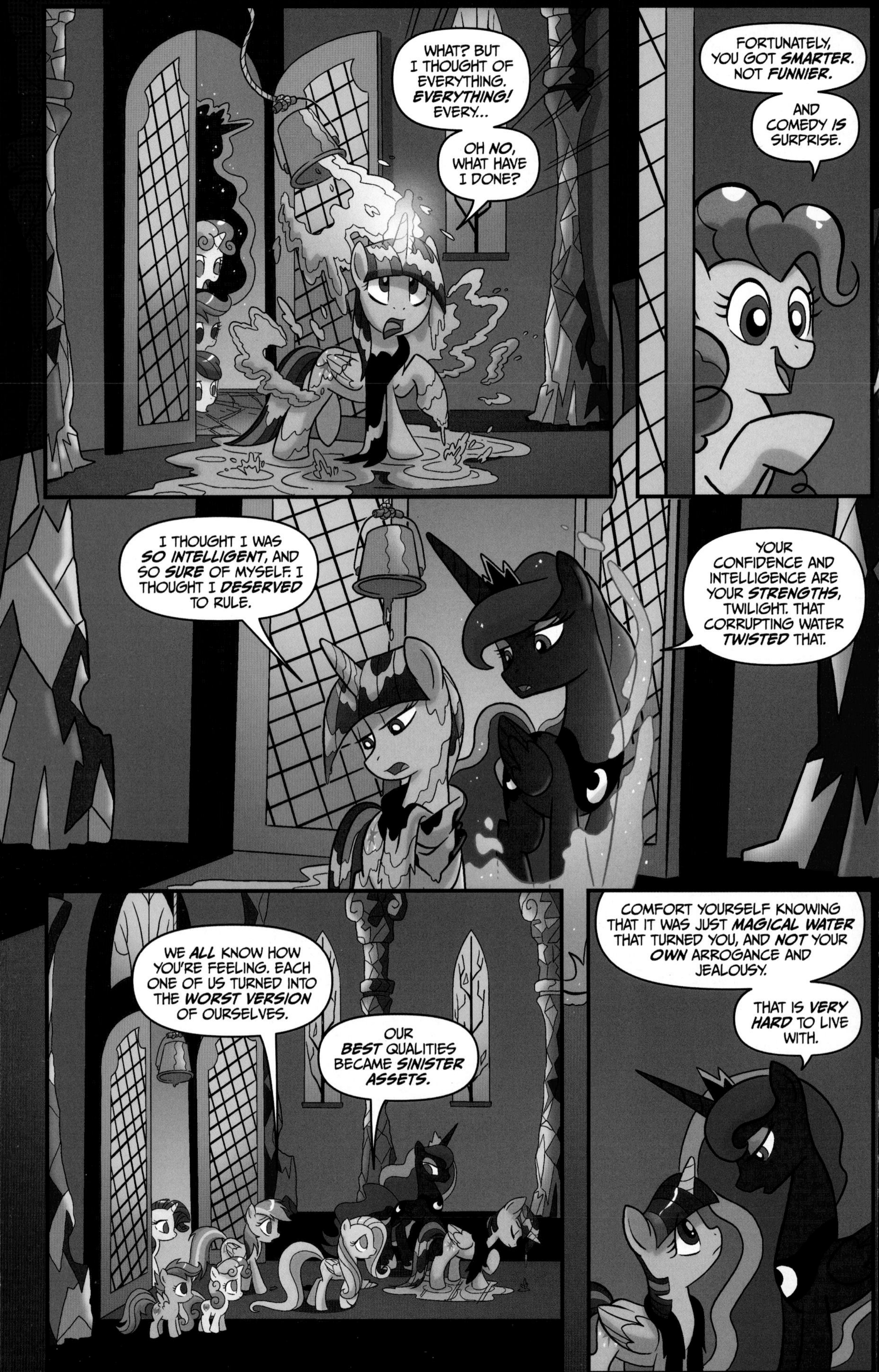
WHAT? BUT I THOUGHT OF EVERYTHING. EVERYTHING! EVERY...
OH NO, WHAT HAVE I DONE?
FORTUNATELY, YOU GOT SMARTER. NOT FUNNIER.
AND COMEDY IS SURPRISE.
I THOUGHT I WAS SO INTELLIGENT, AND SO SURE OF MYSELF. I THOUGHT I DESERVED TO RULE.
YOUR CONFIDENCE AND INTELLIGENCE ARE YOUR STRENGTHS, TWILIGHT. THAT CORRUPTING WATER TWISTED THAT.
WE ALL KNOW HOW YOU'RE FEELING. EACH ONE OF US TURNED INTO THE WORST VERSION OF OURSELVES.
OUR BEST QUALITIES BECAME SINISTER ASSETS.
COMFORT YOURSELF KNOWING THAT IT WAS JUST MAGICAL WATER THAT TURNED YOU, AND NOT YOUR OWN ARROGANCE AND JEALOUSY.
THAT IS VERY HARD TO LIVE WITH.

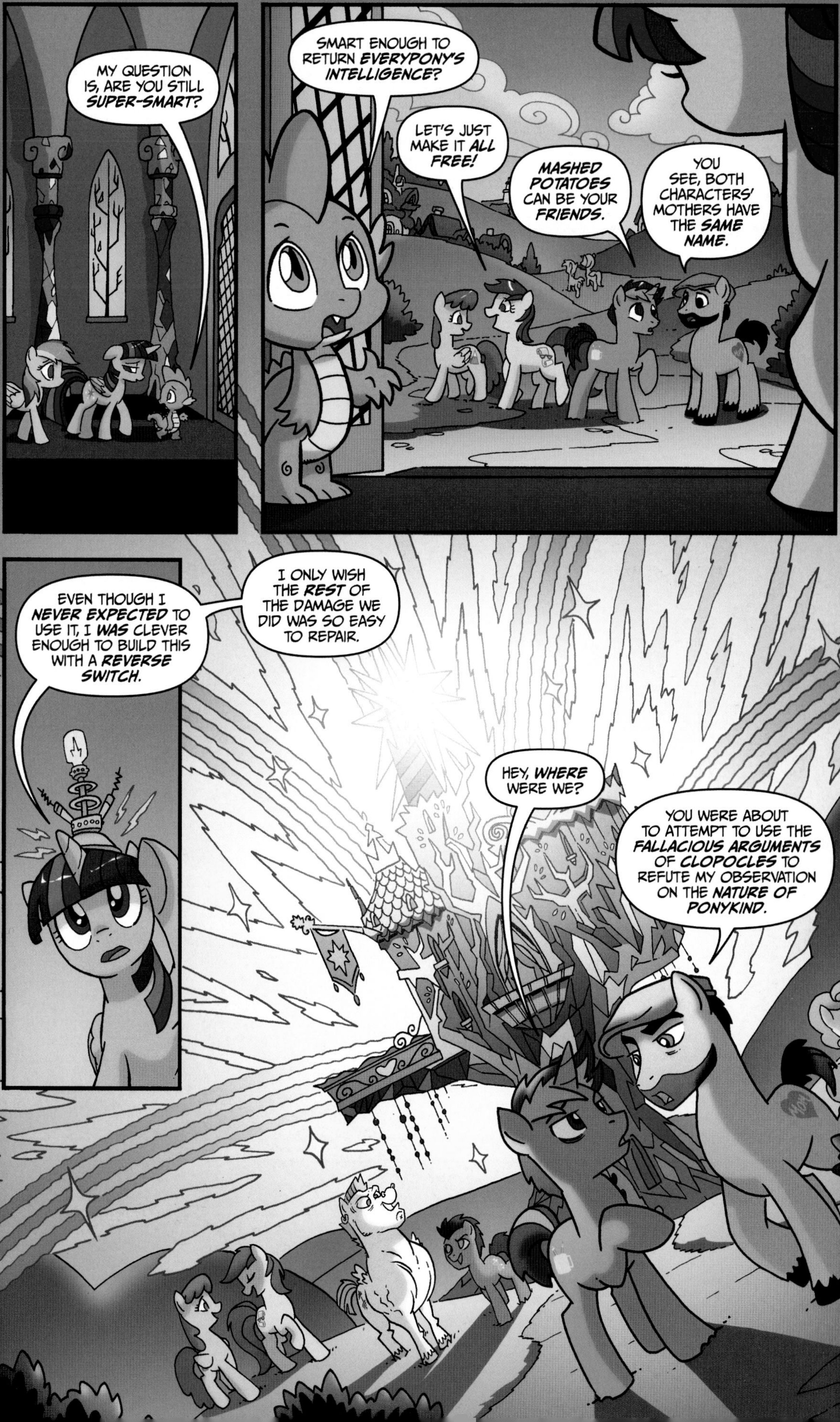
MY QUESTION IS, ARE YOU STILL SUPER-SMART?
SMART ENOUGH TO RETURN EVERYPONY'S INTELLIGENCE?
LET'S JUST MAKE IT ALL FREE!
MASHED POTATOES CAN BE YOUR FRIENDS.
YOU SEE, BOTH CHARACTERS' MOTHERS HAVE THE SAME NAME.
EVEN THOUGH I NEVER EXPECTED TO USE IT, I WAS CLEVER ENOUGH TO BUILD THIS WITH A REVERSE SWITCH.
I ONLY WISH THE REST OF THE DAMAGE WE DID WAS SO EASY TO REPAIR.
HEY, WHERE WERE WE?
YOU WERE ABOUT TO ATTEMPT TO USE THE FALLACIOUS ARGUMENTS OF CLOPOCLES TO REFUTE MY OBSERVATION ON THE NATURE OF PONYKIND.

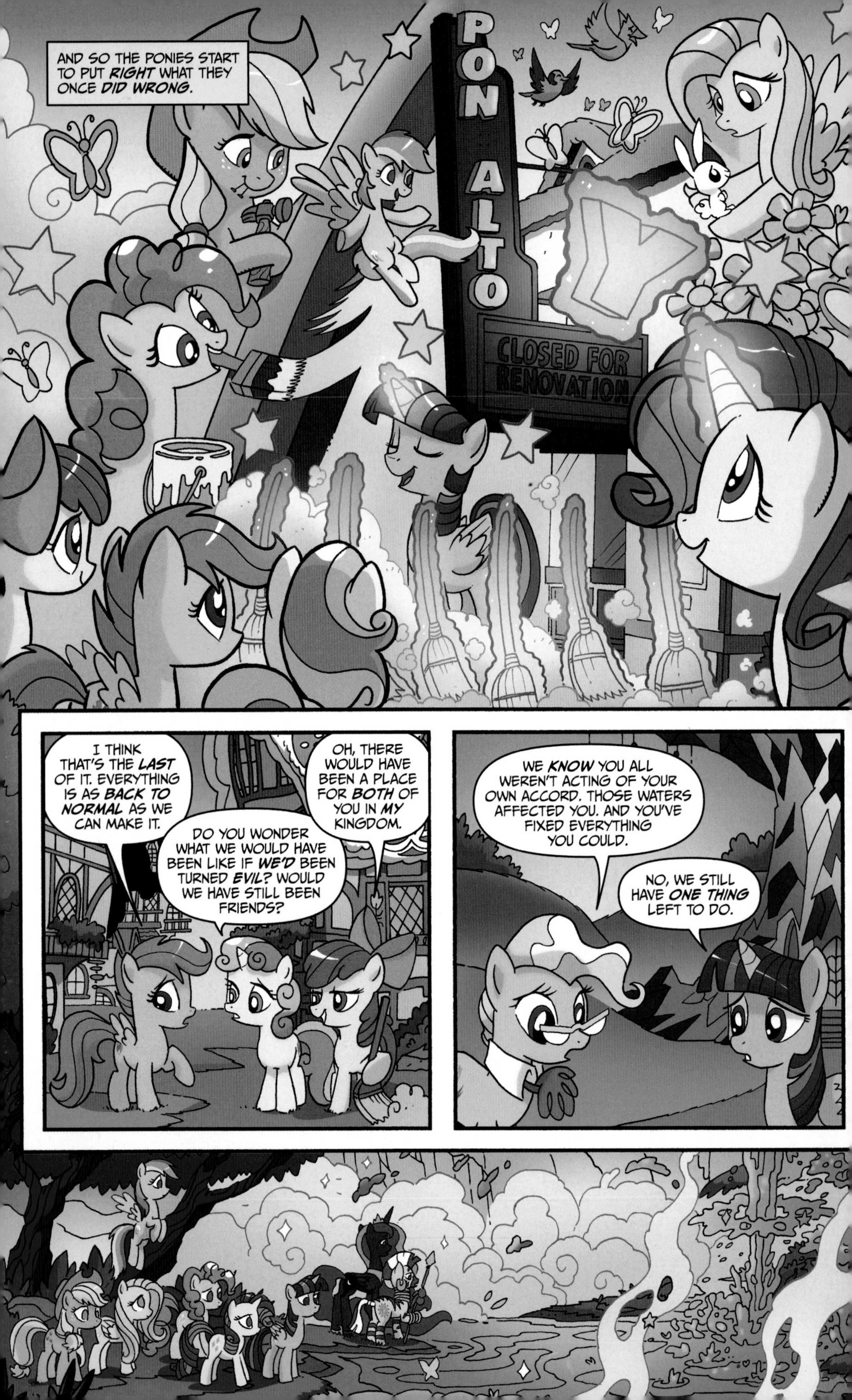
AND SO THE PONIES START TO PUT *RIGHT* WHAT THEY ONCE *DID WRONG*.
PON ALTO
CLOSED FOR RENOVATION
I THINK THAT'S THE *LAST* OF IT. EVERYTHING IS AS *BACK TO NORMAL* AS WE CAN MAKE IT.
DO YOU WONDER WHAT WE WOULD HAVE BEEN LIKE IF *WE'D* BEEN TURNED *EVIL*? WOULD WE HAVE STILL BEEN FRIENDS?
OH, THERE WOULD HAVE BEEN A PLACE FOR *BOTH* OF YOU IN *MY* KINGDOM.
WE *KNOW* YOU ALL WEREN'T ACTING OF YOUR OWN ACCORD. THOSE WATERS AFFECTED YOU. AND YOU'VE FIXED EVERYTHING YOU COULD.
NO, WE STILL HAVE *ONE THING* LEFT TO DO.

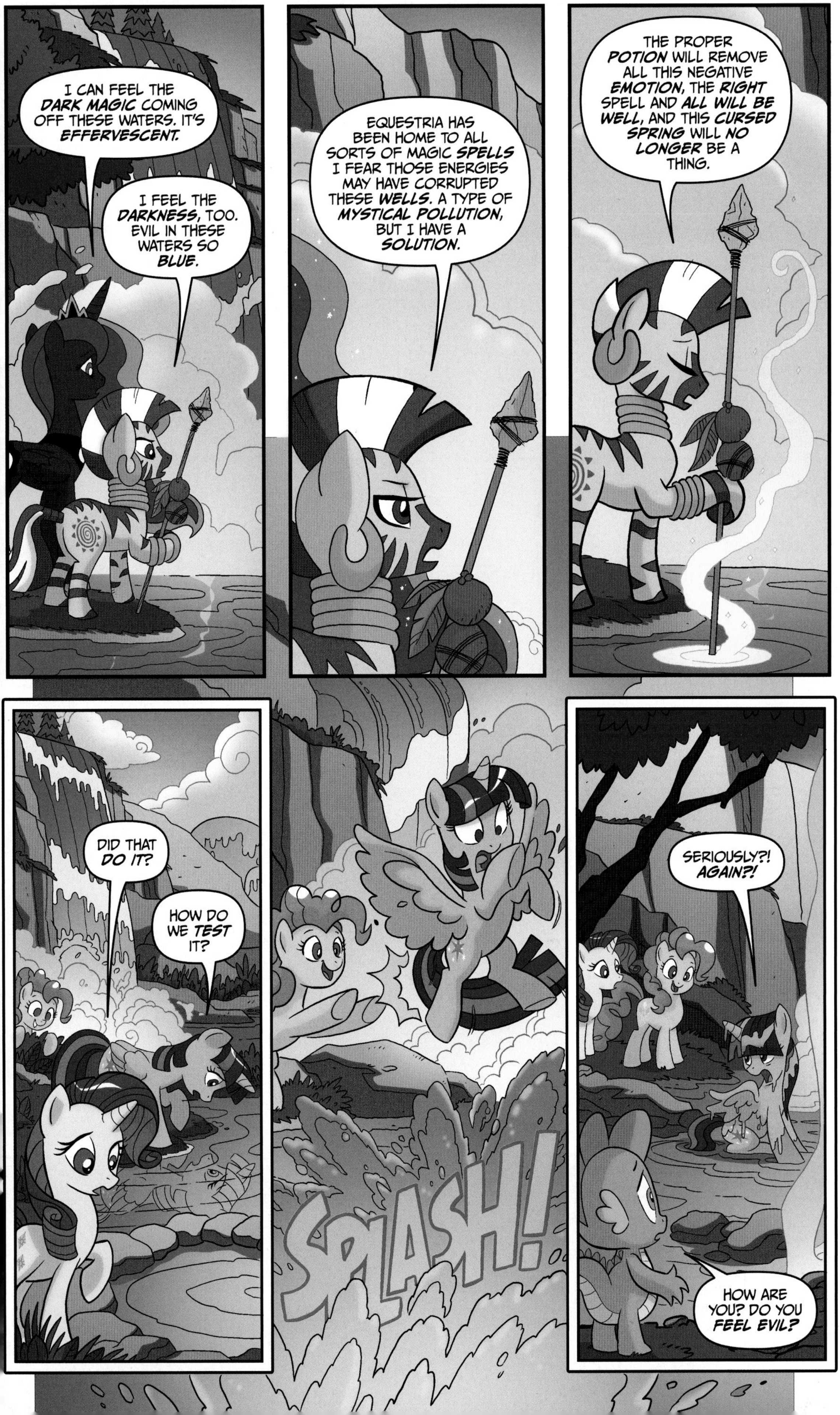
I CAN FEEL THE DARK MAGIC COMING OFF THESE WATERS. IT'S EFFERVESCENT.
I FEEL THE DARKNESS, TOO. EVIL IN THESE WATERS SO BLUE.
EQUESTRIA HAS BEEN HOME TO ALL SORTS OF MAGIC SPELLS I FEAR THOSE ENERGIES MAY HAVE CORRUPTED THESE WELLS. A TYPE OF MYSTICAL POLLUTION, BUT I HAVE A SOLUTION.
THE PROPER POTION WILL REMOVE ALL THIS NEGATIVE EMOTION, THE RIGHT SPELL AND ALL WILL BE WELL, AND THIS CURSED SPRING WILL NO LONGER BE A THING.
DID THAT DO IT?
HOW DO WE TEST IT?
SPLASH!
SERIOUSLY?! AGAIN?!
HOW ARE YOU? DO YOU FEEL EVIL?

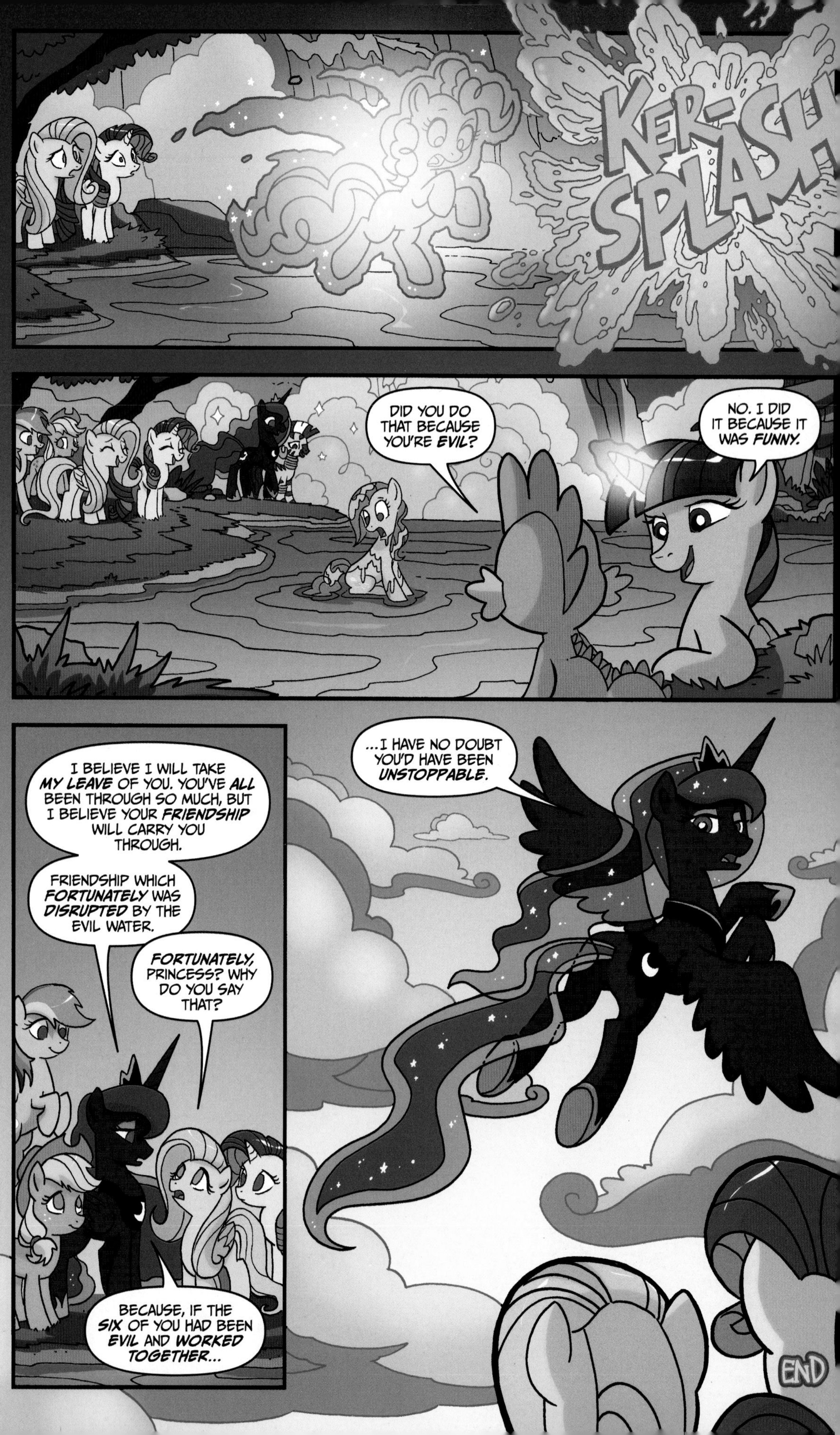
KER-SPLASH!
DID YOU DO THAT BECAUSE YOU'RE *EVIL*?
NO. I DID IT BECAUSE IT WAS *FUNNY*.
I BELIEVE I WILL TAKE *MY LEAVE* OF YOU. YOU'VE *ALL* BEEN THROUGH SO MUCH, BUT I BELIEVE YOUR *FRIENDSHIP* WILL CARRY YOU THROUGH.
FRIENDSHIP WHICH *FORTUNATELY* WAS *DISRUPTED* BY THE EVIL WATER.
FORTUNATELY, PRINCESS? WHY DO YOU SAY THAT?
BECAUSE, IF THE *SIX* OF YOU HAD BEEN *EVIL* AND *WORKED TOGETHER*...
...I HAVE NO DOUBT YOU'D HAVE BEEN *UNSTOPPABLE*.
END

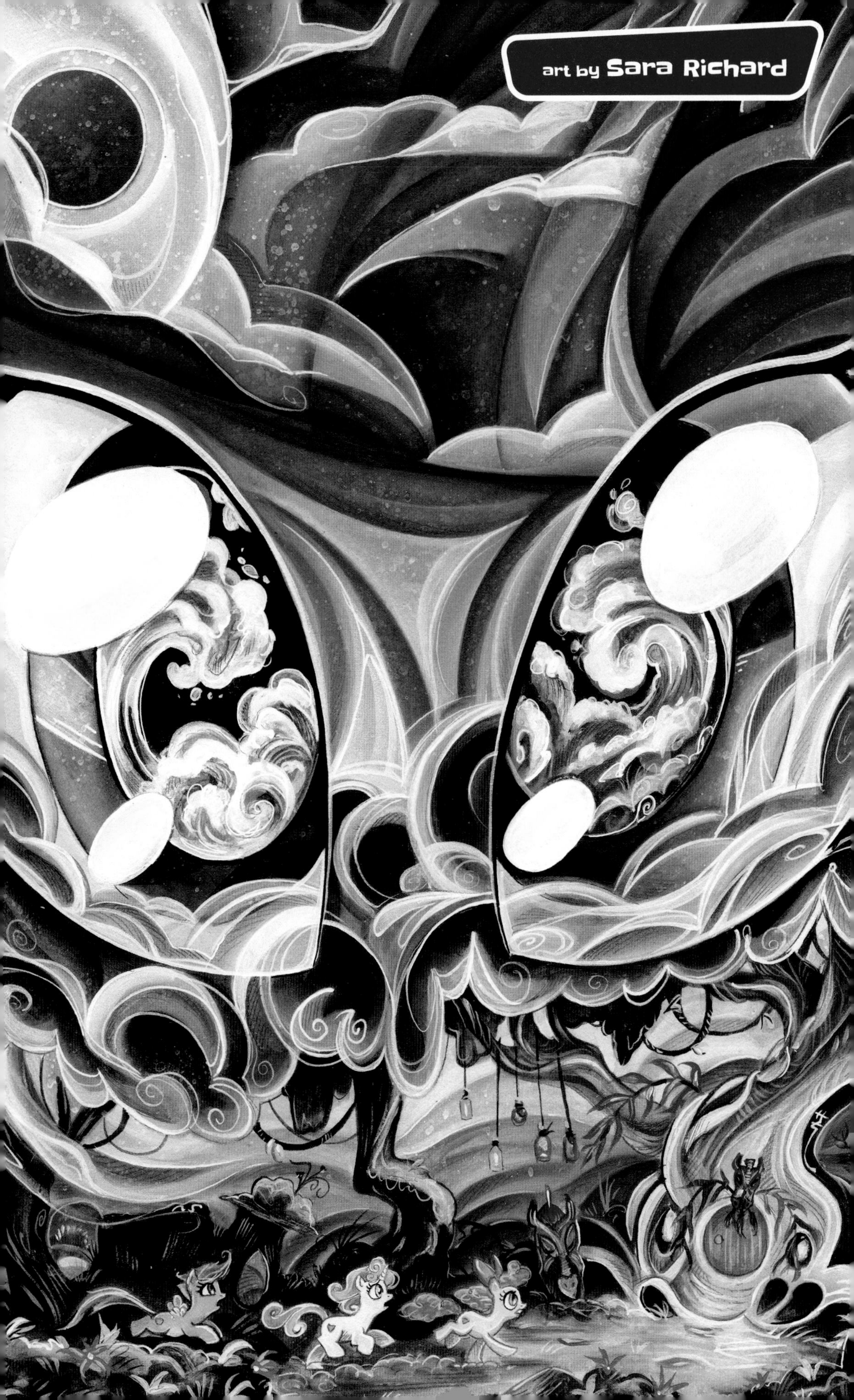
art by Sara Richard

art by Agnes Garbowska

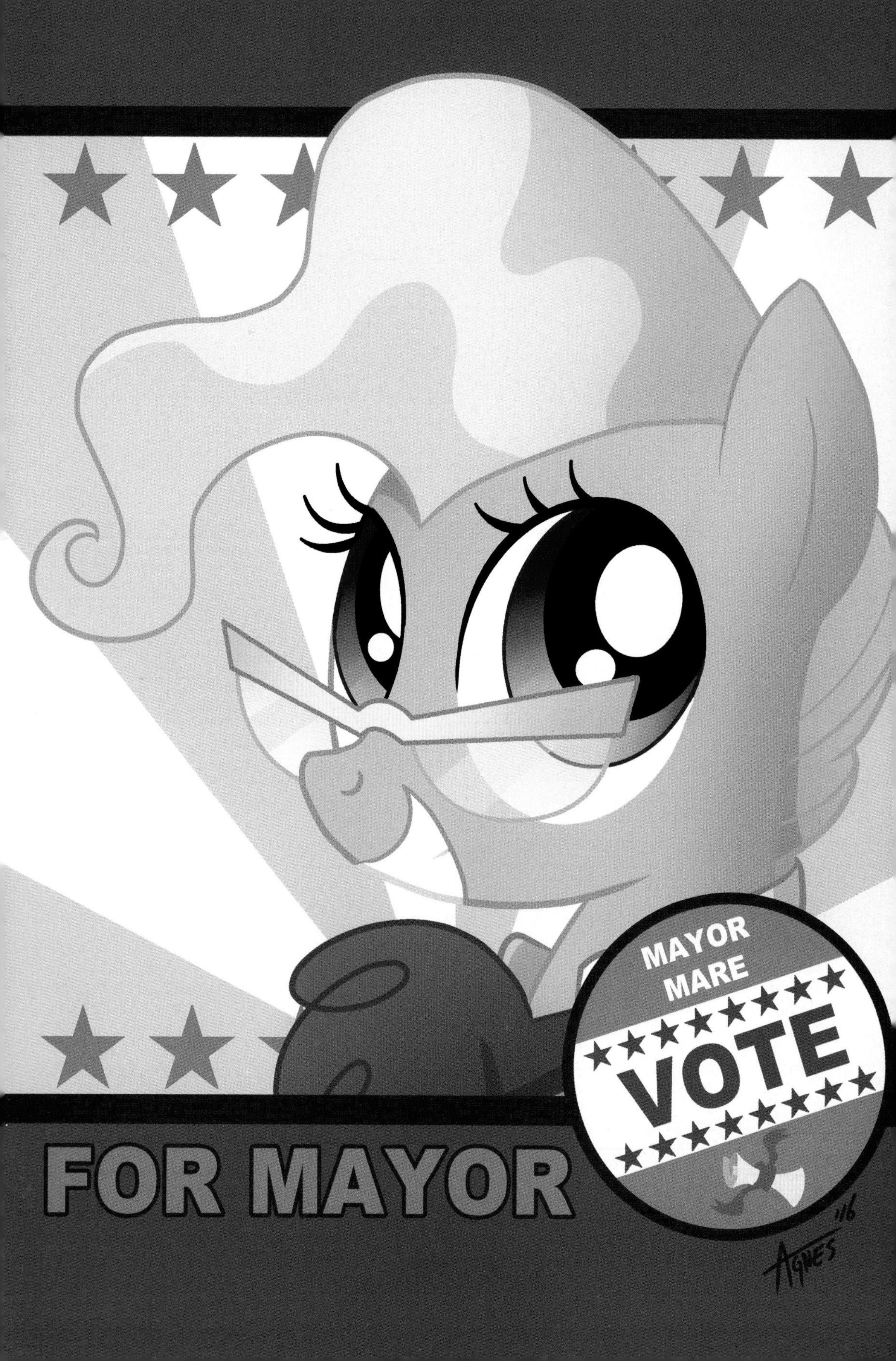
MAYOR
MARE
VOTE
FOR MAYOR
'16
AGNES

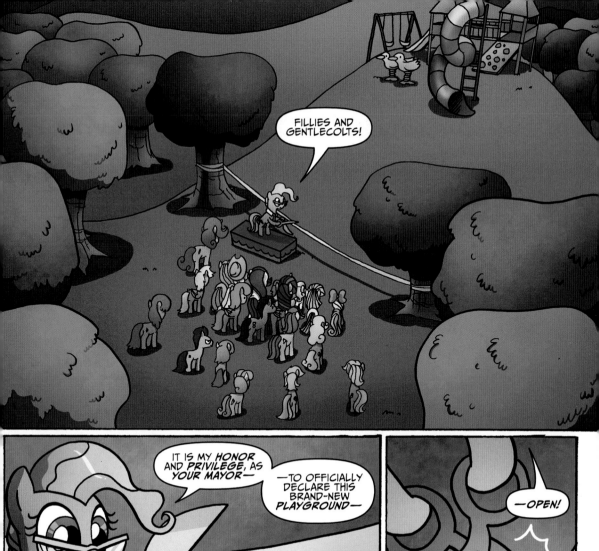

FILLIES AND GENTLECOLTS!

IT IS MY *HONOR* AND *PRIVILEGE*, AS YOUR MAYOR—

—TO OFFICIALLY DECLARE THIS BRAND-NEW PLAYGROUND—

—OPEN!

SNIP

CLAP CLAP CLAP CLAP CLAP CLAP CLAP

MAYOR MARE REALLY KNOWS HOW TO *PUT ON* AN *EVENT!*

YOU GOT THAT RIGHT!

YEAH!

NEW PLAYGROUND!

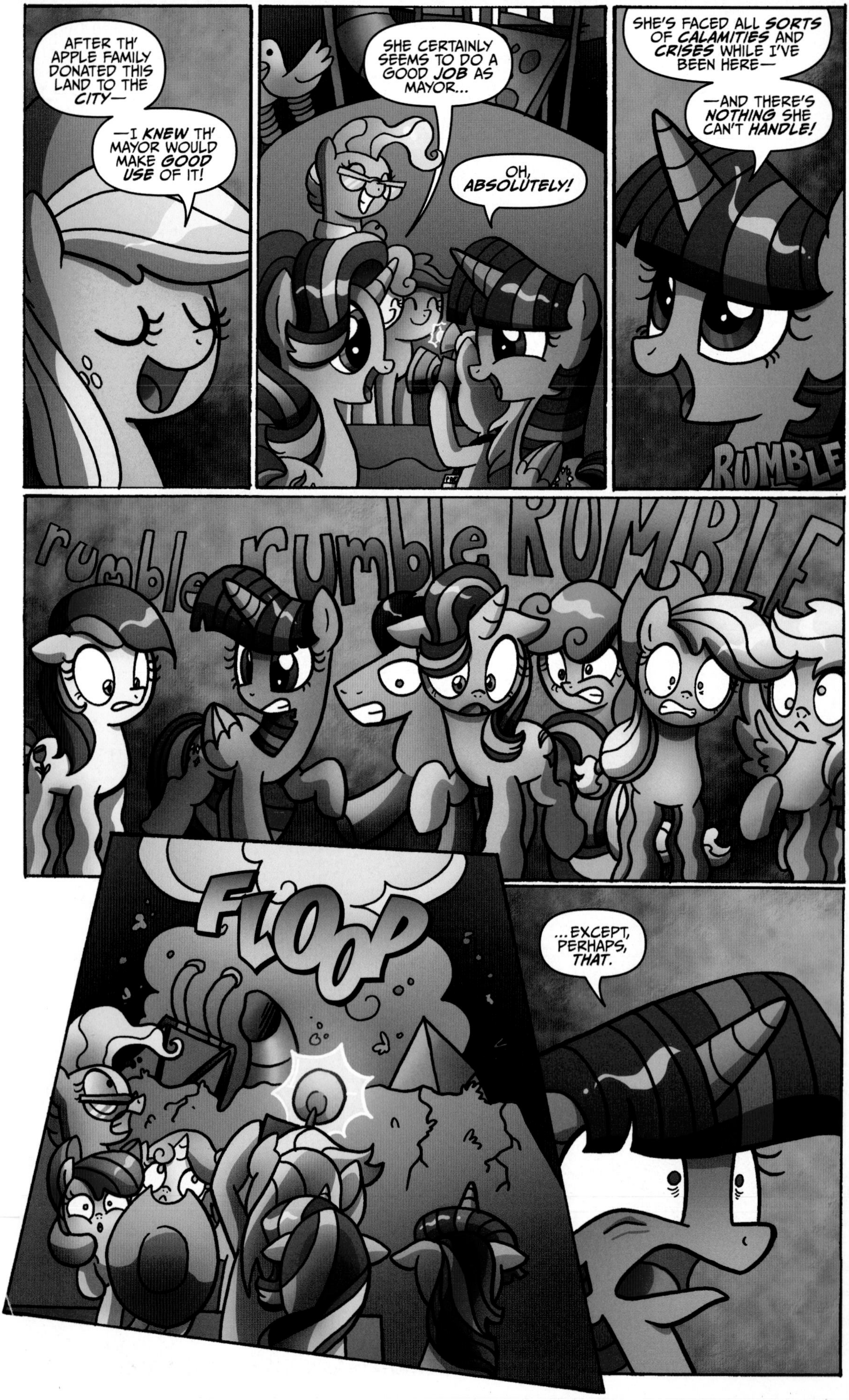
AFTER TH' APPLE FAMILY DONATED THIS LAND TO THE CITY—
—I KNEW TH' MAYOR WOULD MAKE GOOD USE OF IT!
SHE CERTAINLY SEEMS TO DO A GOOD JOB AS MAYOR...
OH, ABSOLUTELY!
SHE'S FACED ALL SORTS OF CALAMITIES AND CRISES WHILE I'VE BEEN HERE—
—AND THERE'S NOTHING SHE CAN'T HANDLE!
RUMBLE
rumble rumble RUMBLE
FLOOP
...EXCEPT, PERHAPS, THAT.

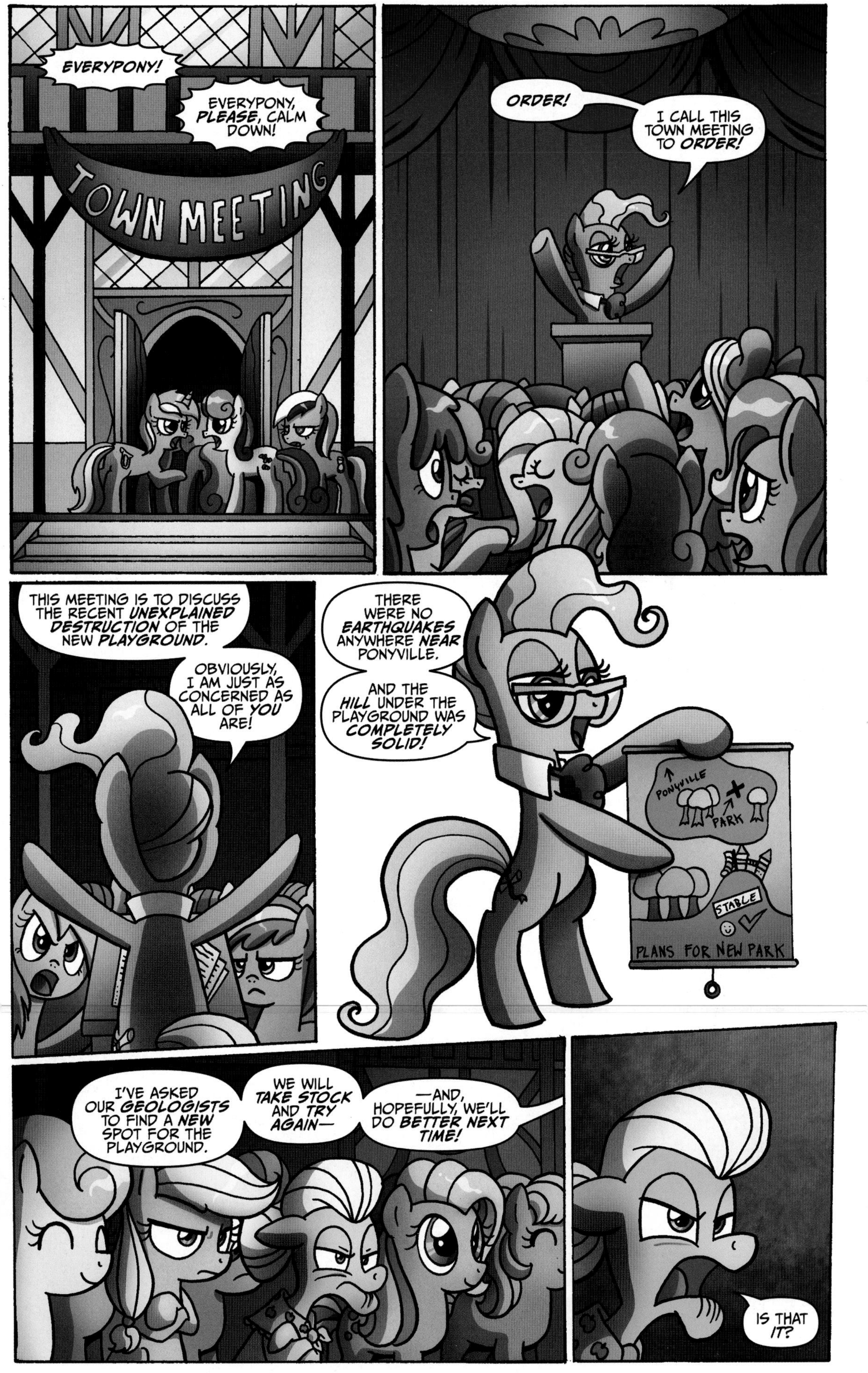
EVERYPONY!
EVERYPONY, PLEASE, CALM DOWN!
TOWN MEETING
ORDER!
I CALL THIS TOWN MEETING TO ORDER!
THIS MEETING IS TO DISCUSS THE RECENT UNEXPLAINED DESTRUCTION OF THE NEW PLAYGROUND.
OBVIOUSLY, I AM JUST AS CONCERNED AS ALL OF YOU ARE!
THERE WERE NO EARTHQUAKES ANYWHERE NEAR PONYVILLE.
AND THE HILL UNDER THE PLAYGROUND WAS COMPLETELY SOLID!
PONYVILLE
PARK
STABLE
PLANS FOR NEW PARK
I'VE ASKED OUR GEOLOGISTS TO FIND A NEW SPOT FOR THE PLAYGROUND.
WE WILL TAKE STOCK AND TRY AGAIN—
—AND, HOPEFULLY, WE'LL DO BETTER NEXT TIME!
IS THAT IT?

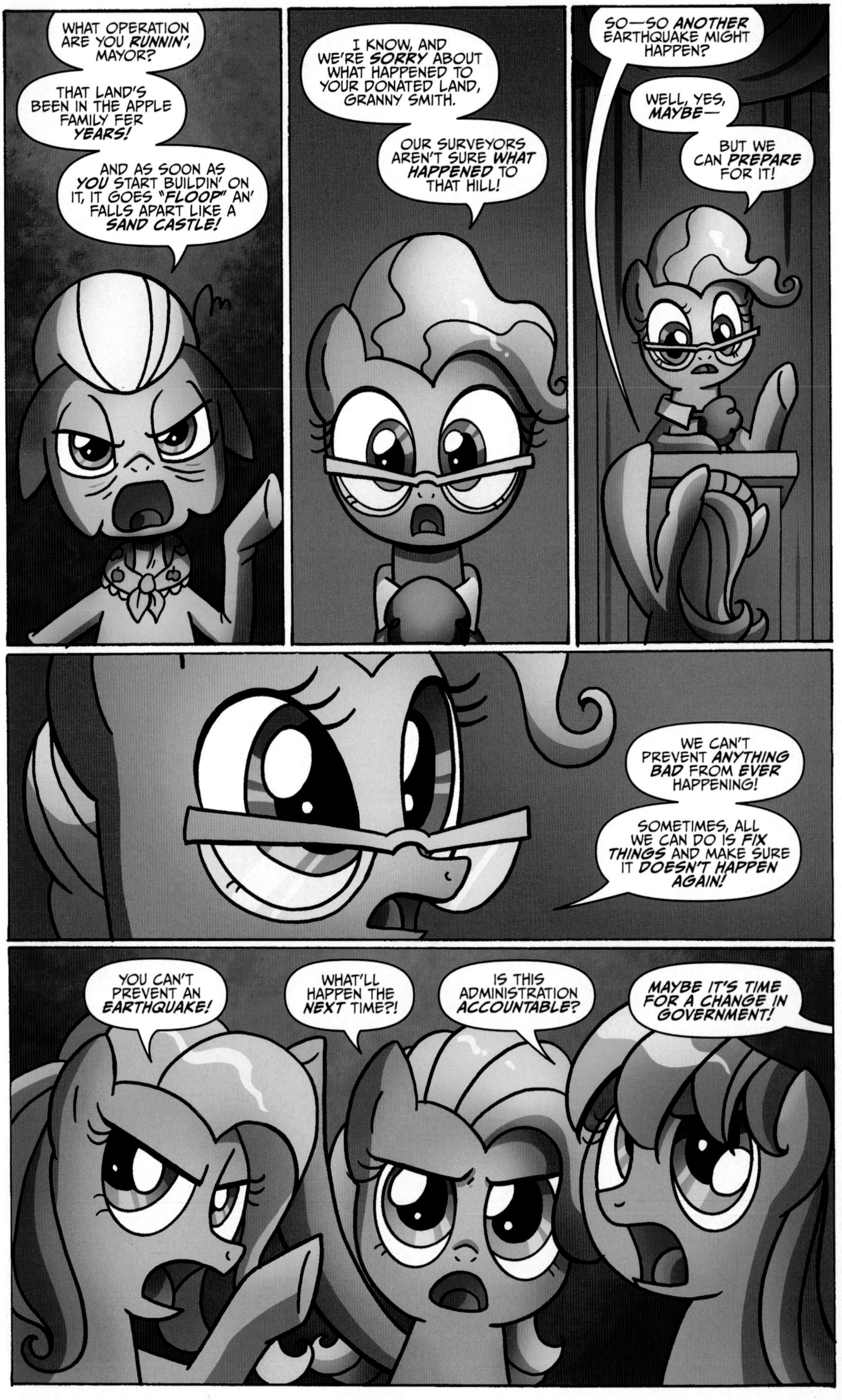
WHAT OPERATION ARE YOU RUNNIN', MAYOR?
THAT LAND'S BEEN IN THE APPLE FAMILY FER YEARS!
AND AS SOON AS YOU START BUILDIN' ON IT, IT GOES "FLOOP" AN' FALLS APART LIKE A SAND CASTLE!
I KNOW, AND WE'RE SORRY ABOUT WHAT HAPPENED TO YOUR DONATED LAND, GRANNY SMITH.
OUR SURVEYORS AREN'T SURE WHAT HAPPENED TO THAT HILL!
SO—SO ANOTHER EARTHQUAKE MIGHT HAPPEN?
WELL, YES, MAYBE—
BUT WE CAN PREPARE FOR IT!
WE CAN'T PREVENT ANYTHING BAD FROM EVER HAPPENING!
SOMETIMES, ALL WE CAN DO IS FIX THINGS AND MAKE SURE IT DOESN'T HAPPEN AGAIN!
YOU CAN'T PREVENT AN EARTHQUAKE!
WHAT'LL HAPPEN THE NEXT TIME?!
IS THIS ADMINISTRATION ACCOUNTABLE?
MAYBE IT'S TIME FOR A CHANGE IN GOVERNMENT!

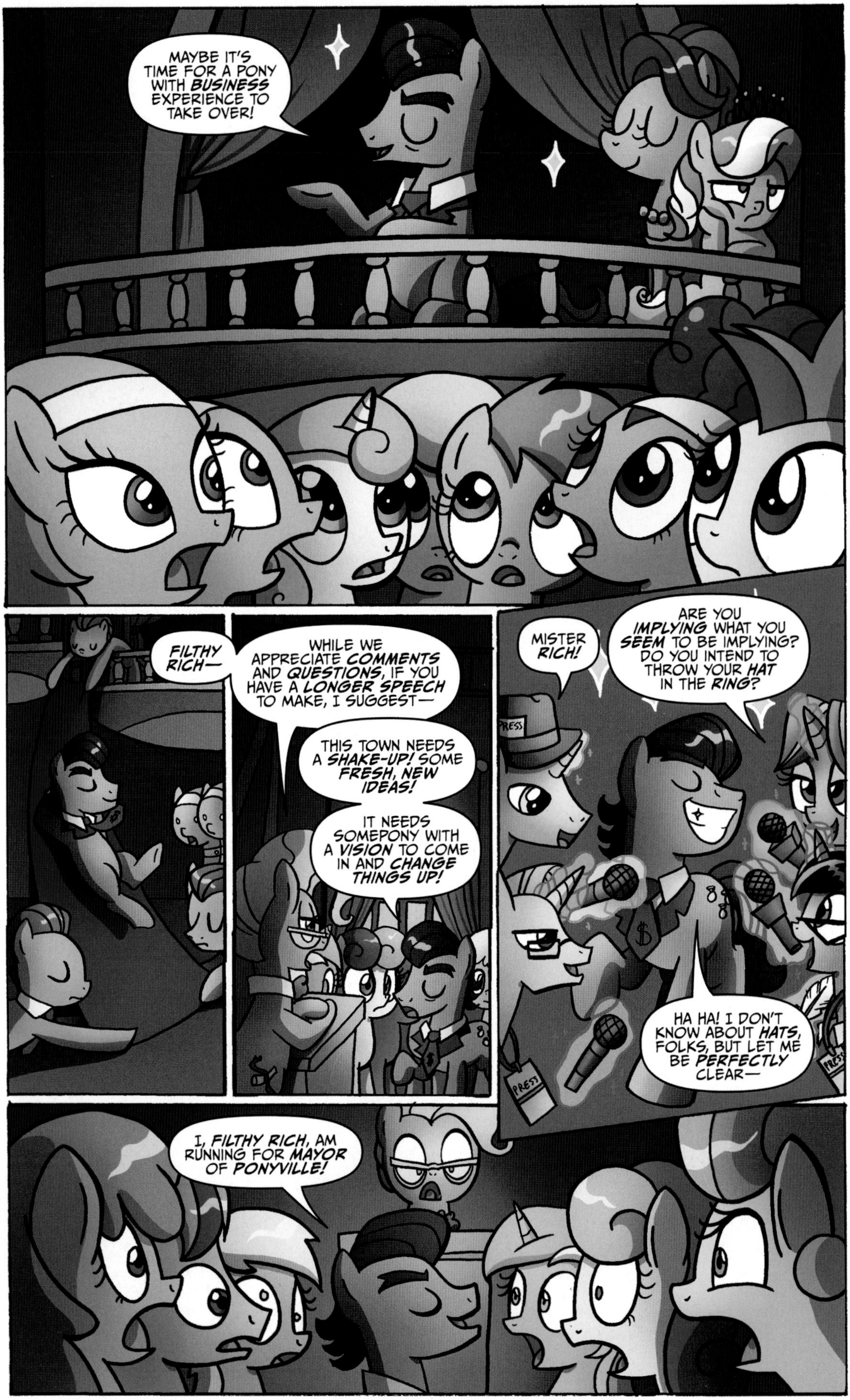
MAYBE IT'S TIME FOR A PONY WITH BUSINESS EXPERIENCE TO TAKE OVER!
FILTHY RICH—
WHILE WE APPRECIATE COMMENTS AND QUESTIONS, IF YOU HAVE A LONGER SPEECH TO MAKE, I SUGGEST—
THIS TOWN NEEDS A SHAKE-UP! SOME FRESH, NEW IDEAS!
IT NEEDS SOMEPONY WITH A VISION TO COME IN AND CHANGE THINGS UP!
MISTER RICH!
ARE YOU IMPLYING WHAT YOU SEEM TO BE IMPLYING? DO YOU INTEND TO THROW YOUR HAT IN THE RING?
PRESS
HA HA! I DON'T KNOW ABOUT HATS, FOLKS, BUT LET ME BE PERFECTLY CLEAR—
PRESS
PRESS
I, FILTHY RICH, AM RUNNING FOR MAYOR OF PONYVILLE!

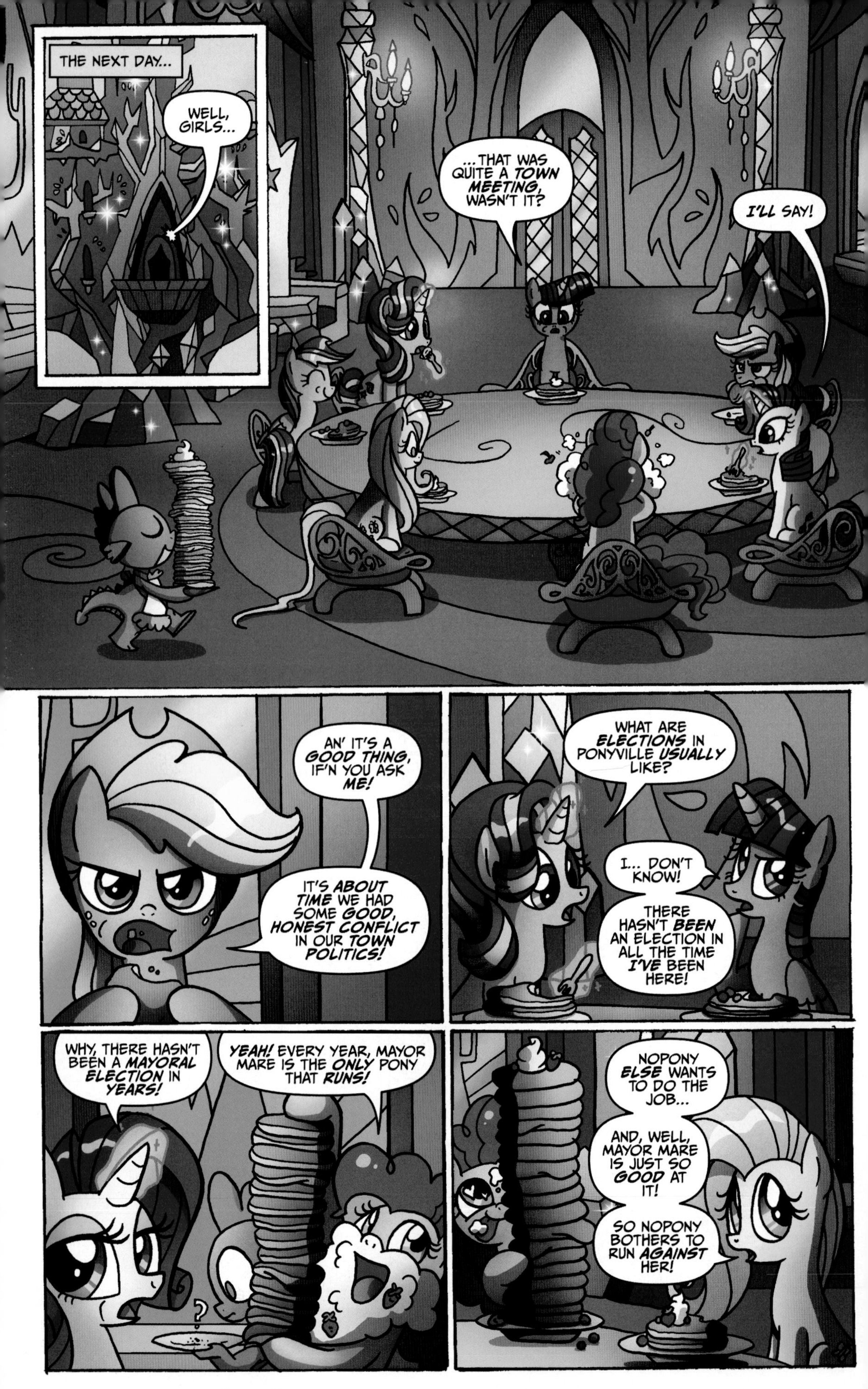
THE NEXT DAY...
WELL, GIRLS...
...THAT WAS QUITE A TOWN MEETING, WASN'T IT?
I'LL SAY!
AN' IT'S A GOOD THING, IF'N YOU ASK ME!
IT'S ABOUT TIME WE HAD SOME GOOD, HONEST CONFLICT IN OUR TOWN POLITICS!
WHAT ARE ELECTIONS IN PONYVILLE USUALLY LIKE?
I... DON'T KNOW!
THERE HASN'T BEEN AN ELECTION IN ALL THE TIME I'VE BEEN HERE!
WHY, THERE HASN'T BEEN A MAYORAL ELECTION IN YEARS!
YEAH! EVERY YEAR, MAYOR MARE IS THE ONLY PONY THAT RUNS!
?
NOPONY ELSE WANTS TO DO THE JOB...
AND, WELL, MAYOR MARE IS JUST SO GOOD AT IT!
SO NOPONY BOTHERS TO RUN AGAINST HER!

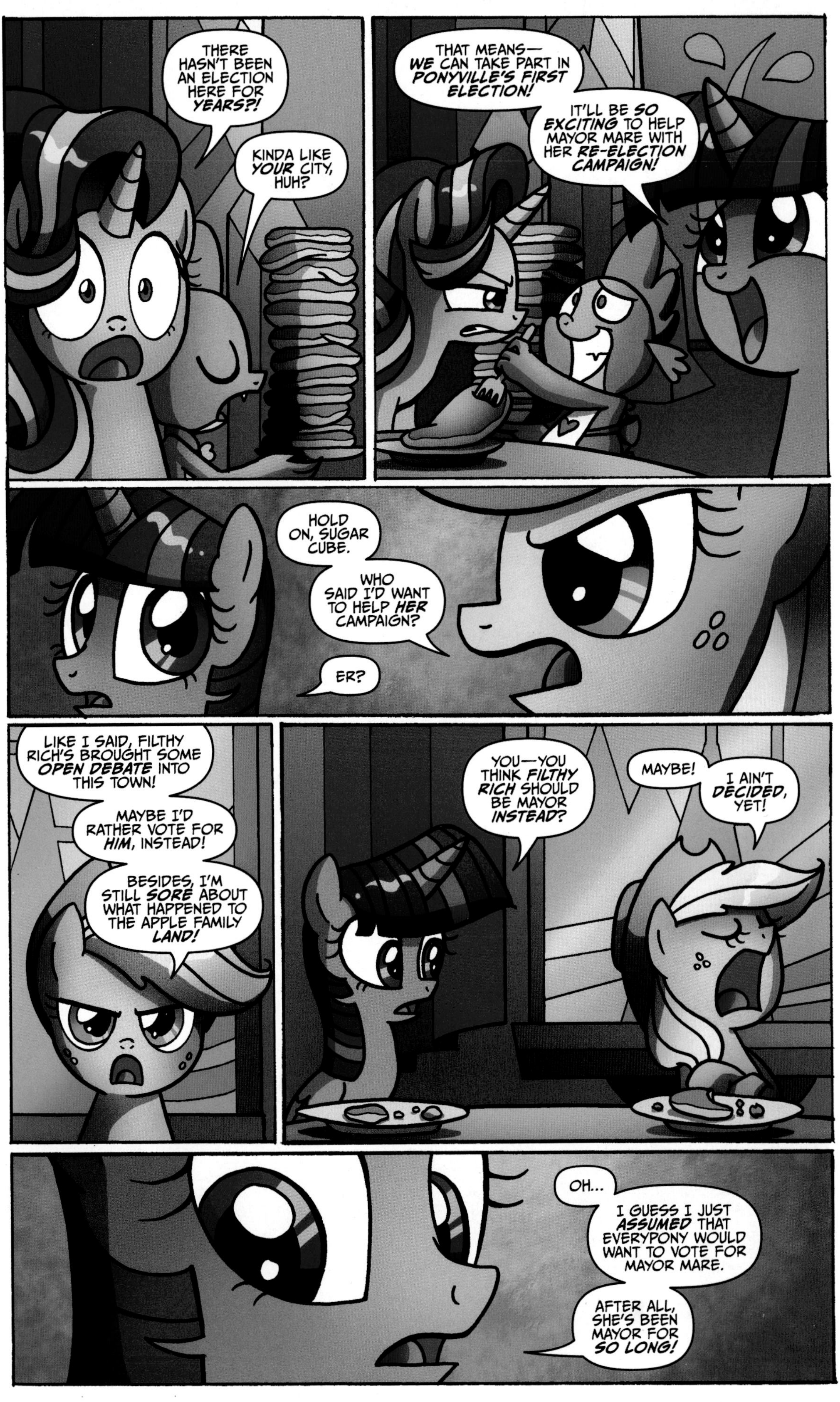
THERE HASN'T BEEN AN ELECTION HERE FOR YEARS?!
KINDA LIKE YOUR CITY, HUH?
THAT MEANS— WE CAN TAKE PART IN PONYVILLE'S FIRST ELECTION!
IT'LL BE SO EXCITING TO HELP MAYOR MARE WITH HER RE-ELECTION CAMPAIGN!
HOLD ON, SUGAR CUBE.
WHO SAID I'D WANT TO HELP HER CAMPAIGN?
ER?
LIKE I SAID, FILTHY RICH'S BROUGHT SOME OPEN DEBATE INTO THIS TOWN!
MAYBE I'D RATHER VOTE FOR HIM, INSTEAD!
BESIDES, I'M STILL SORE ABOUT WHAT HAPPENED TO THE APPLE FAMILY LAND!
YOU—YOU THINK FILTHY RICH SHOULD BE MAYOR INSTEAD?
MAYBE!
I AIN'T DECIDED, YET!
OH...
I GUESS I JUST ASSUMED THAT EVERYPONY WOULD WANT TO VOTE FOR MAYOR MARE.
AFTER ALL, SHE'S BEEN MAYOR FOR SO LONG!

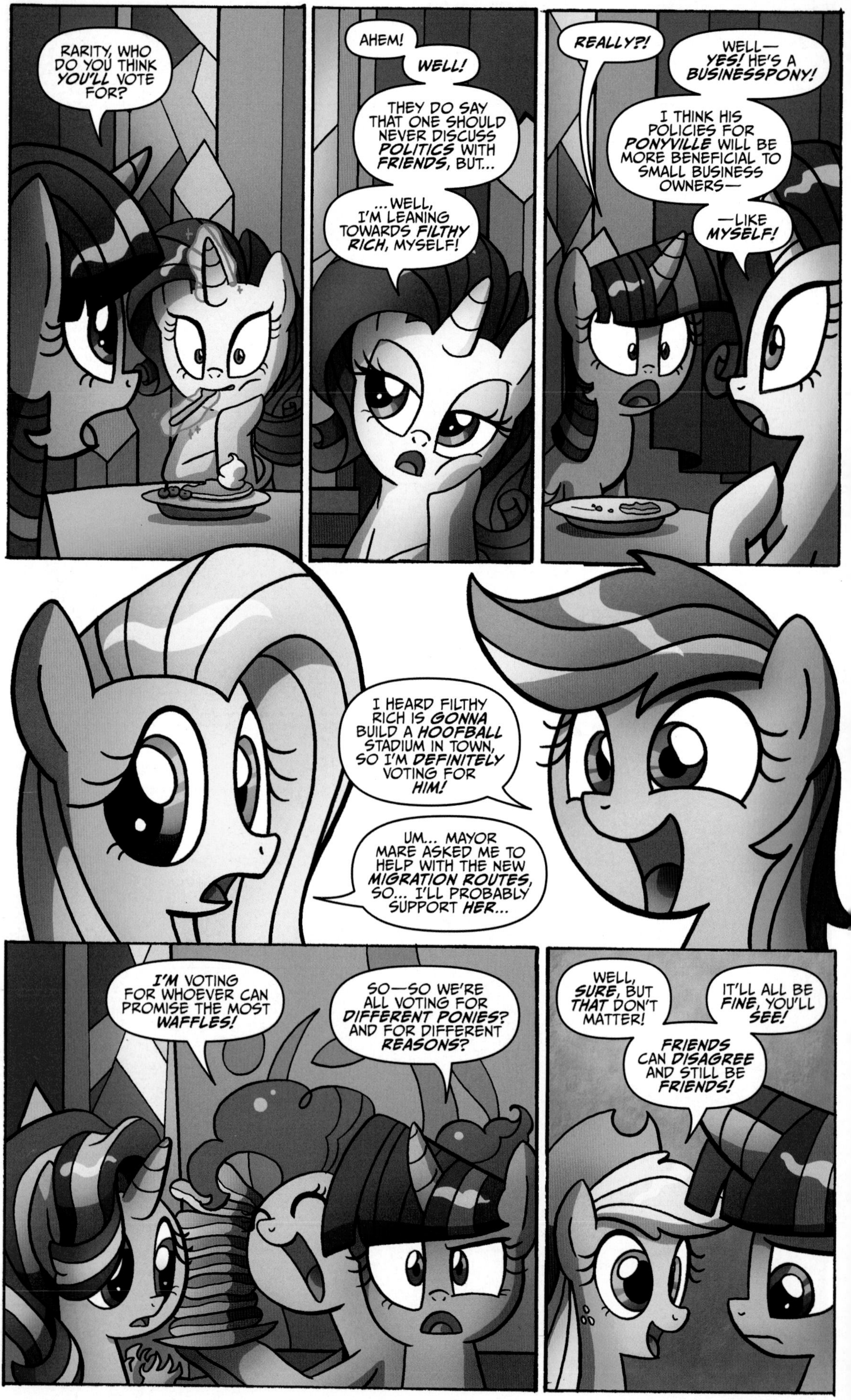
RARITY, WHO DO YOU THINK *YOU'LL* VOTE FOR?
AHEM!
WELL!
THEY DO SAY THAT ONE SHOULD NEVER DISCUSS *POLITICS* WITH *FRIENDS*, BUT...
...WELL, I'M LEANING TOWARDS *FILTHY RICH*, MYSELF!
REALLY?!
WELL— *YES!* HE'S A *BUSINESSPONY!*
I THINK HIS POLICIES FOR *PONYVILLE* WILL BE MORE BENEFICIAL TO SMALL BUSINESS OWNERS—
—LIKE *MYSELF!*
I HEARD FILTHY RICH IS *GONNA* BUILD A *HOOFBALL* STADIUM IN TOWN, SO I'M *DEFINITELY* VOTING FOR *HIM!*
UM... MAYOR MARE ASKED ME TO HELP WITH THE NEW *MIGRATION ROUTES*, SO... I'LL PROBABLY SUPPORT *HER*...
I'M VOTING FOR WHOEVER CAN PROMISE THE MOST *WAFFLES!*
SO—SO WE'RE ALL VOTING FOR *DIFFERENT PONIES?* AND FOR DIFFERENT *REASONS?*
WELL, *SURE*, BUT *THAT* DON'T MATTER!
IT'LL ALL BE *FINE*, YOU'LL *SEE!*
FRIENDS CAN *DISAGREE* AND STILL BE *FRIENDS!*

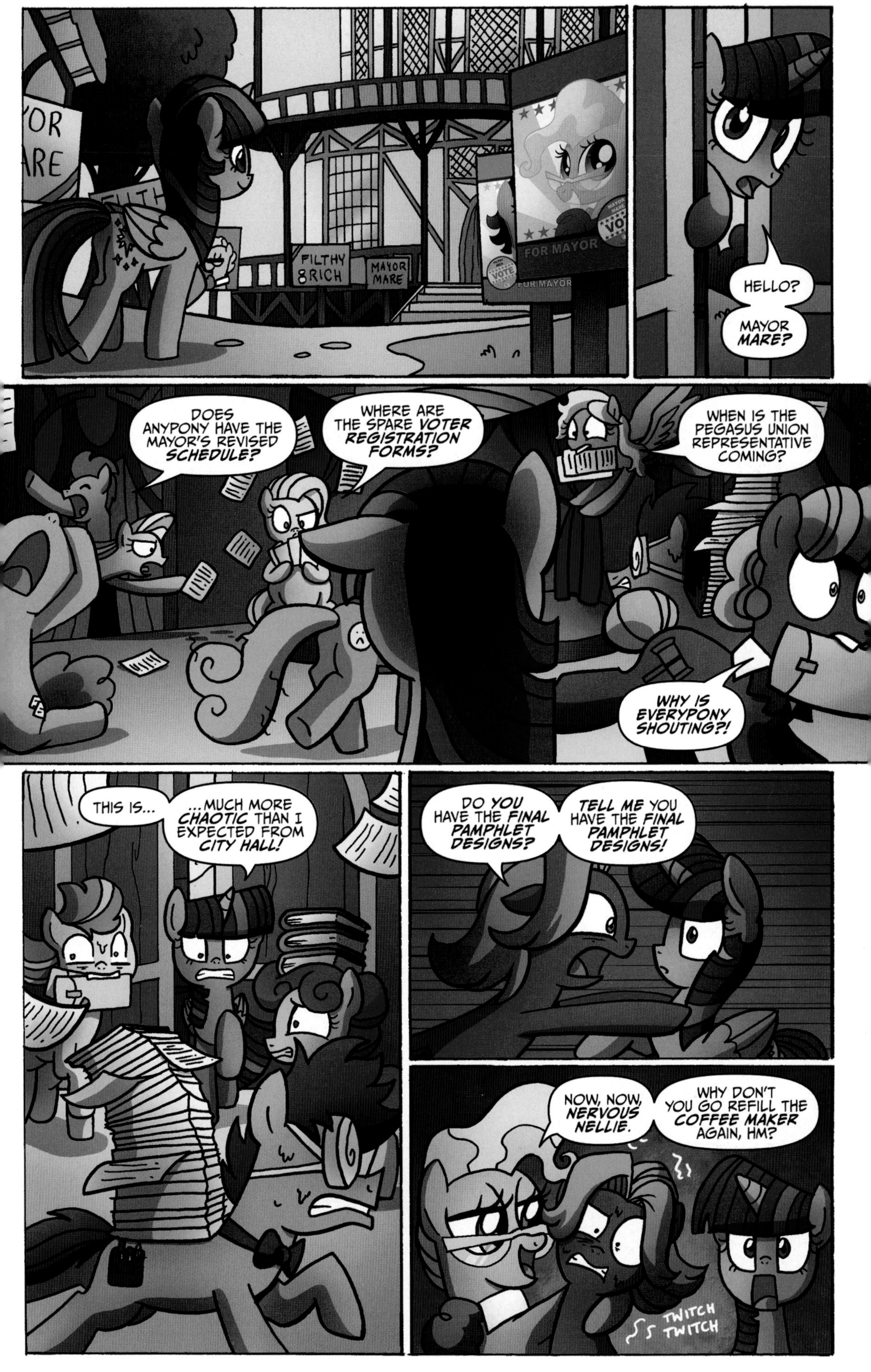
MAYOR MARE
FILTHY RICH
FILTHY RICH
MAYOR MARE
FOR MAYOR
VOTE
FOR MAYOR
HELLO?
MAYOR MARE?
DOES ANYPONY HAVE THE MAYOR'S REVISED SCHEDULE?
WHERE ARE THE SPARE VOTER REGISTRATION FORMS?
WHEN IS THE PEGASUS UNION REPRESENTATIVE COMING?
WHY IS EVERYPONY SHOUTING?!
THIS IS...
...MUCH MORE CHAOTIC THAN I EXPECTED FROM CITY HALL!
DO YOU HAVE THE FINAL PAMPHLET DESIGNS?
TELL ME YOU HAVE THE FINAL PAMPHLET DESIGNS!
NOW, NOW, NERVOUS NELLIE.
WHY DON'T YOU GO REFILL THE COFFEE MAKER AGAIN, HM?
TWITCH TWITCH

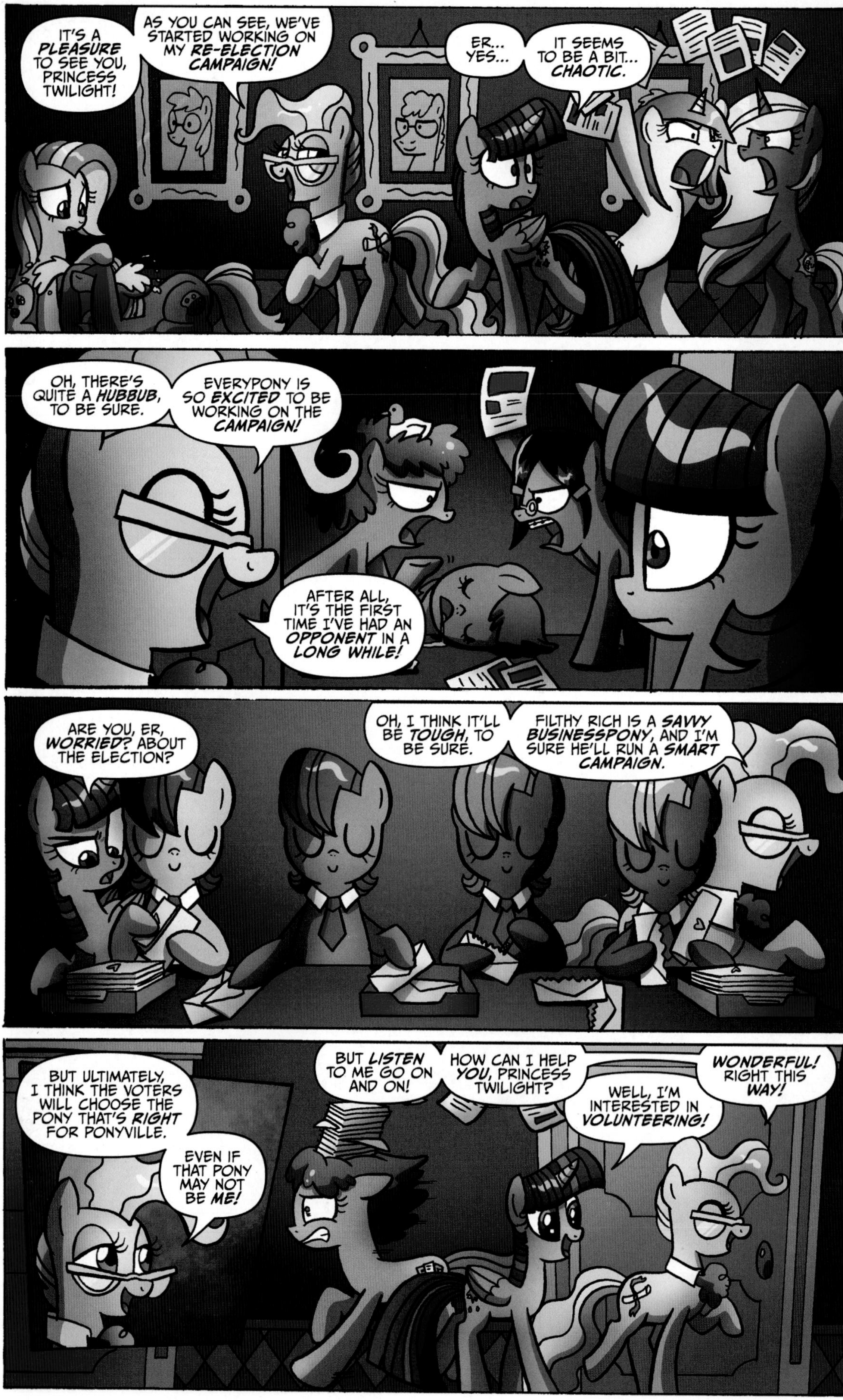
IT'S A PLEASURE TO SEE YOU, PRINCESS TWILIGHT!
AS YOU CAN SEE, WE'VE STARTED WORKING ON MY RE-ELECTION CAMPAIGN!
ER... YES...
IT SEEMS TO BE A BIT... CHAOTIC.
OH, THERE'S QUITE A HUBBUB, TO BE SURE.
EVERYPONY IS SO EXCITED TO BE WORKING ON THE CAMPAIGN!
AFTER ALL, IT'S THE FIRST TIME I'VE HAD AN OPPONENT IN A LONG WHILE!
ARE YOU, ER, WORRIED? ABOUT THE ELECTION?
OH, I THINK IT'LL BE TOUGH, TO BE SURE.
FILTHY RICH IS A SAVVY BUSINESSPONY, AND I'M SURE HE'LL RUN A SMART CAMPAIGN.
BUT ULTIMATELY, I THINK THE VOTERS WILL CHOOSE THE PONY THAT'S RIGHT FOR PONYVILLE.
EVEN IF THAT PONY MAY NOT BE ME!
BUT LISTEN TO ME GO ON AND ON!
HOW CAN I HELP YOU, PRINCESS TWILIGHT?
WELL, I'M INTERESTED IN VOLUNTEERING!
WONDERFUL! RIGHT THIS WAY!

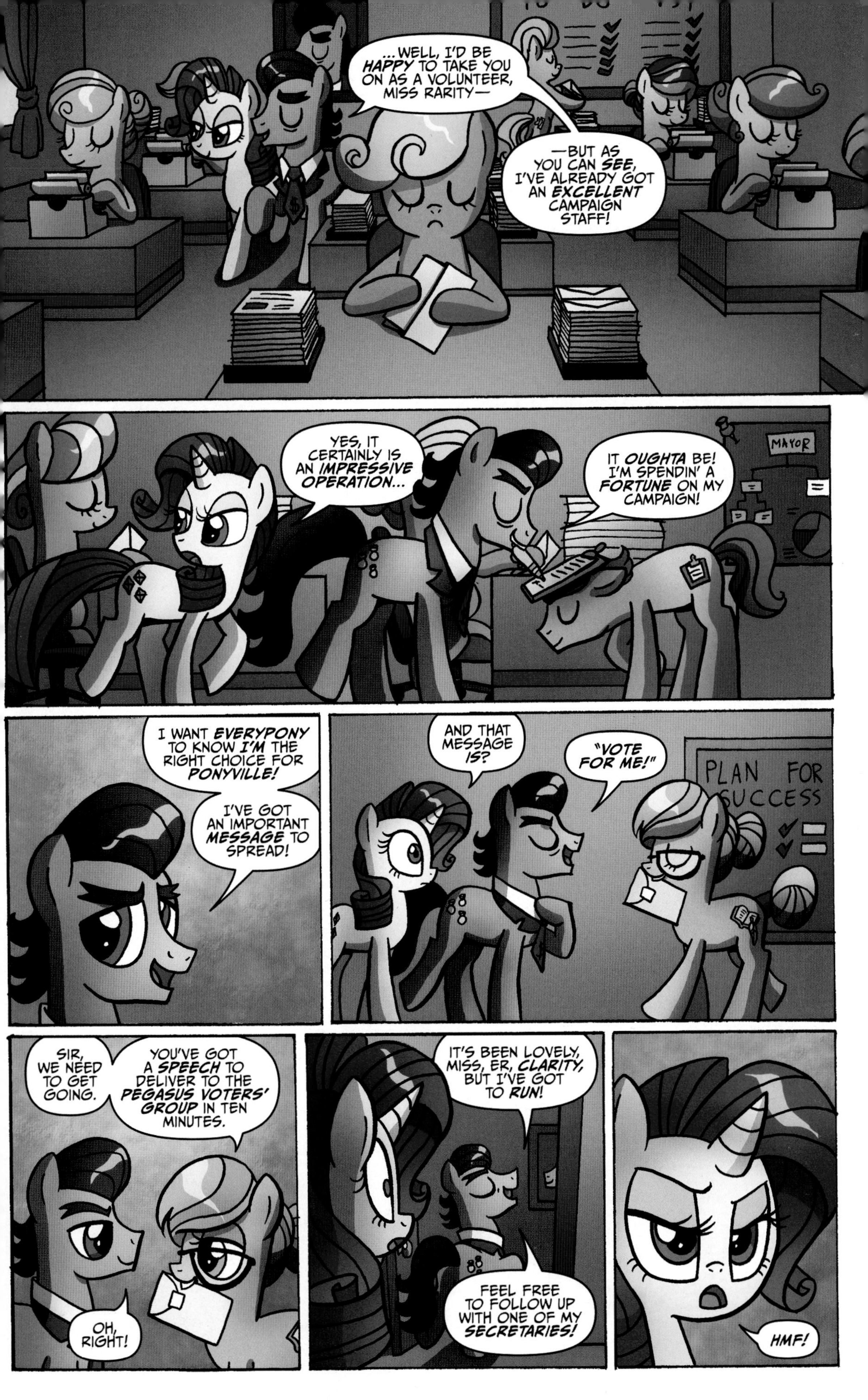
...WELL, I'D BE HAPPY TO TAKE YOU ON AS A VOLUNTEER, MISS RARITY—
—BUT AS YOU CAN SEE, I'VE ALREADY GOT AN EXCELLENT CAMPAIGN STAFF!
MAYOR
YES, IT CERTAINLY IS AN IMPRESSIVE OPERATION...
IT OUGHTA BE! I'M SPENDIN' A FORTUNE ON MY CAMPAIGN!
I WANT EVERYPONY TO KNOW I'M THE RIGHT CHOICE FOR PONYVILLE!
I'VE GOT AN IMPORTANT MESSAGE TO SPREAD!
AND THAT MESSAGE IS?
"VOTE FOR ME!"
PLAN FOR SUCCESS
SIR, WE NEED TO GET GOING.
YOU'VE GOT A SPEECH TO DELIVER TO THE PEGASUS VOTERS' GROUP IN TEN MINUTES.
OH, RIGHT!
IT'S BEEN LOVELY, MISS, ER, CLARITY, BUT I'VE GOT TO RUN!
FEEL FREE TO FOLLOW UP WITH ONE OF MY SECRETARIES!
HMF!

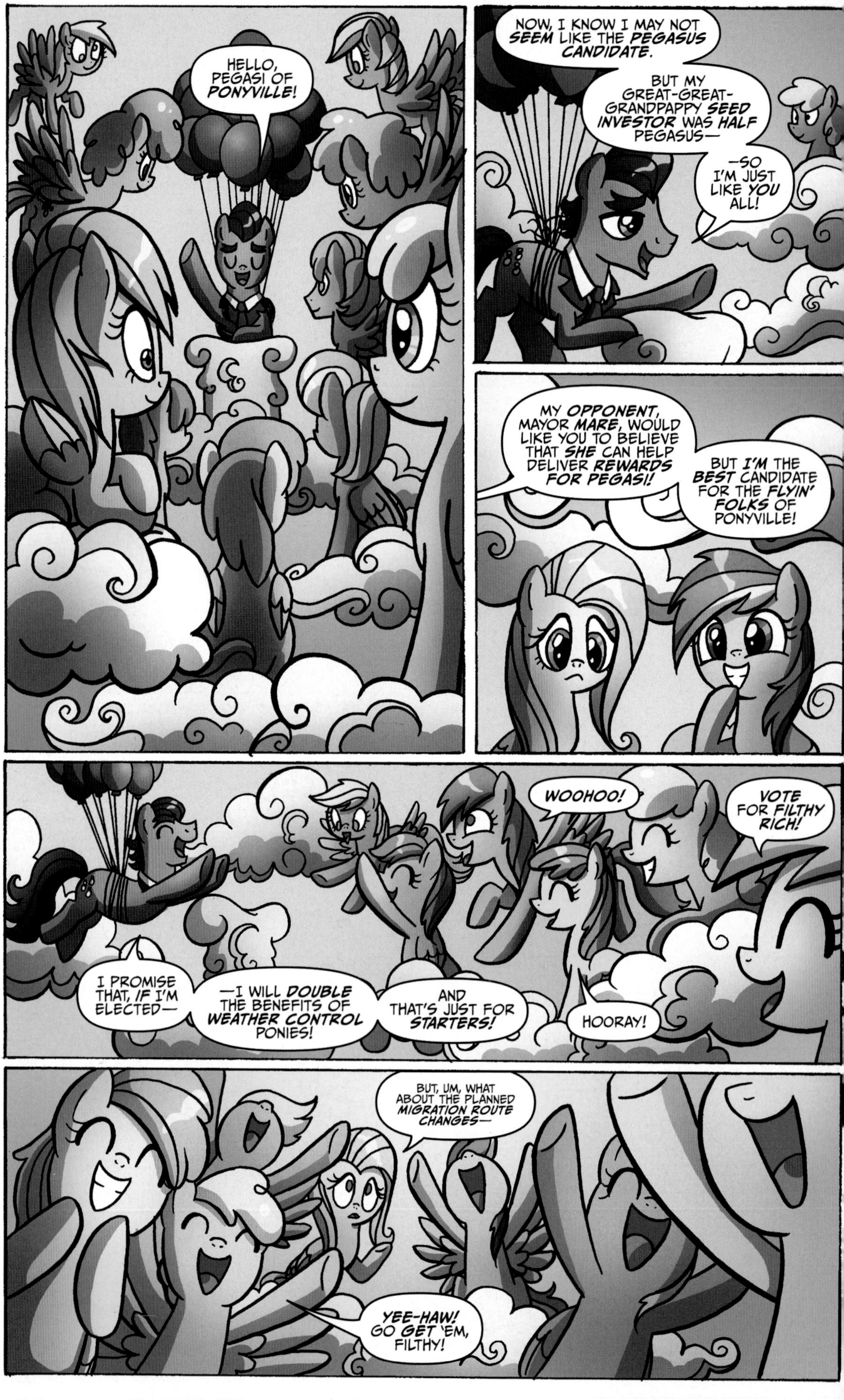
HELLO, PEGASI OF PONYVILLE!
NOW, I KNOW I MAY NOT SEEM LIKE THE PEGASUS CANDIDATE.
BUT MY GREAT-GREAT-GRANDPAPPY SEED INVESTOR WAS HALF PEGASUS—
—SO I'M JUST LIKE YOU ALL!
MY OPPONENT, MAYOR MARE, WOULD LIKE YOU TO BELIEVE THAT SHE CAN HELP DELIVER REWARDS FOR PEGASI!
BUT I'M THE BEST CANDIDATE FOR THE FLYIN' FOLKS OF PONYVILLE!
WOOHOO!
VOTE FOR FILTHY RICH!
I PROMISE THAT, IF I'M ELECTED—
—I WILL DOUBLE THE BENEFITS OF WEATHER CONTROL PONIES!
AND THAT'S JUST FOR STARTERS!
HOORAY!
BUT, UM, WHAT ABOUT THE PLANNED MIGRATION ROUTE CHANGES—
YEE-HAW! GO GET 'EM, FILTHY!

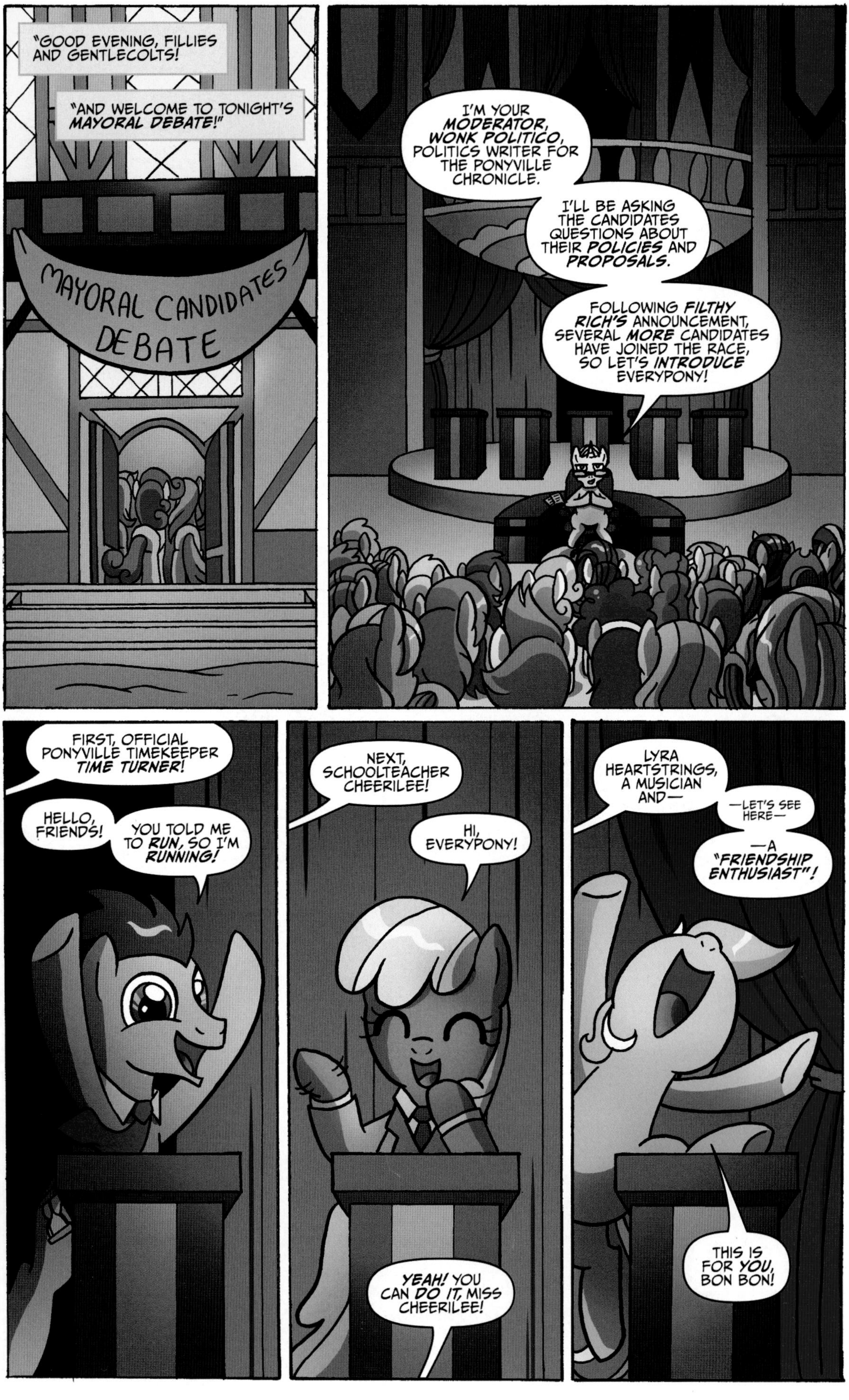
"GOOD EVENING, FILLIES AND GENTLECOLTS!
"AND WELCOME TO TONIGHT'S MAYORAL DEBATE!"
MAYORAL CANDIDATES DEBATE
I'M YOUR MODERATOR, WONK POLITICO, POLITICS WRITER FOR THE PONYVILLE CHRONICLE.
I'LL BE ASKING THE CANDIDATES QUESTIONS ABOUT THEIR POLICIES AND PROPOSALS.
FOLLOWING FILTHY RICH'S ANNOUNCEMENT, SEVERAL MORE CANDIDATES HAVE JOINED THE RACE, SO LET'S INTRODUCE EVERYPONY!
FIRST, OFFICIAL PONYVILLE TIMEKEEPER TIME TURNER!
HELLO, FRIENDS!
YOU TOLD ME TO RUN, SO I'M RUNNING!
NEXT, SCHOOLTEACHER CHEERILEE!
HI, EVERYPONY!
YEAH! YOU CAN DO IT, MISS CHEERILEE!
LYRA HEARTSTRINGS, A MUSICIAN AND—
—LET'S SEE HERE—
—A "FRIENDSHIP ENTHUSIAST"!
THIS IS FOR YOU, BON BON!

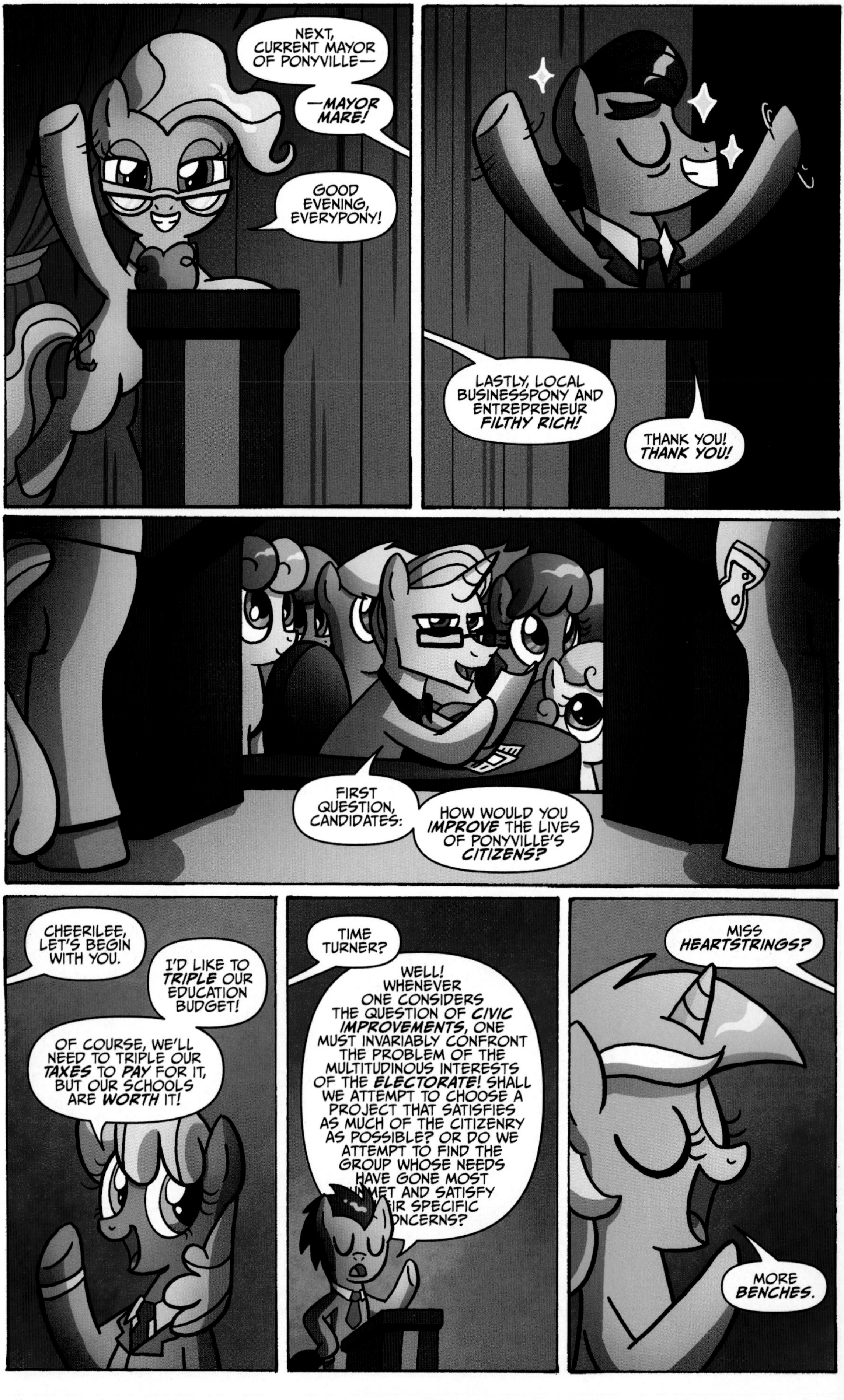
NEXT, CURRENT MAYOR OF PONYVILLE—
—*MAYOR MARE!*
GOOD EVENING, EVERYPONY!
LASTLY, LOCAL BUSINESSPONY AND ENTREPRENEUR *FILTHY RICH!*
THANK YOU! *THANK YOU!*
FIRST QUESTION, CANDIDATES:
HOW WOULD YOU *IMPROVE* THE LIVES OF PONYVILLE'S *CITIZENS?*
CHEERILEE, LET'S BEGIN WITH YOU.
I'D LIKE TO *TRIPLE* OUR EDUCATION BUDGET!
OF COURSE, WE'LL NEED TO TRIPLE OUR *TAXES* TO *PAY* FOR IT, BUT OUR SCHOOLS ARE *WORTH* IT!
TIME TURNER?
WELL! WHENEVER ONE CONSIDERS THE QUESTION OF *CIVIC IMPROVEMENTS*, ONE MUST INVARIABLY CONFRONT THE PROBLEM OF THE MULTITUDINOUS INTERESTS OF THE *ELECTORATE!* SHALL WE ATTEMPT TO CHOOSE A PROJECT THAT SATISFIES AS MUCH OF THE CITIZENRY AS POSSIBLE? OR DO WE ATTEMPT TO FIND THE GROUP WHOSE NEEDS HAVE GONE MOST NMET AND SATISFY IR SPECIFIC ONCERNS?
MISS *HEARTSTRINGS?*
MORE *BENCHES.*

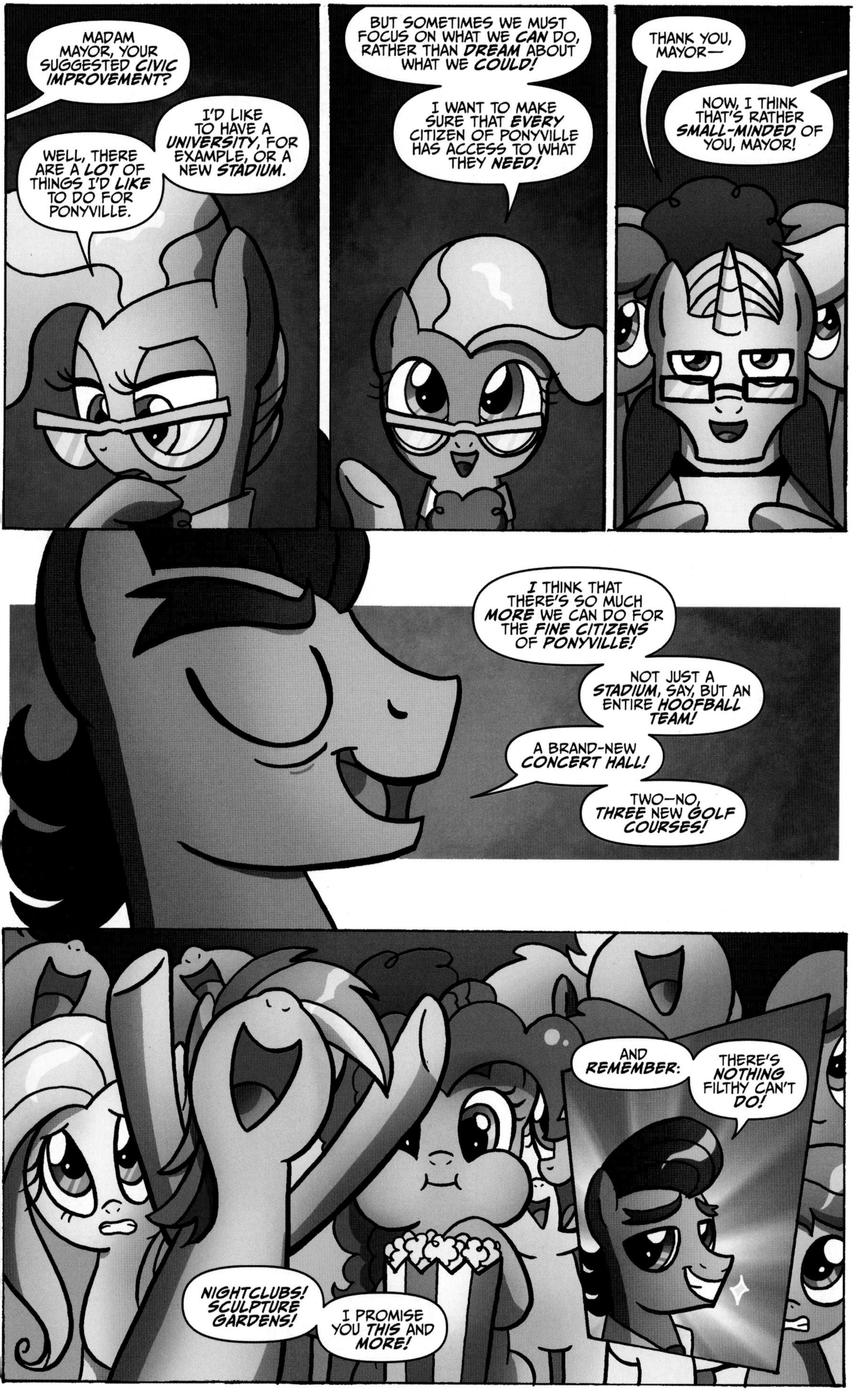
MADAM MAYOR, YOUR SUGGESTED CIVIC IMPROVEMENT?
WELL, THERE ARE A LOT OF THINGS I'D LIKE TO DO FOR PONYVILLE.
I'D LIKE TO HAVE A UNIVERSITY, FOR EXAMPLE, OR A NEW STADIUM.
BUT SOMETIMES WE MUST FOCUS ON WHAT WE CAN DO, RATHER THAN DREAM ABOUT WHAT WE COULD!
I WANT TO MAKE SURE THAT EVERY CITIZEN OF PONYVILLE HAS ACCESS TO WHAT THEY NEED!
THANK YOU, MAYOR—
NOW, I THINK THAT'S RATHER SMALL-MINDED OF YOU, MAYOR!
I THINK THAT THERE'S SO MUCH MORE WE CAN DO FOR THE FINE CITIZENS OF PONYVILLE!
NOT JUST A STADIUM, SAY, BUT AN ENTIRE HOOFBALL TEAM!
A BRAND-NEW CONCERT HALL!
TWO—NO, THREE NEW GOLF COURSES!
NIGHTCLUBS! SCULPTURE GARDENS!
I PROMISE YOU THIS AND MORE!
AND REMEMBER:
THERE'S NOTHING FILTHY CAN'T DO!

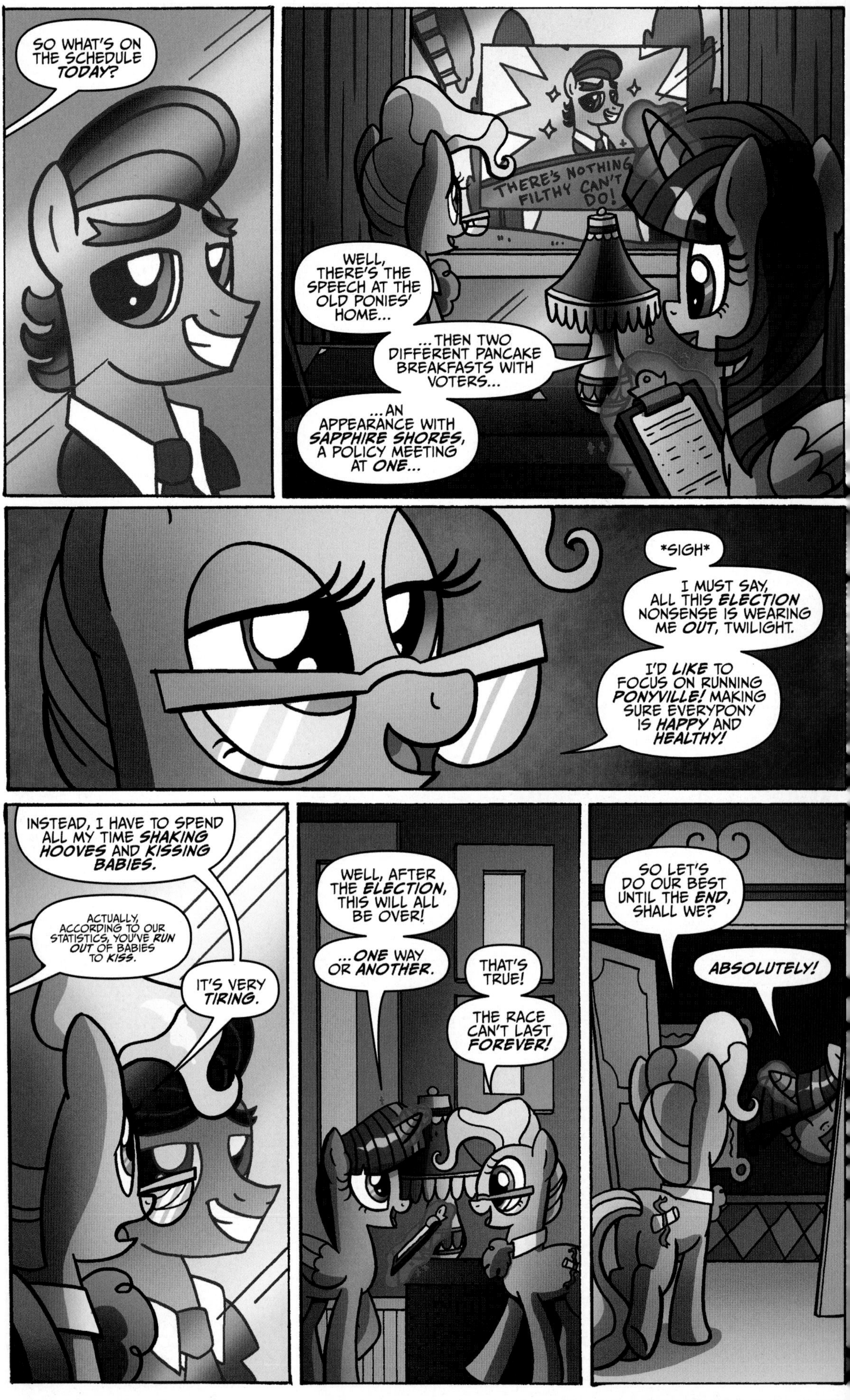
SO WHAT'S ON THE SCHEDULE TODAY?
THERE'S NOTHING FILTHY CAN'T DO!
WELL, THERE'S THE SPEECH AT THE OLD PONIES' HOME...
...THEN TWO DIFFERENT PANCAKE BREAKFASTS WITH VOTERS...
...AN APPEARANCE WITH SAPPHIRE SHORES, A POLICY MEETING AT ONE...
SIGH
I MUST SAY, ALL THIS ELECTION NONSENSE IS WEARING ME OUT, TWILIGHT.
I'D LIKE TO FOCUS ON RUNNING PONYVILLE! MAKING SURE EVERYPONY IS HAPPY AND HEALTHY!
INSTEAD, I HAVE TO SPEND ALL MY TIME SHAKING HOOVES AND KISSING BABIES.
ACTUALLY, ACCORDING TO OUR STATISTICS, YOU'VE RUN OUT OF BABIES TO KISS.
IT'S VERY TIRING.
WELL, AFTER THE ELECTION, THIS WILL ALL BE OVER!
...ONE WAY OR ANOTHER.
THAT'S TRUE!
THE RACE CAN'T LAST FOREVER!
SO LET'S DO OUR BEST UNTIL THE END, SHALL WE?
ABSOLUTELY!

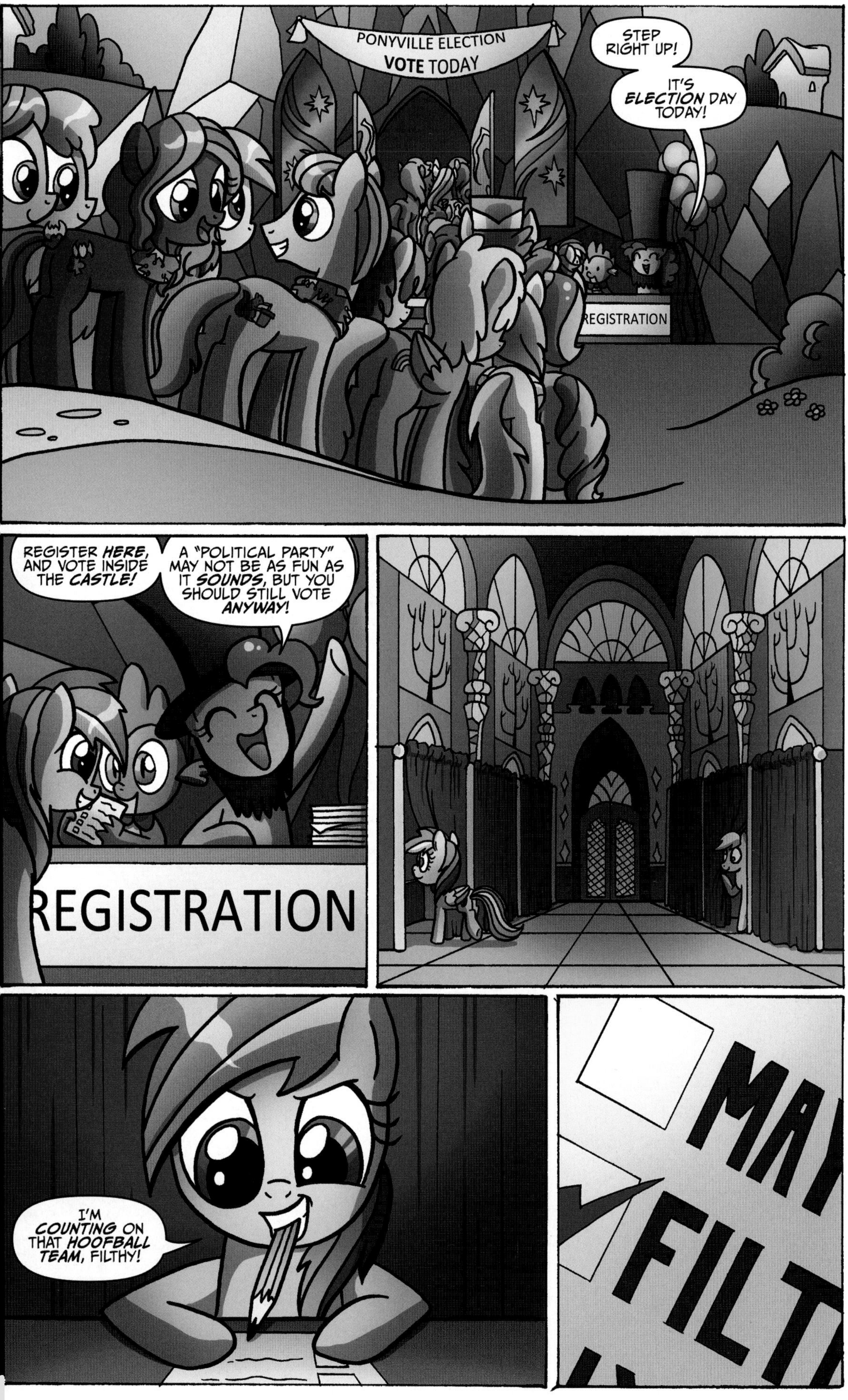
PONYVILLE ELECTION
VOTE TODAY
STEP RIGHT UP!
IT'S ELECTION DAY TODAY!
REGISTRATION
REGISTER HERE, AND VOTE INSIDE THE CASTLE!
A "POLITICAL PARTY" MAY NOT BE AS FUN AS IT SOUNDS, BUT YOU SHOULD STILL VOTE ANYWAY!
REGISTRATION
I'M COUNTING ON THAT HOOFBALL TEAM, FILTHY!
MA
FILT

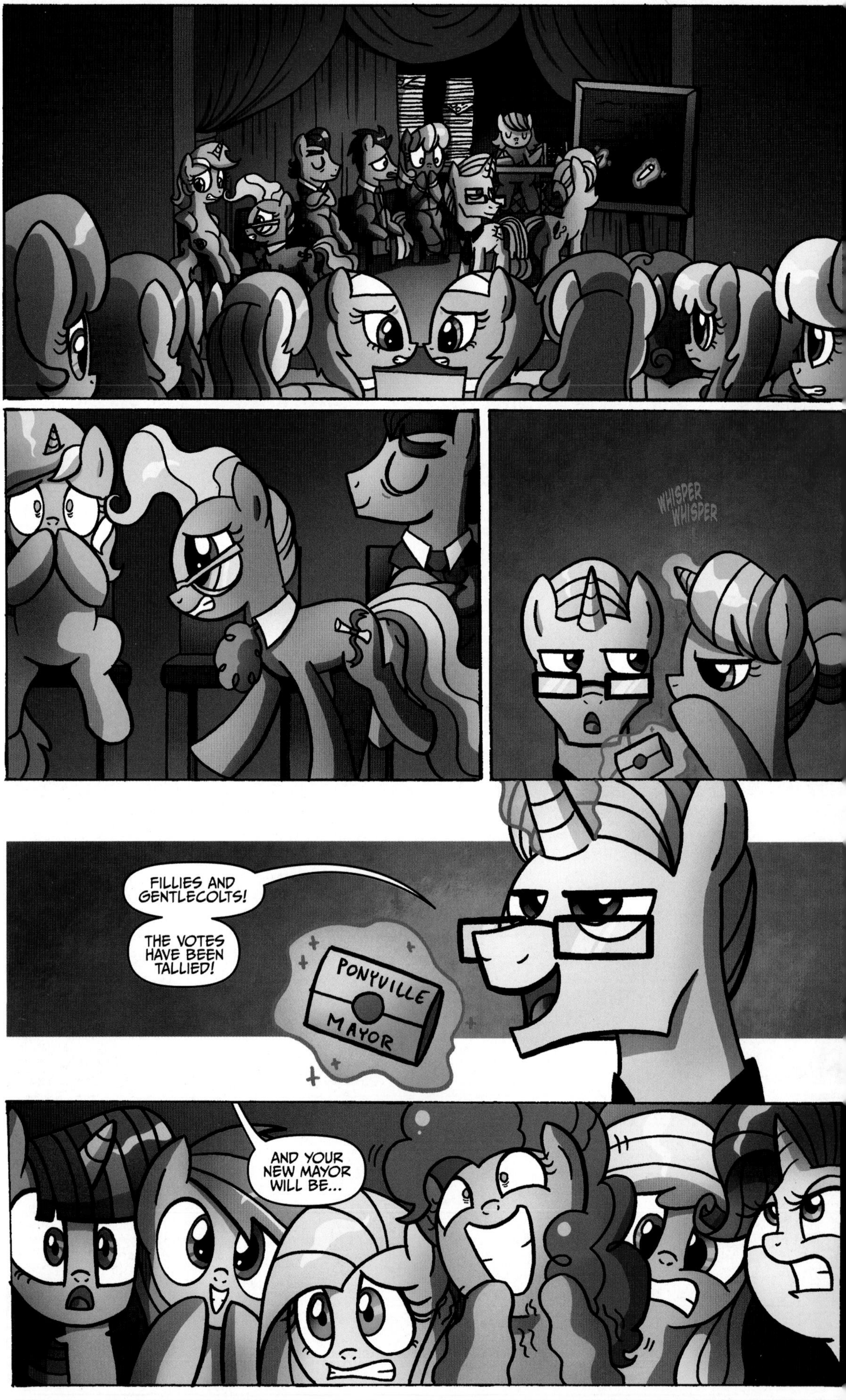
WHISPER WHISPER
FILLIES AND GENTLECOLTS!
THE VOTES HAVE BEEN TALLIED!
PONYVILLE MAYOR
AND YOUR NEW MAYOR WILL BE...

...FILTHY RICH!

THANK YOU! *THANK YOU,* EVERYPONY!

IT'S AN *HONOR* TO SERVE!

THERE'S GONNA BE A *WHOLE LOTTA CHANGES* AROUND PONYVILLE!

I WANT TO MAKE THIS *TOWN* BIGGER AND *BETTER* THAN EVER!

THIS ADMINISTRATION'S GOING TO BE *DYNAMIC!* AGGRESSIVE! FORWARD-THINKING!

YOU'RE GOING TO SEE A *WHOLE NEW* PONYVILLE!

RUMBLE RUMBLE RUMBLE

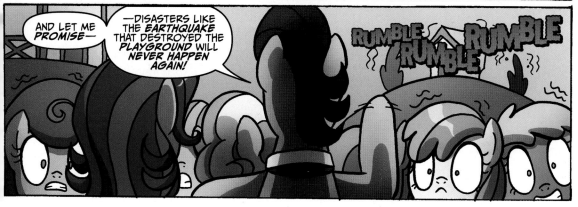

AND LET ME *PROMISE*—

—DISASTERS LIKE THE *EARTHQUAKE* THAT DESTROYED THE *PLAYGROUND* WILL *NEVER HAPPEN AGAIN!*

RUMBLE RUMBLE RUMBLE

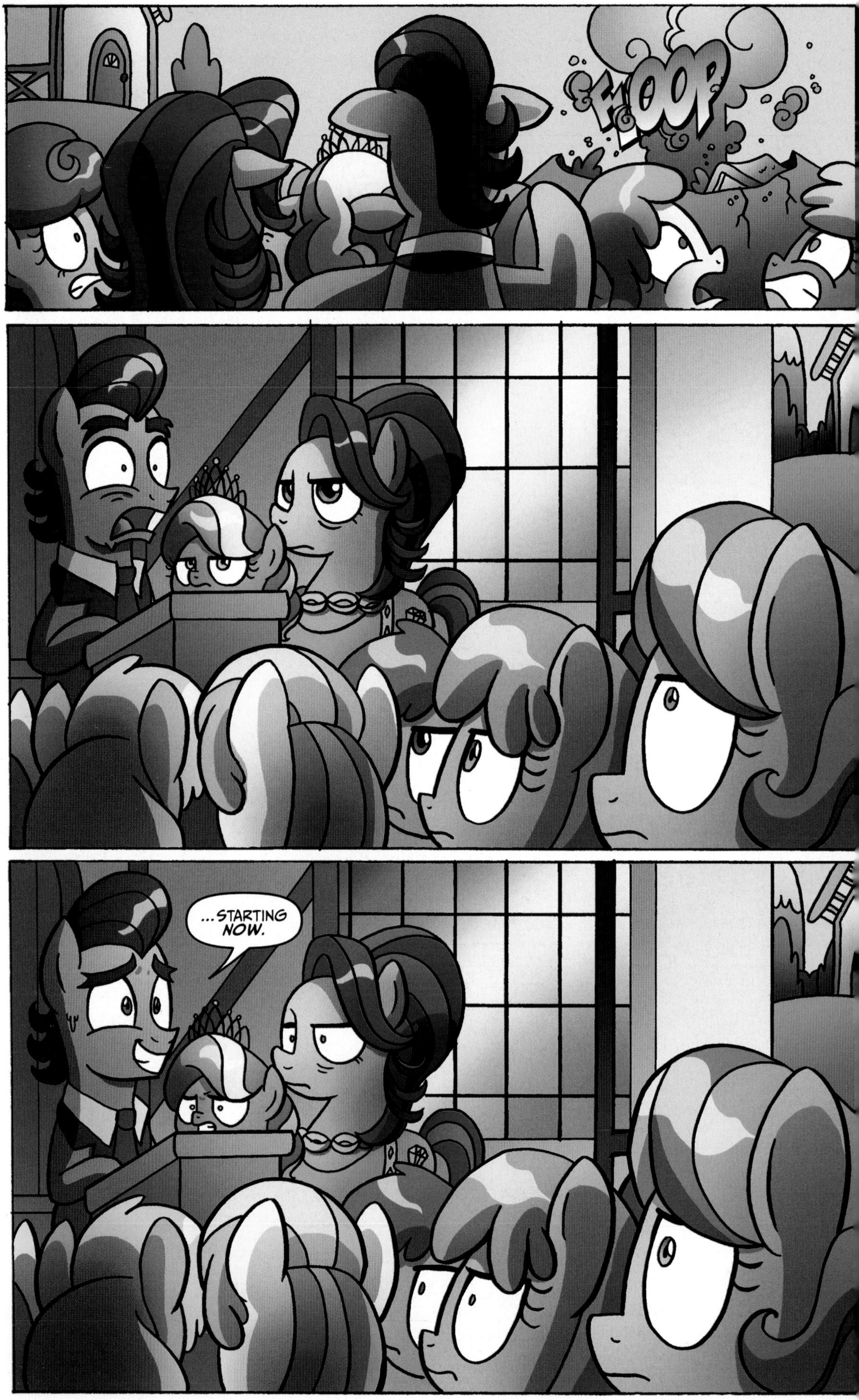
FOOP
...STARTING NOW.

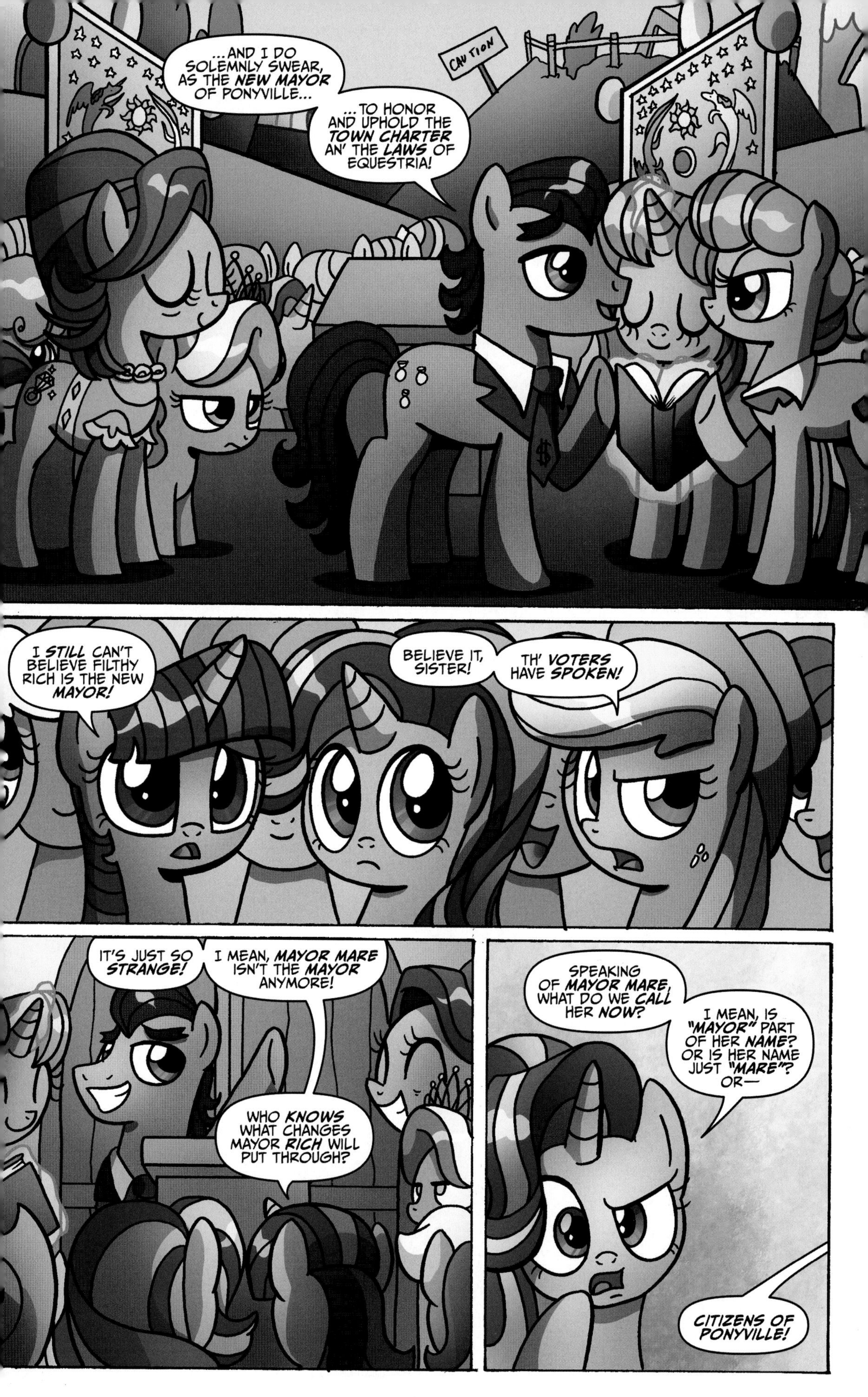

CAUTION
...AND I DO SOLEMNLY SWEAR, AS THE NEW MAYOR OF PONYVILLE...
...TO HONOR AND UPHOLD THE TOWN CHARTER AN' THE LAWS OF EQUESTRIA!
I STILL CAN'T BELIEVE FILTHY RICH IS THE NEW MAYOR!
BELIEVE IT, SISTER!
TH' VOTERS HAVE SPOKEN!
IT'S JUST SO STRANGE!
I MEAN, MAYOR MARE ISN'T THE MAYOR ANYMORE!
WHO KNOWS WHAT CHANGES MAYOR RICH WILL PUT THROUGH?
SPEAKING OF MAYOR MARE, WHAT DO WE CALL HER NOW?
I MEAN, IS "MAYOR" PART OF HER NAME? OR IS HER NAME JUST "MARE"? OR—
CITIZENS OF PONYVILLE!

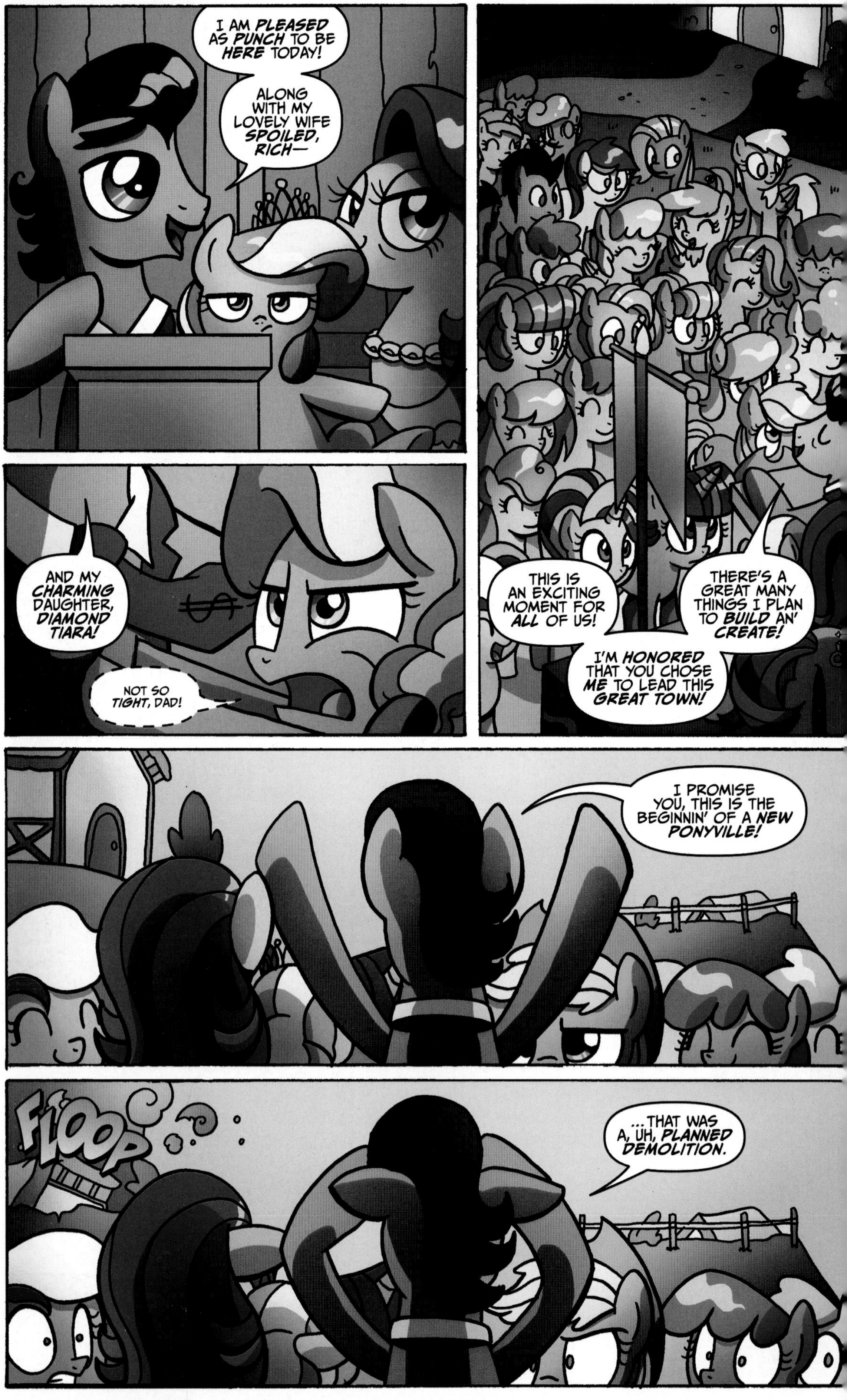
I AM PLEASED AS PUNCH TO BE HERE TODAY!
ALONG WITH MY LOVELY WIFE SPOILED, RICH—
AND MY CHARMING DAUGHTER, DIAMOND TIARA!
NOT SO TIGHT, DAD!
THIS IS AN EXCITING MOMENT FOR ALL OF US!
I'M HONORED THAT YOU CHOSE ME TO LEAD THIS GREAT TOWN!
THERE'S A GREAT MANY THINGS I PLAN TO BUILD AN' CREATE!
I PROMISE YOU, THIS IS THE BEGINNIN' OF A NEW PONYVILLE!
FLOOP
...THAT WAS A, UH, PLANNED DEMOLITION.

THE NEXT DAY...

BANG

CRUNCH

SMASH

AAAAA!

KA-CHNGO

OKAY, CHARLIE, BACK IT UP!

PUT THE DONUTS OVER *THERE*, DIGGER!

VVVRRRRRR

DONUTS

E-EXCUSE ME!

OH, GOOD *MORNING*, MISS!

HOPE WE DIDN'T *WAKE* YOU!

W-W-WHAT'S GOING *ON* OUT THERE?

CONSTRUCTION, MISS!

FOR THE NEW *STADIUM!*

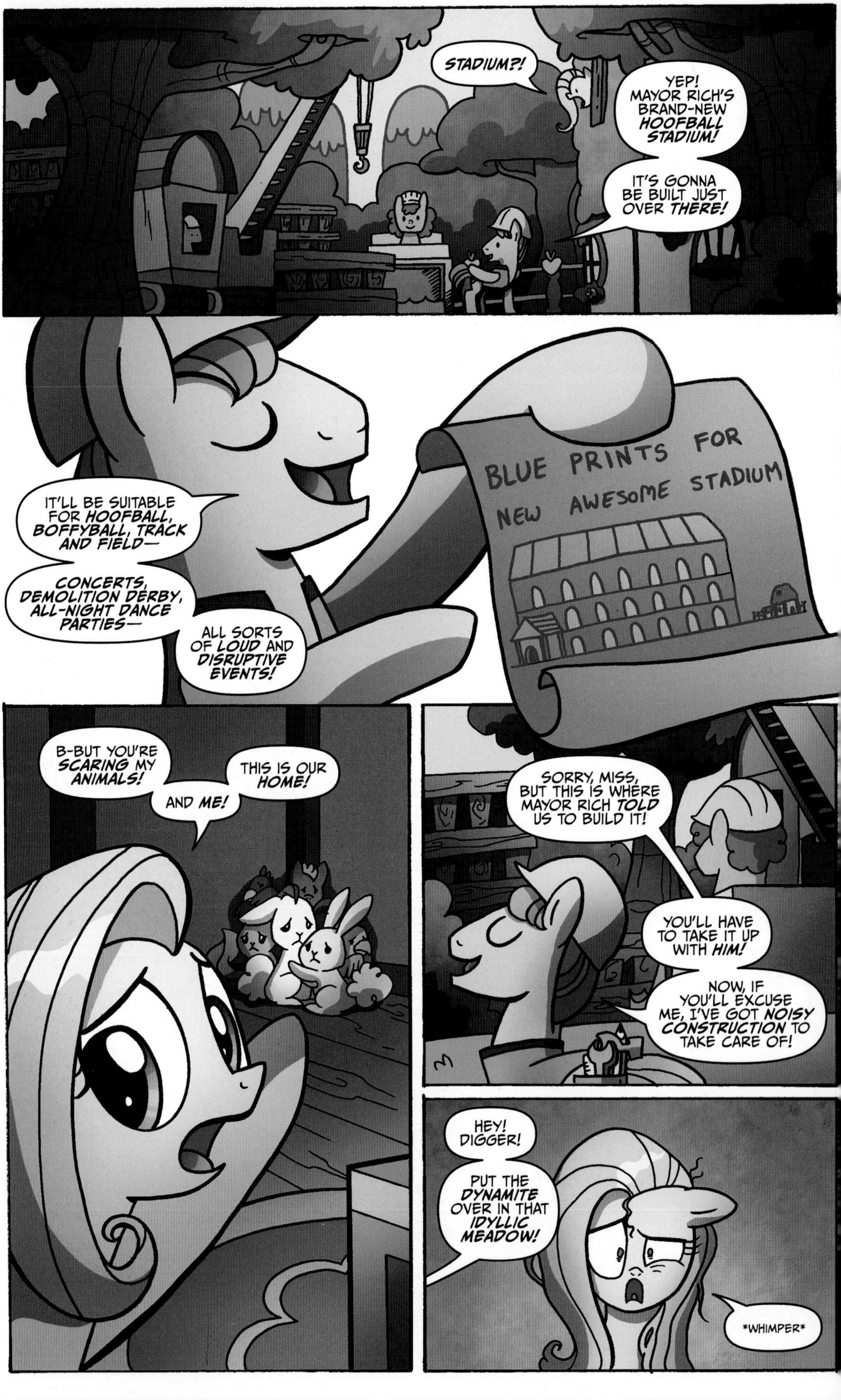
STADIUM?!
YEP! MAYOR RICH'S BRAND-NEW HOOFBALL STADIUM!
IT'S GONNA BE BUILT JUST OVER THERE!
BLUE PRINTS FOR NEW AWESOME STADIUM
IT'LL BE SUITABLE FOR HOOFBALL, BOFFYBALL, TRACK AND FIELD—
CONCERTS, DEMOLITION DERBY, ALL-NIGHT DANCE PARTIES—
ALL SORTS OF LOUD AND DISRUPTIVE EVENTS!
B-BUT YOU'RE SCARING MY ANIMALS!
AND ME!
THIS IS OUR HOME!
SORRY, MISS, BUT THIS IS WHERE MAYOR RICH TOLD US TO BUILD IT!
YOU'LL HAVE TO TAKE IT UP WITH HIM!
NOW, IF YOU'LL EXCUSE ME, I'VE GOT NOISY CONSTRUCTION TO TAKE CARE OF!
HEY! DIGGER!
PUT THE DYNAMITE OVER IN THAT IDYLLIC MEADOW!
WHIMPER

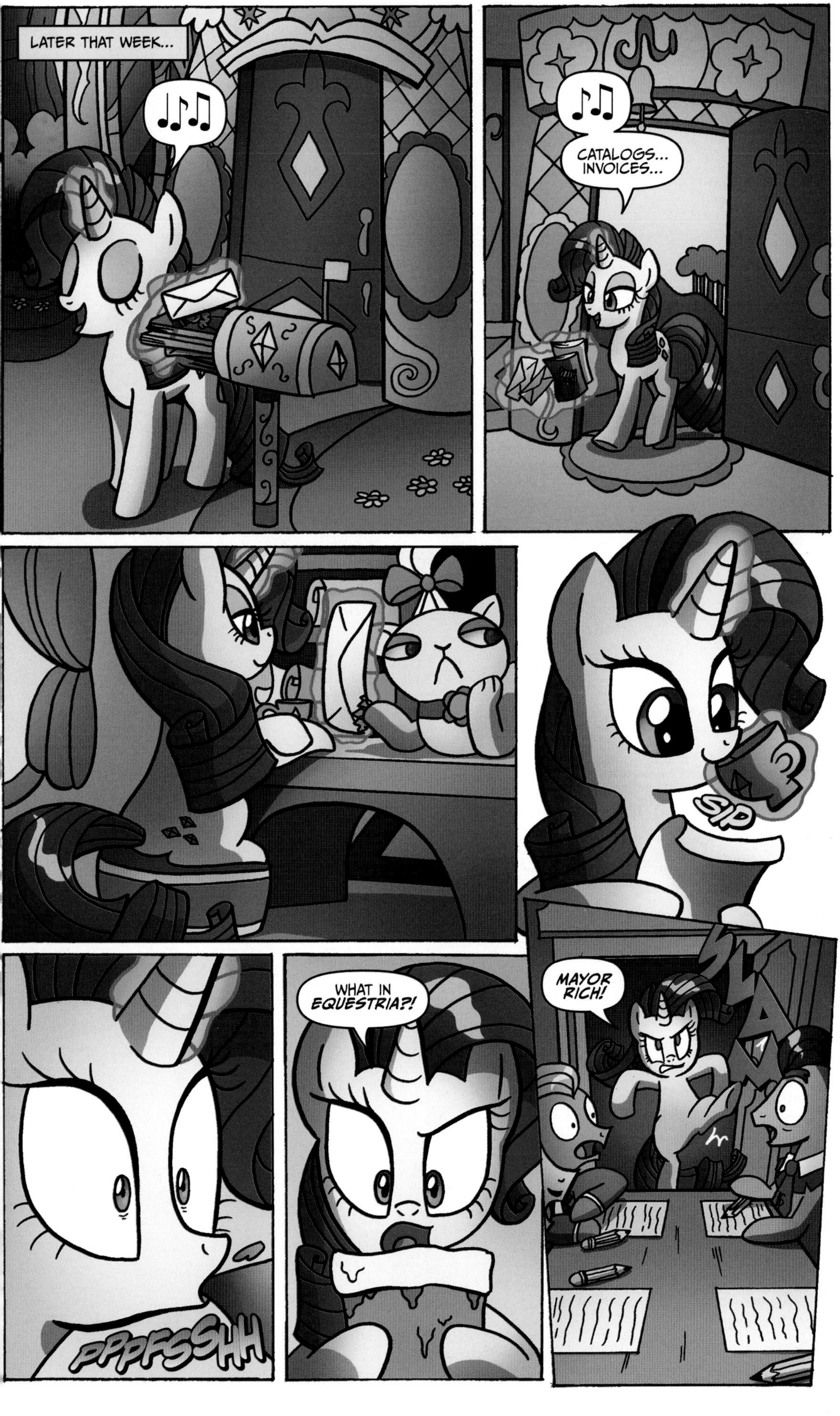
LATER THAT WEEK...
♩♪♫
♪♫
CATALOGS... INVOICES...
SIP
PPPFSSHH
WHAT IN EQUESTRIA?!
MAYOR RICH!

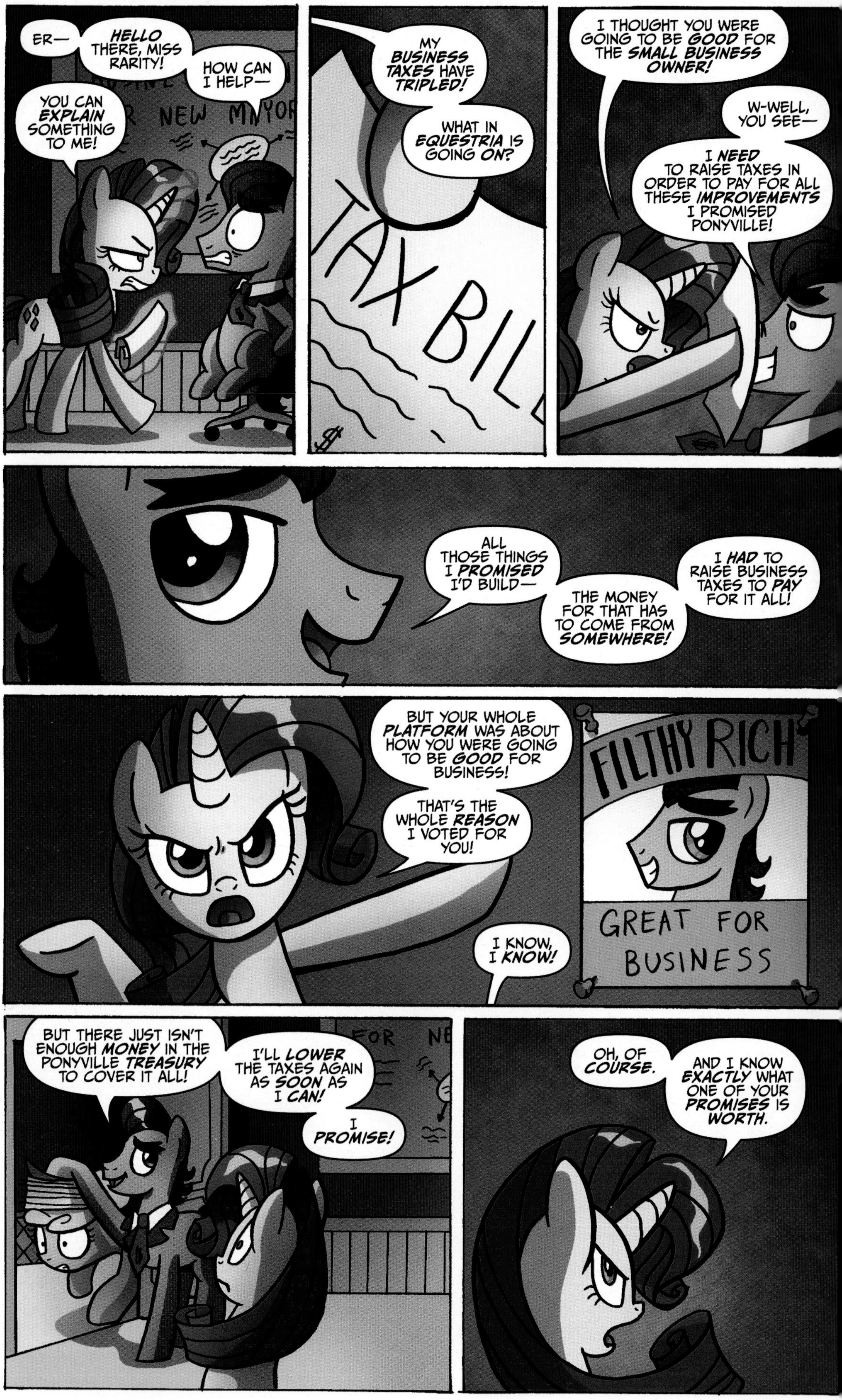
ER—
HELLO THERE, MISS RARITY!
HOW CAN I HELP—
YOU CAN EXPLAIN SOMETHING TO ME!
MY BUSINESS TAXES HAVE TRIPLED!
WHAT IN EQUESTRIA IS GOING ON?
I THOUGHT YOU WERE GOING TO BE GOOD FOR THE SMALL BUSINESS OWNER!
W-WELL, YOU SEE—
I NEED TO RAISE TAXES IN ORDER TO PAY FOR ALL THESE IMPROVEMENTS I PROMISED PONYVILLE!
ALL THOSE THINGS I PROMISED I'D BUILD—
THE MONEY FOR THAT HAS TO COME FROM SOMEWHERE!
I HAD TO RAISE BUSINESS TAXES TO PAY FOR IT ALL!
BUT YOUR WHOLE PLATFORM WAS ABOUT HOW YOU WERE GOING TO BE GOOD FOR BUSINESS!
THAT'S THE WHOLE REASON I VOTED FOR YOU!
FILTHY RICH
GREAT FOR BUSINESS
I KNOW, I KNOW!
BUT THERE JUST ISN'T ENOUGH MONEY IN THE PONYVILLE TREASURY TO COVER IT ALL!
I'LL LOWER THE TAXES AGAIN AS SOON AS I CAN!
I PROMISE!
OH, OF COURSE.
AND I KNOW EXACTLY WHAT ONE OF YOUR PROMISES IS WORTH.

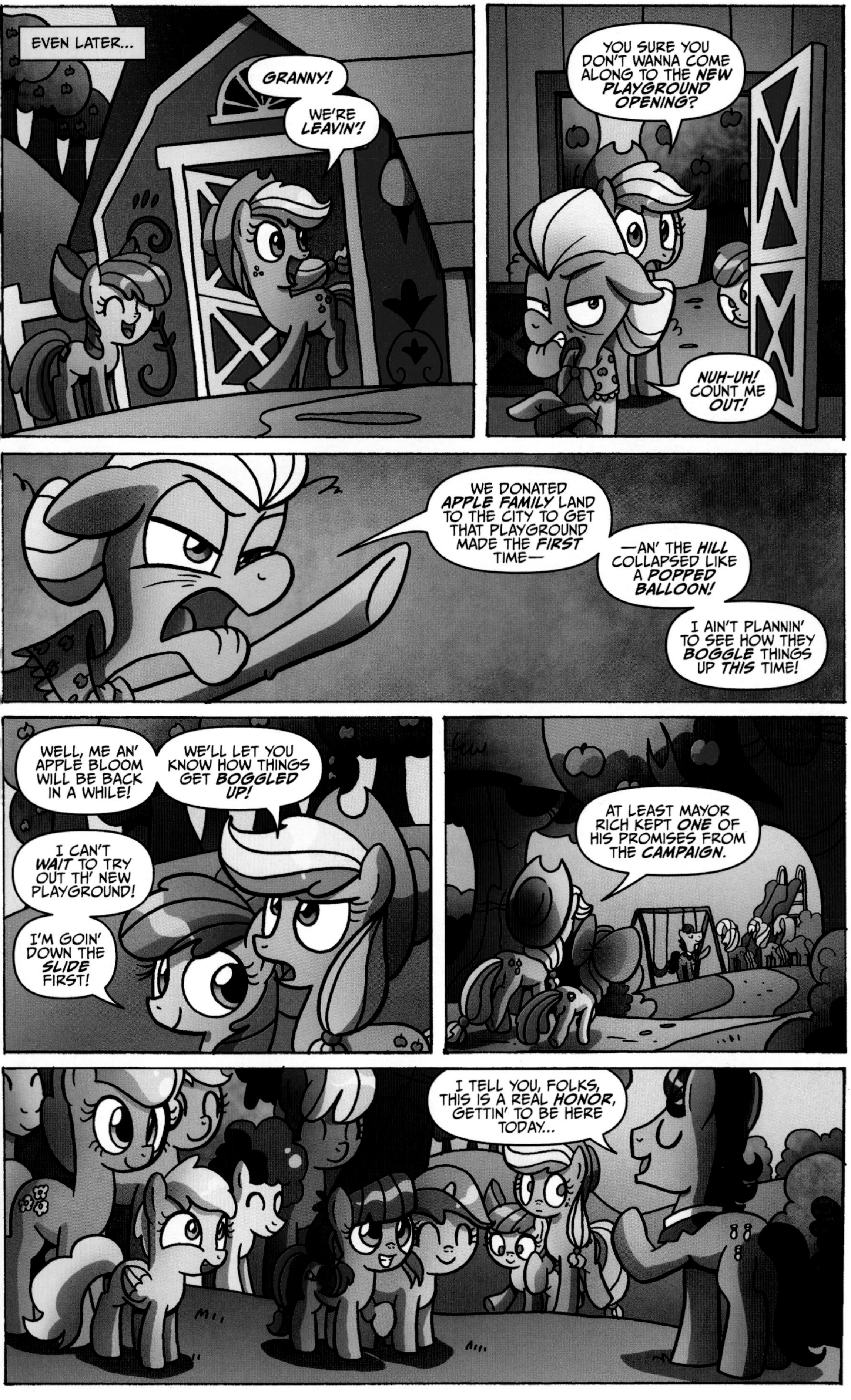
EVEN LATER...
GRANNY!
WE'RE LEAVIN'!
YOU SURE YOU DON'T WANNA COME ALONG TO THE NEW PLAYGROUND OPENING?
NUH-UH! COUNT ME OUT!
WE DONATED APPLE FAMILY LAND TO THE CITY TO GET THAT PLAYGROUND MADE THE FIRST TIME—
—AN' THE HILL COLLAPSED LIKE A POPPED BALLOON!
I AIN'T PLANNIN' TO SEE HOW THEY BOGGLE THINGS UP THIS TIME!
WELL, ME AN' APPLE BLOOM WILL BE BACK IN A WHILE!
WE'LL LET YOU KNOW HOW THINGS GET BOGGLED UP!
I CAN'T WAIT TO TRY OUT TH' NEW PLAYGROUND!
I'M GOIN' DOWN THE SLIDE FIRST!
AT LEAST MAYOR RICH KEPT ONE OF HIS PROMISES FROM THE CAMPAIGN.
I TELL YOU, FOLKS, THIS IS A REAL HONOR, GETTIN' TO BE HERE TODAY...

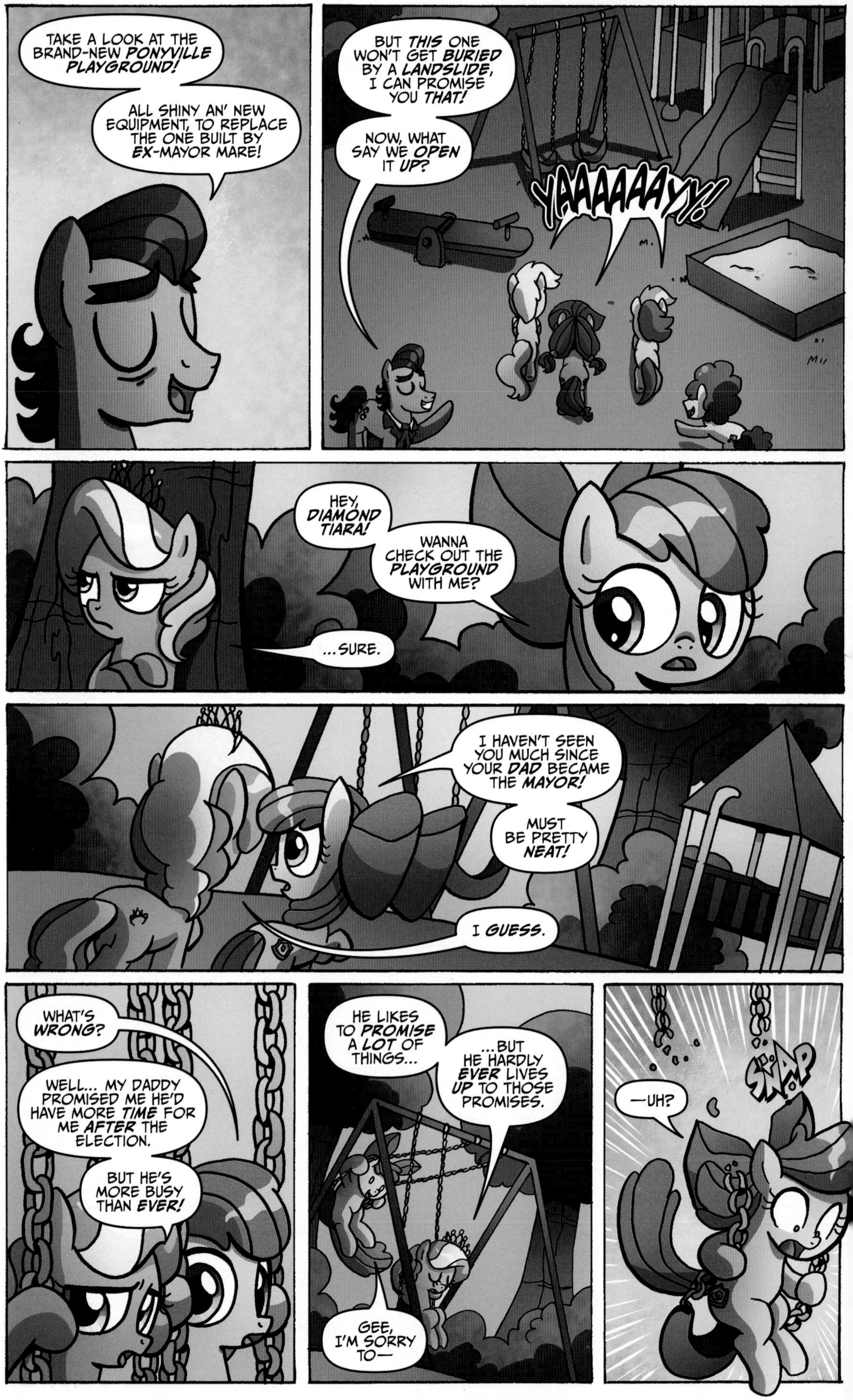
TAKE A LOOK AT THE BRAND-NEW PONYVILLE PLAYGROUND!
ALL SHINY AN' NEW EQUIPMENT, TO REPLACE THE ONE BUILT BY EX-MAYOR MARE!
BUT THIS ONE WON'T GET BURIED BY A LANDSLIDE, I CAN PROMISE YOU THAT!
NOW, WHAT SAY WE OPEN IT UP?
YAAAAAAYY!
HEY, DIAMOND TIARA!
WANNA CHECK OUT THE PLAYGROUND WITH ME?
...SURE.
I HAVEN'T SEEN YOU MUCH SINCE YOUR DAD BECAME THE MAYOR!
MUST BE PRETTY NEAT!
I GUESS.
WHAT'S WRONG?
WELL... MY DADDY PROMISED ME HE'D HAVE MORE TIME FOR ME AFTER THE ELECTION.
BUT HE'S MORE BUSY THAN EVER!
HE LIKES TO PROMISE A LOT OF THINGS...
...BUT HE HARDLY EVER LIVES UP TO THOSE PROMISES.
GEE, I'M SORRY TO—
SNAP
—UH?

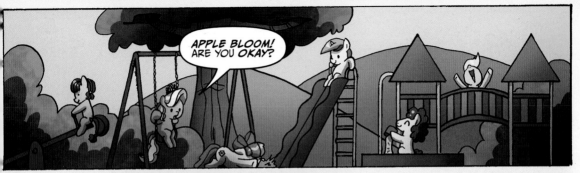

APPLE BLOOM! ARE YOU *OKAY?*

WHAT IN THE *HAY—?!*

CRACK

SNAP

KLUNK

THE *SWING* BROKE!

ALL THE STUFF IS BREAKING!

WHAT TH'—WHAT'S *HAPPENING?*

ALL YER PLAYGROUND EQUIPMENT IS *BREAKIN'!*

AND I *THINK* I *KNOW WHY!*

THIS IS THE *CHEAPEST, CRUMMIEST, SHODDIEST* PLAYGROUND EQUIPMENT I EVER *SEEN!*

IT LOOKS LIKE THIS STUFF WAS MADE OUTTA *CARDBOARD!*

WHAT'RE YOU TRYIN' TO *PULL,* MAYOR?

WELL, UH—

I GOT THE *CHEAPEST* CONSTRUCTION COMPANY I COULD FIND TO *BUILD* THE PLAYGROUND.

T-TO SAVE THE CITY *MONEY,* Y'KNOW?

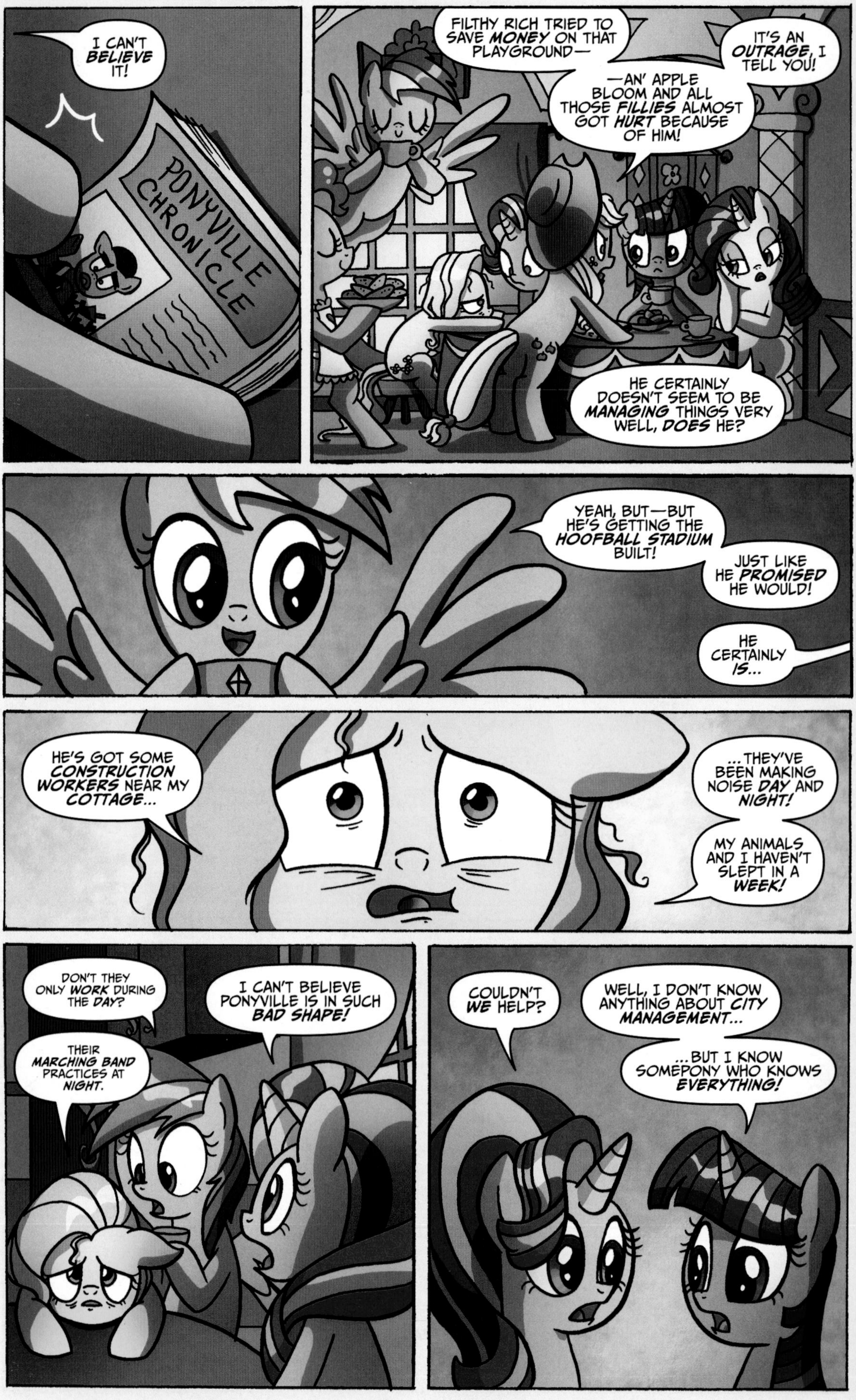

I CAN'T BELIEVE IT!
PONYVILLE CHRONICLE
FILTHY RICH TRIED TO SAVE MONEY ON THAT PLAYGROUND—
—AN' APPLE BLOOM AND ALL THOSE FILLIES ALMOST GOT HURT BECAUSE OF HIM!
IT'S AN OUTRAGE, I TELL YOU!
HE CERTAINLY DOESN'T SEEM TO BE MANAGING THINGS VERY WELL, DOES HE?
YEAH, BUT—BUT HE'S GETTING THE HOOFBALL STADIUM BUILT!
JUST LIKE HE PROMISED HE WOULD!
HE CERTAINLY IS...
HE'S GOT SOME CONSTRUCTION WORKERS NEAR MY COTTAGE...
...THEY'VE BEEN MAKING NOISE DAY AND NIGHT!
MY ANIMALS AND I HAVEN'T SLEPT IN A WEEK!
DON'T THEY ONLY WORK DURING THE DAY?
THEIR MARCHING BAND PRACTICES AT NIGHT.
I CAN'T BELIEVE PONYVILLE IS IN SUCH BAD SHAPE!
COULDN'T WE HELP?
WELL, I DON'T KNOW ANYTHING ABOUT CITY MANAGEMENT...
...BUT I KNOW SOMEPONY WHO KNOWS EVERYTHING!

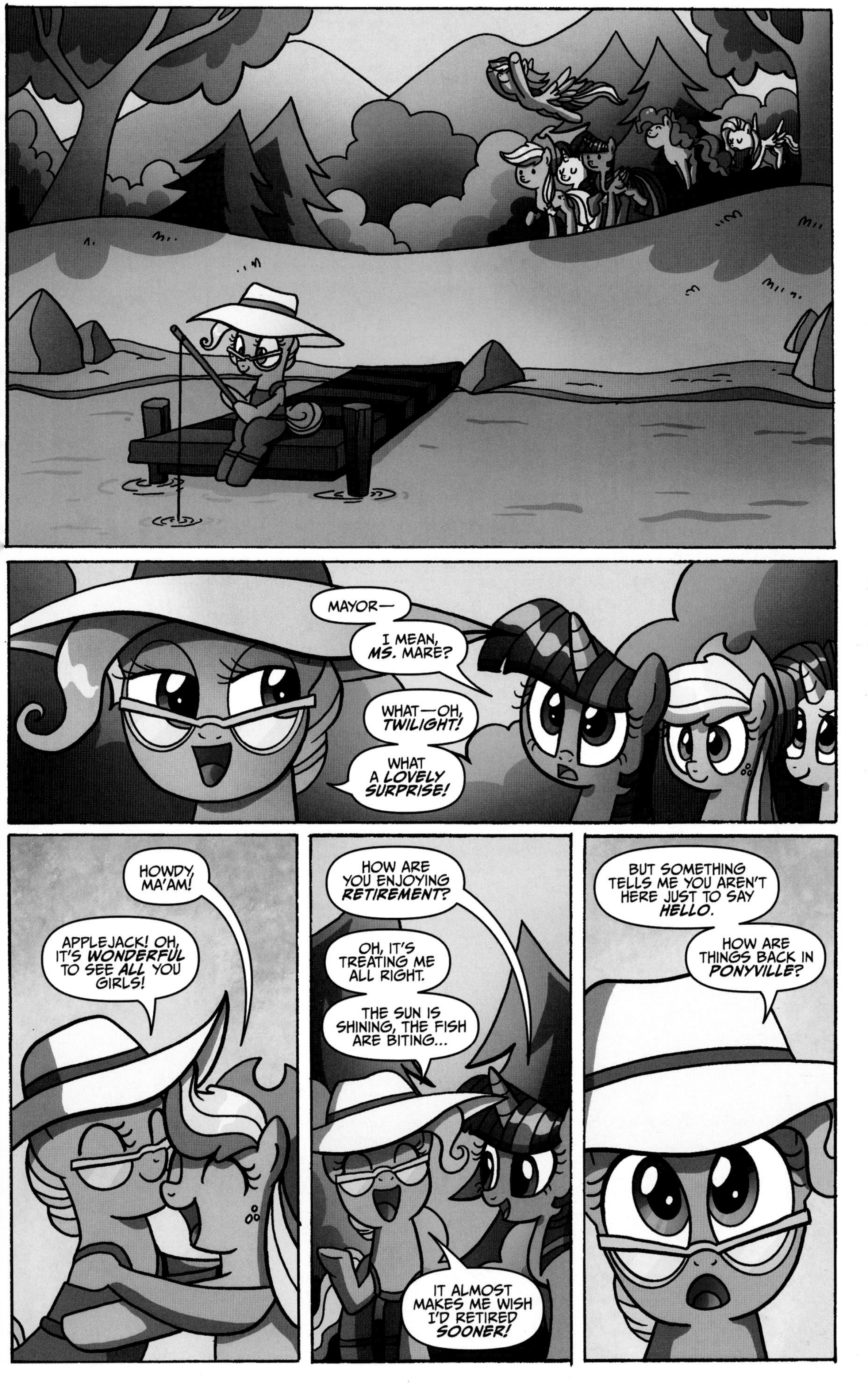

MAYOR—
I MEAN, MS. MARE?
WHAT—OH, TWILIGHT!
WHAT A LOVELY SURPRISE!
HOWDY, MA'AM!
APPLEJACK! OH, IT'S WONDERFUL TO SEE ALL YOU GIRLS!
HOW ARE YOU ENJOYING RETIREMENT?
OH, IT'S TREATING ME ALL RIGHT.
THE SUN IS SHINING, THE FISH ARE BITING...
IT ALMOST MAKES ME WISH I'D RETIRED SOONER!
BUT SOMETHING TELLS ME YOU AREN'T HERE JUST TO SAY HELLO.
HOW ARE THINGS BACK IN PONYVILLE?

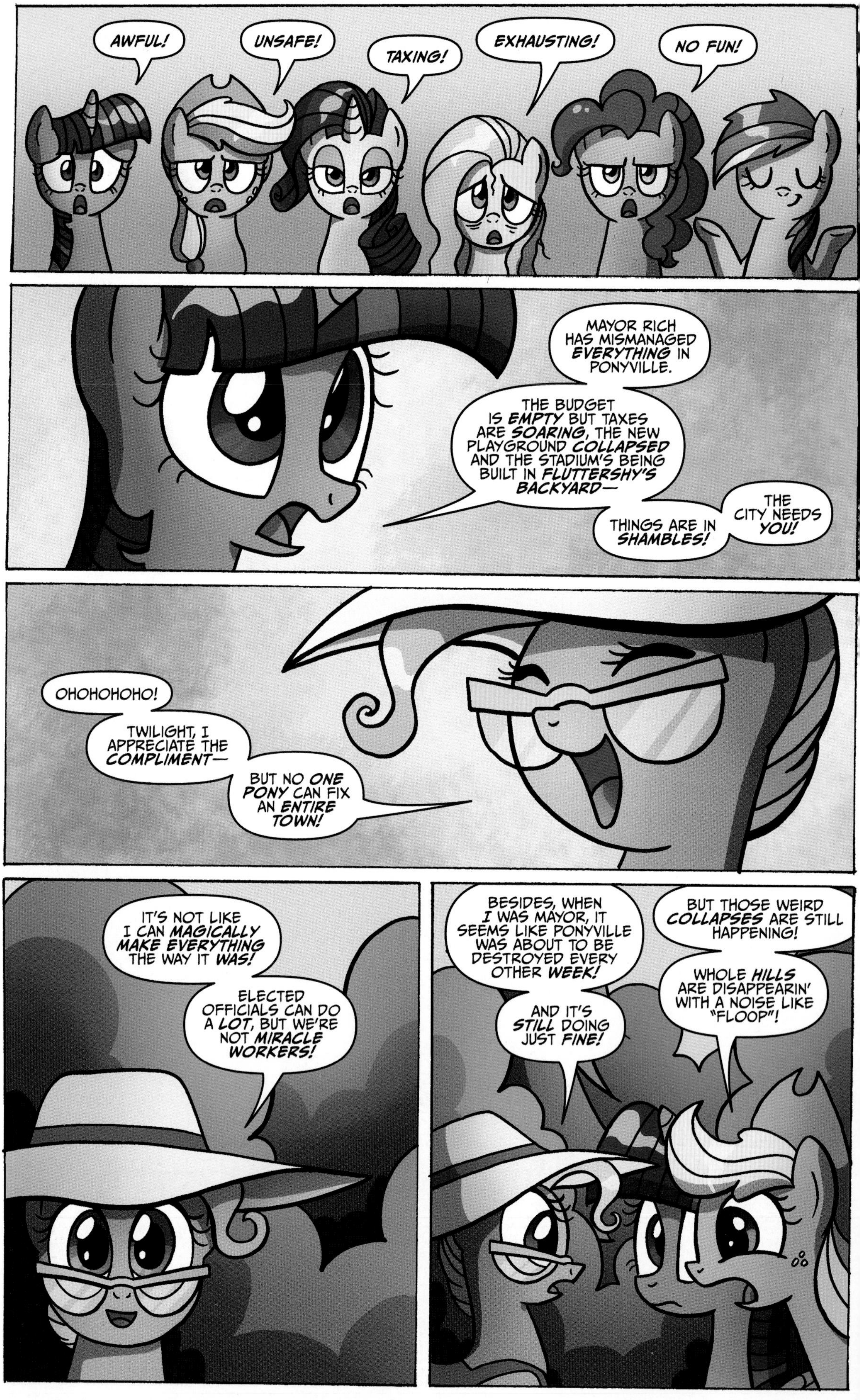
AWFUL!
UNSAFE!
TAXING!
EXHAUSTING!
NO FUN!
MAYOR RICH HAS MISMANAGED EVERYTHING IN PONYVILLE.
THE BUDGET IS EMPTY BUT TAXES ARE SOARING, THE NEW PLAYGROUND COLLAPSED AND THE STADIUM'S BEING BUILT IN FLUTTERSHY'S BACKYARD—
THINGS ARE IN SHAMBLES!
THE CITY NEEDS YOU!
OHOHOHOHO!
TWILIGHT, I APPRECIATE THE COMPLIMENT—
BUT NO ONE PONY CAN FIX AN ENTIRE TOWN!
IT'S NOT LIKE I CAN MAGICALLY MAKE EVERYTHING THE WAY IT WAS!
ELECTED OFFICIALS CAN DO A LOT, BUT WE'RE NOT MIRACLE WORKERS!
BESIDES, WHEN I WAS MAYOR, IT SEEMS LIKE PONYVILLE WAS ABOUT TO BE DESTROYED EVERY OTHER WEEK!
AND IT'S STILL DOING JUST FINE!
BUT THOSE WEIRD COLLAPSES ARE STILL HAPPENING!
WHOLE HILLS ARE DISAPPEARIN' WITH A NOISE LIKE "FLOOP"!

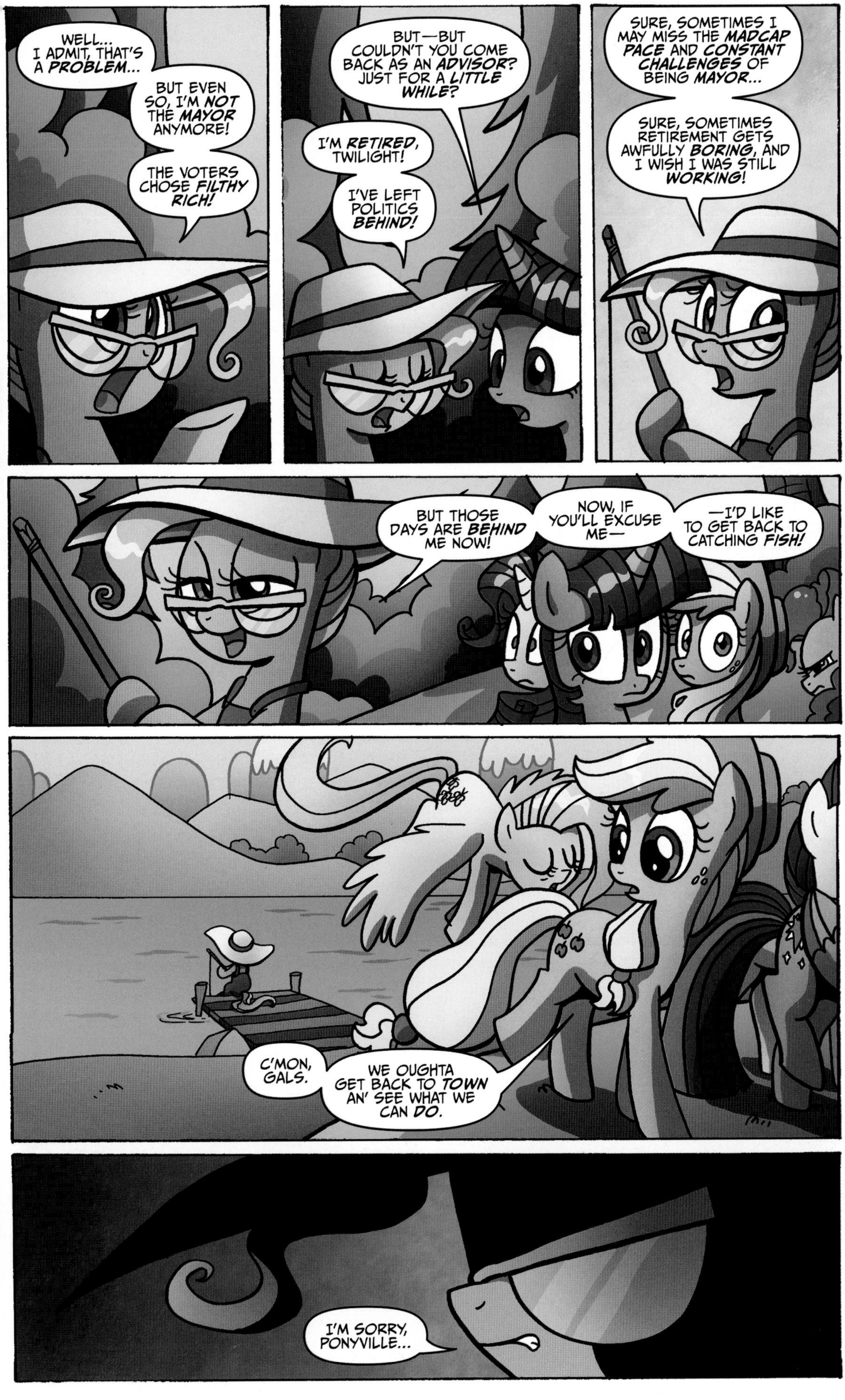
WELL... I ADMIT, THAT'S A *PROBLEM*...
BUT EVEN SO, I'M *NOT* THE *MAYOR* ANYMORE!
THE VOTERS CHOSE *FILTHY RICH!*
BUT—BUT COULDN'T YOU COME BACK AS AN *ADVISOR*? JUST FOR A *LITTLE WHILE*?
I'M *RETIRED*, TWILIGHT!
I'VE LEFT POLITICS *BEHIND!*
SURE, SOMETIMES I MAY MISS THE *MADCAP PACE* AND *CONSTANT CHALLENGES* OF BEING *MAYOR*...
SURE, SOMETIMES RETIREMENT GETS AWFULLY *BORING*, AND I WISH I WAS STILL *WORKING!*
BUT THOSE DAYS ARE *BEHIND* ME NOW!
NOW, IF YOU'LL EXCUSE ME—
—I'D LIKE TO GET BACK TO CATCHING *FISH!*
C'MON, GALS.
WE OUGHTA GET BACK TO *TOWN* AN' SEE WHAT WE CAN *DO*.
I'M SORRY, PONYVILLE...

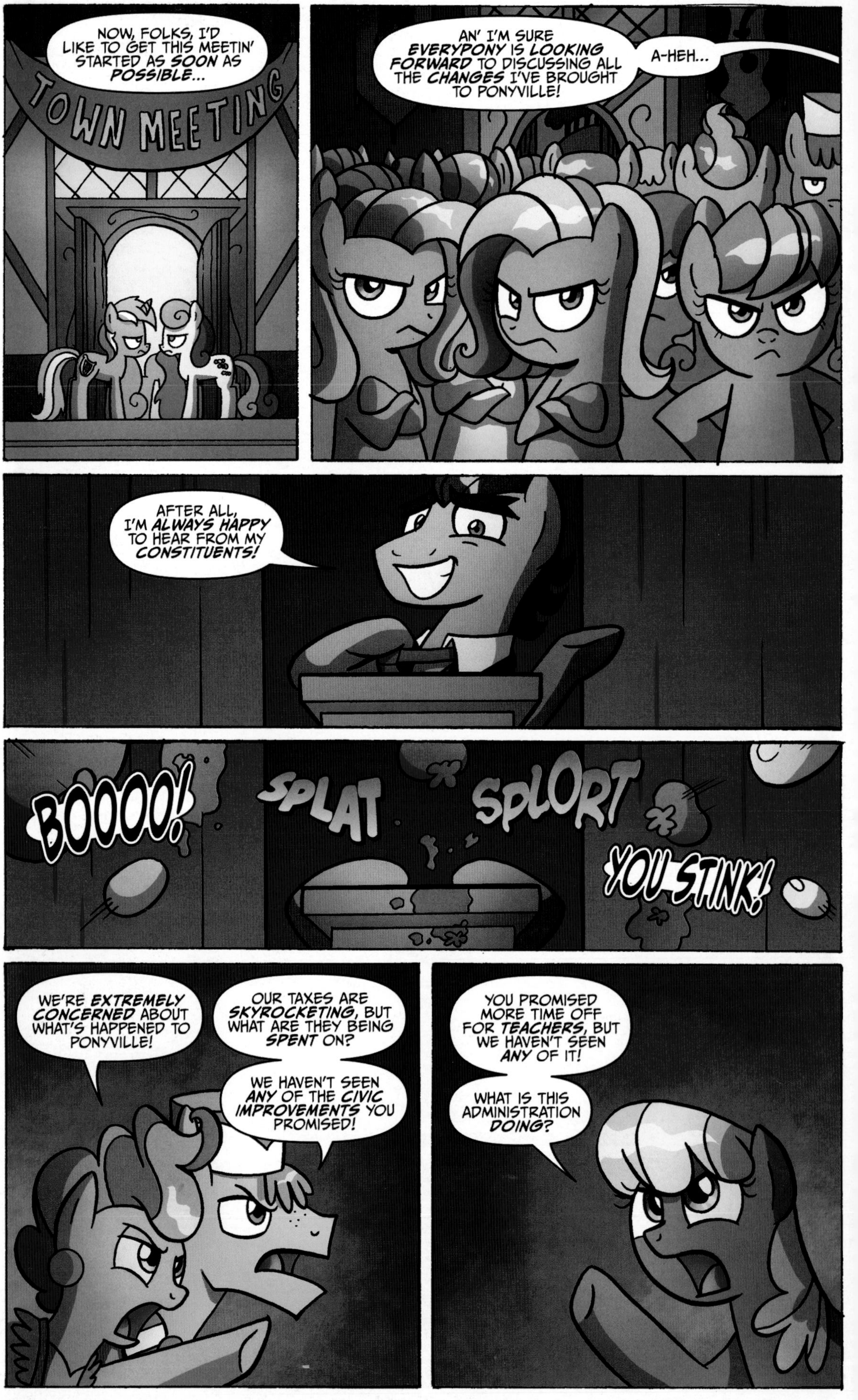
NOW, FOLKS, I'D LIKE TO GET THIS MEETIN' STARTED AS SOON AS POSSIBLE...
TOWN MEETING
AN' I'M SURE EVERYPONY IS LOOKING FORWARD TO DISCUSSING ALL THE CHANGES I'VE BROUGHT TO PONYVILLE!
A-HEH...
AFTER ALL, I'M ALWAYS HAPPY TO HEAR FROM MY CONSTITUENTS!
BOOOO!
SPLAT
SPLORT
YOU STINK!
WE'RE EXTREMELY CONCERNED ABOUT WHAT'S HAPPENED TO PONYVILLE!
OUR TAXES ARE SKYROCKETING, BUT WHAT ARE THEY BEING SPENT ON?
WE HAVEN'T SEEN ANY OF THE CIVIC IMPROVEMENTS YOU PROMISED!
YOU PROMISED MORE TIME OFF FOR TEACHERS, BUT WE HAVEN'T SEEN ANY OF IT!
WHAT IS THIS ADMINISTRATION DOING?

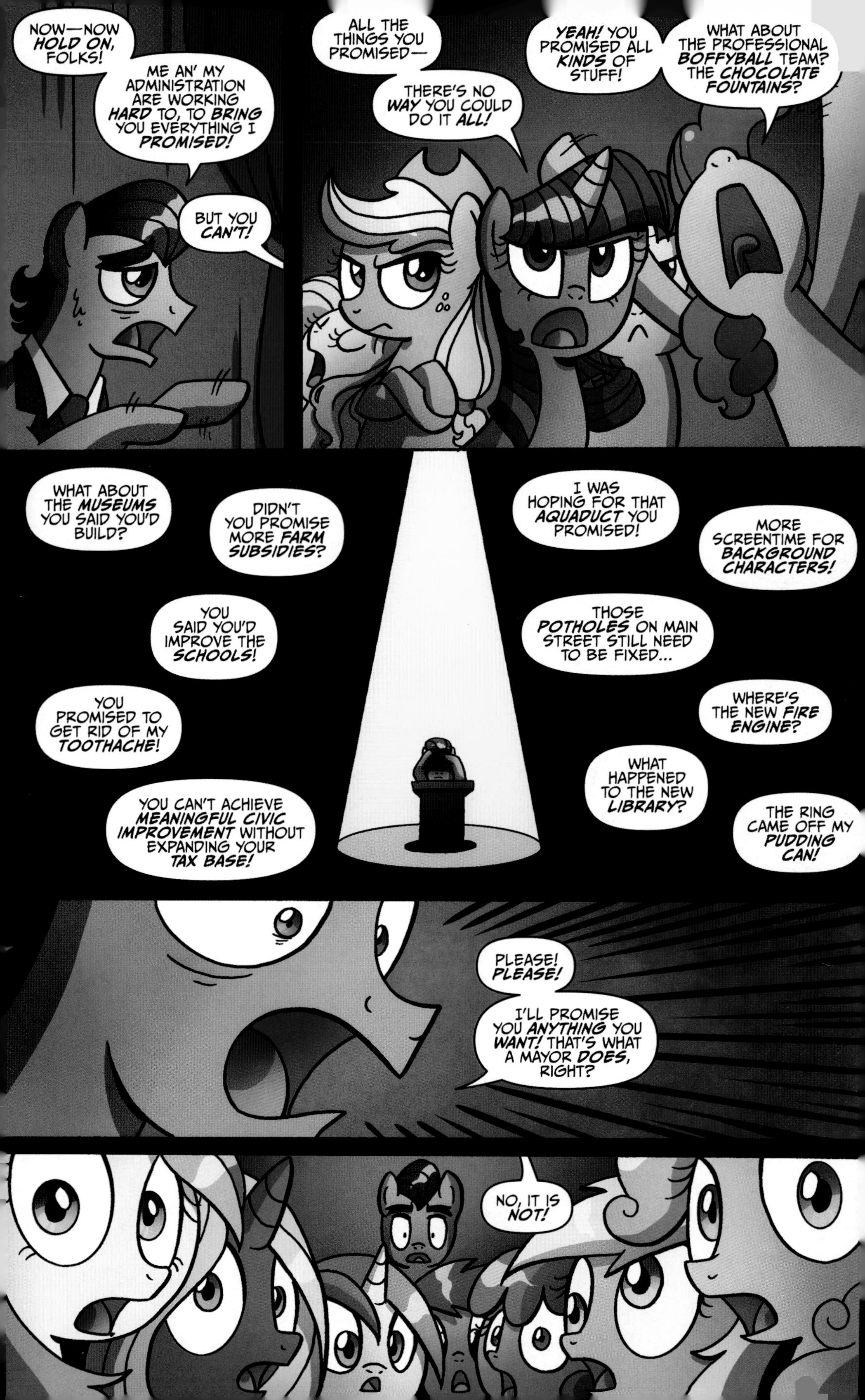
NOW—NOW *HOLD ON,* FOLKS!
ME AN' MY ADMINISTRATION ARE WORKING *HARD* TO, TO *BRING* YOU EVERYTHING I *PROMISED!*
BUT YOU *CAN'T!*
ALL THE THINGS YOU PROMISED—
THERE'S NO *WAY* YOU COULD DO IT *ALL!*
YEAH! YOU PROMISED ALL *KINDS* OF STUFF!
WHAT ABOUT THE PROFESSIONAL *BOFFYBALL* TEAM? THE *CHOCOLATE FOUNTAINS?*
WHAT ABOUT THE *MUSEUMS* YOU SAID YOU'D BUILD?
DIDN'T YOU PROMISE MORE *FARM SUBSIDIES?*
I WAS HOPING FOR THAT *AQUADUCT* YOU PROMISED!
MORE SCREENTIME FOR *BACKGROUND CHARACTERS!*
YOU SAID YOU'D IMPROVE THE *SCHOOLS!*
THOSE *POTHOLES* ON MAIN STREET STILL NEED TO BE FIXED...
YOU PROMISED TO GET RID OF MY *TOOTHACHE!*
WHERE'S THE NEW *FIRE ENGINE?*
WHAT HAPPENED TO THE NEW *LIBRARY?*
YOU CAN'T ACHIEVE *MEANINGFUL CIVIC IMPROVEMENT* WITHOUT EXPANDING YOUR *TAX BASE!*
THE RING CAME OFF MY *PUDDING* CAN!
PLEASE! *PLEASE!*
I'LL PROMISE YOU *ANYTHING* YOU *WANT!* THAT'S WHAT A MAYOR *DOES,* RIGHT?
NO, IT IS *NOT!*

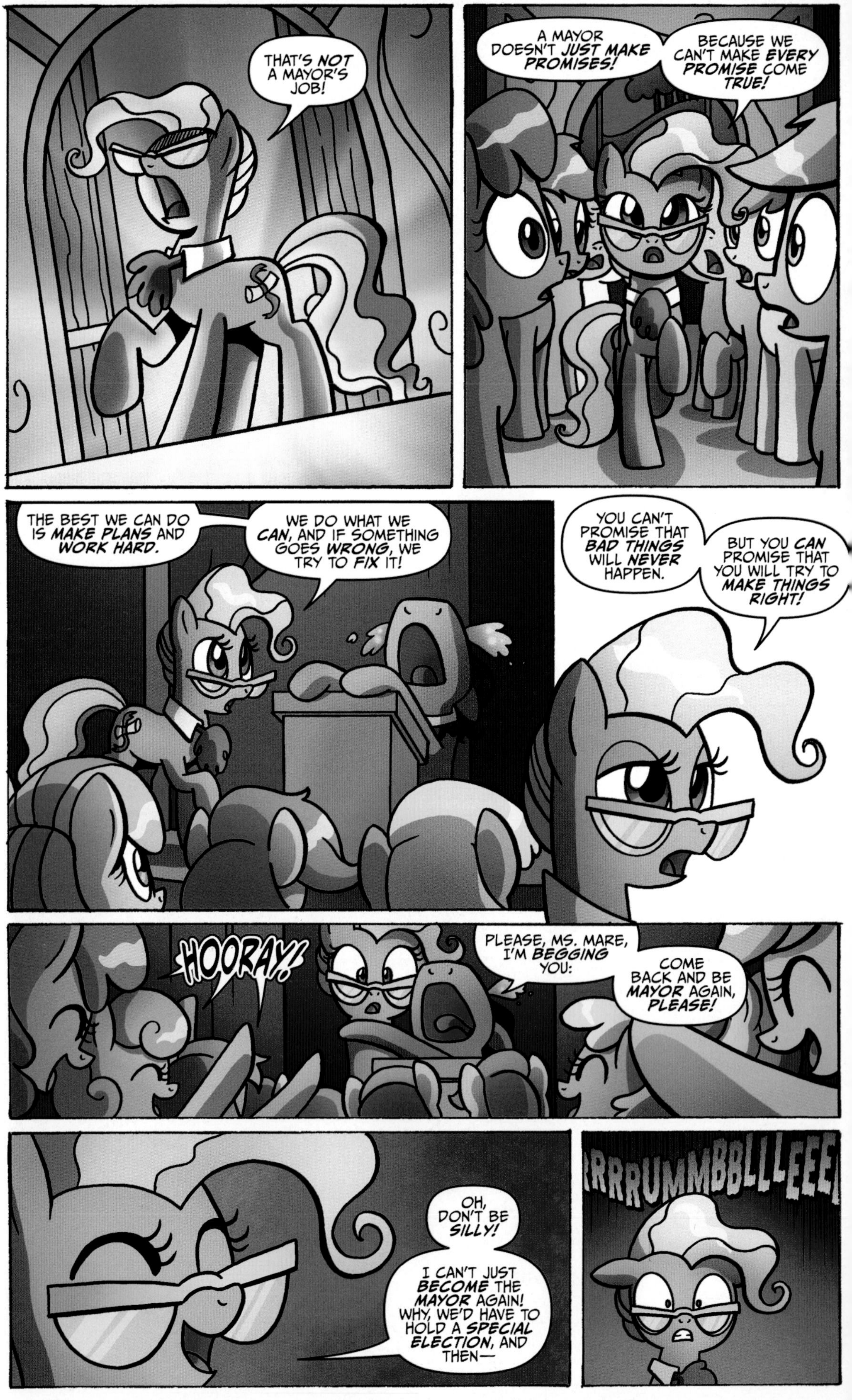

THAT'S NOT A MAYOR'S JOB!
A MAYOR DOESN'T JUST MAKE PROMISES!
BECAUSE WE CAN'T MAKE EVERY PROMISE COME TRUE!
THE BEST WE CAN DO IS MAKE PLANS AND WORK HARD.
WE DO WHAT WE CAN, AND IF SOMETHING GOES WRONG, WE TRY TO FIX IT!
YOU CAN'T PROMISE THAT BAD THINGS WILL NEVER HAPPEN.
BUT YOU CAN PROMISE THAT YOU WILL TRY TO MAKE THINGS RIGHT!
HOORAY!
PLEASE, MS. MARE, I'M BEGGING YOU:
COME BACK AND BE MAYOR AGAIN, PLEASE!
OH, DON'T BE SILLY!
I CAN'T JUST BECOME THE MAYOR AGAIN! WHY, WE'D HAVE TO HOLD A SPECIAL ELECTION, AND THEN—
RRRRUMMBBLLLEEEE

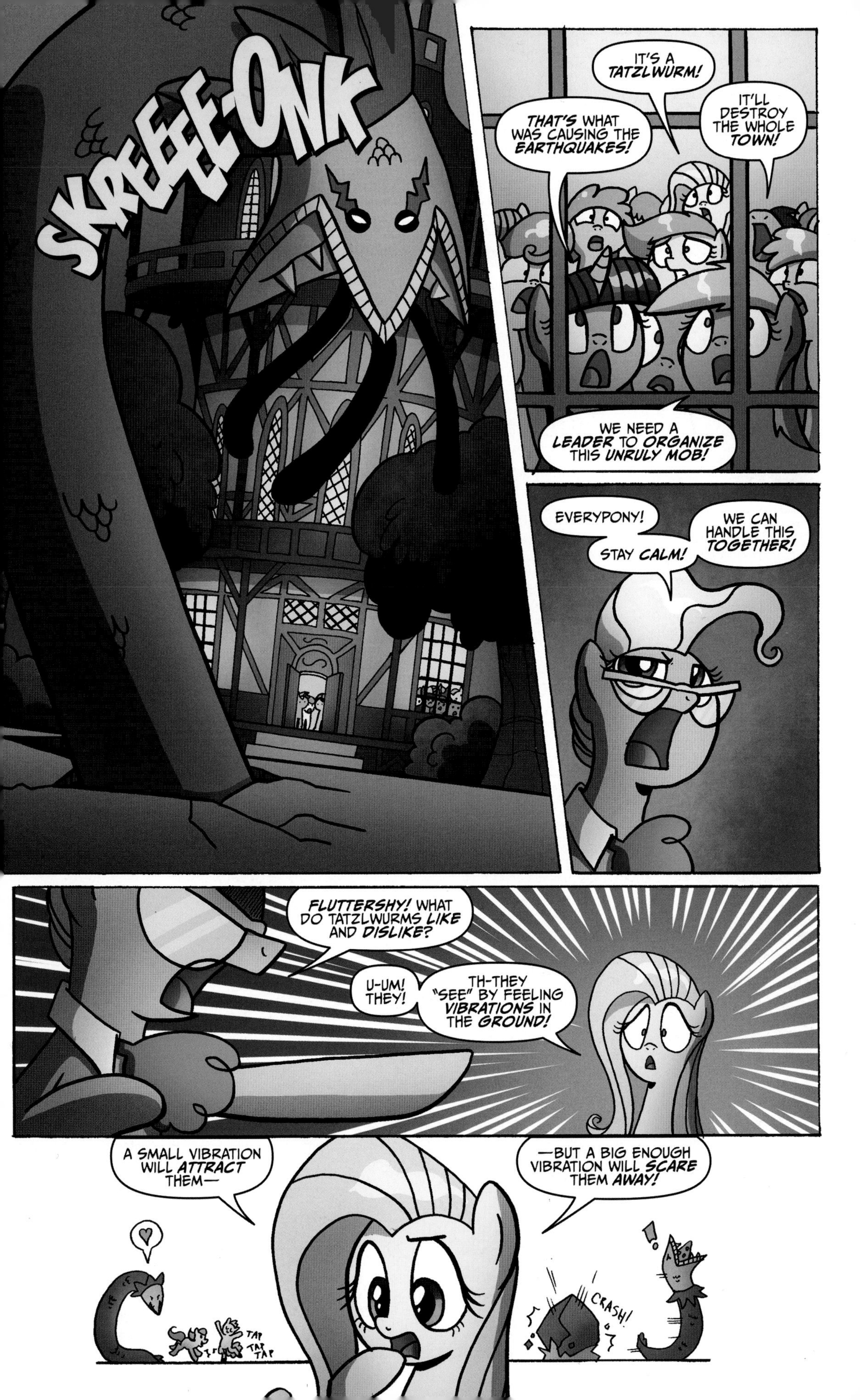
SKREEEE-ONK
IT'S A TATZLWURM!
THAT'S WHAT WAS CAUSING THE EARTHQUAKES!
IT'LL DESTROY THE WHOLE TOWN!
WE NEED A LEADER TO ORGANIZE THIS UNRULY MOB!
EVERYPONY!
STAY CALM!
WE CAN HANDLE THIS TOGETHER!
FLUTTERSHY! WHAT DO TATZLWURMS LIKE AND DISLIKE?
U-UM! THEY!
TH-THEY "SEE" BY FEELING VIBRATIONS IN THE GROUND!
A SMALL VIBRATION WILL ATTRACT THEM—
—BUT A BIG ENOUGH VIBRATION WILL SCARE THEM AWAY!
TAP TAP TAP
CRASH!

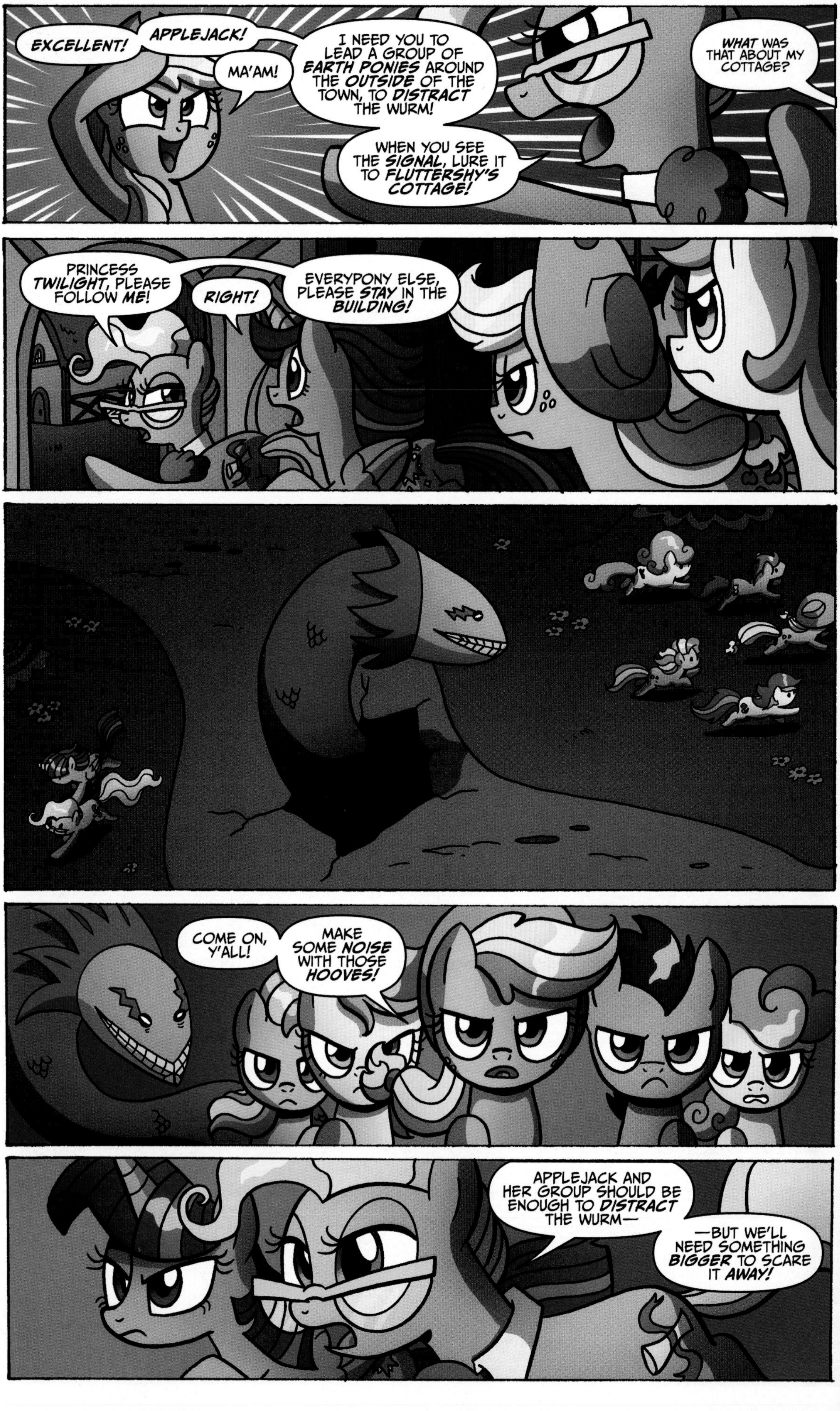

APPLEJACK!
EXCELLENT!
MA'AM!
I NEED YOU TO LEAD A GROUP OF EARTH PONIES AROUND THE OUTSIDE OF THE TOWN, TO DISTRACT THE WURM!
WHEN YOU SEE THE SIGNAL, LURE IT TO FLUTTERSHY'S COTTAGE!
WHAT WAS THAT ABOUT MY COTTAGE?
PRINCESS TWILIGHT, PLEASE FOLLOW ME!
RIGHT!
EVERYPONY ELSE, PLEASE STAY IN THE BUILDING!
COME ON, Y'ALL!
MAKE SOME NOISE WITH THOSE HOOVES!
APPLEJACK AND HER GROUP SHOULD BE ENOUGH TO DISTRACT THE WURM—
—BUT WE'LL NEED SOMETHING BIGGER TO SCARE IT AWAY!

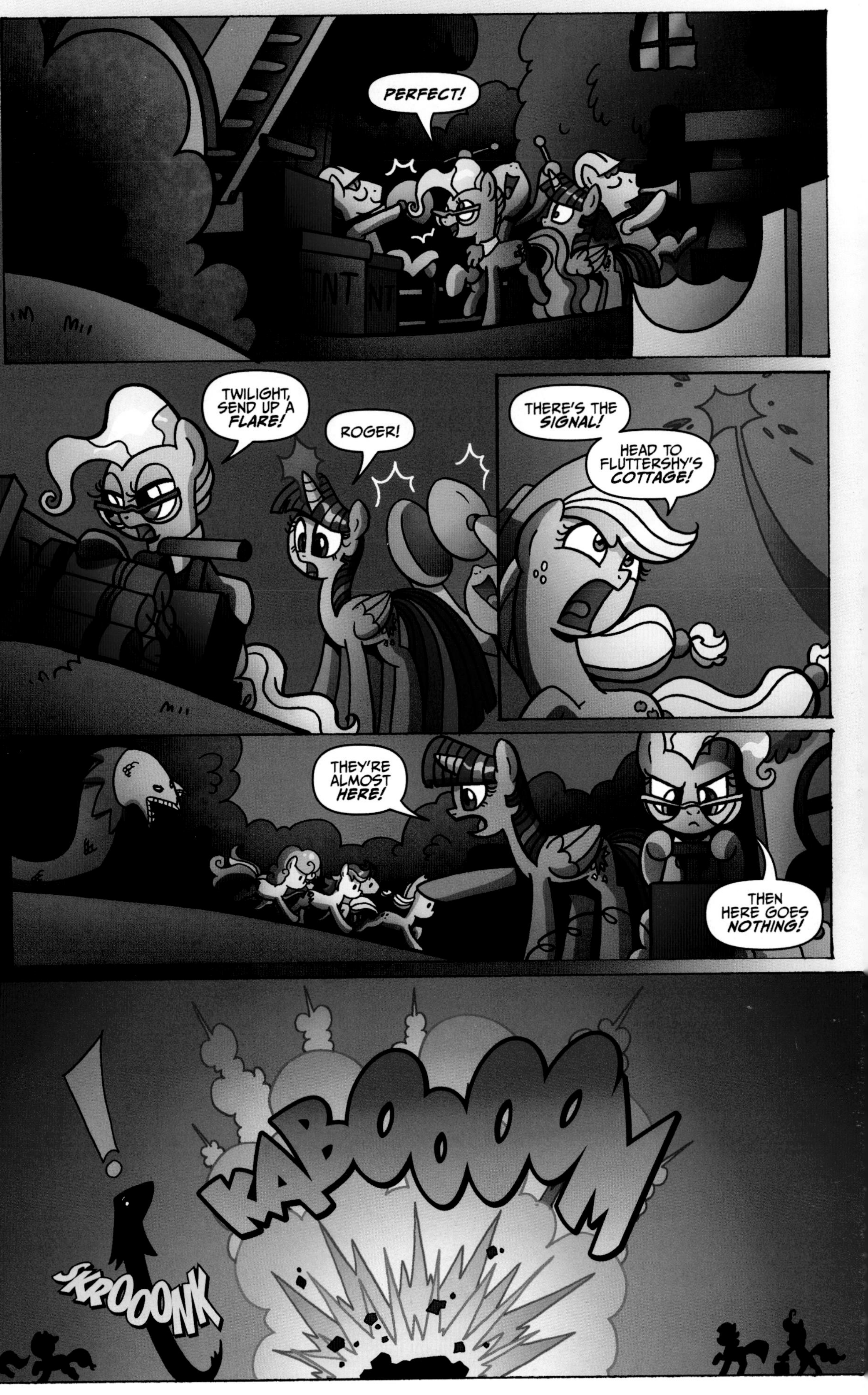
PERFECT!
TWILIGHT, SEND UP A FLARE!
ROGER!
THERE'S THE SIGNAL!
HEAD TO FLUTTERSHY'S COTTAGE!
THEY'RE ALMOST HERE!
THEN HERE GOES NOTHING!
!
KABOOOM
SKROOOONK

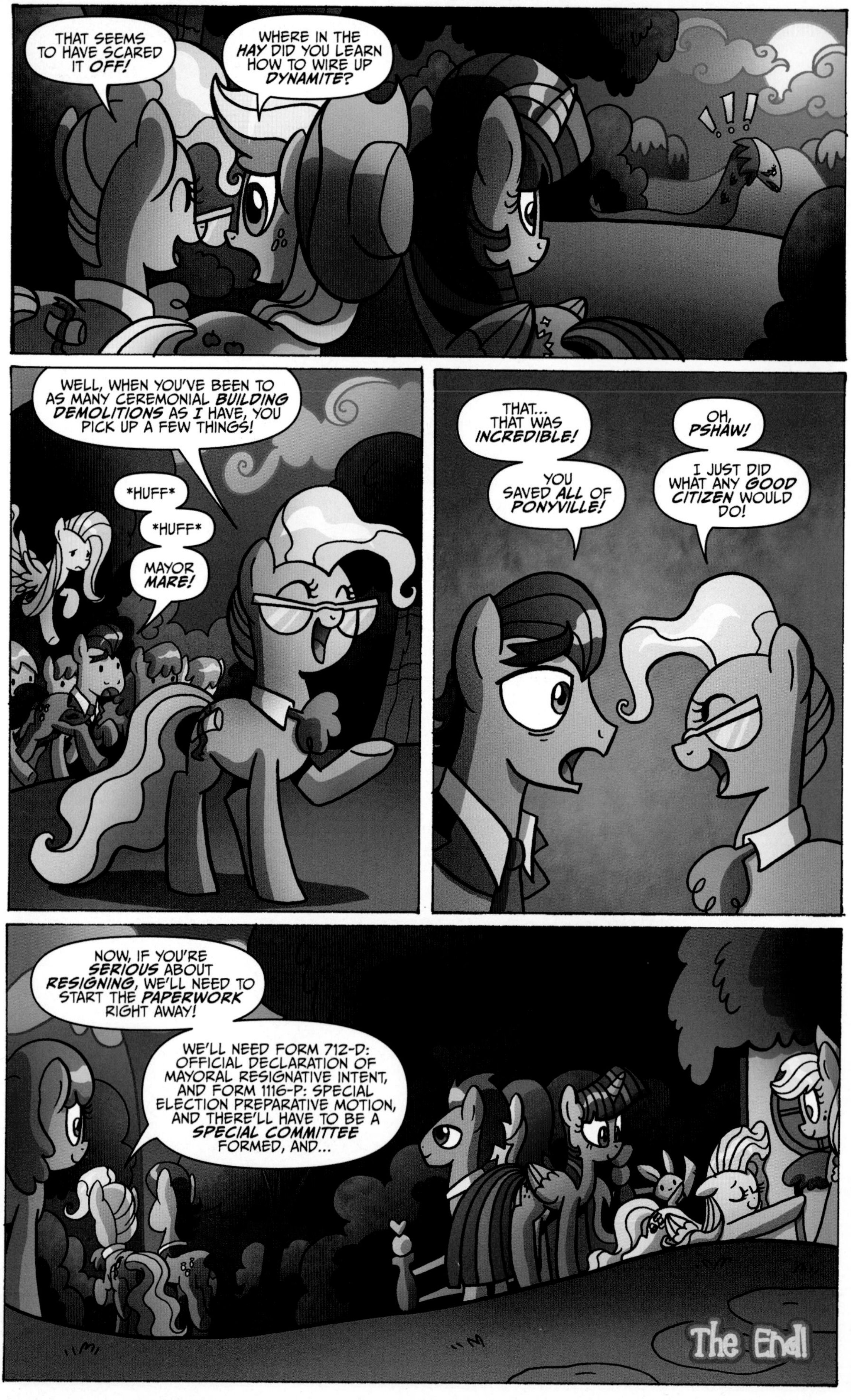
THAT SEEMS TO HAVE SCARED IT OFF!
WHERE IN THE HAY DID YOU LEARN HOW TO WIRE UP DYNAMITE?
!!!
WELL, WHEN YOU'VE BEEN TO AS MANY CEREMONIAL BUILDING DEMOLITIONS AS I HAVE, YOU PICK UP A FEW THINGS!
HUFF
HUFF
MAYOR MARE!
THAT... THAT WAS INCREDIBLE!
YOU SAVED ALL OF PONYVILLE!
OH, PSHAW!
I JUST DID WHAT ANY GOOD CITIZEN WOULD DO!
NOW, IF YOU'RE SERIOUS ABOUT RESIGNING, WE'LL NEED TO START THE PAPERWORK RIGHT AWAY!
WE'LL NEED FORM 712-D: OFFICIAL DECLARATION OF MAYORAL RESIGNATIVE INTENT, AND FORM 1116-P: SPECIAL ELECTION PREPARATIVE MOTION, AND THERE'LL HAVE TO BE A SPECIAL COMMITTEE FORMED, AND...
The End

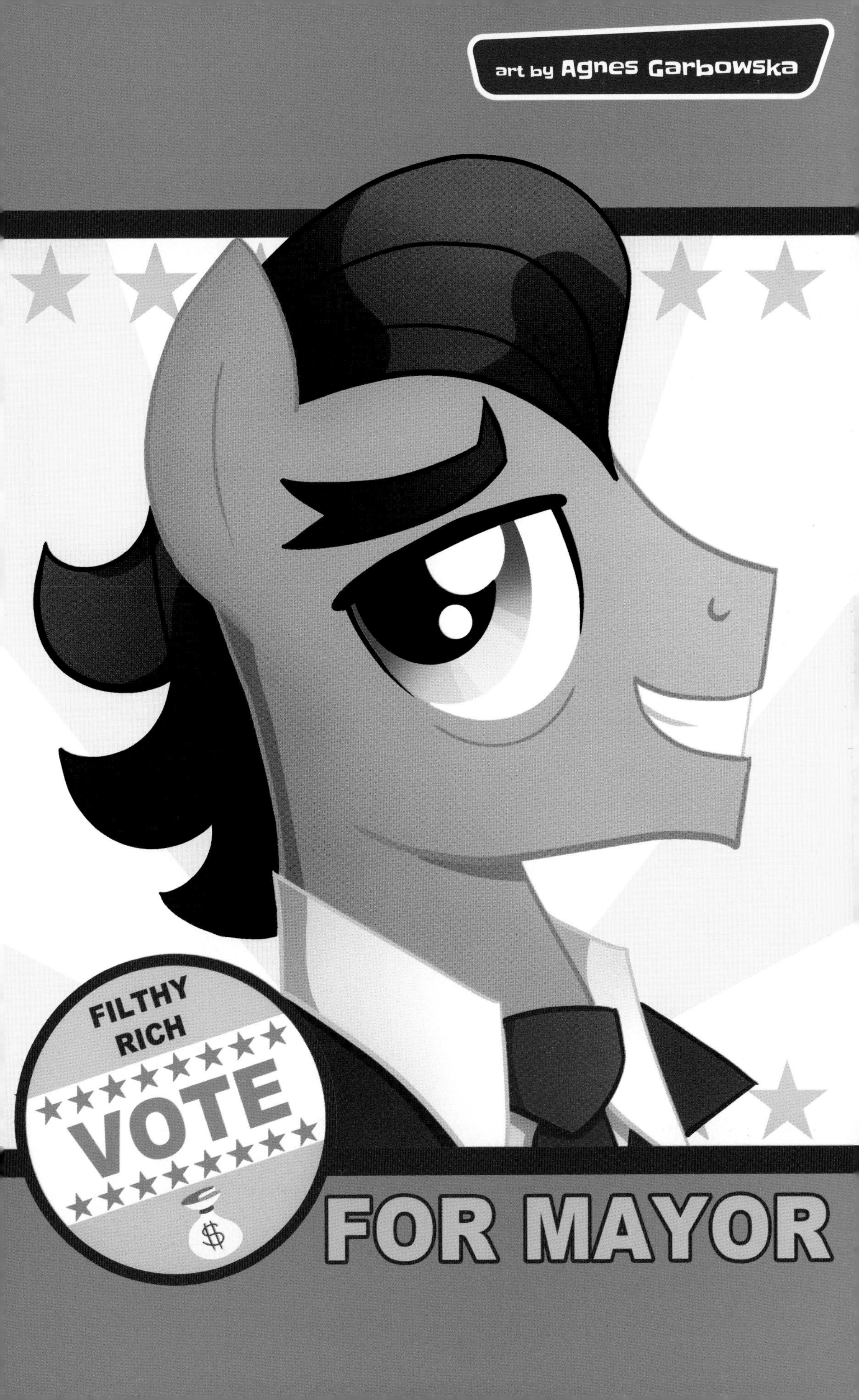
art by Agnes Garbowska
FILTHY RICH
VOTE
FOR MAYOR

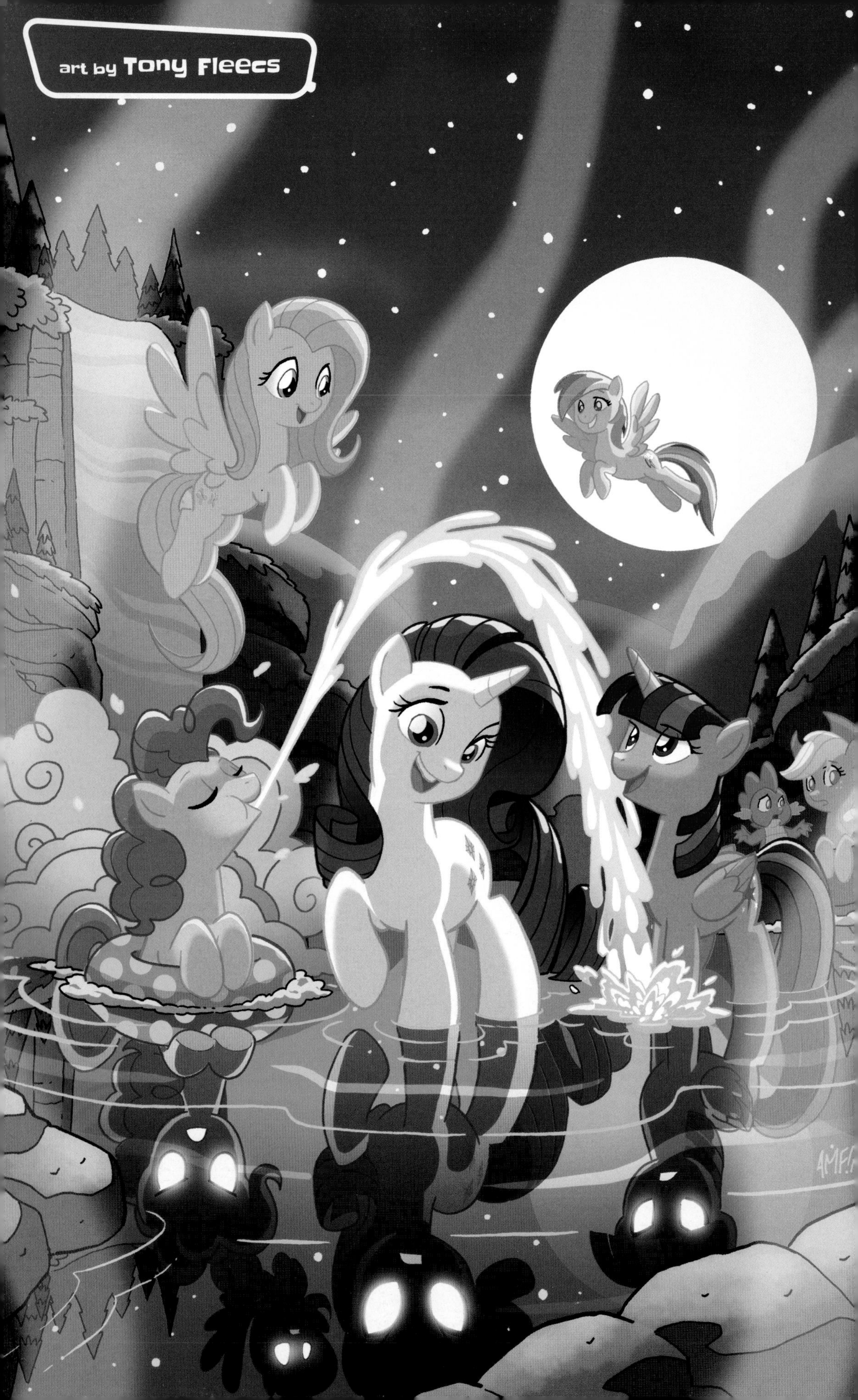

art by Tony Fleecs

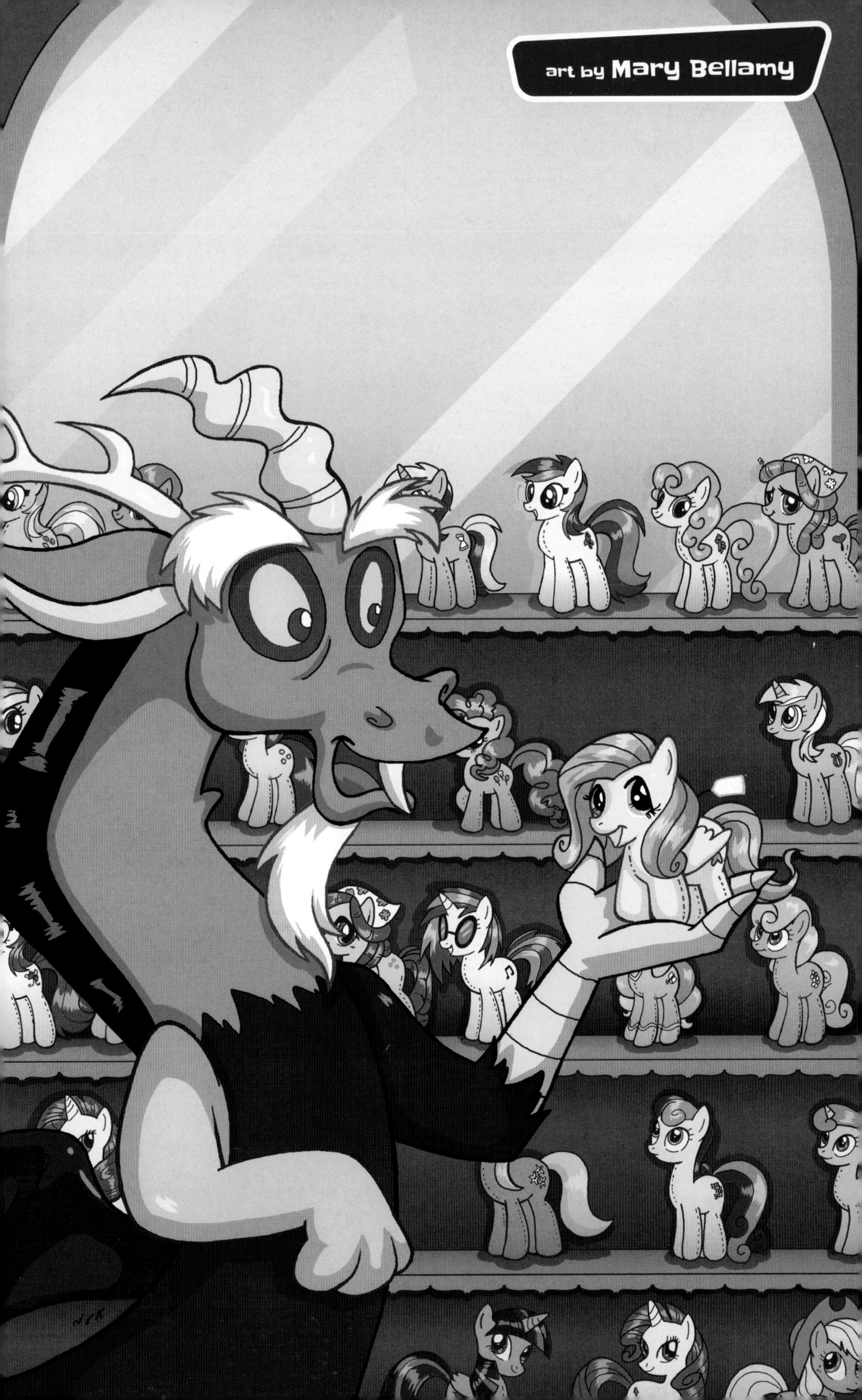
art by Mary Bellamy

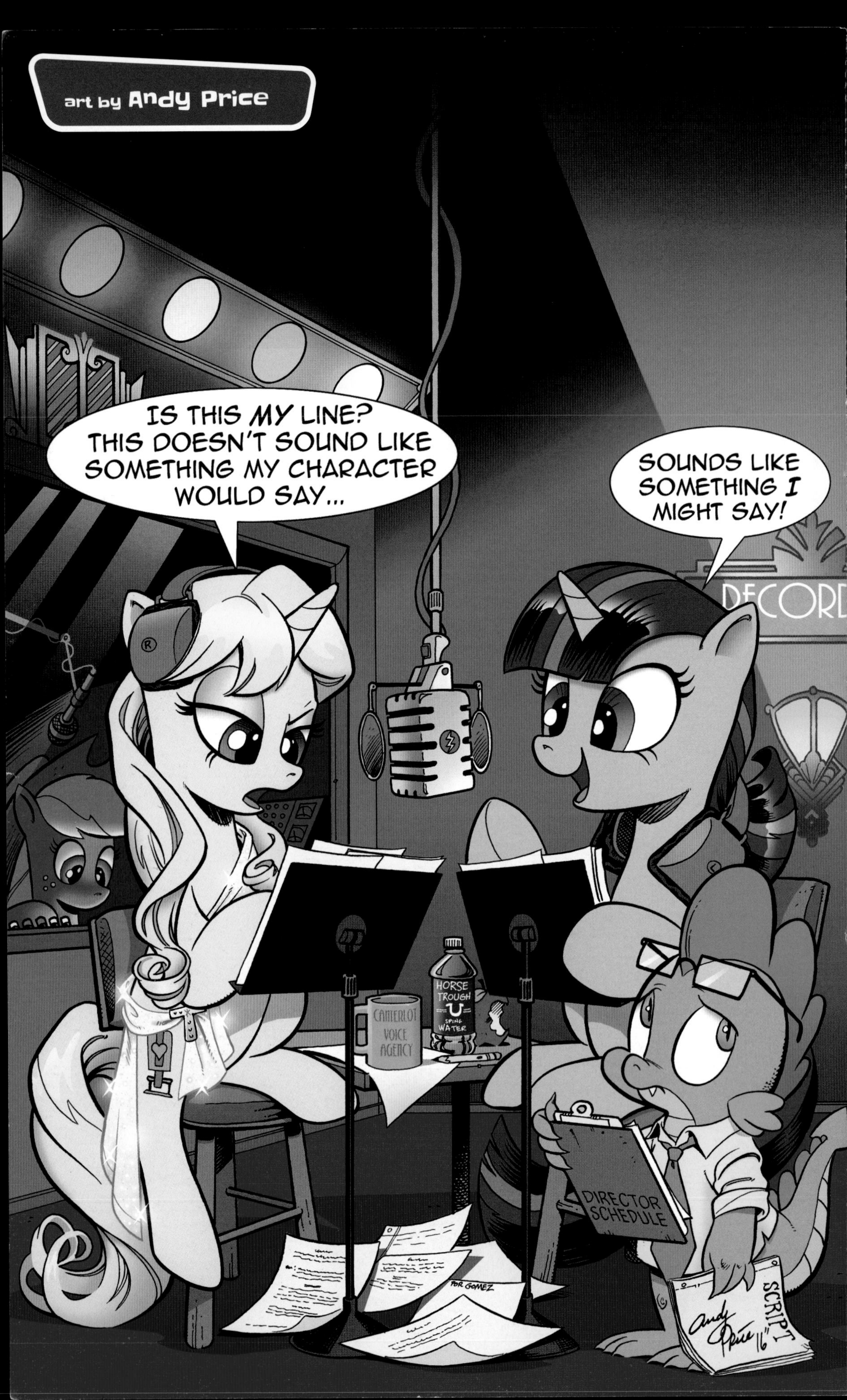
IS THIS *MY* LINE? THIS DOESN'T SOUND LIKE SOMETHING MY CHARACTER WOULD SAY...
SOUNDS LIKE SOMETHING *I* MIGHT SAY!
DECORD
CANTERLOT VOICE AGENCY
HORSE TROUGH
WATER
DIRECTOR SCHEDULE
SCRIPT
FOR GOMEZ
art by Andy Price

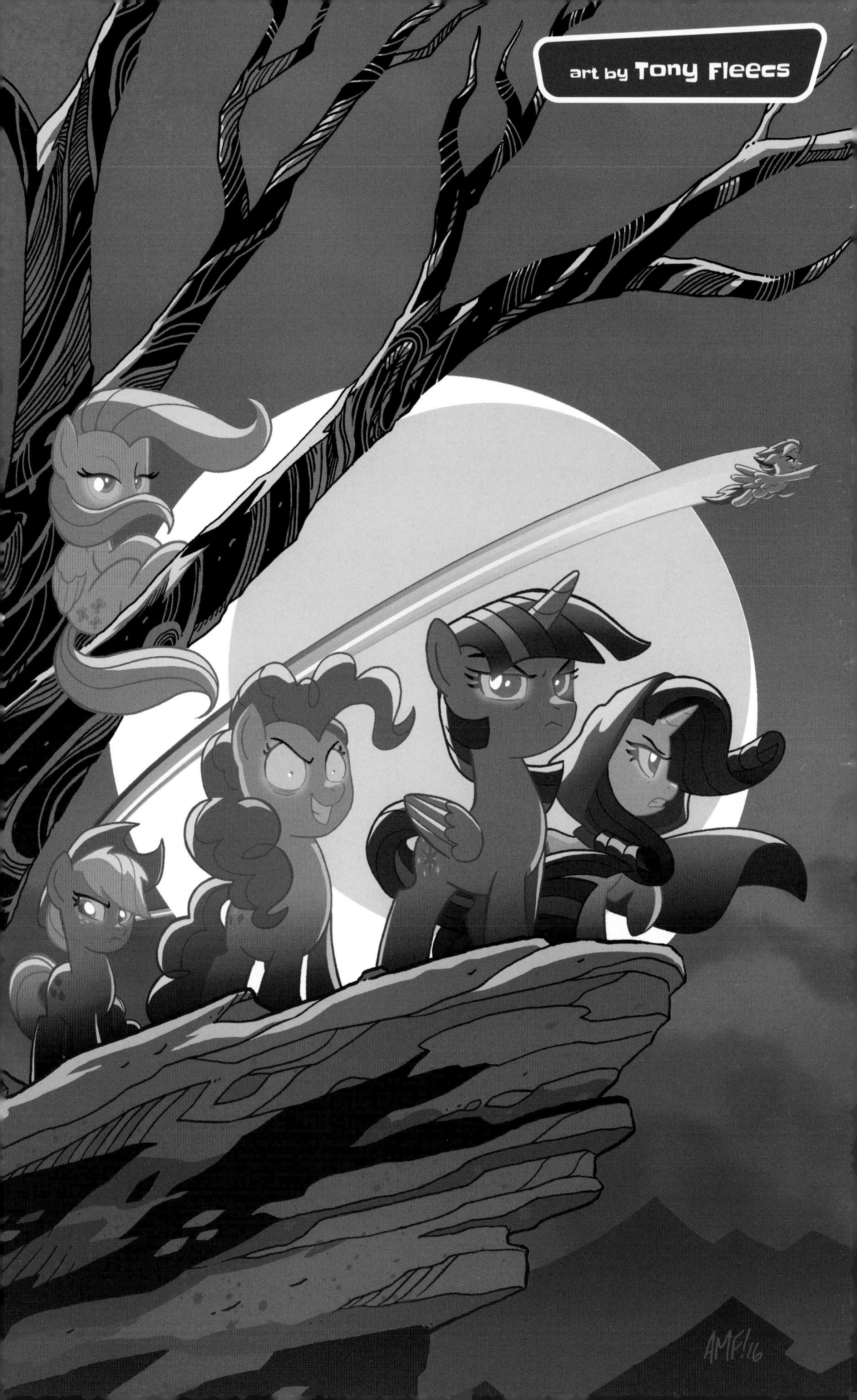

art by **Tony Fleecs**

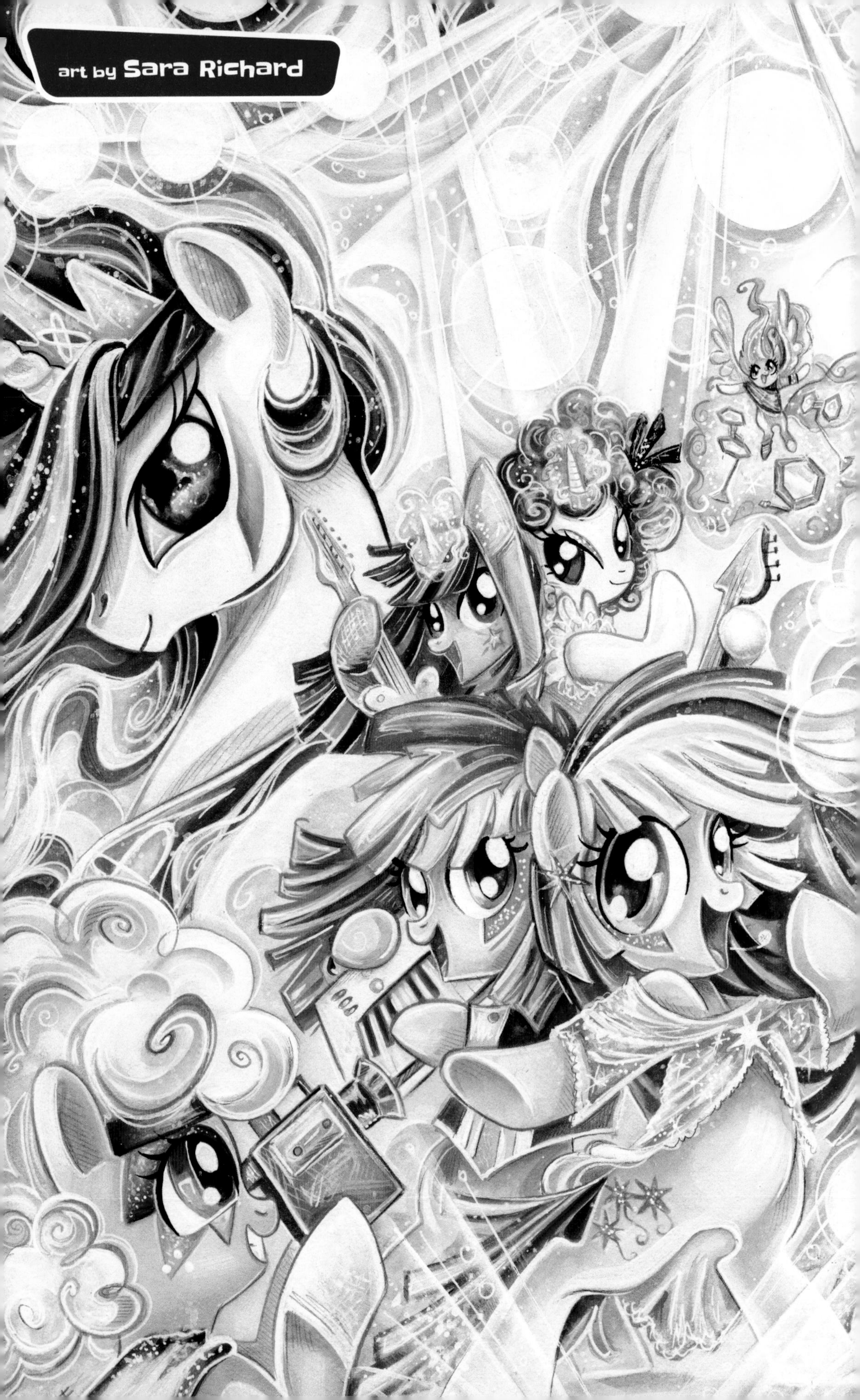
art by Sara Richard

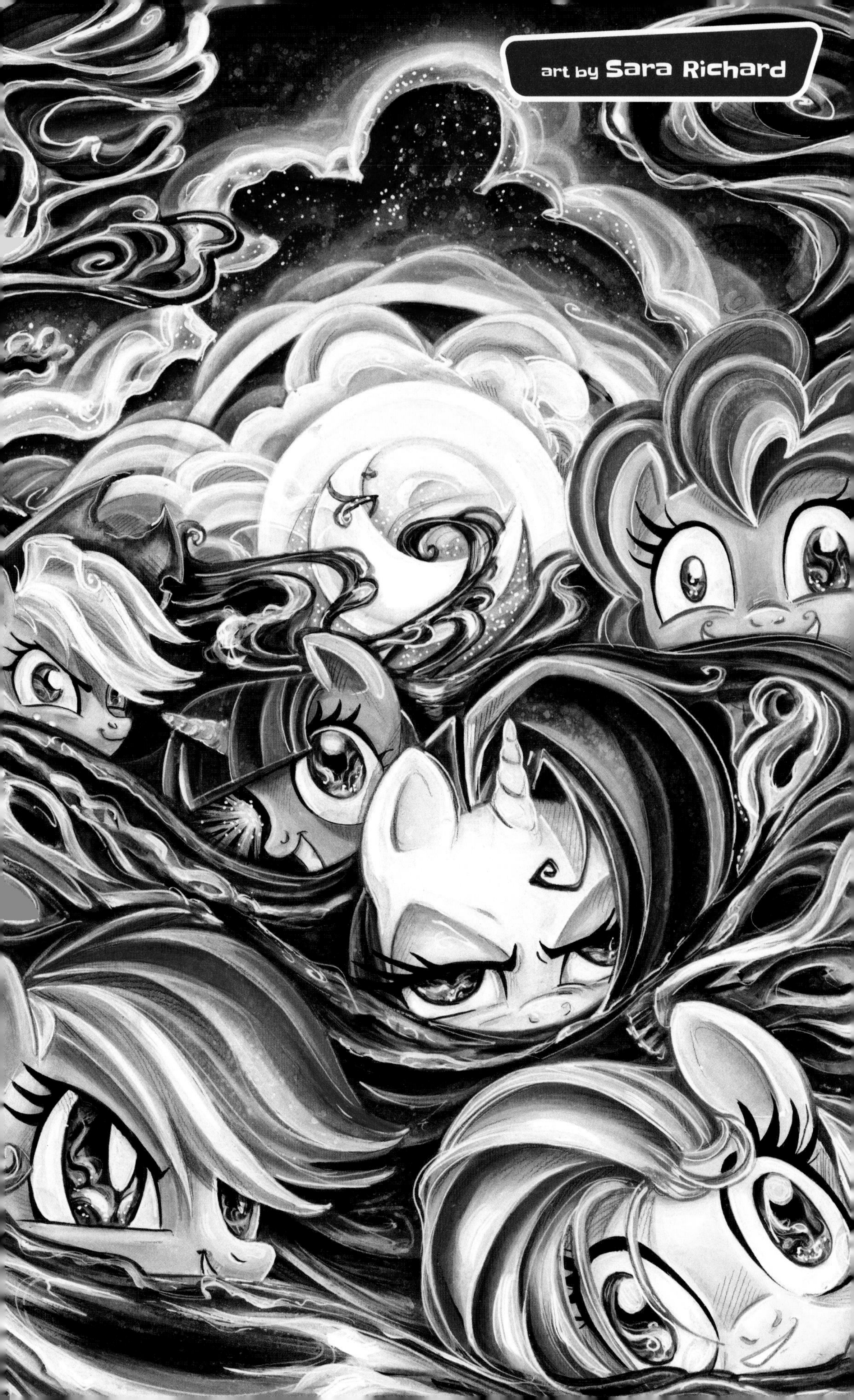
art by Sara Richard

art by Andy Price

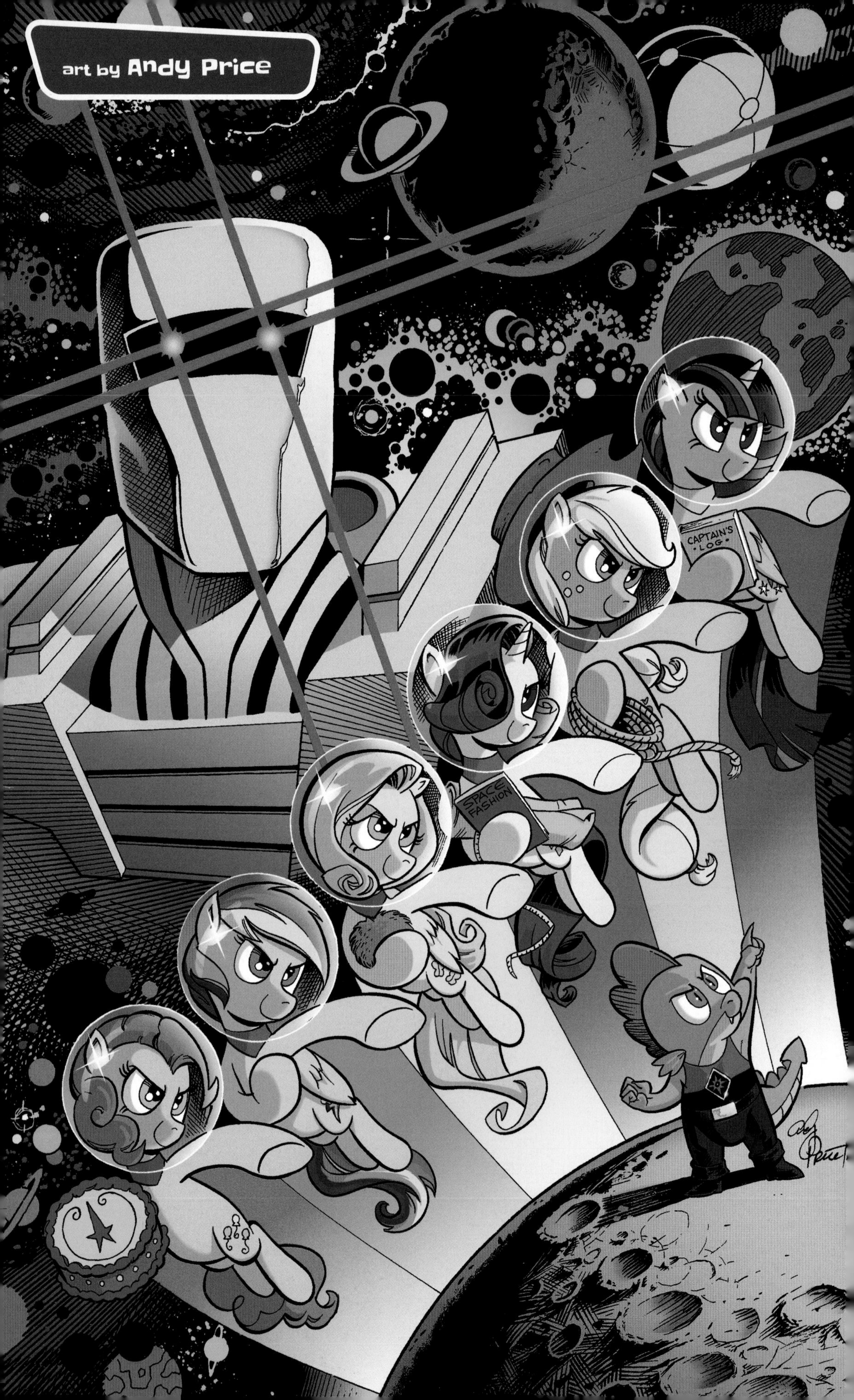

CAPTAIN'S LOG
SPACE FASHION

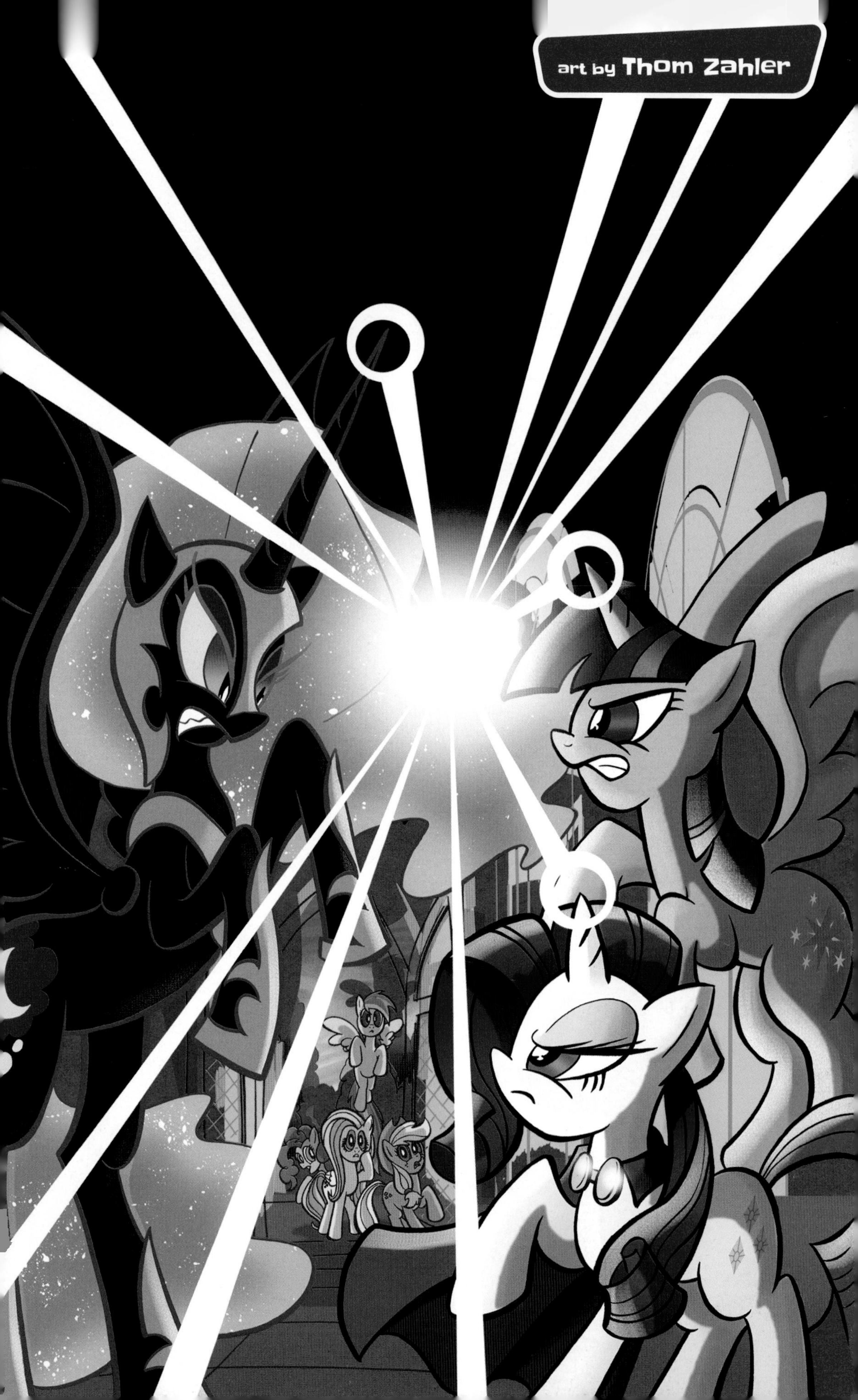
art by Thom Zahler

art by Sara Richard

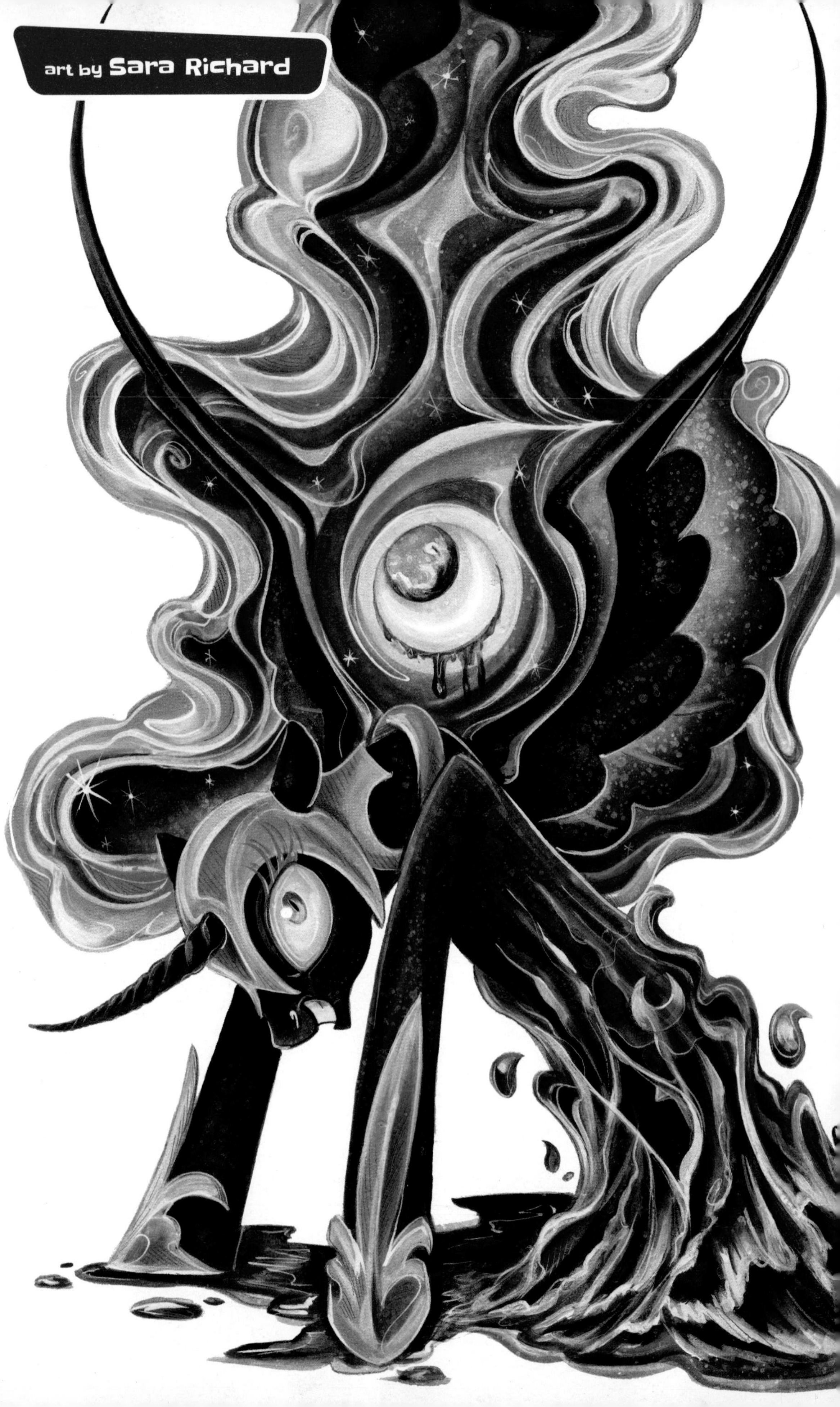

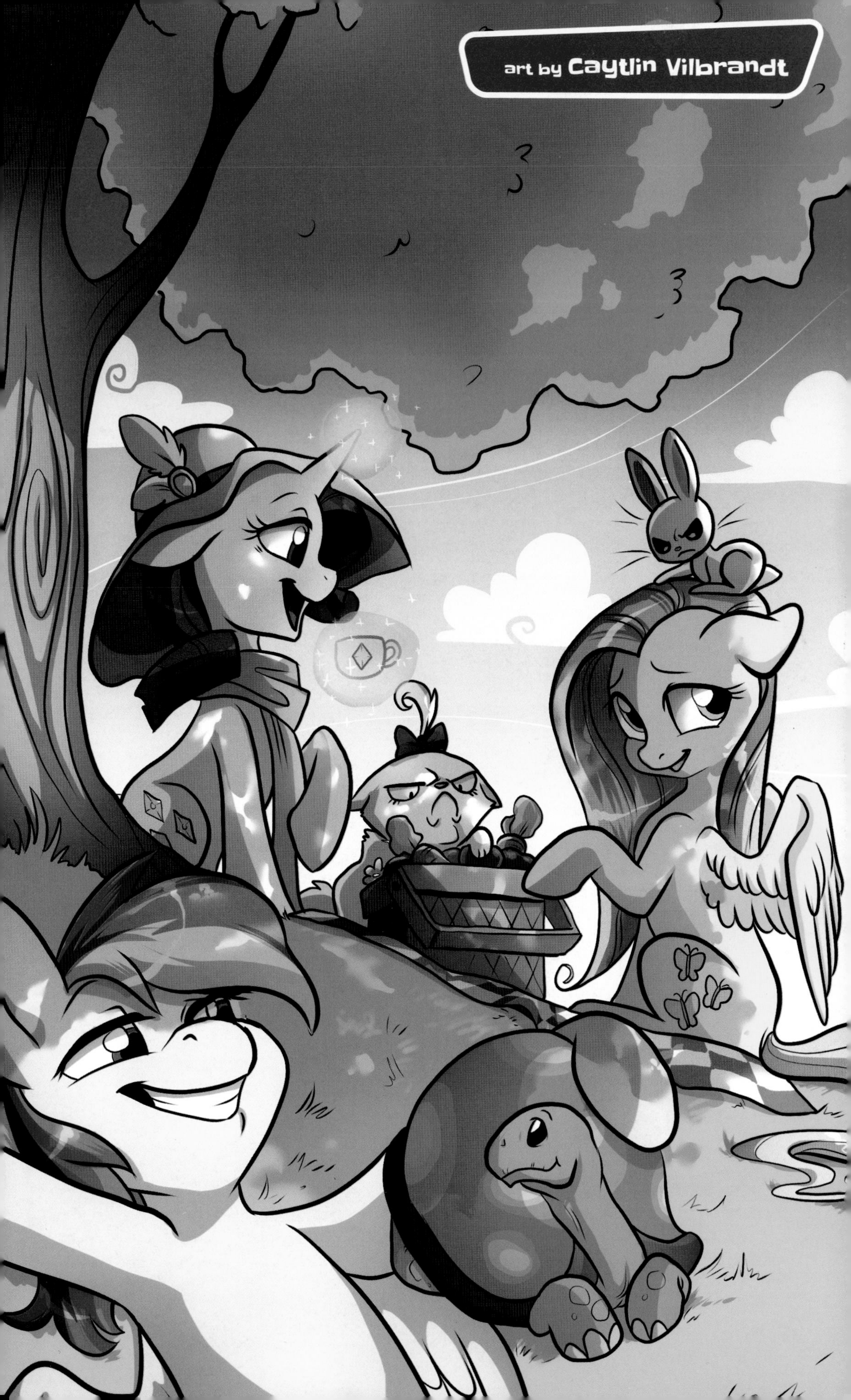
art by Caytlin Vilbrandt

art by Sara Richard

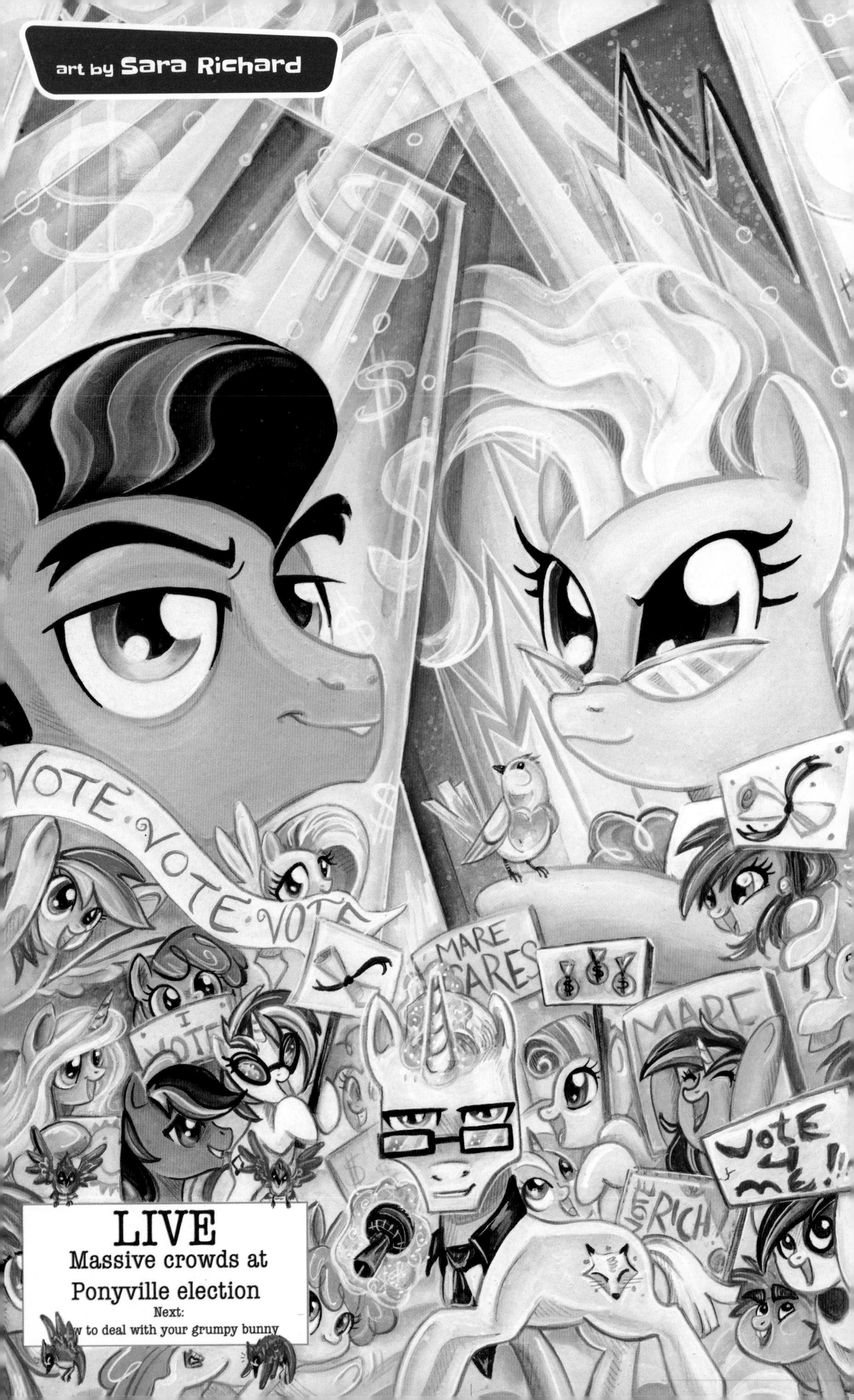
VOTE VOTE VOTE VOTE
MARE CARES
I VOTE
MARE
VOTE 4 ME!!
RICH
LIVE
Massive crowds at
Ponyville election
Next:
w to deal with your grumpy bunny

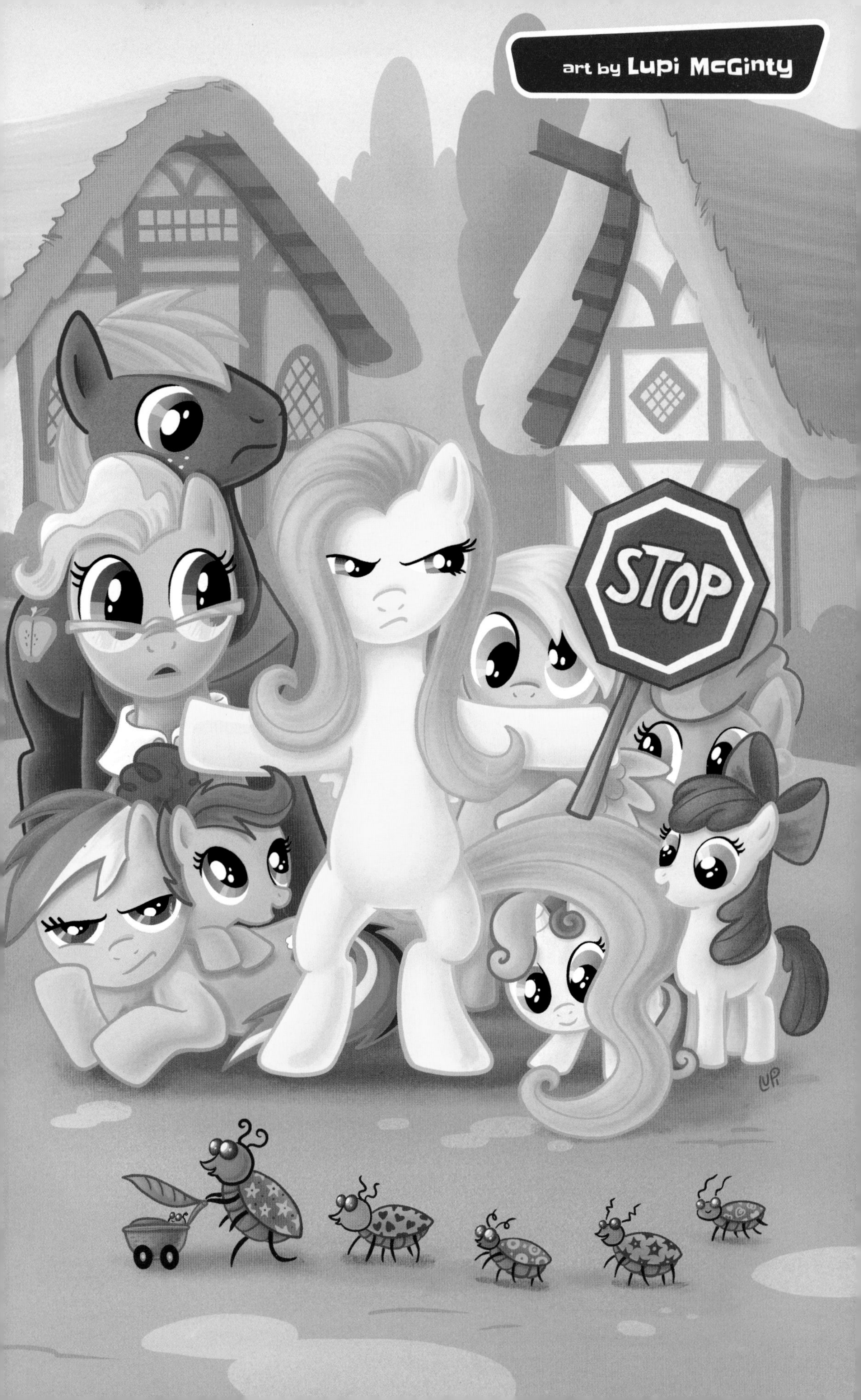
STOP
art by Lupi McGinty

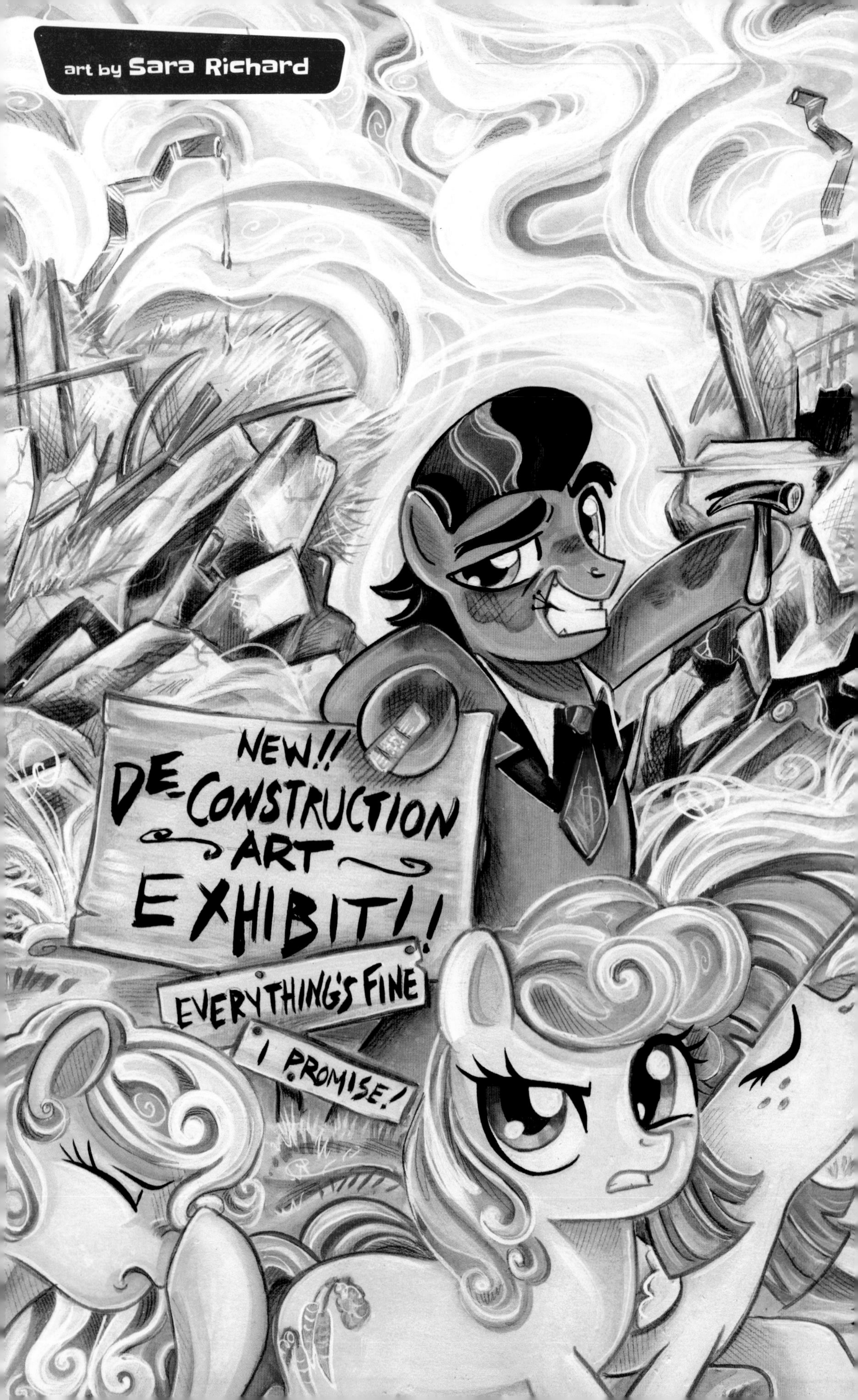
NEW!!
DE-CONSTRUCTION
ART
EXHIBIT!!
EVERYTHING'S FINE
I PROMISE!
art by Sara Richard